max monroe

Wildcat
A Mavericks Tackle Love Novel
Published by Max Monroe LLC

ISBN-13: 978-1984153364
ISBN-10: 1984153366

This is a work of fiction. Names, characters, places, brands, media, and incidents are either the product of the author's imagination or are used fictitiously. The author acknowledges the trademarked status and trademark owners of various products referenced in this work of fiction, which have been used without permission. The publication/use of these trademarks is not authorized, associated with, or sponsored by the trademark owners.

Editing by Silently Correcting Your Grammar
Formatting by Champagne Book Design
Cover Design by Peter Alderweireld
Photo Credit: Wander Aguiar
Title Font by: Font Forestry

You know how it goes with dedications.
You scan to the page, only to find that the book is once again *not* dedicated to you.
Not this time, (insert your name here).

Because we are the best of friends/are absolutely crazy about each other/haven't seen each other in a long, long time/are in some way related/have only shared a fleeting, longing glance/have the funniest conversations/have never actually met but already know we'll love each other…

You're funny/funny/funny/funny…
Yeah, we only really like funny people.

And this sexy, long, *thick*…book is for you.
(You thought we were gonna say cock, didn't you?)

intro

Quinn Bailey
The New York Mavericks
#9 | Quarterback
Height: 6-6 | **Weight:** 228 lbs. | **Age:** 28
Alma Mater: Alabama
Last Season Stats: TDS: 32 | INT: 7| YDS: 4,478 | RTG: 103.1

You see all of those O's? That's my team, The New York Mavericks.

And that little circle in the center with the letters QB? That's me, Quinn Bailey. I'm the quarterback, and funnily enough, my initials match my job title. Some call it coincidence, but I call it kismet. I was born to eat, sleep, and breathe Mavericks football.

Now, the X's, well, they're the other team. You can forget about those because they don't fucking matter.

When I get done with them, all you'll remember is *me*.

Trust me, I'll make it good.

Are you ready to play?

Chapter One

Quinn

My phone buzzed as I ducked my head to fit through the door on to my flight, and I glanced down to see who it was.

Instantly, pain exploded above my eye and pulsed along with my heartbeat.

"Ow. Fuck," I muttered, rubbing at the spot I'd just knocked against the hard metal of the airplane's exterior. Day after day of eating dirt and turf, compliments of some of the biggest guys *in the world*, and I was going to end up in the hospital from something as simple as boarding my flight.

"Walking and texting," a flight attendant said with a sigh, shaking his head. "Hazardous to your health, I tell ya. Just last week, I missed a step on the sidewalk in front of Bloomingdale's."

"Wow," I commiserated. "That sucks. Did you get hurt?"

His voice was somehow grave and shrill at the same time. "I spent four hundred dollars in there after I fell into the sale sign! Four hundred dollars meant for things like eating and self-maintenance. I had to skip breakfast this morning, and my eyebrows are making a bid to become one. Trust me, it's *still* hurting."

I laughed at his tale of woe and decided immediately I liked him. I glanced up again to survey his features, noting he was groomed to the nines—even his so-called overgrown eyebrows—had plump, friendly cheeks, and blue eyes that sparkled.

I wonder if he's my brother's type?

Taking my life into my own hands, I focused back on my phone as I navigated the short aisle to my seat in the second row.

A text from my brother sat waiting for me.

Speak of the devil.

Denver: Did you make it on to the off-brand deathtrap yet?

Kicking my bag under the seat, I settled into the leather and typed out a response.

Me: Just sat down. And there were no flights left on any of the major airlines, so it was either this, FedEx, or you don't see me.

Denver: RoyalAir sounds like a one-guy operation with a Prince Harry complex. At least FedEx is a global corporation. They probably could have fit you into their cargo bay. They must haul oversized loads occasionally, right?

Apparently, my brother was an airline snob. You'd think he worked for Delta or something. RoyalAir was actually a pretty nice, new-to-the-scene airline. Sure, their seats could've been a little more accommodating for a man my size, but it wasn't like the major airlines had La-Z-Boy recliners.

Me: Ha. Ha. I'm laughing so hard my sides hurt. And to think I was going to set you up with a cute guy I just met.

Denver: My straight brother picking out men for me? Jesus take the wheel. Tell me, how big was the pool of gay men you selected him from today? Negative one?

Me: So what if he's the only potential mate I met for you today? He could be great. You don't know.

Denver: Right.

Me: Fine. But you're missing out.

Denver: Sweet baby kittens. You've bonded with the random gay man.

Me: He's funny!

I shifted and squirmed, trying to make room for my shoulders in the miniature-sized airplane seat and pulled my Beats headphones up from around my neck to settle on my ears. Candy bars, shampoo, even horses—all cute when you make them little. Seats that I had to be confined to for more than five minutes? Not so much.

Even the first-class seat struggled to accommodate the width of a professional football player like myself, but a few hours of discomfort was worth the end result—three blissful days with my family before the grind of the upcoming Mavericks season took over my life.

Once the season started, I never even considered flying home for fear of losing focus. It was too easy to slow down and slip into a different frame of mind when I set foot in Boone Hills. An hour and a half south of Birmingham with a population of three hundred, it put the small in *small town* and the simple in *simple life*. Frankly, it was everything I loved in life—homey, personal, completely feel-good in its eccentricities—but it wasn't conducive to maintaining the mental focus required to lead a football team at the professional level.

My phone vibrated against my thigh.

Denver: Funny ha-ha, or funny-looking? I'm still young and beautiful. I'm not ready for someone with a "good personality" yet.

I smiled to myself and shook my head as "Rockstar" by Post Malone featuring 21 Savage pumped into my ears.

Me: Maybe you're right. Remotely hooking you up with someone probably isn't a good idea. You sound a lot less likable via text.

I smiled as I thought about how true that was—in person, my brother Denver was remarkably pleasant. Truth be known, he was one of my favorite people in the whole world, and I didn't see him nearly enough. He was still in college at the University of Alabama, and my schedule with the New York Mavericks was extensive and long. My trips home were few and far between, and this would be the last one I'd be able to make for a while. Hell, I'd spent last Christmas in a cabin in the Catskills with my coach, his family and closest friends, and several other players, so dedicated was my vow to avoid hometown comfort during the season.

"Excuse me," I heard from my immediate right. A guy in his early thirties with a flashy suit and perfectly gelled comb-over hadn't even made ass-to-seat contact, but he was already flagging down the flight attendant. I couldn't see Mr. Bloomingdale's behind the line of people still boarding the plane, but based on the snap of the stupid fuck's fingers in impatience, I immediately felt sorry for the funny flight attendant.

Darkness enveloped me as I closed my eyes, pushed my head back into the headrest as best as I could at my height, and tried to let the music drown out everything else. 21 Savage rapped about having a twelve-car garage despite only having six cars, one of my favorite lines of the song, but the annoying hum of the guy next to me pulled me out of the moment and made me crack an eye—just barely.

"Forty percent vodka, fifty percent cranberry, ten percent lemon juice. Don't try to cheapen it with less vodka, okay, sweetheart? Take care of me here."

Jesus Christ. I guess it's Merry Douche-mas in July to us today.

I closed my eyes again without looking over, not at all interested in the play-by-play of this self-acclaimed sweet talker.

But a female voice was not what I was expecting, especially one that vibrated in my chest like it was physically scraping against me. It had a delicate rasp, almost like she was losing her voice to sickness, but the end of every word came out soft and smooth like silk.

"I'm sorry, sir, but we don't have any lemon juice on board. I'd be happy to make the cranberry and vodka for you, though."

Simple and to the point, she did her best to remain professional, and like some kind of hypnosis, it pulled my eyes open again—both of them.

Her skin was like a glass of hot chocolate, the mocha swirling smoothly over the surface. Its only imperfection was a tiny smattering of dots—brown freckles sprinkled like cinnamon across her nose—and the deep brown of her eyes worked to look warm despite the dickhead they were pointed at.

Je-sus, she's pretty.

All of a sudden, comb-over in 2B's use of *sweetheart* made a lot more sense. He was on the prowl.

"Fifty-fifty then, babe. But you should really talk to your superiors about catering to your VIP passengers more specifically," the guy said with a derogatory undertone. Like somehow making her feel less worthy was going to get him somewhere.

I couldn't seem to pull my eyes away from her face to look at him, but I had a feeling if I'd been able to, the smug bastard would have looked like he actually thought he could talk to her like that *and* get *in* there.

In my experience, being a condescending asshole and calling women you'd never met *babe* never helped in the flirting game.

She smiled minutely—an expression I could tell was forced but I suspected he couldn't—and gave the asshole what he wanted, if only in an effort to get the fuck out of there. "No problem, sir."

"It's Luke," the guy said, giving her his name but not bothering to get hers. She nodded, her creamy pink-tipped fingernails squeezing into the leather of the headrest in front of us reflexively.

Somewhere deep in my mind, I had a moment of disappointed reflection that I wouldn't be seeing any more than necessary of the beautiful woman in front of me this flight. Lucas Dickhead Doucherson had made sure of that.

Her eyes came to me then, and I pulled my headphones off, settling them on my neck to better hear her as she spoke. "Can I get you anything, sir?"

I glanced down at my phone to check the time. It was already 7:55 p.m., and we were supposed to be wheels up in ten minutes. Anything I asked of her would take too much of her time before takeoff.

I searched out her name tag, finding it a few inches down from her shoulder, nestled in the crisp white fabric of her shirt, and then met her eyes, trying to make my face as remotely friendly as possible, and shook my head. "No thanks, *Catharine*. I'm good for now."

She smiled again, this time big enough to empty the flesh from the dimples in her cheeks, and her nonverbal gratitude ran through me like a current.

God, why does her smile feel so personal?

A quick glance to Luke told me he was completely oblivious to the fact that I'd just addressed her by her actual name and received a warm smile in return.

Some fools can't be taught.

I forced myself to put my headphones back in place and close my eyes as she walked away, but my imagination finished the image for me as clearly as though I'd actually seen it. The sway of her hips, the lines of navy that seamed together her hose along her calves, and the perfect sweep of her dark hair across her back—all of it burned on my eyelids and trickled into a special bank of memories.

A place behind a lock and key—and then a coded keypad for good measure—where I kept inappropriate things hidden away from public discovery.

That's right, Quinn. Take that sexy little montage to the grave.

I'd done this flight—on my way home to Boone Hills—what felt like a thousand times, usually via one of the major airlines and out of Newark rather than JFK, but it was all the same. Usher herd of people on to plane as quickly as possible, cram bags into overhead bins, cater to those of us lucky enough to be in the front of the plane, go over a bevy of safety information that no one paid attention to, and then push back from the gate to get the show on the road and the big metal bird in the air.

Catharine was prettier than most of the flight attendants I'd encountered in the past, but she was also just another face in the sea. After this flight, I'd never see her again. Frankly, once the season started up, most of the faces I'd see would be ugly, male, and coming at me at full speed with every intention of breaking my body.

Ah, football. Good times.

My playlist rolled on to a Selena Gomez song, and I felt my cheeks pull up into a smile. My teammate and one of my best friends, Sean Phillips, was always stealing my phone and adding random music to my playlist. Funny thing was, I normally liked everything he added. Britney, Selena, Beyoncé, Kesha, Lady Gaga—they were all empowered women. And I got a certain kind of excitement out of women who knew their own worth. Not that I shared that kind of information with Sean—he wouldn't keep adding to my music collection if he thought I was actually enjoying it.

I felt a presence return and tensed. A cramping, tight chest and clenching hands—symptoms of want and curiosity—tried to sway me to give in to the urge to take a peek.

Was Catharine back with the drink? Would she smile my way again? Would I be able to keep my loose tongue from running away and saying something embarrassing?

It was serious battle, a war waged with nothing but desperation and self-preservation on my side, but I managed to keep my eyes closed. Just *barely.*

I did turn the volume down on my music so I could listen in, though. I was only fucking human.

The voice I heard surprised me. It was hard, to the point—and it definitely wasn't hers.

"Your drink, sir."

I opened my eyes then, seeing Mr. Bloomingdale's leaned over, the offensive drink offered up to Luke like a trophy. My brother's almost-boyfriend was the picture of poise, his face fixed into an almost-smile—but make no mistake, there was nothing friendly about it.

Just as I'd suspected, I wouldn't be seeing too much of the pretty flight attendant from before. Even through my disappointment, I was glad for it. Glad she had the intelligence to avoid a guy like Luke despite his obvious money, and glad she had friends who were willing to help her do it.

I could feel my face settling into a grin just as the male flight attendant looked over—and winked.

My smile deepened.

He looked surprised for the barest hint of a moment, and then turned to hustle back up to the front of the plane. He spoke rapidly to Catharine, and I watched raptly, unable to stop myself. Her eyes flicked up in surprise and landed right on mine.

All I could do was hold them.

Moments passed as time slowed, her surprised gaze opening up a virtual tether between us where she tried to infiltrate my mind and I tried everything I could think of to be superhuman enough to let her.

Fuck being only human. I could Clark Kent the shit out of this moment and open up my mind.

Just as concentration started to feel a little more like constipation, my abilities to let her mind meld with mine officially limited by the constraints of something called science, the speaker crackled, breaking the connection. Released from her grasp, I moved my scrutiny to the male flight attendant standing at the front of the plane, right in front of the cockpit doors, an old-style beige phone to his ear.

"Hello, my name is Casey," he announced over the speakers, his voice about two-hundred percent cheerier than it had been while addressing my seatmate, Luke. "I'd like to be the first to welcome you to RoyalAir Flight 2107. If you're going to Birmingham, you're in the right place. If you're not going to Birmingham, you're about to have a really long evening." He chuckled into the intercom as Catharine moved out of the galley and to the center of the aisle and turned to face the entire plane, ducking her head as she turned back to glance at him. Her long, dark, smoothly curled hair covered her face like a curtain.

"With the help of lovely Catharine, we'd like to tell you now about some important safety features of this aircraft," he continued. Catharine smiled at us, her professional persona in place.

I had a moment of hysteria where I imagined she was smiling only for me, from the center of my bed.

Holy Christ, I said with a mental slap as I started to undress her in my mind. *You better get your shit together, Quinn. Stop being a pervert.*

Quickly, my daydream followed orders, pulling her shirt closed and doing up the buttons. But my mind was a rebel, and no matter how hard I tried, I couldn't get it to refasten the last button.

Poor Catharine would forever be sporting a hint of cleavage in my mind.

Goddamn, I'm an asshole.

Really, though, fantasizing about random women was a reality thrust upon the male gender by biology. The Quinn in my pants was always ready to rut—a genius plan by our creator to ensure the survival of the race.

But male-female interaction wasn't always that simple, and P didn't always stand for penetration.

"The most important safety feature we have aboard this plane is…*the flight attendants.* Treat them well, and you have a much better chance of getting out of this flight alive. Please move your attention to the pretty one in the front of the aircraft now."

Catharine smiled toward us, a hint of blush covering the mocha hues of her cheeks at the mention of being pretty.

Catharine.

Jesus Christ. I was thinking about her like I actually *knew* her. *Don't get attached to the flight attendant you don't plan on ever seeing again.*

"There are five exits aboard this plane, two at the front, two over the wings, and one out the plane's rear end," Casey continued while the female flight attendant—I rolled my eyes at myself… *Good try, Quinn, but just because you don't use her name in your thoughts doesn't mean you're good to go*—used two finger motions with both hands to gracefully point out the exits. "Please take a moment to look around and find the nearest exit. In the event that the need arises to find one, trust me, you'll be glad you did, even if it's the one in the rear."

This was their stand-up routine, a thing they did on a regular basis to liven up the mundane. I smirked to myself.

My pregame routine was legend among my teammates, gossiped about on tabloid sites, and a staple of the unorthodox way I went about life.

Kindred personalities, Catharine and I.

Oh my God, Quinn, stop. This is not a dating show.

"We have pretty blinking lights on the floor that will blink in the direction of the exits. White ones along the normal rows, and sparkly red ones at the exit rows." Casey's voice pulled me from my delusion.

Catharine giggled and offered a smirk toward her coworker as she pointed toward the lights, before grabbing a prop oxygen mask from an empty seat and holding it up for everyone to see.

I choked on my own saliva. *Good God, that laugh.* It was so perfectly awkward.

"In the event of a loss of cabin pressure, the baggy thing that Cat is holding will drop down over your head. You stick it over your nose and mouth like she is doing now. The bag won't inflate, but there's oxygen there, I promise." He grinned. "If you are sitting next to a small child…" He moved his gaze very pointedly to me and emphasized, "or someone who is acting like a small child, please do us all a favor and put your mask on first."

I chuckled and nudged Luke with an elbow. "I'll get yours right after I do my own, okay, buddy?"

His eyebrows shot together. "Do I know you?"

The question wasn't completely out of the blue. As a professional quarterback for the New York Mavericks, I got recognized all the time. But this guy looked like he knew as much about football as I did about knitting—not fucking much.

"I doubt it."

Catharine smirked discreetly, the corners of her lips curling up in such perfect synchronization with my own that I nearly felt it, and tucked her head down to put her prop away.

"If you are traveling with two or more children, please take a moment now to decide which one is your favorite. Help that one first, and then work your way down," Casey added as Cat switched out the oxygen mask for a safety pamphlet.

She held it in front of her body and then started to teasingly use it as a fan, smirking as she did.

"In the seat pocket in front of you is a pamphlet about the safety features of this aircraft. I usually use it as a fan when I'm having my own personal summer, just like Cat is demonstrating for you," he said with a soft chuckle. "Please take it out and play with it now."

"There is no smoking in the cabin on this flight or in the lavatories. If we see smoke coming from the bathroom, we will assume you are on fire and then put you out. Don't worry, this is a free service we provide, and we're experts at keeping the spray of the fire extinguisher off of ourselves," he joked, and Catharine nodded toward us with big, amused eyes.

"In a moment, we will be turning off the cabin lights, and it's going to get really dark. If you're afraid of the dark, now would be a good time to reach up and press the yellow button. The yellow button turns on your reading light. Please don't press the orange button unless you absolutely have to. The orange button is your seat ejection button."

I glanced up to see the orange button was, in fact, the flight attendant call button.

A soft chuckle left my lips. I guess I'd been wrong. This flight was different. These two were a nice change of pace from the usual dull flights I'd become accustomed to.

"I can say on behalf of myself, Cat, and the rest of our crew, we're glad to have you on board. Thank you for choosing RoyalAir and giving us your business…and your money." He grinned. "If there's anything we can do to make you more comfortable, please don't hesitate to ask," he finished, smirked, and then winked toward us as he added one last sentiment, "but ask Cat first."

Every passenger on the plane laughed, and then, surprisingly, gave the dynamic duo a round of applause.

Shit. Even I was laughing and clapping. It was rare to keep a plane full of New Yorkers happy, much less get them to actually listen to the safety instructions.

I watched as Cat and Casey did their final checks before strapping themselves into their jump seats at the front of the plane, and then I grabbed my phone to send my brother a final text.

There was one from him already waiting for me from our earlier exchange. Somehow, I'd missed it. I blamed the douchebag sitting next to me, but my mind said otherwise, whispering, *you were too distracted by the pretty flight attendant.*

Denver: That's because you can see my charming smile in person. It takes some of the edge off.

Me: I guess it's good that I'll see you in person soon, then. You can remind me why I like you. About to take off. Should be there in about 2.5 hours.

"Good evening, this is your captain speaking. Thank you for choosing to fly with RoyalAir tonight. We are pleased to have some of the best and most professional flight attendants in the industry, but as you can see, none of them are on this flight…"

Cat smirked and Casey rolled his eyes, but he couldn't hide the hint of a smile on his lips.

"We'll be taxiing for the runway for another two minutes," the pilot added, "and then our takeoff toward Birmingham will begin. Please sit back, relax, and enjoy the flight."

After one last look at Catharine, I decided to do just that. Closing my eyes and settling into my seat, I shut out the world and let myself look forward to heading home—even if just for a little while.

Chapter Two

Cat

"I'll take another vodka and cranberry, *babe*," Luke, the over-zealous dickhead in first class, requested with a cursory raise of his empty glass as I stepped by his seat.

His condescending tone made a slight headache pulsate above my brow.

God, I'll be glad when this flight is over…

Babe. If tossing out demeaning nicknames and demanding booze was this guy's way of schmoozing women, he needed a reality check. Not to mention, how many drinks did he really need? We'd been in the air for ninety minutes, and already, this man had consumed no fewer than three drinks.

There was one certainty in this situation: any sign of slurred words or disruptive behavior, and I'd cut off his alcohol supply quicker than a doctor cuts an umbilical cord.

It was times like these, when dealing with assholes like Luke in 2B, that I started to question my decision to be a flight attendant. *It'll be so much fun*, I'd naïvely thought. *I'll get to travel the world, meet new people, and have daily adventures.*

I'd forgotten to take into account the whole serving other people thing. *Or* the times when things like puke occurred outside of the lavatory.

Honestly, I did love my new job, but I was only human. I had good days, as well as days when I had to deal with douchebags.

I nodded and plastered on my very best "I'll get right on that" smile, but once I stepped into the first-class galley, I rolled my eyes and let Casey know his favorite passenger on the plane needed another drink.

"*Babe* would like another vodka cranberry."

Lucky for me, my best guy friend was also my fellow flight attendant—who also happened to be very gay and extremely protective. He was my biggest buffer for asshole male passengers who came on too strong.

Case and I flew together on a weekly basis, and because he always had my back, I was more than thankful our flight schedules were generally in sync.

He snorted in response. "Considering we're taking a detour to Atlanta because of the weather, Mr. First Class Dickhead can live without another drink." Casey punctuated his statement by holding his middle finger up in the air, high and proud, but sadly, behind the safe constraints of the galley wall.

I'd say I wasn't the only one tired of *Babe's* bullshit.

"Although..." Casey cleared his throat and waggled his brows. "I haven't minded looking at Babe's seatmate every time I've dropped off his vodka and cranberry."

"Seatmate?" I feigned confusion—as though I didn't fucking remember who he'd meant.

I knew damn well who he was referring to—the tall drink of water in seat 2A.

Deep blue eyes, big and broad shoulders, a svelte, muscular frame, and full lips to boot, the mystery man in 2A was a looker, that was for fucking sure. Not to mention the perfectly mussed light brown hair that framed his face and the soft Southern drawl that accompanied his words. Those locks and that accent would make any woman's mind wander toward thoughts of beds and sleep and *sex*.

I'd spent the majority of this flight sneaking glances in his direction, wondering, *What does a guy like that look like underneath his clothes?*

My brain screamed, *Strong and big and thick in all of the right places.*

Thankfully, since the freakishly long moment he'd met and held my eyes before takeoff, 2A had spent most of the flight with his eyes closed, head resting on the seat back, and his headphones covering his ears. Otherwise, he might've caught me mid-ogle.

Although, if I was being honest with myself, I wasn't sure if it was a good thing he hadn't realized that my gaze had taken notice of him or not. I felt torn between wanting him *not* to see me looking at him and wanting him to *know* I was looking at him.

Attraction is a weird phenomenon.

"Oh, don't play coy with me," Casey outright refuted with a hand to his hip. "I know you know who I'm talking about. Just two hours ago, you listened while I pledged my virginity to him and him alone if he would take me as his he-wife. He's so freaking fine, I'm honestly curious if he is the sole reason Tropical Storm Rita decided to switch up her path."

"Pretty sure, no matter how good-looking the man is, he doesn't have the power to change weather patterns. And God will smite me if I don't, again, laugh in your face at your inference that you're still a virgin."

"Aha!" He wiggled a knowing finger in my direction. "So, you *do* remember him, you little harlot!"

I just laughed it off and used my best tactic of defense before he started tossing out ideas of how to get 2A's phone number. "Do you think we'll be able to finish up inflight service?" I questioned and quickly busied myself with emptying out the coffee machine.

Casey looked up from his new current task: refilling the drink cart with coveted boxes of orange juice. It was a true wonder of the modern world why airplanes urged cravings of sugared-up oranges in liquid form, but the proof was in the pudding, or should I say, the constant passenger requests for OJ.

"Doubtful, but we'll try to make the best of it," he answered with a little shrug of his shoulders. "Captain Billy should be making the final announcement to land in the next few minutes, and with the way the turbulence has been the whole way, I have a feeling he'll demand we keep our asses in our jump seats."

He had a point. We'd been fighting a bumpy ride ever since we'd reached altitude out of JFK. Word on the street was that a tropical storm from the Atlantic had taken an abrupt turn and fucked up our expected weather pattern. Hence the need for an early landing in Atlanta, which was only about an hour flight from our intended destination of Birmingham—one of those trips where you basically only had time to go up and come right back down.

"Oh no, honey," Casey muttered, and I moved my eyes away from the coffee machine to look at him. I followed the path of his gaze until I realized he'd spotted a giant run in my panty hose.

"Son of a bitch." I followed the nylon wreckage with my index finger. From the top of my kneecap to just slightly above my ankle, I had somehow ruined yet another pair of panty hose.

"*Those hoes ain't loyal*," Casey teased, and I couldn't not laugh.

"I swear to God, how many pairs of panty hose do I need to bury before RoyalAir changes their uniform requirements?"

He grinned. "Like that'll ever happen."

"Don't squash my dreams."

"Honey, RoyalAir prides themselves on their uniforms," he said with a wink. "And trust me, I didn't sign on with them just because of the benefits and travel opportunities. They are literally the only airline with actual fashion taste."

I put a free hand to my hip and pointed a box of coffee filters toward him. "When you have to wear panty hose underneath your perfectly fitted suit, then maybe your constant need to defend the dress code can be taken seriously. But until that day comes, I'm not hearing it."

"Uh oh." Casey chuckled. "Someone's feisty…"

"Hell yeah, I'm feisty, Mr. '*I get two days off in a row after this flight*,'" I complained and put—*more like tossed*—all of the coffee supplies away into the overhead cabinet. "I'm the one who has to figure out how in the hell I'm going to sweet talk the RoyalAir agents in Atlanta to help me get to Birmingham by six in the morning *or* get me off that flight altogether."

"Yeah. Okay. Sorry, honey." He pinched his face together in a grimace. "You have every right to be pissy right now. I can't deny the A-T-L is like the seventh circle of hell, and that's on a good day. And don't even get me started on the ladies in the staffing office there. Can you say *divas*?"

"Pissy?" I questioned with a quirk of my brow. "I thought you said I was feisty?"

"Out of everything I just said, that was all you heard?" he questioned with a quirk of his lips. "And yes, that's exactly what I said. Pissy and feisty." He blew me a kiss. "But I still love you all the same, honey."

"Good evening, folks." The overhead speakers crackled as Captain Billy greeted the plane. "Due to the continued occurrence of unexpected weather conditions and Tropical Storm Rita's abrupt change in path, we will be landing in Atlanta in about ten minutes," he announced. "Everyone, for your safety and the safety of the aircraft, please remain seated with your seat belts fastened in place."

Tropical Storm Rita had moved over the southern states, hooking a hard right after making landfall in Texas, a lot quicker than originally predicted. The only safe choice was to take an early landing and let it pass, instead of staying in the air and getting stuck within the storm's unpredictability.

Once the seat belt light dinged loud and clear, I stopped refilling the cart's pretzel supplies and looked at Casey.

Immediately, he gave me his take on the current situation without uttering a single word. With a simple shrug of his shoulders, followed by pushing the cart into its final resting spot underneath the cabinet, he locked it into place. He might as well have just shouted toward the middle of the plane, "*That's a wrap, folks! No sodas or pretzels for you!"*

"Well, I guess we now get to experience the joys of walking the aisles and dealing with the unhappy and disgruntled..." I mused, and a laugh bubbled up from his lips.

"Buckle *your* seat belt, honey. This customer service is going to get bumpy."

While Casey finished locking up the overhead cabinets in the galley, I started my walk-thrus.

Surreptitiously, as I passed the first few rows of first class, my eyes strayed, moving across the rows and seats until they reached the spot where lucky number 2A was located. From my viewpoint, I could see the way his hand rested on his thigh, his long fingers tapping out the beat to whatever music filled his ears. I had the urge to backtrack my steps just so I could see his face and take inventory of his handsome features—his strong jaw, full lips, and warm blue eyes.

Somehow, my brain had already memorized his most striking features like this was someone I would see more than once in my life.

Before my feet could move an inch, a passenger cockblocked me from engaging in another ten-second ogle session.

"Miss," a middle-aged woman called my attention from the last row in first class. "I am supposed to be in Birmingham by tomorrow morning. I have an important work meeting. I need you to make sure I have a flight available *immediately*."

Oh, man. It was already starting.

I walked the ten steps it took to get to her row, the bottoms of my heels crinkling against the carpet of the aisle, and stopped right beside her seat. "We're very sorry for the inconvenience." I erred on the side of apology first. "But the weather conditions are no longer safe for us to be in the air. You'll just have to be patient until we get to Atlanta, and a gate agent will be able to assist you with rescheduling your flight."

"Do we really need to take this detour?" she questioned, and I watched as her hands adjusted and fiddled with the fanny pack strapped across her waist. "I think everyone on the plane can handle a little bit of turbulence in order to get to our *planned* destination."

I wanted to let her know her idea of a little bit of turbulence didn't actually account for hurricane-force winds and unpredictable storm paths, but I bit my tongue. "I understand your frustration, but I can assure you this is not a matter of convenience, but safety. Our top priority will always be the safety of our passengers."

She rolled her eyes and sighed at the same time. "Oh, don't give me that bullshit safety spiel. This early landing is going to fuck up my whole schedule. I'll be lucky if I can find a flight to Birmingham by tomorrow night."

I'd only been a flight attendant for about six months, but I'd flown the majority of my flights with Captain Billy. He had nearly thirty years of flying under his belt, so it went without saying that he didn't just make an early landing for the hell of it. If he was landing us in Atlanta, it was because we needed to fucking land in Atlanta.

I looked at the woman, her blond hair resting high on top of her head in a severe, ballerina-style bun, her hazel eyes squinting in disdain, her fanny pack constricting her abdomen, and I put her in her place—*via mental telepathy.*

Listen up, Fanny Pack. I have no desire to fall thirty thousand feet from the air in a metal deathtrap just because you need to be somewhere, thank you very much. We'll be landing in Atlanta, so just keep your mouth shut and your ass in your seat and deal with it.

Once I'd gotten that off my chest, and she still continued to stare at me like her eyes had the power to physically stab me, I proceeded to give her the sugary-sweet, RoyalAir "customer is always right" bullshit answer, but *out loud* this time. "Again, I'm very sorry this happened, but let me assure you this isn't by choice or a matter of convenience. It's for everyone's safety. Air traffic control has requested that all planes within two hundred miles of our current location land as soon as possible to ensure the safety of everyone in the air."

She blinked. Once. Twice. And then stared. She was still visibly pissed, and her hands vibrated with irritation as she readjusted herself in her seat and started rummaging through her fanny pack.

Instantly, I noted she no longer had her seat belt on.

God, could this lady just do as she was told?

We weren't trying to be assholes here. We were trying to, you know, make sure no one died in the case of an emergency.

"I'm also going to have to ask you to take your fanny pack off and buckle your seat belt," I instructed with a saccharine smile. "For your safety, of course."

"This is my fanny pack." She huffed out a breath, and her bangs billowed above her forehead from the forced air. "I'm not taking it off. I never take it off. *Ever.*"

I couldn't stop my face from scrunching up in confusion. Obviously, we'd missed this thing during takeoff. No way in hell Casey wouldn't have blabbed about the Battle of the *Abdominal* Bulge.

Wow, Cat, I mused, impressed. *Seems you did manage to maintain a little bit of high school history knowledge.*

And what did she mean, she never took it off? Like, she showered with the fanny pack? Had sex with the fanny pack? *Everything* with that fucking fanny pack on?

"Listen, ma'am," Casey chimed in as he started his overhead bin checks up the aisles. "Unless you want to be escorted off this plane by the air marshal for disruptive behavior when we land, you need to take that fanny pack off. We are not going to ask you again."

Oh boy. And he called me the feisty one…

The woman blustered. And huffed again. Until she unclicked the fanny pack from her waist and properly buckled her seat belt just in time for Captain Billy to begin our final descent toward Atlanta.

Casey and I double-and triple-checked our passengers, the overhead bins, the lavatories, and the aisles. Once we ensured everything was as it should be, we strapped ourselves into our jump seats for landing.

"Sheesh. Fucking fanny packs," I muttered toward him, and he laughed.

"Yeah, the shit you have to request to keep people safe on a plane," he agreed with a grin. "Listen, sister, the instant we land, just move your ass. I'll do the final check and make sure everything is clean as a whistle before I go."

"You're the best," I whispered. Luckily for both of us, I was the only one who needed to make a return flight in the next twelve hours. Casey had two days off to get his schedule situated.

Casey blew me a kiss. "I know."

The instant we landed, I did exactly as I was told.

Legally, I had to wait as the passengers filed out, but as soon as they were done, I abandoned my responsibilities and moved my ass.

I grabbed my black carry-on and walked as fast as my navy patent leather heels would take me. After a serious delay and then a goddamn detour from the original planned flight, I was in Atlanta, should've been in Birmingham, and I had no idea what my next steps were.

Only six months into the flight attendant game, and without my flight attendant bestie by my side, I was a newbie. A little fish in a big ole airport pond trying to find her way back to Birmingham. Not to mention, RoyalAir was currently severely short-staffed, so the odds of being taken off my Birmingham to NYC flight completely were probably slim to none.

As I took the tram from Terminal D to Terminal A, where RoyalAir's hub was located, I silently prayed the flight manager on staff this evening could find a way to help me.

The airport was insanely busy for the hour of the day. Eleven at night was generally blessed with calm and quiet, but not tonight. Tonight, the usual hustle and bustle of airline employees and people rushing about to reach their terminal or their next connecting flight had been put on steroids because of all of the detours and weather delays.

I weaved in and out of the crowd, doing my best not to bump into anyone, and my heels click-clacked across the tile at a rapid pace.

The flight manager's office, located on the opposite end of the terminal and tucked into a small, obscure and darkened corner of a hallway, looked like something out of a customer service horror film. The phones were ringing off the hook, and two out of the three agents were already talking to other flight attendants. Paperwork littered the floor to the back and side of the long desk and blood was smeared all over the walls.

Okay, there wasn't any blood, but it felt like there could have been.

A rescheduling war had been fought here.

"Name," a woman with a short, jet-black bob and the darkest, thickest eyebrows I'd ever seen—the only person not occupied—demanded as soon as she noticed me stepping through the door.

Oh, fantastic. This should go well since she's obviously in such a great mood...

"Cat, uh, well, Catharine Wild," I responded and slid my carry-on bag to a stop with a little help from the counter. The bang of wheels against wood made *The Eyebrows* draw together, and I winced. "Oops. Sorry," I apologized. She glared. "Most people call me Cat, though."

"Well, it looks like RoyalAir calls you *Catharine*."

Sheesh. This woman. She's a real sweetheart, huh?

I glanced at her name tag. *Carol,* it read.

Well, Carol, you can blow me, I thought. *You're not the only one who's had a long night.*

"I'm supposed to be in Birmingham for a nine a.m. flight," I explained, and Carol raised one eyebrow high on her forehead.

Looking more like black caterpillars than facial hair, those eyebrows of hers were distracting as hell. They had a power that rivaled the sun, and it took all of my willpower to not stare directly at them.

"Well..." She looked up from her screen and pinched her lips together in a firm line. "You're not in Birmingham. You're in Atlanta."

Wow. Thanks. I hadn't realized I was in a completely different city and state from where I was supposed to be. I mean, I had been on the flight that took the detour, but I just had no fucking clue what was going on.

I kept my sassy in check and bit my tongue. "I realize that."

"I have no flights to Birmingham tonight," she muttered and pursed her lips. "The next flight to Birmingham isn't until noon tomorrow."

"That doesn't really help me," I attempted to explain my dilemma...*again.* "I'm supposed to be on the nine a.m. Birmingham to JFK flight tomorrow."

"That sounds like a problem."

Ya think?

"Is there any way I can get off that flight, then?" I asked, too hopeful for my own good. This was why they had backup flight attendants stationed at various airports, for situations like this. *Right?* "I mean, I'm not sure how I'm going to get there in enough time..."

She shook her head, and I couldn't keep my eyes off her eyebrows. Good Lord, those things were an anomaly. Big, bushy, and yet, well-maintained somehow. They were distracting. And ironic. And, considering I was in a bit of a situation, I honestly had no idea why I was even analyzing Carol's fucking eyebrows like there was a quiz on them later.

"They need you in Birmingham," she stated firmly. "There is only one other flight attendant for your flight to JFK, and all of the backups are accounted for thanks to the shortage. You're just going to have to find another way to get there."

And how in the heck was I going to manage that? A goddamn hot air balloon?

I looked at Carol, and Carol looked at me.

And, after another twenty or so seconds passed, I realized Carol and her eyebrows weren't going to offer up any solutions. I glanced at the mess of paper on the floor behind her and then back to her cold eyes. Any fuck she'd had to give, she'd given out a long time ago.

"So," I started in an attempt to carefully pry a solution out of her, "if you were me, how would you get to Birmingham?"

She shrugged. "The train, probably."

There's a train? Like, a real one? Or is she just bullshitting me?

"So, I could take a train?" I asked to confirm. Her eyebrows weren't pleased, turning down on the ends. "A train from Atlanta to Birmingham?"

"Yep. Amtrak."

Amtrak. Remember that, Cat…

"Okay… Well… Do you happen to have any information for me?" I asked and rested my elbows on the counter. "You know, like, where is the train located? How do I get there?"

C'mon, Carol. Work with me here.

She sighed, long and exaggerated, and then sat there, wordless, for what felt like an eternity.

Whose will would break more quickly?

To my surprise, I won that round, and she eventually opened a drawer on the left side of her desk and started to rummage through its contents.

"How long have you been with RoyalAir?"

"Six months."

"That explains it," she muttered under her breath.

Wow. Another point for Carol, I guess.

I bit my tongue *for the second time*. I feared if I didn't get out of Carol's office in the next five minutes, I might bite the damn thing straight off.

"Here," she said and slapped a white envelope onto the counter.

Done with our game and done with me, Carol didn't provide any instructions after that. I silently prayed she hadn't just shoved an old Chinese food menu into an envelope, lifted my elbows from the counter, and grabbed the handle of my carry-on.

Fingers and toes crossed, I strode out of the office, sat down on an empty bench, and opened up the white flap of paper on the back.

My eyes scanned the text, and relief filled my stomach, heavy and warm. Carol had *actually* given me information that could help me find my way to Birmingham before my nine a.m. flight.

Hallelujah, praise Jesus.

Unfortunately, when I got a load of the nightly Amtrak train schedule, the relief quickly dissipated.

Next train to Birmingham: 12:00 a.m.

I looked at my watch. 11:30 p.m.

Google was my bitch as I typed in the train station and plotted a foot route from my current location. Estimated time it would take for me to get to the train: twenty minutes.

"Son of a bitch," I muttered and hopped out of my seat at a dead sprint.

Chapter Three

Quinn

"You're kidding, right?" I asked my previous seatmate, Luke, as he slid into the line at customer service ahead of me. Me and the thirty people behind me had been patiently waiting our turn to try to reschedule our way to Birmingham after being diverted to Atlanta about half an hour ago.

The airport was pure chaos with a slew of Deep South flights that had been rerouted due to weather, and after a failed attempt to get anything accomplished at the gate counter and twenty brain-bleeding minutes spent on hold with the airline via the phone while I'd been waiting in line here, I wasn't in the mood for bullshit from anyone—and certainly not from Luke.

Luke looked back over his shoulder, slipping one of his grins into place to try to charm me and the rest of the crowd, but we had leg cramps, dehydration, and severe frustration on our sides—we wouldn't be swayed. "I've got an important business meeting to get to. I'm sure you understand."

"No," I said instantly. "I don't."

His grin turned condescending as he focused on my black track-style pants and the plain white T-shirt stretched over my chest. "Right. Well, trust me. This business is important—the kind of thing that can't wait."

I stepped out of my place in line, fully prepared to suffer the consequences of rejoining it at the rear, and made my way past the few people between myself and Luke.

I towered over him, and a dull roar of whispers picked up behind me.

"No," I said quietly to Luke. "What can't wait is the thirty-five people you cut who have business to attend, families to see, sick to care for, and babies to get to bed. So why don't you and I take a walk to the back of the line where we belong and let them get their rightful turn."

Luke's grin slipped into a hard mask. "I see you're intent on making a scene, but I'm hardly inconveniencing them. I'm just one person."

"Holy shit, dude," I heard one of the guys directly behind me whisper. "You're right. It is him."

Like a sixth sense, I could feel the phones being held up and switched on to record instantly. My publicist for sure wouldn't like that I'd made a scene, but the idea of putting Luke in his place in front of millions of people didn't bother me—I'd just have to make sure I made it worthwhile.

"One person, sure. One *very self-entitled* person."

"I'm not sure what your problem is—"

"You really aren't paying attention, then," I interrupted him. He glared. "You and I," I explained, "are gonna head on back to the back of the line and let these nice folks go before us. I'll even sacrifice my own spot just to keep you company. Now, come on."

"Do I need to call security?" he threatened, seemingly noticing my size for the first time but too self-righteous to back down.

"Oh, how I wish you would," I told him sweetly, batting my eyelashes as I did.

He sneered and moved to step forward as the service desk employee called the next person up, but I caught him with a gentle hand to the shoulder and pulled him back. "Not so fast," I told him, turning to usher the guys behind me forward with a jerk of my chin.

They looked at me in awe but made no move to scuttle by in the space I'd freed.

"Get your hands off me!" Luke yelled. I took my hand off of his shoulder in an effort not to push it. My publicist would whine about a scene, but he'd straight break my kneecaps over an arrest.

"Dude. Epic," the guy whispered to his friend who still hadn't moved, and then raised his voice to address me directly. "You're Quinn Bailey, right?"

I nodded.

"Fucking hell! Quinn Bailey fighting for our spot in line! You're, like, a football god. I've had you on my fantasy team for the last three years in a row."

I glanced up to see that Luke, opportunist that he was, hadn't used my fans gushing as a lesson in respect for others, but had instead bellied up to the counter to try to solve his own issues as quickly as possible while my attention was otherwise occupied.

I felt momentarily disappointed at my failure to protect these strangers' honor, but the rest of the line didn't give me long to think about it as a ripple quickly informed everyone as to who I was.

In no time, I had a group of fifteen people around me, all waiting with scraps of paper they'd dug out of their belongings and passing around a pen for me to use to sign.

"Don't worry about that dude, Quinn," one kid said. "Karma will make him her bitch soon."

"Jeremy!" a woman I suspected was his mother snapped. "Language!"

He shrugged. "Sorry, Mom. But this is Quinn Bailey, and he just tried to give up his spot in line for us! He should be on a private plane or some sh—stuff."

I laughed and smiled at the kid and then his mother. "Listen to your mama, Jeremy. Manners are important." I cocked my head to Luke at the counter. "That guy never listened to his mama. Guaranteed."

Jeremy laughed and jerked up his chin.

I signed a few more autographs, letting people move up to the counter as they passed me in line and only stepped away when my phone rang in my pocket.

"Hello?" I answered, leaning into one of the walls in a little hallway that jutted off to the side to try to get some privacy. The main terminal was jam-packed with bodies weaving in and out, trying to be polite to the people around them and cutting them off with no remorse at the same time. It was funny to watch from the sidelines.

"I called the airline, and there aren't any flights with seats on them until Tuesday," my assistant, Jillian, said in my ear without any pleasantries or greeting.

She'd been with me for the last three years, and she was more efficient than anyone else I knew. My world was hers to command, such was her badassery.

Her voice wasn't happy now, though, obviously feeling a little bitter about working when I'd supposedly given her three days off.

"So, basically, unless I want to stay in Atlanta until it's time to go home again, I'm fucked on the flight side."

"Basically."

"So, what are my other options?"

"Teleportation?" she replied testily.

I rolled my eyes. "Look, I'm sorry I called you. But I was on hold for fifteen minutes, and the line at customer service was hella long. Then I got into it with a guy from my flight—"

"Got into it? Jesus Christ, Quinn! Now Nathan is going to be calling me. This was supposed to be my chance to have sex with my boyfriend uninterrupted."

"Oh God. Too much information, Jilly."

"Deal with it."

I collected my thoughts as I took her order to heart. Nathan, my publicist, *was* going to be calling her nonstop. And then, when he couldn't reach me—because no way in *fuck* was I going to answer his calls—he'd be bothering her even more. Her ability to have some kinky orgy with her boyfriend would be grossly diminished, and if it were me getting my sex party interrupted, I'd be annoyed too.

"So, what are my options here? And don't say goddamn teleportation again. If I had the ability, I would have done that from the start."

"A rental car."

"Perfect." I smiled and shoved to standing at full height again. "I'll head over there now."

Jilly sighed in my ear. "Don't bother. I already called, and they're all gone."

Denial ran strong through my veins. "All of them?"

"All."

"Even the Mini Coopers?" No way every fucking rental car in this airport was accounted for. Right?

She scoffed. "As if you could fit in a Mini Cooper."

"I—"

"And yes, they're gone too."

Goddammit.

"So…"

Planes, trains, automobiles, I recited in my head.

"What about a train?"

"Ding, ding, ding," she cooed. "You got it, big guy. Midnight train bound for Birmingham. I got you a ticket. You just have to pick it up at the train station ticket office."

"And you couldn't have just told me that from the beginning?"

"Definitely not."

"Jesus Christ. You're fired."

She laughed. Guffawed, really. "You wish. By the way, the train leaves in forty minutes. You're going to want to move your ass. See you in seventy-two hours, Quinndolyn."

Quinndolyn. She'd been talking to my brother.

"Jilly!" I snapped, but there was no one there. No one but dead air.

Chapter Four

Cat

My purse flopped against my hip with every long stride while my carry-on bag teetered on its wheels behind me. I lifted my wrist up toward my face and did my best to check the time as the screen of my watch bounced up and down with the movements from my hurried pace.

11:55 p.m.

I had five minutes to get my ass on the train platform, and I was still making—*more like sprinting*—my way through the station and toward the ticket counter.

"Ticket counter?" I shouted toward a security guard standing watch near an empty entrance hallway.

He pointed toward the open doorway directly across from him, and I nodded in acknowledgment, calling "Thank you!" over my shoulder as I redirected my body to the left.

The warm humidity of a July night in Atlanta had permeated the station's walls, making my skin feel sticky and my lungs damn near suffocated.

No doubt, my clothes and hair were a fucking mess at this point—uniform in wrinkled disarray, the long run in my hose probably reaching my waist, and my hair frizzy and damp with humidity and perspiration.

Sweat rolled down the skin of my back, and I could feel my heart throbbing inside of my chest. All of this fucking polyester RoyalAir required me to wear made me feel like I was roasting inside of my own body.

My heels click-clacked loudly across the tiled floor, echoing off the large walls as I made my way to the ticket counter at the end of the hall.

I was exhausted, and I'm sure I proved that point to the lady behind the Plexiglas window when I came to an abrupt stop in front of her, flopping my purse on top of the counter and grabbing my knees with my hands.

"I'm sorry," I muttered through erratic breaths as I strove to get my shit together and not pass out right in front of her. "I basically ran from the airport to get here," I added, each of my words coming out in a short, abrupt burst.

Between my lungs being one inhale away from bursting and the Sahara that had taken up residence in my throat, I needed water. And a nap.

"The midnight train," I forced out. "I need the midnight train to Birmingham."

"That'll be forty-two dollars." She tapped her fingers across her keyboard in quick succession. "And you have exactly two minutes to get to the platform," she updated, and her pink-painted lips frowned ever so slightly for my cause.

"Oh God," I muttered and with a shaky hand, swiped my credit card to pay.

"You can do it," she encouraged and slid my ticket toward me.

"And where exactly is the platform?"

"Back that way." She pointed her finger behind me. "Take a right at the end of the hall and follow the signs toward Platform Nine. If you run, you can make it. And good news," she said with a hopeful smile, "it looks like the train might be running about three minutes late."

"Okay! Thank you!" I shouted as I snatched my ticket off the counter, threw my purse over my shoulder, and ran back the way I came.

I bolted down the hallway and followed the signs toward Platform Nine like an Olympic champion at the starting gun, ticket clutched tightly in my sweaty hand. I quickened my pace to an all-out sprint when what sounded like the screeching arrival of a train filled my ears. The clacking noises of my high heels resonated around the vandalized walls of the hallway with a clanging echo.

When I reached the platform, showed my ticket to the Amtrak agent, and pushed open the door that led toward the outside platform, the sticky, hot Georgia air hit my face like a sack of potatoes.

Sweet baby pickles, it's hot as balls outside.

I looked around to find at least ten other people standing on the cement platform, waiting patiently.

"Did I make it?" I asked an older man with a gray baseball cap covering his eyes and a newspaper resting beneath his right arm. "This is the train to Birmingham, right?"

"Yes, ma'am." He nodded. "They just made an announcement. The train is a few minutes behind schedule."

"Okay. Thanks."

The train was late. I'd never been so happy for tardiness in my life.

I set my purse on the ground beside my feet and picked at my hair. It was useless, though. My normally straightened, long brown hair had been struck by the humidity plague of the South. Surely, criminal curls had gone rogue, finding their way into my tresses and encouraging frizz and chaos.

I sighed and blew out a breath.

Choosing convenience over style, I pulled out a ponytail holder from my purse. My hair was up, gloriously off my shoulders, and secured in a messy bun just as a raucous, metallic shriek announced the arrival of the train.

It sped to a stop at the platform, standing in defiance of its current condition—all corroded iron and tacky upholstery. The doors reluctantly eased open with the force of an old station guard as if gripped by age, the handles stiff with arthritis.

As I boarded, I realized there was one benefit of taking a midnight train—hardly anyone was on it, and I managed a nice, roomy window seat all to my lonesome.

Adrenaline still pumping, I placed a hand to my chest and took several deep inhales. All of that rushing around had my heart rate cruising at a higher than normal pace.

Okay. I can relax now.

Somehow, someway, I'd fucking made it.

Settling into my self-entitled throne, I set my purse by my feet, pulled my phone out of the front pocket, and enjoyed the fact that I was no longer running through a train station like a crazed maniac.

My phone vibrated in my hands as the train started to plunge forward at an excruciating pace. Rocking back and forth, its initial whining and groaning eventually settled into a soft hum as we found our optimal speed and rhythm.

I checked the screen to find a text from Casey.

Casey: Did they take you off the flight?

Me: Hell no. Carol with the eyebrows was not having that. I'm currently sitting on a midnight Amtrak toward Birmingham.

Casey: Damn, girl, were you wearing roller skates? How in the hell did you make it to the train station that quickly?

Me: God, I wish. But I can pretty much skip going to the gym for the next month.

Not that I ever really fit gym time into my busy schedule, but that was neither here nor there. I had good intentions. Ones that generally fell through, but the motivation was still there…sort of.

Casey: I'd love to know the last time your little ass was actually in the gym.

Me: Shut up.

Casey: :) Be safe tonight. Let me know when you make it to Birmingham, okay?

Me: You got it.

Before I could put my phone back in my purse, it started ringing and vibrating in my hands. ***Incoming Call: Casey***

What the heck?

I tapped the green phone icon with my index finger and held the phone to my ear.

"Hel—" I started to greet, but Casey's melodic voice interrupted me.

"Just a—" he sang into the receiver, and I grimaced the instant his booming voice banged against my eardrum. He might have said something about me being a small town girl, but I was too busy trying to recover from the brain bleed.

"Oh my God," I muttered as he went on about my lonely world, and I held the phone away from my face.

But he didn't care. He was a man on a mission—a Journey, "Don't Stop Believin'" mission. His voice still reached me with ease through the receiver that was no longer pressed to my ear, such was the level of his volume.

I stared down at the screen of my phone, shaking my head, amused more than anything else.

I didn't need him to sing on about being on a midnight train to know where he got his inspiration to sing this song to me now, but he did anyway.

He belted, he enunciated—he fucking slayed—but an echo emerged anyway. It only took a few more words to realize it was *two* different voices, each singing to me with their own accent and inflection.

Huh? I scrunched up my nose and lifted my gaze from the screen of my phone, scanning the area around my seat to find the source.

I saw full lips moving in sync with Casey's voice, and then I was met with familiar, way too alluring blue eyes staring back at me from across the aisle.

Holy moly. It was 2A. The handsome as hell mystery man from my flight.

With my phone still clutched in my hand, every muscle in my body froze, and my face washed blank with confusion. It was like the wheels of my brain couldn't spin fast enough to take in the information presented in front of me.

He witnessed the surprise register on my face before I could hide it, and a small smile played on his lips. And his voice, as he sang along with Casey, was sweet and decadent like cheesecake, the richness of his tones luxurious and intense.

Internally, my brain felt like it might explode, and my heart pounded erratically in my chest as fluttering wings moved up from my belly and into my chest. Externally, I had no idea what my reaction was, but I silently prayed it wasn't something weird like drooling or going slack-jawed.

Mr. 2A grinned, and I couldn't do anything but stare—half shocked and completely mesmerized.

But, eventually, a grin crept on to my face and soon stretched from one side of my mouth to the other, even forcing my cheeks up toward my eyes.

They both sang in harmony about not having a particular destination, Casey through the phone, and mystery man turned vocalist from the train seat across from my mine. I hoped to all that was holy they weren't right. *This fucker better be headed for Birmingham.*

Casey stopped, but my ridiculously handsome trainmate kept singing, while he simultaneously—and smoothly as hell—moved to the seat beside mine.

His soft Southern accent only added to his surprisingly natural singing ability, and I got sucked deeper and deeper into his honey trap.

"What the what, Cat? Who's singing backup with me?" Casey asked from the phone, and my new seatmate just smirked and kept on singing, through the next verse and until he reached the part about strangers in the night and the smell of wine and cheap perfume.

"Hell-o? Cat?" Casey's voice called from my phone, pulling me out of my mindless gawk. I lifted the phone to my ear again.

"Yeah, Case?"

"Girlfriend, are you being serenaded right now?"

"Um... *Apparently?*" I shrugged and giggled nervously at the same time, all the while the man who should've felt like a complete stranger was acting like we were anything but. He was seemingly comfortable with sharing the spot beside mine, and I watched as he pulled his duffle bag over to his feet and slid it underneath his seat.

"Apparently?" Casey questioned. "What does that even mean? Who was that?"

"Well..." I muttered and met the charming stare of Mr. Blue Eyes.

"Quinn," he kindly answered for me, obviously privy to my phone conversation thanks to Casey's notoriously loud voice.

Quinn. He had a name. And I imagined it would roll off my tongue perfectly.

"Who's Quinn?" Casey asked, and then answered his own question with, "He sounds like someone I'd like to meet."

My phone vibrated, and I looked at the screen to find a FaceTime request.

"Oh my God," I said, and an exasperated laugh escaped my lips. "I'm not FaceTiming you right now."

Both Casey and Quinn laughed.

"I'm also ending this call," I added, and before quickly tapping the red phone icon, I added, "Bye, Case. I'll text you when I make it to Birmingham."

My phone pinged with an irate text message a moment later.

Casey: Oh no, you didn't just hang up on me...

Me: Whoops. My bad.

Casey: Before you turn off your phone and start ignoring me, tell me who the Casanova on the phone was. Girl, his voice was so dreamy...

Me: You're never going to believe this, but...

I hit send. And, since Quinn and I were apparently the best of buddies, I turned toward him and pointed the camera of my phone toward his face. "Can you smile real quick while I take a picture?"

Casey will die when he finds out who was singing with him.

Quinn didn't bat an eye, grinning directly toward me and showing no signs of insecurity. "Just make sure you get my good side, okay?"

"Your good side?" I questioned with a laugh, and he nodded.

From my viewpoint, there were no bad sides to be seen. Only good, better, and *ah-fucking-mazing.*

"We can't all have flawless skin and gorgeous smiles from all angles like you, Cat," he said with a sexy little wink and tilted his head slightly to the left. "This is my good side, by the way."

There was no difference. Left, right, backward, forward, upside-fucking-down, every side looked like perfection from where I sat.

Wait... Was he hitting on me?

I sure fucking hope so...

My cheeks heated and flushed. Hell, they were probably one more sly compliment away from bursting into flames.

This man was dangerous, and I wasn't sure if it was in the very best or worst way.

In the wise words of Uncle Jesse, *Have mercy.*

As I snapped a picture, I couldn't stop myself from taking additional inventories of his face, his body, his overall demeanor. You'd think I'd managed enough ogling opportunities on the plane, but for some insane reason, I still craved more.

It's because he's so fucking beautiful to look at.

I quickly decided no one feature made Quinn so crazy handsome, though his blue eyes came close. People often spoke of the color of eyes, as if that were of importance, yet Quinn's would probably be beautiful in any shade. From them came this intensity, a playfulness, an honesty, a gentleness, and this unquestionable, yet very palpable, charm.

My phone vibrated in my hands, and I startled, my eyes flicking down to the screen.

Casey: Hello???

Casey: WHAT AM I NEVER GOING TO BELIEVE???

I grinned, and as I attached the picture to my text response, Quinn asked, "Well, did you get my good side?"

I sent the message to Casey and met his blue as the ocean eyes. "You looked all right, I guess."

His lips crested into a smirk, and this sexy as hell, soft laugh slipped past his lips.

His response to my teasing only made me like him more.

There was a part of me that felt like I already knew him, which was crazy. Technically speaking, I hadn't even really met him.

Yes! Introduce yourself. It will be the perfect icebreaker.

"So…uh…I feel like we know each other's names, but we haven't really been introduced…" I smiled and held out my hand. "I'm Cat. Well, my full name is actually Catharine, but everyone calls me Cat. Oh, it's Catharine Wild, by the way. Or Cat Wild, if you take the whole nickname thing into consideration."

Wow, Cat. Real fucking smooth introduction.

His eyes glimmered with a smile. "It's a pleasure, Cat." He took my hand in his. "I'm Quinn Bailey. No nickname, though."

With my small hand engulfed within the warmth of his and our eyes locked, we stayed like that for way longer than two people normally would.

I think you're insanely handsome, my brain whispered as we released hands. *Can I keep you?*

A slow, warm as honey smile crested his mouth, and I had the insane urge to run my tongue across it just to get a taste.

Good God. Was I really going to get to spend a nearly four-hour train ride sitting beside this man?

What he was, what was so alluring about him, I couldn't quite put my finger on. It was like it came from somewhere deep within.

And the intrigue, well, it was beyond my control. It just *was.*

I barely knew the guy, but hell if I wasn't fascinated as fuck.

My phone vibrated in my lap, and I looked down at the screen.

Casey: O-M-fucking-G. That's my husband!

It looked like I wasn't the only one who remembered Quinn.

Casey: I'm so jelly right now. Quick, tell him I love him.

Nor the only one to understand the overpowering allure.

Me: Sorry. You're breaking up. I must not be getting good service.

Casey: We're texting, you whore! You either get the message or you don't.

Me: Then I'm definitely not getting yours.

Casey: Wow. Bold-faced lying. That's cold. I wasn't going to say anything, but bitches get stitches. Carol can't make you take a train to make your flight. Either they get you there, or you don't fly. Too bad you're already on the train. Buh-bye now!

Well, fuck. Carol probably laughed her fucking eyebrows off after I'd left.

But I was already on my way now, and thanks to Quinn, things were just getting interesting.

God, I just hoped I could manage to keep awkward rambles under wraps.

As I adjusted myself in my seat, I remembered how my arrival to the train station had been—a thirty-minute sprint, frizzy hair, and makeup that was pretty much sweated off.

Instantly, nerves fluttered inside of my belly.

Fucking hell.

Why couldn't I have at least had a moment to freshen up before this train ride?

Chapter Five

Quinn

She'd introduced herself on a ramble, and it had only made me more smitten with her presence. This girl, Cat Wild, was fucking adorable.

Now frazzled and blushing, she searched for the most comfortable position in the seat beside me. She was antsy and maybe a little uncomfortable, and the way she flopped her bag around like a fish on the floor beside her feet made me smile.

Thanks to Casey and Journey, it'd been easy to break the ice.

Even though the train had been running behind schedule, she'd still whirled onto it in a flurry, giving me one of the best surprises of my life.

She hadn't even noticed my presence, or really, anyone else's for that matter, and as she strode down the aisle, erratically looking for a seat, a wave of her delicious scent had hit me like a lightning bolt. Orangy and light, every note of it felt fresher than the last. It was a scent I'd become wholly familiar with after two hours in a metal tube in the sky, and one I thought I'd never smell again.

She twisted in the seat, back and forth, trying to calm down, and I couldn't help but tease her about it.

"You accidentally sit on an anthill since the last time I saw you?" I asked softly. Her eyes jerked up to mine, and her body settled immediately on the command of her embarrassment.

I watched intently as a pink stain bloomed across the apple of her closest cheek.

"What? Oh. No," she stuttered. "I just had to rush to get here, and the adrenaline crash has me a little..." She jiggled her hands in front of herself instead of using a word.

I smiled.

"Plus, these hose are about to drive me to insanity."

I blinked, trying to understand, before letting out a little chuckle when I couldn't. "I'm sorry, what?"

"My..." She blushed again, looking down to her lap as she spoke, "panty hose. They're cutting off my circulation."

My cock jerked awake on the word panty, and suddenly, I was glad for her inability to look directly at me. *Nuns, grandmothers, grandfathers, wrinkled ball sacs,* I recited in my mind, quickly trying to calm my half chub back to no chub.

"Well, don't feel obligated to keep up the uniform for me," I told her, trying to be solicitous but flushing when I realized it sounded flirtatious.

She looked up at me then, chewing nervously on her lip and then looking over to the restroom. I followed her gaze to see the little light above it shone red, with a big X through the picture of people above it.

She chewed her lip some more, and all I could do was watch, transfixed by the manipulation of plump flesh, until she got up the guts to speak again. "Would you... Do you mind covering your eyes? I'm literally two seconds away from murder if I don't get these things off."

I smiled and immediately covered my lookers with a beefy hand. "I'm looking to live, Cat," I mumbled through my fingers. "Take all the time you need."

She laughed, the sound echoing around in my self-imposed darkness, and I tried to fight against my body's desire to soak it all in.

What is it about this girl?

Pulling my hand away from my eyes enough to look down at the floor and let in some light as the train moved from side to side, thinking that might assuage my body's bid for companionship, I caught a glimpse of her feet as she slipped her heels off one at a time. Her toes were long and painted, and I swear to God, she had some of the sexiest little feet I'd ever seen.

Feet? Really? What the hell is wrong with me?

I willed my eyes to close again, but they disobeyed me. The slide of her panty hose as they slipped off of her feet and left her skin bare made me shiver.

Oh God. My brain swam inside my skull.

"Almost done, Kitty Cat? I'm getting a little motion sick with my eyes covered like this."

"Oh, shoot," she squeaked. "Yeah, of course. All good."

I uncovered my eyes as she slipped her heels back on and tucked a hunk of curlier hair behind her ear. The humidity had obviously been to work on it. "Sorry about that," she apologized.

I shook my head and scrunched my face. "It's fine…as long as you feel less like killing me now."

Her laugh was melodious. "No worries. The murderous rage is all gone."

I slapped my hands together playfully in a prayer position and looked to the ceiling. "Thank God."

We were silent for a moment, the train rocking and clacking on the tracks. Lights from outside flashed through the dark windows like a strobe, lighting Catharine's face so much her eyes glowed and then plunging it back into darkness in an erratic rhythm.

"I'm surprised to see you here," I commented softly when all the flashing light finally blurred into a soft glow.

"Really? Why?"

I laughed and shrugged, crossing one ankle over my other knee and sinking farther into the worn fabric of the seat. "Well, you are an employee of the airline. I figured if anyone would be able to get on another flight, it would be you."

She pulled her feet up into the seat, leaning her knees into the side so she could cuddle up comfortably without flashing me. "Sadly, no. I'm relatively new, and RoyalAir is relatively small. There were other stranded fish, and they were much bigger than me. And I need to be on a flight out of Birmingham tomorrow morning." She shrugged. "So here I am."

"Here you are," I murmured to myself. She heard me, of course, because I wasn't silent by some form of magic, so it seemed a little creepier than intended. I kept talking to try to play it off.

"I'm on my way home to see my brother and my folks. A real quick trip, and the soonest they could get me there on a plane was Tuesday."

"Ouch," she remarked, scrunching her nose. "Sorry about that. If I ever get to talk to upper management, I'll tell them to make a note to change that."

I laughed. "Ah, Luke. He was a real peach, huh? You'll be thrilled to hear I ran into him again at customer service."

"Oh, no." She sat up straighter, her face draining of every drop of amusement.

"Yeah, he was just as lovely."

Her giggle was delicate as she found her humor again in my playfulness. "There's almost always one on every flight."

"A douchebag?" I asked, and she laughed. Hands together in a cute knot, she lifted them up and settled them under her chin.

I watched her slender wrists flex as she nodded on top of them.

"I'm sure. Are you always on the flight to Birmingham?"

"Mostly," she confirmed. "Occasionally, I have to do another route. But they just transferred me over to JFK for my home base, and I do this run five days a week." She blushed a little, looking at her lap and back up again. "Truthfully, though, I only started about six months ago."

"Oh, wow. A fledgling flight attendant," I teased with a smile. "Is it everything you thought it would be?"

"Not really," she admitted. The train rocked hard as we rounded a curve in the track, and one of her navy pumps teetered in front of her seat and fell over. She reached down to right it, but I was already there. The skin of her fingers was cool against my own.

She paused briefly, her eyes jumping to mine as she gathered her train of thought again. "But I really like it, and I have some good friends."

I smiled and tried to ignore her touch as it lingered like a phantom. "Yeah, Casey seems like a hoot."

She nodded easily. She might occasionally play the part of annoyed when it came to her friend Mr. Bloomingdale's, but under the surface, there was nothing but a whole lot of love and respect.

"Five days a week, huh?" That was a normal work schedule, but it seemed like an awful lot of days to spend so far away from home. Of course, who was I to talk? During the season, I was almost never at my own fucking place. "What do you do in your free time? Play any sports?"

Her nose wrinkled, and I laughed outright. "Not into sports, then?"

"Not particularly. I'm more the type to trip over my own feet."

I shrugged. "I'm sure you could get enough people together to start a league for that if you really wanted."

She laughed, rolling belly laughs like she thought maybe I was a lunatic.

Hopefully, psychopaths are her type…

"What about you? What do you like to do?" she asked as she gathered herself, sighing hard like the laughter had tired her out before nuzzling deeper into the seat.

I rubbed at the back of my neck, suddenly eager to lie down. Preferably with her next to me, in a bed big enough to sustain some sexual gymnastics, but if an opportunity presented itself, I'd try not to be picky. "A little bit of everything, really. Rock-climbing, hiking, skiing…"

"Geez, stop rubbing it in."

I chuckled. "I'm pretty good at drinking beer and watching TV too."

Her eyes lit up. “What shows?”

“Uh oh. I feel distinctly like this is a test.”

Her smirk was enthralling—sexy and edgy and confident. “Only to see how honest you are.” I liked this side of her.

“Well, let’s see. I like *NCIS* because Abby is a badass, and *Live PD* because criminal America is endlessly entertaining, and *Teen Mom OG* because—”

“*Teen Mom OG*?” she asked, her voice shaking with laughter.

“Of course. Tell me you could watch Tyler’s vows to Catelyn and not tear up. Tell me, and I’ll call you a liar.”

She laughed and settled deeper into her seat, finally relaxing in a way that said she was comfortable around me. Her arms fell to her sides, and her chest opened up, her shoulders rolling back to allow it. I let out a deep breath I didn’t know I’d been holding.

“And what’s your favorite show, kitten? MSNBC?”

She bit her lip, blushing slightly at the nickname, and admitted, “I don’t know about favorite, but the one I watch most often is the *Kardashians*.”

“Ahh. Now it comes out. “

“They run those dang reruns all the time!” she shouted. “This is a timing and availability thing!”

“Sure,” I taunted. “Like you weren’t hanging on to Kim’s Instagram last Christmas just waiting to see Kylie’s baby bump along with everyone else.”

Her cheeks turned so red I laughed harder.

“Speaking of a gang of attractive siblings,” I segued. “How about you? Do you have any?”

She shook her head slightly, a fond smile curling her mouth as she thought about her family. “Nope. Just me and my mom and dad. But Casey and my other friend, Nikki, might as well be. They’re just as annoying anyway.”

I laughed at that. I knew the feeling.

“You?” she asked.

“Yep. I have one brother by blood and a whole bevy of asshole friends who act like they are."

She nodded with a smile, but her face softened sweetly then. "It's nice."

"It is," I agreed.

Nicer than I ever could have expected, I thought as I looked at a woman I hadn't known six hours ago.

At a woman that I suddenly couldn't get enough of.

Chapter Six

Cat

"Well..." Quinn started and looked toward me with a soft, maybe even slightly gloomy smile. "I guess this is it, huh?" The question hung in the air, heavy and thick with hesitation and melancholy, as our train pulled into the station in Birmingham.

"Yeah." I felt my lips turn down at the corners of their own accord. "I guess so."

We both stood when the train came to a stop, and like a gentleman, Quinn motioned me out of the way and proceeded to pull my carry-on down from the overhead rack.

"Thanks," I said, and his blue eyes shone.

I felt compelled to say something witty, something memorable, but my brain wasn't up to the task. I guessed it was still reeling from the fact that I'd just spent three and a half hours on a train—speeding through the middle of nowhere Alabama in the late hours of night—and I'd done the exact opposite of what I'd expected.

Instead of napping or finding solace from boredom with Candy Crush and random playlists on iTunes, I'd chatted with a complete stranger until it felt like we weren't strangers anymore.

Quinn Bailey—a man who held the power of comfort and ease and apparently knew all of the right things to say to a girl. He was a force to be reckoned with, an enigma among my usual male acquaintances.

Where most men would have come across as pushy and too overzealous, his vibe was the opposite. A Southern gentleman to his core, he was playful and flirtatious, but only when he understood those qualities were welcomed.

And good God, he was funny.

I honestly couldn't remember the last time I'd laughed so much with another human being.

"You know what I think?" he asked, and my eyes met his.

"What do you think?"

"I think you should give me your phone number. Just in case of emergency. Or, you know, just so I can call you."

A soft laugh escaped my lips. "Okay."

His blue eyes lightened. "Yeah?"

"Yeah," I responded with one simple word, even though on the inside, I was jumping up and down like a giddy lunatic. It took all of my willpower to appear cool and collected.

Quinn pulled his cell phone out of his pocket, and as I recited my phone number to him, he saved my info into his contacts.

The doors of the train opened with a loud creak, and people started to file out in a surprisingly slow and easy manner. I guessed it was hard to be in a rush after spending the entire night on a train.

Preparing for our turn to exit, I started to wrap my hand around my carry-on handle, but I had to redirect it when my phone started ringing inside my purse. I pulled it out of my bag to realize it was an incoming call from a number I had never seen before.

"Just checking," Quinn mused, and I turned and looked up to find him gazing down at me with a little smirk.

I hadn't really calculated how tall he was until that moment—him standing behind me while we waited to file off the train. At five foot seven, I wasn't a short girl by any means, but Quinn was well over six foot.

He raised the screen of his phone, and when Cat Wild shone

back at me, I quickly realized he was the one calling me.

What the heck?

A second later, he ended the call with a quick tap to the screen and slid his phone back into his pocket.

"Wait…" I paused for a brief moment as my brain put the puzzle together. "Were you just checking to make sure I didn't give you a bogus number?"

Quinn shrugged and sent a sexy little wink in my direction. "You never know, Kitty Cat."

I had a hard time imagining that type of situation had ever happened to a man like him. If anything, women probably Sharpie-tattooed their numbers all over their bodies, just hoping he'd catch a glimpse of one.

"But good news," he added. "Now you can call me whenever you like."

"Emergency purposes?" I teased and promptly added him as a contact.

"*Any* purposes," he clarified, and I blushed under his flirtatious gaze. "All the fucking purposes."

I blushed harder. Smiled. And then giggled nervously.

Good God, he is dangerously charming.

It was our turn to file off the train, and before I managed to walk down the exit steps that led to the platform, Quinn gently squeezed my shoulder from behind, whispering into my ear, "I'll call you. Have a safe flight back to New York."

"Okay." I smiled at him over my shoulder. "And you too."

Our eyes locked as we stepped onto the platform, and for one brief yet very reluctant moment, our feet grew roots that held us in our spots. The crowd from the train moved around us, but neither of us seemed to care.

A hesitant goodbye suspended in time.

Eventually, in the name of getting to the airport on time, I had to break the trance. With a soft smile and a little wave, I felt his name roll off my tongue. "Bye, Quinn."

"Bye, Cat."

And that was that. Quinn walked in one direction, and I went in the other, both of us heading toward completely different destinations.

As my heels smacked across the cement platform, I felt disappointment over the idea of time. It was moments like these when I realized it passed too quickly. I wanted a redo of my train ride to Birmingham with Quinn.

But it wouldn't really be a redo, because I wouldn't have changed a thing. I just wanted to experience it again for the first time and try to find a way to savor how good being in his presence had made me feel.

It probably didn't take a rocket scientist to figure out I was insanely attracted to Quinn. I'd felt that attraction the instant I'd seen him in seat 2A, and it only grew stronger when he'd joined Casey's Journey rendition and made himself comfortable in the seat next to mine.

Attraction was a thought inside your head that said, "There's something about this…"

And believe me, when it came to Quinn, there was definitely something about him.

I couldn't stop myself from gravitating toward this man who so easily had captured my attention, and the more time I'd spent with him and the more I learned about him, the more I wanted to learn about him, the more I wanted to experience all that was *him.*

Over and over again.

If Quinn Bailey was the metal, I was the fucking magnet.

With my purse securely on my shoulder and my carry-on sliding behind me, I followed the signs that directed me toward the main area of the train station—where I would find a taxi to take me to the airport.

And thankfully, I had plenty of time to actually get to the airport, check in with my gate agent, and get my plane ready for the flight back to NYC.

Although, as Casey had finally pointed out, I could have avoided this altogether.

You wouldn't trade last night for anything, my mind taunted. *Not even less hassle.*

I couldn't even argue with myself. I knew my mind was right.

The platform was busier than I'd expected at nearly four in the morning, but my tired legs navigated the cement path just fine, moving with ease around motionless bystanders and stationary bags.

By the time I reached the door that led toward the inside of the train station, the chatter behind me grew louder until I heard a familiar name being called out several times.

I stopped in my tracks and turned to find a small crowd of excited people surrounding Quinn on the other side of the platform. His back was toward me at that point, but it was apparent he was laughing and smiling with the crowd, the screens of their phones catching his every move, some lucky enough to even get a selfie with him.

I imagined this was what it would look like if Kim Kardashian had stepped off that platform.

Shocked, I watched as he took several of their pens and scribbled what I assumed was his name across newspapers and notebooks and pretty much anything they could find for him to sign.

Am I hallucinating?

I mean, considering I'd just taken a late-night, nearly four-hour train ride after working most of the day, it was possible. But the scene that lay before me was too real. Too vivid.

Each flash of a camera and excited murmur was not fogged over or hazy in a dreamlike way. No. It was most definitely happening.

But what I couldn't understand was *why.*

Was Quinn Bailey someone important? Or more than that, someone famous?

And if that was the case, how in the heck had I not known that?

If one of The Real Housewives or Khloe Kardashian had been sitting beside me on a four-hour train ride, you could bet your ass I'd have known who they were. I might have been overworked as a flight attendant, but I didn't live under a rock. I was hip to the pop culture game. I kept up with *US Weekly*, and pretty much every show on E! was on regular rotation on my television.

I felt like an idiot for not understanding why the person I'd just spent most of my night with was being treated like royalty. Without drawing any attention to myself, I exited the platform and found a quiet, secluded spot inside the train station to pull my cell phone out of my purse.

And then I did what anyone in my situation would do.

I consulted Google.

My fingers tapped out the letters of his name until Quinn Bailey stood proud in the search bar. With one quick tap to the enter button, Google gave me everything I needed to know.

About 1.5 million search results to be exact.

My eyes read the first little snippet of a result, which just so happened to be Quinn Bailey's Wikipedia page.

He has a fucking Wikipedia page?

Quinn Matthias Bailey is an American football quarterback for the New York Mavericks of the National Football League (NFL).

Holy moly. He was a professional athlete.

I honestly wasn't an expert when it came to anything sports-related, but I knew enough to know that NFL meant he was a *huge* deal, and I was reasonably certain the quarterback was pretty much the most important guy on the team.

Quinn Bailey was an NFL quarterback. For the New York freaking Mavericks.

And I'd just spent four hours talking to him like he was just some regular guy off the street. How had I not asked what he did for a living? Was I that distracted by his good looks and easy lead of the conversation?

Not to mention, I'd given him my phone number with the

internal hope that there was an actual chance he'd call me and ask me out on a date.

The outlook of a phone call from Quinn was feeling less positive by the second.

I mean, didn't celebrities and famous people generally stick to each other?

I was a flight attendant from Cincinnati. Not Selena Gomez.

Sure, I had a pretty rocking greeting card shop on Etsy that I'd been doing with my dad for years, but that was about it. My life was probably boring compared to what Quinn saw on a daily basis.

Hell, the only red-carpet event I'd been to was Black Friday at Target.

Ten minutes passed, my head in my phone in the exact same spot in the train station, scrolling through Quinn Bailey's page on the Mavericks roster, followed by three pages of his Google Image results. I'd thought he was dreamy in his everyday clothes, but Lord Almighty, he looked fucking ah-mazing in a football uniform.

Had I really just spent an entire night sitting next to this guy?

He hadn't even *hinted* at the fact that he was someone whose handsome face was known by millions of people across the world.

The whole thing was surreal. Hands down, it was the weirdest day I'd ever had in my entire life, and it had literally just gotten started.

Okay, Cat. It's time to stop gawking and move your ass again.

I had a flight to catch, and that meant I didn't have time for OCD-level fixation and overanalyzing. But as I grabbed my carry-on and headed toward the taxi line, I couldn't stop myself from thinking, *Pfft. Yeah. Probably don't hold your breath waiting for Mr. Famous Quarterback to call you…*

Chapter Seven

Quinn

It took nearly forty-five minutes to sign all of the autographs I needed to in order to actually make it *out* of the train station and into a taxi.

I never minded it, giving my fans a little piece of myself as they waited patiently with excitement wherever I happened to be. I remembered what it was like to be one of them, to look up to the guys in the league with adoration and goals fluttering through my mind. I saw myself in all of them, and so I gave with the same amount of care and attention I would have wanted from one of my heroes.

Unfortunately, this time came with a price—having to live with the look of shock I'd seen on Cat's face as she'd taken me in with them. Her step had stuttered and her eyes had widened, and I swore there'd been a brief glimpse of betrayal in her features.

And holy hell, that made me feel rotten.

It'd been clear from the beginning—hell, from the plane—that she hadn't known who I was. It seemed so clichéd, but I'd done the stupid thing, been the girl in the horror movie who hides under the bed, and I'd kept it secret from her—all for the thrill of feeling her open up to me, laugh openly, and talk to me like a regular human being.

It felt good to be teased—something anyone other than my

teammates, brother, and Jilly rarely had the guts to do—and linger in the background while I focused on getting to know *her*.

As soon as people knew I was any kind of celebrity, all focus shifted to me. And frankly, I was bored with myself. Focusing on someone else, delving into their likes and wants and dreams, felt soul-enriching—like I was filling a hole inside myself.

I shook off my negative thoughts and got over it.

Those four hours had been some of the best of my life. I was still going to call her, and I'd deal with the fallout when I did.

Resolved to my new plan, I took out my phone and texted my traitor brother.

Me: I'm in Birmingham. Not that you care since you decided not to pick me up and MADE ME GET A CAB, ASSHOLE.

Denver: Busy…sleeping…bye

Me: I'm flipping you off.

He didn't answer.

Just for fun, I sent him one more line of text in one-word increments.

Me: I'll
Me: Call
Me: You
Me: When
Me: I
Me: Get
Me: To
Me: Mom
Me: And

The buzz of my phone interrupted me.

Denver: I WILL END YOU

I laughed out loud, and the cab driver's eyes came to me in the rearview mirror.

And then he did a double take.

Busted.

It took him a minute to work up the courage to ask, but when he did, his voice was strong. "Are you…are you Quinn Bailey?"

I smiled my charming public smile. "Guilty."

"Oh, shit, dude!"

The car swerved, and I grabbed on to the seat in front of me as I laughed. "Easy, buddy."

"Oh, shit!" he yelled, swerving back into the appropriate lane.

"Don't worry." I glanced at his GPS with my home address programmed in. "It looks like we've got about an hour and fifteen minutes to get to know one another. You just take your time."

His eyes were manic as they flashed to the road, back to me in the mirror, and back again several times. "No shit? You don't mind talking?"

I shrugged and extended a long arm against the top of the whole back seat. "Just as easy as sitting here, I figure." I was tired as all hell, but that wasn't my driver's fault. For him, this was a once-in-a-lifetime opportunity, and I tried not to fucking crush people's dreams when I could help it.

"Kick. Ass. My friends are never gonna believe this."

When I climbed out of the taxi an hour and a half later, we'd talked about last season, this year's draft, training schedules, teammates, favorite stadiums, and my favorite team picks for the year—other than us, of course.

And through all of it, I'd managed to keep thinking about Cat to a scorching-low grand total of forty-seven times.

I smiled distractedly for a picture with my driver—as I was still climbing out of the car—and pulled my phone from my pocket. I scrolled to her contact information and hovered over the button to draft a message.

I wasn't sure what to say, but I couldn't stop myself from being curious about whether she had made it safely to her flight or not.

"Thanks so much! For the picture and talking and yeah…the ride's on me," my driver blathered on, pulling me out of my thoughts and making me concentrate.

My eyebrows pulled together as I protested. "No way, dude. I just brought you well out of your way from normal airport pickups."

I reached into my pocket to pull out my wallet, and his smile deepened even further. "Man, Quinn Bailey. Football legend *and* nice guy."

I smiled. Now that, my publicist would be happy to hear.

I pulled a hundred-dollar bill off my stack and handed it to him. "Keep it. But promise me you've got the Mavericks front and center in your fantasy picks."

He nodded excitedly. "Of course."

I gave a wave and started across the dirt drive toward the front door of my childhood house when the door burst open and an angry six-foot-four man came charging out.

"You're dead to me!" my brother whisper-yelled.

Thankfully, when I glanced back, Paul the taxi driver was waving and pulling away.

"Whoa," I called on a smile. "What'd I do?"

"It's what you didn't do!" he explained. "Someone didn't call Mom to tell her that his *plane got diverted*. So when you didn't show up, *I'm* the one who got the angry phone calls in the middle of the night!"

I laughed. "Serves you right, traitor. You should have picked me up in Birmingham, and maybe I could have shared some of the heat."

"As if. You're the golden boy. You shit rainbows and pee sunshine, and I'm your gay misfit knock-off."

"Hey," I chastised. "Definitely gay. Maybe misfit. But you're no knock-off. One hundred percent Bailey original right here," I teased, knocking my fist against his chest.

"Yeah, you're hilarious too. Could God have paired me against a steeper opponent?" he called to the sky, as though he were reaching out to God himself.

"Den," I said seriously, pulling him into me with an arm around his neck. "Stop now. We're a team, not opponents. You know I am *always* in your corner."

"Yeah," he breathed, leaning into my embrace. "I know. It's just Mom and Dad." He shook his hands as though he was wringing an imaginary neck. "You know they make me crazy."

I smiled. "I know they do. What are you doing here so early anyway? I figured after you bailed on being my ride, you'd delay your arrival as long as possible."

He grimaced. "We're supposed to help out over at high school football tryouts, remember?"

"Ohh," I moaned. "Yeah, I'd forgotten."

"Well, I hadn't," Denver grumbled. "I don't know why Dad insists on my being there too. I'm not a professional football player."

I rolled my eyes. "You play for the University of Alabama—one of the best college football programs in the country."

"Only because Dad would drop dead if I didn't."

"Aw, see," I teased. "You care about his survival. So that's something."

"He's all," Den deepened his voice to sound more like my dad, "'I produced two of the best football players in the country from my loins, and damned if I'm not going to exploit it a little. Those high school boys'll piss their jockstraps with the two of you there during tryouts. Really up the ante.'"

I chuckled as I opened the front door and shoved Denver inside.

"Quinn?" my mom called out instantly, her voice the perfect mix of poise and Southern sophistication. "Is that you?"

"Yes, ma'am," I called back, drumming up my Southern manners and settling in for an interaction with my parents.

Traditional thinkers—real grassroots Southern people—my parents were conservative in a way that was really more like conservative's older, more conservative friend.

They believed in three things: Family, Jesus, and Football—and not in that order.

Denver wasn't completely overdramatic with the way he talked about them and the life he'd lived. He was a gay man in rural southern Alabama, but in our house, he wasn't. Not because he hadn't told our parents—he actually had, and I'd never been prouder of him than I had been in that moment—but they refused to acknowledge it. They didn't set him out or make a stink—they just pretended his deepest confession had never happened.

From time to time, they even tried to set him up with well-bred girls from town.

I was heartbroken for Denver, but I didn't know how to fix it. I didn't pretend he wasn't gay around my parents, and I supported him whenever he chose to share with someone else, but beyond that, I felt trapped.

I couldn't even imagine how he felt.

Denver tried to escape my hold and scoot up the foyer staircase, but I ratcheted my elbow tighter and pulled him to me.

"Quinn," he hissed.

"Come on, Den. *I* want to see you. Just hang out. I'll do all the talking with—"

"Hitler and his mistress."

I shook my head with a smile. Denver was always nicknaming our parents—really awful things. I'd like to say I was above it, but secretly, my anticipation was eternally high, waiting to see what he would come up with.

"Mom and Dad," I corrected, "and you can keep a running tally in your head of things you'd like to say to them for later. I'll let you rant about them while we binge on *Sons of Anarchy*."

He squinted his unhappiness, but he stopped fighting to get free from my grip. "Goddamn you. You know Jax Teller is my weakness."

I raised my eyebrows as I waited for his full commitment.

"Fine. I have to spend the morning with you and Assbag McBallsac anyway. I might as well get a warm-up in."

"Den."

He swung a dramatic arm and made big eyes at me. "Well? What are you waiting for? Lead the way into the depths of hell."

I gave his shoulder a squeeze and released him from my hold, heading down the long hall to the kitchen at the back of the house. It was big and stately with ceiling-high cabinets and tan-and-gold-flecked stone counters, and my mom stood in the center of it, twisting a pie that she'd just pulled out of the oven on a cooling rack.

The air smelled like apples and cinnamon.

Her short, blond bob was perfectly kempt, and a string of pearls fell into the hollow of her neck. She was thin—thinner than necessary, if I was honest—but keeping a trim figure had always been something that was important to her.

When Denver was born, I was already seven years old, and I could still remember the manic desperation with which she'd strived to be skinny again.

When I glanced over my shoulder, Denver was halfway through the doorway of the half bath, already going back on his word.

I scowled, and he jumped back out, pretending he hadn't been caught.

"Quinn," my mom greeted with a smile, her voice as soft as a vat of Paula Deen's beloved butter.

"Hey, Mom," I responded, rounding the island to pull her tiny body into my arms.

She hugged me demurely—formally, even—but for her, that was about as warm as her affection got. She didn't scream or shout her excitement, and she didn't bury her head in your chest to get a good smell. Her outfit was too prone to wrinkles, and her skin was the same. It was all to be handled with care.

My dad was the opposite, loud and rowdy and tough. He

wrestled and shoved his hellos and felt the thing every growing boy needed most was a metaphorical ass-kicking.

Hard workouts, hard labor—anything that drenched your clothes in sweat and brought you to the brink of physical exhaustion.

Not that I ever liked to picture my parents *together*, but the logistics had always boggled my mind. Her so delicate, and him so…*not.* And yet, there were two of us, products of their very lovemaking that proved it was, in fact, possible.

As my mom turned back to the oven to put in another pie, I suddenly realized how weird this was. It was only six thirty in the morning, and my mom was fully coiffed and baking pies.

"What's with the pies?" I asked her, scooting out of the way while she shut the oven door. Denver, silent and stalwart, took a seat on one of the stools at the island and started playing with a cloth napkin off of my mom's stack.

"The town bake sale is tomorrow. I have twenty-eight more to bake."

Twenty-eight pies? Holy hell. My eyes nearly bugged out of my head.

"Wow, that's a lot of pie," I remarked. A quick glimpse at Denver caught him in the middle of mouthing *That's what he said.*

My mom, thankfully, didn't notice.

"I volunteered you to be the MC when they do the bachelor auction," she stated, and I shrugged. I never minded town activities. "And make sure to really talk up your brother when he comes up for bid. Bethany Logan has her eye on him, but her mother can barely afford to keep herself in facials. I'd rather Tiffany Lynn."

Den's smile was caustic. My chest squeezed. "Mom, maybe Den doesn't need to be in the auction—" I started just as my father made his entrance. He had on his Boone Hills coaching gear and a pair of khaki shorts, his whistle already around his neck.

He didn't pause as he pulled me into a rough hug and barked, "Horseshit," at the same time. "This is a town thing, your mother's worked hard, and both of you are going to do your part. If it weren't for your schedule, you'd be up for sale too."

I opened my mouth to protest again, but Denver cut me off with a hushed command. "Don't bother, Quinn."

My parents acted as if he hadn't even spoken.

My father looked me up and down, and my mom stared blankly at her newest pie. "Get changed," my dad ordered. "Both of ya. We've got tryouts to get to. If you're not ready in five minutes, your ass can walk."

If there was one thing that was a certainty in my parents' home, it was that I wasn't anyone to them but their son. Even after I'd gone on to win college football championships at Alabama and had been drafted to the Mavericks in the first round, they treated me like they'd always treated me.

I hoped that aspect of our relationship would never change.

It was things like that that kept me grounded, sane, and able to handle the constant spotlight I faced as a professional athlete.

"Beau," my mom murmured. "Language, please."

Déjà vu from the boy at the airport made my synapses misfire. By the time I shook off the moment, Den was gone from the kitchen, and my dad was hauling ass for the garage door.

I moved forward, gave my mom a quick kiss on the cheek, and made a run for my room.

Beau Bailey's declarations were legendary. If I wasn't there in five minutes, I would, indeed, be walking to the high school. And then when I got there, inevitably late, I'd have to run sprints to pay for it.

The instant I stepped into my childhood bedroom, I was hit with the comforting sense of nostalgia. My mother still hadn't changed a single thing. It was like stepping into a time machine, everything just the way I'd left it when I was just an eighteen-year-old kid ready to find his place in the world and heading off to college.

Bag unzipped, I rummaged through it quickly, looking for my athletic shorts and a clean T-shirt.

My phone lay on the bed, forlorn.

I wonder if I have time to text Catharine really quickly?

I paused, just about to do it, when Denver's knock sounded on my door. "Fucking hustle," he whisper-yelled. "I'm not walking, and I'm not riding alone with Gary Goodtimes either."

His face was pinched in pure misery, and any thought of delaying getting ready flew out of my mind. I couldn't do that to him.

Finally finding what I was looking for, I pulled the shirt and shorts out of my bag and pushed my cargo shorts down off my hips. Denver leaned in my doorway watching, so with practiced ease, I stepped out with one foot and swung my discarded shorts up and into his face with the other.

"Quinn!" he yelled as I laughed, pulling on my other shorts and jamming my feet into my tennis shoes—*as a Southerner, tennis shoes are what my northern friends call sneakers, whether they're used for tennis or not.* Hand between my shoulder blades, I reached back and pulled my shirt over my head, grabbed my deodorant to roll on a few strokes, and replaced it with my fresh T-shirt.

Denver straightened from my door when I made it to him.

"Boys!" my dad yelled from downstairs. "Thirty seconds."

Neither of us said anything as we took off down the stairs at a run.

Denver worked with a couple of the quarterback prospects while I ran the offensive line through some drills with my dad.

Keeping them separated eased the tension in Denver's shoulders and gave him the freedom to actually make a difference in some of these young guys' training. Under the watchful eye of my dad, he never played his best. I, however, thrived under Beau's brand of pressure.

Who knew why, but when he yelled and cursed and chased after me with a clipboard, it fed the monster inside me that knew it was better than that, better than him, better than any opponent in the game.

Originally, he'd wanted to run full game drills, but I wasn't really into it. I didn't think it was all that fair to pit me against a high school defense. I was a fucking professional quarterback, and some of these kids were fourteen years old. I knew what playing against a pro would have been like for me at fourteen, and trust me, it would have been nearly spirit-crippling. But working with the offense on timing was a different animal. It was fun *and* useful, and when I gave the kids pointers, they lit up inside.

No matter what, the game was always fast, whether at the high school level, college, or beyond, and as players of the game, we were always trying to keep up.

"Hut, hut," I called, willing the ball into my fingers as a young freshman center did his best to do what I'd asked. He had potential, but he needed repetition. Hundreds and hundreds of practice snaps would have his mind throwing to the exact distance I needed without even thinking about it.

Honestly, it was amazing what you could train muscle memory to do with enough practice.

The line scrambled, blocking the pads in front of them with force and persistence. The running back did a sweep behind me where I pretended to hand it off, while both receivers broke off and ran their routes at full speed. I looked up and let it fly, putting the ball where the receiver was supposed to be—unfortunately, not exactly where he was.

As the quarterback, it was my job to put the ball where they were. But I knew my job, and they were still learning theirs. And as receivers, their job was to be where they were *supposed* to be.

It was essential to the viability of plays, to run them how they were choreographed and make it easier for the guy with the ball—namely, me—to find them.

My dad yelled and screamed, forever the bad cop in his coaching style. But today, I got to be the good guy.

Easy steps crunched in the semi-dry July field grass as I made my way over to the sophomore receiver and grabbed him right in the crease of his neck and shoulder, where I could get to flesh beyond his pads.

"Speed was good, route was accurate, but your timing was off. You gotta pay attention to your yard lines, and you have to have sideline awareness."

He nodded, his "Yes, sir," gruff with embarrassment.

I gave him a shake. "Hey," I challenged. "Get over who I am, and focus on what I'm saying." His gaze shifted quickly from the ground to my face. "Learn from this, don't live in it. It was a moment, plain and simple. Even in games, you're gonna fuck up. It's how you move on from that, how you fight back against the failure. Understand?"

"Yes, sir," he said again, this time, with confidence.

I nodded. "Let's run it again, then, okay? Know your route," I coached. "Follow it, trust it. And when the time is right, I'll put the ball right in your hands. Got it?"

His nod was sharp, and his eyes—they were life.

Sore and sweaty, Den and I climbed out of my dad's truck and headed for the house in a rush. Den, I suspected, was running from any more time with my father, while I was just running from time.

I'd been focused all day on technique and timing and trying not to fucking roast in the southern Alabama summer sun. They'd all taken an expert level of concentration and a fair number of hours, and now that I was home, I just wanted to shower off and sleep for-fucking-ever. But first, I wanted to find my phone and try to touch base with the woman I'd met on a midnight train.

With Den no more than two steps ahead of me, I lunged toward him, grabbing at his hips to slam him out of the way as we made it to the door.

He fought back, of course, shoving me off of him and pulling the big wooden thing open with ease.

I stumbled but recovered easily, laughing as I yelled, "Den! Hold up, loser! I'm gonna kill you for that!"

"You have to catch me first!" he yelled back from the top of the stairs, already up them after taking them four at a time.

"Cut it out!" my dad yelled as he dropped his bags inside the front door and pushed it closed.

God, sometimes it was good to be home. Even with my dad yelling at us like we were still teenagers hopped up on hormones and testosterone, it felt good to be able to rely on that stability.

Hell, if anything, it probably only egged me on further to let loose and joke around with my baby brother like I'd done for so many years growing up in this house.

"Beau?" my mother called. "Are you home?"

"Yes, Dixie," he yelled back, his voice a deep boom.

"Wash up, then, and tell the boys. Dinner will be ready in ten minutes."

Ten minutes. *Shit.* I guessed sleeping wasn't going to happen any time soon.

When it came to my mother, her dinner table was like my dad's truck. You were at it on time, or there'd be hell to pay.

I picked up the pace to my room, hearing Den's shower turn on as I passed his room, and quickly shut my door behind me.

My phone lay on my bed, exactly where I'd left it that morning. Desperate despite the crunch of time, I picked it up and lit the screen to try to touch base with Catharine. But the picture of Denver and me on my background may as well have had teeth, red bubbles and notices littering the fucking thing like a booby trap.

I had forty missed calls from my publicist and ten threatening texts from Jilly, and the stress of both made my chest get tight.

Determined to get past it, I clicked the button to draft a fresh message when it started ringing in my hands.

Nathan, my publicist, *again.*

Jesus Christ.

I dropped it like it was on fire and swept some clean clothes from my bag to head for the shower instead.

After dinner, I told myself. Surely, I'd have time after dinner.

Chapter Eight

Cat

Two full days and still no call, text, *any sort of contact* from *him.*

Trust me. I'd checked. With the way my senses were attuned to my phone, it might as well have been a bomb waiting to go off inside my pocket.

I kind of hated how consumed my brain was with the guy I'd spent only a few real hours with.

I shouldn't have been surprised, though.

Quinn Bailey wasn't some normal, average guy. He was freaking famous, and from what I'd seen on Google, there were hordes of female—*and male*—fans who professed their undying love to him on a daily basis. Some of them even proposed marriage through social media and blog posts.

But you're definitely disappointed…

Silently, I reminded myself the lack of contact was just *confirmation* of what I'd already known the instant I saw a crowd of people standing outside the train station waiting for photo ops and autographs from the man I hadn't realized was a football superhero.

He was a certified celebrity, and sports fans looked at him as if he were an actual god.

And let's face it, I was a mere mortal.

Gods didn't mess around with mortals.

Despite my better judgment, I looked down at my phone for what was probably the one millionth time in the past forty-eight hours, and every time, with the sole purpose of checking to make sure I hadn't missed anything.

Still *nothing.*

Get ahold of yourself, Cat. This is starting to smell a lot like desperation...

All of this preoccupation was starting to make me feel a bit crazy.

I mean, he wasn't Joe Schmo off the street.

He was *Quinn Bailey*, a flipping professional athlete, an NFL quarterback. You know, the guy that everyone loved, the one who threw the ball and made the home runs... *Or is it baskets? Field goals? Touchdowns?*

Touchdowns. That's what it was.

He was the guy who threw the fucking touchdowns.

Obviously, I was completely clueless when it came to sports, but my internet resources told me he was a big fucking deal.

And he played for the *New York Mavericks*. They were a freaking dynasty, the kind of team you couldn't go out in public without seeing people sporting their merchandise—hats, T-shirts, phone cases...it was an endless list.

I slid my phone into my jacket pocket and forced my focus to the tasks at hand—*my job.* I had another round of New York to Birmingham and Birmingham to New York flights to complete.

To the tune of Rhianna singing *work work work work work* in my head, I stepped into the galley kitchen and prepared coffee. Once I'd filled the machine and set it to brew, my eyes met the main doors of the plane. A line of people, holding their various versions of carry-ons, had already started to file in as Casey greeted them on board with a smile.

Before I knew it, first class was filled to the brim, every seat holding an expectant occupant. Seeing as this was one of my usual flights, more than a few of the faces were familiar.

Row three, seat B: Older gentleman in a fitted navy suit and gray hair, otherwise known as one of our biweekly regulars, Mr. Phillip Johnson.

Word on the street said he was a multimillionaire who ran an investment firm. From what I'd gathered over the last few months, his family was in Birmingham, and his company's headquarters were located in the prestigious Financial District of New York.

Mary Jane Matthews filled the spot in row six, seat C. She rode this flight weekly. Apparently, she was an up-and-coming, twenty-something vlogger on YouTube.

Why she needed flights to and from Birmingham was still a mystery I was trying to solve, though. Not to mention, how in the hell she kept her eyebrows so perfect. Every flight, homegirl's eyebrows were never anything less than *on fleek.*

I had found out that her vlogs were directed toward fashion, and one overnight in Birmingham last month, Casey and I had sat in our hotel room and watched no less than fifty videos on her channel.

Fingers crossed *MaryJaneFashion* posts a tutorial on eyebrows soon.

Quickly, I glanced at my watch and noted the time. 5:55 p.m.

Shit. We'd be wheels up and in full takeoff mode in less than ten minutes. I had to finish my preflight prep or else both Casey and Nikki would kick my ass once they realized our onboard service of drinks, cocktails, and snacks was about thirty minutes behind schedule.

Time was of the essence when you were a flight attendant, which meant I didn't have the luxury of sitting around and daydreaming about the New York Mavericks' quarterback calling me or taking inventory of flight regulars.

I had shit to do, two flight attendant buddies to keep from strangling me, and a whole plane full of passengers to keep happy. You hadn't seen pissed off until you were 30,000 feet in the skies, and your passengers realized you forgot to stock the cart with cookies.

During my first thirty days on the job, I'd let that happen once, and the overall response had been pretty close to a riot.

As I restocked my cart with cans of soda and juice, I glanced toward the back of the plane to see Nikki doing the same with her cart in the coach galley, and Casey assisting passengers with their luggage into the overhead bins.

Thankfully, tonight's flight would be our regular crew—Captain Billy, Co-Captain Lori, Nikki, Casey, and myself. Over the past few months, we'd found a good flow of getting down to business and always finding time to make the job fun—*aka screw around and be a little goofy, and maybe even slightly unprofessional, without pissing off the passengers.*

It was a necessary mix when you were faced with a grueling flight schedule.

And, this round, we were facing arduous head on.

I preferred my Birmingham flights to bring me straight back to New York the same day. This round, I had no such luck. I'd be stuck with an overnight in Alabama and then faced a 6:30 a.m. flight back to New York the next morning.

It was no wonder my first priority of preflight prep was coffee. To hell with the passengers, caffeine was my sweet nectar for survival.

"Ready for final checks, Cat?" Captain Billy asked as he peeked out the cockpit door, and I moved my gaze toward the other end of the plane again.

Casey assisted the last two rows of coach into their seats, and Nikki appeared all set with her cart in the back galley.

"It looks like Nikki and Casey are about two minutes away from being ready."

"And you?" Captain Billy asked with a knowing, hearty chuckle that appeared to come straight from his toes.

"Are you trying to say I'm running behind schedule?"

He was always a jokester, and his salt-and-pepper beard moved as his lips crested into a giant grin. "I'm just ascertaining if you would like me to give you a few extra minutes, *which* I *could* manage since we'll have to taxi on the runway for about three minutes."

"No extra minutes," I said as I shut the bottom drawer of my cart and flashed him a victorious smile. "I'm all set to start final checks."

"Perfect." With one hand resting on the cockpit door, he adjusted the navy tie of his pilot's uniform and gave a little nod of approval. "Intercom us when final checks are done," he added before shutting the door closed behind him.

I grabbed the beige phone from the holder. "Begin final checks," I announced, and Casey nodded toward me, while Nikki started going aisle by aisle to check for seat belts and make sure all belongings were stored underneath seats or in overhead bins.

I did the same, starting in first class, and by the time we met in the middle, she asked, "We good?"

I nodded, and Nikki gave Casey a thumbs-up toward the back of the plane.

"Aye, aye, Captain! Final checks are *good* to go!" he gladly announced into the beige phone he'd pulled away from the wall.

"Copy that," Billy responded through the overhead speakers with a soft, amused chortle leaving his lips and crackling through the speakers. "Good evening, folks, this is your captain speaking. I'd like to be the first to welcome you aboard RoyalAir Flight 2107 to Birmingham. We'll only have to taxi down the runway for a few quick minutes and should be wheels up toward Alabama in no time. Flight attendants stand by for departure."

"Girl, I call dibs on safety," Casey whispered to me as he grabbed the needed props from the first-class galley cabinet.

I rolled my eyes and laughed at the same time.

"I'm convinced one day you'll leave RoyalAir for Broadway."

He clasped his hands together like he was praying. "Please, God, listen to Cat."

Always the drama queen, Casey loved putting on a show.

A giggle escaped my lips. "I call dibs on *not* being your assistant-slash-demonstrator."

He grabbed the beige phone again. "Nikki, we need you front and center," he announced and then tossed a wink in my direction.

I could hear her answering sigh from the back of the plane.

I hear ya, girl, but I had to deal with Casey's happy, comedic ass last flight.

Her hazel eyes met mine, and a few faint wrinkles formed between her brow as she glared directly at me. Long, wavy hair, sparkling eyes, and a figure that showed she actually went to the gym, Nikki was as pretty as she was likable.

Happily married and with two college-aged sons, Nik was much further into her life than I was, but somehow, we'd instantly become friends during RoyalAir training in Cincinnati.

Her life, her wisdom, were always a much-needed change of pace for me.

I liked that she'd been with her husband for thirty years, especially when she often shared funny anecdotes of what it was like to be married to Mr. Marty Miller—notorious karaoke lover and owner of seven hundred pairs of socks that all managed to have holes in them.

I liked that her two sons drove her crazy with their antics.

And I loved that she was my friend.

"Sorry," I mouthed toward her, but she was having no part of my silent apology for forcing her to participate in Casey's safety show.

She shook her head in response, her auburn hair brushing across her shoulders as she did. "Liar," she mouthed back with her red-painted lips and a quirk of her brow.

All I could do was shrug one shoulder in response, while guilt in the form of amusement crested my lips at the corners.

"Hello." The overhead speakers crackled as Casey geared up for his big performance.

I wondered if he'd eventually find some way to add a tap dance and Barbra Streisand ballad into the routine.

"My name is Casey," he announced giddily as Nikki walked up toward the front of the plane and snatched the props from his hands. "I'd like to welcome you to RoyalAir Flight 2107. If you're going to Birmingham, you're in the right place. If you're not going to Birmingham, you're about to have a really long evening..."

It didn't take long for me to tune him out. I'd heard this safety spiel so many times, I could probably recite it in my sleep.

It also didn't take long for me to grab my phone out of my pocket to check for missed calls or texts.

I was pathetic.

And yet, still *nothing.*

My gut clenched in disappointment, and I had the irrational urge to punch myself in my own stomach just to knock that unwanted feeling loose.

I didn't want to be disappointed. I wanted to be rational.

Yeah, but none of that works when you really, really want him to call you...

With a frustrated exhale, I started to slide my phone back into my jacket pocket, but when it began vibrating like crazy in my hand, I practically jumped out of my heels and fumbled to bring it back in front of my face.

A soft gasp escaped my lungs, and my eyes popped wide and surprised when I saw the notification flashing on the screen. ***Incoming FaceTime Call: Quinn Bailey.***

Holy hell, he's calling me? He's really calling me right now?

My heart jumped into my throat, but then took a nose dive to my feet when I realized he wasn't just calling me, he was *FaceTiming* me...

As in, he wanted to *see my face* during the call.

Nerves vibrated inside of my belly until they extended their path and reached my fingertips. My hand shook as I gripped the phone in my palm.

Quinn wanted to video chat with me? Right now?

This has to be a mistake.

Who in their right mind chose FaceTime as their first form of contact?

Definitely had to be a mistake.

As Casey started to talk about oxygen masks, I quickly tapped decline with my index finger.

But only five seconds passed before another round of vibrating came from my phone.

I looked at the screen again, only to see the same notification popping up.

Incoming FaceTime Call: Quinn Bailey.

I tried to solve this complicated puzzle of confusion in my brain, but the only thing I could come up with was Quinn Bailey was accidentally butt-dialing me.

I hit decline again and decided to get some balls and send him a text message.

Me: I think you keep accidentally FaceTiming me...

An answering text vibrated my phone a moment later.

Quinn: Take out the word "accidentally."

And then another one followed before I could respond.

Quinn: Wait...are you declining my calls?

Holy moly. He wasn't butt-dialing me?

Me: You're calling me on purpose?

Quinn: Isn't that what people do when they meet someone they like?

He likes me? Quinn Bailey likes me? Hold the fucking phone.

Wait. I was holding the phone. Literally. How in the hell was I supposed to respond to that?

I'm so happy you called! I like you too! I want to see you naked! Let's be naked together!

Obviously, my brain was no use.

I stared down at the blinking cursor of my text message screen and decided to take a nearly honest approach, sans the ramble about being naked.

Me: Okay. Yeah. The call makes sense. But the fact that it's a FaceTime VIDEO call is a little weird...

Quinn: You calling me weird, Kitty Cat? And you still didn't answer why you're declining my calls...

Kitty Cat. Why did that stupid nickname make me smile?

I should've been annoyed. But I wasn't.

I was giddier than Casey during flight safety instructions announcements.

Me: Yeah, I guess I am calling you a little weird. ;) And I'm declining because I'm at work.

Quinn: That's not why you're declining...

He had me there. I could've easily taken a quick call, but internally, I was way too nervous to FaceTime with him. A girl needed a moment to check her makeup in the mirror, maybe brush out her hair, for something like that.

A phone call was one thing. It still allowed you to hide a little, show only as much to someone as you wanted, but having a camera in front of your face during a call was a whole different animal. The very idea of it made me feel a little too vulnerable.

Me: I really am at work.

I snapped a quick photo of my jump seat, the words RoyalAir embroidered into the cushion, and a thumbs-up from yours truly in the center of the photo.

I added the question ***See?*** and sent it to him.

Quinn: Okay…I guess I'll take that excuse, but I'm going to make sure we talk later. :)

Yes, please!

Oh, wait. What did he mean by later? My schedule wasn't exactly conducive to flexibility until tomorrow night when I got back home.

Uncertainty vibrated in my stomach. What if he called when I was in the air?

I didn't want him to think I was ignoring his calls, when in reality, I was in the air and my phone was off.

Me: Later sounds good. :) Just to give you a heads-up, I'm on a flight to Birmingham right now. And tomorrow, I'll be flying back to NYC on the 8:15 a.m. flight.

I read my text after I'd hit send. Had my words made me sound desperate?

Fuck, I hoped not.

God, why can't I be one of those smooth, cool as a cucumber kind of girls?

It really would've made my life a lot easier.

Quinn: Don't worry, Kitty Cat. I'll make sure it happens. ;)

A grin formed across my lips after reading his words, but then realization quickly set in. What exactly did he mean by that? So, like, maybe tomorrow night he'd call me?

Obviously, if he tried the FaceTime thing again, I'd answer, but I'd cover my camera and force his version of appropriate first calls to audio. I mean, who in the hell chooses video calls before knowing someone for more than six months minimum?

Apparently, Quinn Bailey.

I smiled at the thought.

He was a conundrum of confident and humble. A gentleman to his core, but a first-class flirt at the same time. He was a freaking puzzle.

But hell if I didn't want to solve him like my own personal Rubik's Cube.

Chapter Nine

Quinn

"I thought you weren't leaving until tomorrow night," Denver said, pushing my bedroom door closed behind him and plopping down on my bed so hard the whole thing bounced.

"Plans changed."

After two of the longest days of my life with my family, I'd finally found time to make contact with Cat. I'd been backstage at the bachelor auction, and she'd been at work, and despite my best efforts to lay eyes on her face directly, all I'd gotten were a few measly texts.

I needed more. So, like any good athlete, I found a way to make it happen.

"Earlier practice?" he asked, spooning a mouthful of ice cream out of his deep burgundy bowl and closing his lips around it until they touched again. He'd been sold to Gerdie Hawthorne at the auction, and after finding out via their initial meeting that she was handsy as hell, had been drowning himself in cookies 'n cream ever since.

I couldn't say I blamed him.

"No."

"Team meeting?"

"No."

"Weight-lifting session with one of the guys?" he pushed, cycling through all of the things I filled my days with on a regular basis.

"No."

It was only a matter of time before he figured out—

"So…a woman, then."

And there it is.

"Denver," I warned, feeling anxious about discussing a woman I'd just met. I didn't want to jinx it, didn't know what to say—I didn't even know what I was doing, much less how to explain it to an outsider.

"Oh, come on, Quinny. You know this is the only traditional guy talk I get to have. It's like everyone else thinks I play for the girls' team because I'm gay. I'm not going to tattle if you tell me the reason you like her has nipples. I can do tit talk. Lay it on me."

"Den," I hummed through a rough chuckle, shoving a folded clump of shorts into my bag and squishing it down. "The reason I like her doesn't have nipples, and I don't ever do tit talk."

"So you *do* like someone!"

"Denver, drop it," I ordered, tossing the rest of my shirts into the bag and whirling the zipper around the perimeter. One thing I was certain of: Jilly would be happy as hell my mom had had the housekeeper do my laundry.

"Are you kidding me? Why? This is the best thing you've given me since you've been home. Something to focus on. Something to work with. Something to peck over."

"Denver."

"*Quinn.*"

I sighed. I knew that tone, and I knew my brother. When he got in pecking mode, I better goddamn give him a carcass, or he would turn me into one.

I sighed, shoved my bag aside, and dropped down onto my bed in the spot I'd created. "Her name is Cat."

His eyes sparkled. "Yesssss. Cat. Meow. Love it."

When I didn't say anything else, the sparkle in his bright green eyes dimmed noticeably, and he sat up to slam his bowl on my nightstand. The spoon clattered loudly with his rough movements. "That's it?" he snapped. "What are the *plans*, Quinn? I need to know where you're taking her, what you're wearing, what other fabulous people will be there."

I rolled my eyes.

"There aren't plans, per se," I admitted. "She's a flight attendant, and she's working the 8:15 a.m. from Birmingham to JFK. And now, I'm *also* on that plane."

"Stalking her at work?" he practically trilled. "Finally, this is getting good."

"I'm not *stalking* her."

Am I?

"I'm just strategically arranging my schedule to coincide with hers."

He clasped his hands together, his face going waxy as he got excited. "Tell me she has another lover, and you'll have to fight him for her. It'll be all over the news and social media, and the air marshal will have to get involved. You'll end up in—"

"Stop talking," I instructed, shoving him back into the headboard with a splayed hand to his chest. "There's no other guy." Suddenly, I frowned. "I don't think."

"You don't think?" Denver whispered elatedly. "You don't know if she's dating someone else?"

I rolled my eyes and picked at some imaginary lint on my shorts. Suddenly, I felt self-conscious. "We talked for a night. I didn't get around to asking her if she was dating anyone."

"How pretty is she?" he asked, and I glared.

"Okay, so, pretty. Duh. Sorry." He pretended to wince. "She's definitely seeing someone, then."

"You don't know that," I contradicted, feeling a tiny stab in my chest as I worked to convince myself he was wrong. "I'm not bad-looking, and I'm not seeing anyone."

He scoffed. "You're an Adonis, and you're seeing several someones. *Next.*"

"Den—"

"I said, *next!*" he shouted.

"You're going to wake up Mom and Dad," I threatened, and he lowered his voice immediately.

"Fine. But don't you have to wake them up? You're not sneaking out and leaving the goodbye to me!"

"I already told them I was leaving early."

"Wow," he remarked, turning his head and pursing his lips in offense. "I see you've been planning this for a while."

"An hour, Den. I've had this plan for an hour." A tiny discomfort from his implication of manwhoring niggled at me. It wasn't that I hadn't partaken in my full quota of sexual activity. I had. But I hadn't run up the number in a while. "And I'm not seeing several someones."

He raised an eyebrow dramatically, his disbelief too pure to require a verbal statement. "I haven't seen one single someone since before preseason."

He smiled, finally convinced. "Well, then, this is exciting. Though the idea that you were coming up with a plan to sweep your lady friend off her feet while I was being sold to a friend with a little too much lady for my tastes is kind of depressing." I frowned, but he pushed onward. "I wish I were coming with you. I want to see her."

As much as I'd love to have my brother with me, I wasn't so sure it'd make my plays any easier this early in the wooing game. "Den—"

"Relax. I'm not coming with you." He rolled his eyes. "I have to go back up to the high school for more football. Yay."

I shook my head at my little brother and gave him a shove in his. "Maybe some other time."

"You're staying in a hotel tonight?" he asked.

"At the airport. Just to make it easier to make the flight in the morning."

He leaned forward and clasped his hands at his chest. "Take me with you."

I laughed at his desperation and then shrugged. "You can come to the hotel with me if you want."

He smiled at me affectionately and then shook his head with resigned determination. “I can’t. I promised Dad I’d go back to the final tryout in the morning.”

My heart swelled for my brother. He was *such* a good guy. After all my parents had put him through, he still took things that were important to them seriously. He kept his promises, and he honored his responsibilities.

“You’re a good man, Den. Really. When you’re not annoying the shit out of me, I’m really proud to call you my brother.”

He laughed. “So flowery.”

I put out my fist and waited for him to touch his to mine. “Until next time, bro.”

“We’d like to welcome Zone One for RoyalAir flight 2209 to board at this time. Passengers in Zone One,” the gate agent announced. Of course, most of us were already lined up like a bunch of fucking cattle.

I wasn’t sure where the urge came from to be on the plane for longer than absolutely necessary, but all but one or two stragglers left in the seating area seemed to have it.

However, I, myself, had something else driving me to get on board.

Several somethings with wings and little fucking antennas, and they were flying all over my fucking stomach.

I hadn’t been this nervous since my first game as the starting quarterback for the Mavericks. I wasn’t sure if it was the thought of seeing Cat again or my brother’s words about stalking her, but angst was my new pet—and it lived within me.

She won’t think I’m stalking her, will she? I mean, I have to fly back to New York, right? I live there. I work there. This is normal.

I moved with the line and stepped up to the scanner, turning over my phone to scan my boarding pass and listened for the beep that said I could move down the jetway. The machine did its magic, and the woman behind it gave me a professional smile. "Welcome aboard, sir."

I smiled back and hustled away, stretching my steps out to be long and slow as I marched down the little square tunnel.

I tucked my phone into my bag and prepared to duck as I approached the metal doorway, eager to make a better entrance this time. *Walking and texting yourself into injury in front of people is really only funny the first time you do it.*

I had to keep my neck craned to the side as I stepped across the threshold since I was too tall to stand all the way up, but I smiled anyway. I'd managed to make it in without hitting my head this time.

Step one, accomplished.

Almost as if on cue, Casey's head came up from his spot across the galley, and his eyes widened slightly. Recognition ripened the air between us.

"Well, well. Back for another ride, Quinn?"

I almost laughed at his double entendre—a pun I was absolutely certain he'd made on purpose—but I was too busy hoping the reason he remembered my name was because Cat had been talking about me.

"What goes to Alabama, must come back," I teased, and he smirked.

Cat came charging up the aisle right then, several bagged blankets in her hands, and my breath caught in my chest. She was even more beautiful than I'd recalled.

Thankfully, Casey didn't seem to have the same problem as he breathed out a taunt with ease. "Oh, Catharinnnne. Look who it is!"

I smiled—at least, I tried to smile as my cheeks turned into some form of flesh-colored Jell-O—and waited for her to meet my eyes.

Panic, pungent and swift, gripped my every muscle and threatened to paralyze me.

What if she looked disappointed to see me?

Up and up, her eyes climbed my body until they found my own, flaring more with every inch they passed. She knew the ridges of my stomach and the soft swell of my chest, she knew the line of my throat as I swallowed in anticipation, and she *knew* my eyes when she found them. It was even better than I could have hoped.

Wide-eyed and beautiful, she caught her toe on the edge of the aisle runner, and she went tumbling—right into me. The bagged blankets in her hands shot out in all directions, falling unceremoniously onto the seats in her close proximity.

I caught her against me, chest to chest, and watched up close as her pupils dilated at my touch.

Yeah. I'd made the right decision.

This flight was going to be fun.

Chapter Ten

Cat

One second, I'd been focused on my first-class seats, ensuring passengers would have fresh blankets, eye masks, and complimentary earbuds for the flight. And the next, I was tripping over my heels because my brain forgot to instruct my feet how to walk.

It wasn't my brain's fault, though.

The sight before my unsuspecting eyes had been information overload. My brain had tried to understand, all synapses firing erratically in search of a rational explanation, but it was no use.

The shock and view of Quinn Bailey standing in the middle of the aisle had been too much to comprehend. I'd tripped on my own two feet, and had he not managed to catch me within the safety of his strong, firm arms, I would've been one step closer to becoming some kind of airplane lesbian—after eating the aisle carpet.

Holy hell, he was on my flight back to JFK?

I wasn't sure if he was a mere mirage from too many flights and too little sleep, but I knew one thing for sure—he smelled crazy good.

His scent filtered into my nostrils, and instantly, like a kid trick-or-treating for candy on Halloween night, I wanted more.

Discreetly, I inched my nose toward his neck because I couldn't stop myself from taking another inhale. A little spicy, a little sweet, the subtle scents of cinnamon and vanilla filled my olfactory senses. He smelled like heaven wrapped up in a giant red bow with a side of strong and alpha and one hundred percent *man* on the side.

There was no denying—even with just one good, hearty sniff on record—my pheromones were addicted to his pheromones.

With strong hands, he helped me back to my feet. Which was good. Standing was good. Only, standing meant looking, and looking meant saying, and, faced with those intoxicating blue eyes of his, I had no idea what to say.

Uh…hi?

What are you doing here…?

Sorry for falling into you like I'm Jennifer Lawrence at the Academy Awards…?

I needed the right words, but obviously, my brain wasn't offering up anything of value. I think I was still in shock, but I guessed an unexpected visit from Quinn Bailey would do that to a girl—and I do mean *any* girl. His fans, his admirers, and then women like me—who had no idea about the public persona, but had been lucky enough to be charmed by the actual man.

He must have sensed my momentary speechlessness, and he hopped behind the driver's seat and put our conversation back into gear.

"Are you okay? You didn't hurt anything, did you?"

Hurt anything? From what?

The fall, you idiot! my brain shouted, for once, thinking rationally again.

Oh, shit. *Right.* I'd literally just fallen into him like a sack of fucking potatoes. Not to mention the confetti of airplane blankets I'd tossed out on the way down.

"I'm fine," I said, and a self-deprecating smile crested one corner of my mouth. "Thanks to your quick hands."

He winked. "You know, funnily enough, that isn't the first time I've heard that."

"Um…can I get through?" a passenger standing behind Quinn

caught my attention.

I glanced over his shoulder and realized there was a line of people waiting to file on to the plane.

Dear God. It was like I'd completely forgotten where the hell I was.

"Oh, man," Quinn muttered and quickly moved out of the aisle and into row three, where his seat must have been located. "Sorry about that."

"So sorry for the delay," I apologized to the slightly irritated man standing at the front of the passenger line. "I had a little bit of a fall in the aisle."

The man just shrugged and offered a small grunt of acceptance, and then proceeded to shuffle his white Reebok trainers down the aisle, past the first-class curtains, until he reached his seat in the first few rows of coach.

While the rest of our passengers filed on to the plane, I couldn't stop myself from stealing a glance in Quinn's direction.

3A. That was where he'd be for the duration of the flight.

For a brief moment, his eyes met mine. They were soft and warm and that perfect shade of blue that if you painted a room inside your house that very same color, it would only provide feelings of serenity and comfort.

And his gaze whispered promises of more to come.

I was entranced, and it took all of my willpower to break the hold and get back to work, my first order of business being the mess of blankets I'd thrown across the seats.

Holy moly, this flight was about to be very, very interesting.

The wheels of the cart shook as we reached the final row of coach. With me driving and Casey pulling the back end, we worked to finish up our complimentary drink and snack service.

Yes, I was supposed to be running the show in first class during this flight, but the fact that Quinn was sitting in row three, seat A, had urged me to keep myself as busy as humanly possible over the past two hours.

I still couldn't believe he was on my flight. *Again.*

And I definitely didn't trust myself to stay in first class and be so close to him. I feared he was too much of a distraction for me to actually do my job if I had to constantly see his handsome face.

Although, I'd spent the majority of the flight trying to understand exactly why Quinn was on my flight.

I could have sworn, when we'd been talking on the train in the wee hours of the morning, he'd told me his flight home was tomorrow. *Didn't he?* God, I couldn't remember.

But if that were true, that would mean he'd purposefully situated himself on this flight, *my* flight. Had that been what he'd meant by his "Don't worry, we'll talk later" text?

No way that was possible…*right?*

"Would you two like something to drink or eat, sir?" I asked the blond gentleman keeping his preschool-age daughter occupied with a movie on an iPad.

"I want a cookie, daddy!" the little one shouted. Her blond curls bounced off of her shoulders as she looked up at me expectantly.

"What about a chocolate chip cookie?" I asked with a smile. "How does that sound?"

She reached out with both hands and wiggled her fingers around. "Ohhh, gimme! Gimme!"

"Don't forget to say please and thank you, Lucy," her father scolded with an apologetic smile in my direction.

"Gimme, pease and thank you!"

I couldn't not laugh at her manner faux pas, and I set a plastic-wrapped cookie on her tray. "What about something to drink?"

"She'll take some orange juice, and I'll have a Coke."

"Coming right up." I pulled out two cans that matched their orders from my drink drawer, and their glasses were filled halfway a moment later. Carefully, I set their beverages on their trays just as

Casey served his last passenger on the right side of the plane.

And *thank God* for the passengers. I knew as sure as I knew my own name that, had it not been for their presence, Casey would have been six miles deep into his Quinn Bailey interrogation by now. As it was, he'd only had time to give me precursory looks—the ones that usually came directly before the questions—before getting interrupted.

Once we secured the cart back in the galley, I headed toward the front of the plane to take over first class from Nikki—and get away from Casey—as fast as my heels would take me. Casey's arched brow promised future retribution.

"Everything okay?" Nikki asked, and I could feel her assessing every inch of my face.

Shit. They're coming at me from both sides.

"Yep," I responded and busied myself with cleaning out the coffee machine. "Just figured I'd give your feet a break and keep Casey entertained for a bit in coach."

Nikki quirked a brow but didn't say anything.

No doubt, I'd be receiving some questions via group text later tonight.

How in the hell was I supposed to explain that the famous quarterback in first class was someone I knew? After parting ways at the train station the way we had, with a mob of fans landing on Quinn like he was as sticky as glue, I'd decided to withhold from my friends. Normally, talking about new guys, new underwear, and new dreams were all things deserving of an immediate overanalysis among friends. But this felt scarier and less realistic than any other normal meet-cute. And the thought of talking about it made me feel vulnerable.

Frankly, it'd be easier to tell my friends I was resigning from my position at RoyalAir to take a job with NASA as a space rocket stewardess.

I glanced over my shoulder to find Quinn looking straight toward me.

Like, direct eye contact.

I smiled. Or at least, I think I smiled.

I might have looked constipated.

He returned the awkward sentiment, only he did it well.

Vivid blue eyes, soft yet firm cheeks, a strong jaw, and a fantastic fucking smile that instantly put you at ease and practically charmed you right out of your panties at the same time. *That* smile, those full lips, and his perfect white teeth were a dangerous combo, that was for fucking sure.

Once the seat belt sign turned back on, Captain Billy announced our impending landing, notifying the passengers and staff to finish up whatever they were doing and prepare for our final destination: New York City.

Nikki, Casey, and I spent the last twenty minutes of the flight cleaning up both galleys, collecting trash, and rechecking our passengers for buckled seat belts, upright trays and seats, and stowed away luggage. And with a little resourcefulness, I made sure I was doing it wherever I needed to be to avoid Casey's cross-examination.

At four minutes past noon, Captain Billy eased us out of the sky, and our wheels touched down on JFK's tarmac. The brakes engaged with their familiar squeal, and our aircraft kissed the ground gracefully. Billy had been flying planes for twenty plus years and consistently proved the more experience a pilot had under his belt, the more enjoyable the overall flight was for its passengers.

In my short stint on this job, I'd quickly learned that he was one of the best.

"Welcome to New York," he announced through the overhead speakers as we taxied toward our gate. "Weather at our destination is a warm eighty degrees with some broken clouds, but don't worry, they'll try to have them fixed before we reach the gate." I could literally hear the smile in his voice.

Between Billy and Casey, I didn't know who was trying harder to turn our intercom system into their own personal stand-up comedy routine.

"We'd like to thank you folks for flying with us today," Casey added into the beige phone on the wall in front of the cockpit. "And the next time you get the insane urge to go blasting through the skies in a pressurized metal tube, we hope you'll think of us here at RoyalAir."

"Oh," Captain Billy interrupted, "And remember, the last one on the plane has to clean it."

I watched as a few passengers glanced around the cabin at each other, smiles and soft laughter on their amused lips.

Casey cackled and banged his hand against the cockpit door with two swift movements. "Please ignore him," he corrected into the intercom through a soft chuckle, and Captain Billy's responding laugh permeated all the way through the metal door.

"Actually, our pilot will be the one cleaning the plane after we land."

Of course, my flight attendant bestie wasn't finished giving his ending spiel.

"It is important that everyone remains seated until Captain Comedian turns off the seat belt light. And once we reach our gate, and as you exit the plane, please make sure to gather all of your belongings. Anything left behind will be distributed evenly among the flight attendants. Please do not leave children or spouses."

Immediately, more chuckles filled the cabin as we pulled up to the gate.

Nikki and I glanced at each other from opposite ends of the plane. She rolled her eyes with a grin, and my answering facial expression was identical to hers.

I often wondered if one day we'd be called into a meeting with our CEO regarding the constant supply of jokes through the overhead speakers. If it ever happened, you bet your ass I'd sing like a canary.

Kidding. Well, *sort of*. It'd probably depend on how much money Billy and Casey paid me to keep my mouth shut.

"Let's rock and roll," Casey whispered once he finished up having fun with the intercom. "I'd like to be off this plane in no less than ten minutes once we hit the gate."

"Hot date?" Nikki questioned, and he just waggled his eyebrows in response.

"Tell me it's that adorable gate agent from Allied Air." I grinned, and internally, I was thankful his attention was otherwise diverted from asking me about Quinn.

Casey's responding grin was carnal.

"It's definitely the guy from Allied," Nikki whispered toward me, but loud enough for him to hear, and then purposefully poked Casey in the chest with her index finger. "You better tell us everything. Or else."

"Or else what?" Casey questioned with a hand to his hip.

"Or else you can expect an all-out catfight," I chimed in.

If I just kept him talking about the hot guy from Allied Air, he'd completely forget to ask me about Quinn.

"And why is Cat allowed to keep secrets about male suitors and I'm not?"

His question was like a needle straight to my hope balloon.

"What?" I barked out with a shocked laugh. "Male suitors? I don't have any male suitors."

"You totally do," Nikki corrected, and Casey's smirk turned wicked, knowing far too much information.

"I do not," I denied anyway.

"Girl," she started, dragging out the word with an exaggerated tone. "I've been watching you acting weird for the last two flights. Constantly checking your phone, getting giddy as hell over text messages, switching cabins with me for no reason. Something is up with you," she said and flipped my hair. "But don't worry, we'll give you a little space until you're ready to tell us all about him."

"There's nothing to tell."

"Are you *sure* about that?" Casey asked, and I kind of wanted to strangle him.

But luckily, Nikki hadn't caught on, still completely out of the Quinn Bailey loop.

"I expect to hear all of the details from both you by our next flight to Birmingham," she demanded with a smirk. "Lord knows, after being married to the same man for thirty years with grown-ass kids who are currently in college, I need to experience some sort of excitement, even if it's through your lives."

"Oh, I bet Mr. Miller knows how to bring it, sista," Casey teased, and Nikki laughed in response.

Praise Marty Miller and his thirty-year power of distraction.

"The only time Mr. Miller stays up late and brings it is when the Yankees are playing. Other than that, dinner is at seven, and he's in bed by eight."

"Oh, honey." Casey smacked his lips together. "We need to get you out during our next layover in Birmingham."

"Count me in," she agreed as the plane came to a stop and the seat belt light went out. "Now, let's get these people off this plane so I can go home and take a nap."

"Let's do it!" Casey cheered and snapped his fingers in the air three times. "You girls say bye to everyone with Billy, and I'll finish cleaning up the galley."

"I can clean up the galley," I offered, but he wasn't having it.

He gave me a look and then pointedly glanced directly toward first class, seat 3A, to be specific. "Honey, the passengers would much rather see your pretty face standing up at the front than mine."

By passengers, he meant Quinn.

I knew, without a doubt, Casey would be watching me like a rabid dog when Mr. Quarterback himself walked toward the exit.

The little Mariah Carey-loving traitor.

Awkwardly, I stood near the exit doors and waited. There weren't but eight people seated in front of him, all already up and exiting the plane, but Quinn took his time pulling down his carry-on from the overhead bin and walking toward me. With the people in front of him all cleared out, I had an unobstructed view.

My fingers tapped nervously against my hip, and my brain raced with a million thoughts at once.

Oh God. Is he going to say something?

Is this going to get weird?

Am I going to blurt out something inappropriate?

My lungs constricted from the anxiety of it all.

"Great flight," he said with a gentlemanly smile. "Thanks for everything." His eyes held mine for an extra second, but to my surprise, he didn't offer anything else before walking off the plane and out of my life.

Well, shit, that had gone a lot better than I'd thought.

Or worse, my mind taunted. *Maybe he* isn't *interested in me.*

My stomach might as well have hit the tops of my heels. I didn't like that thought. Not one fucking bit. And I wasn't sure what that said about me.

Was I already too hopeful about the whole Quinn Bailey situation?

I barely knew the guy, and I'd thought I'd kept any flighty musings about kismet and love under control. Clearly, the calibration of my self-awareness was a little off. Too bad resetting it was a little more complicated than the figure eight motion the compass on my iPhone required.

God, I need to get it together.

After a long, deep breath, I forced my focus to the tasks at hand—cleaning up the plane and getting the hell home.

Ten minutes later, I watched Casey and Nikki walk off the plane, bags in hands and smiles on their faces, and five minutes after that, I followed their lead.

At the end of the gate ramp, my heels skidded to a stop.

Quinn Bailey.

He stood, tall and confident and beautiful as ever, just outside of our gate and looking straight in my direction. All the while, he quickly signed some autographs for fans standing around him.

I wasn't sure seeing him sign autographs and being fawned over by complete strangers was something I could ever get used to.

But did anyone really get used to that? I silently wondered. *Even the celebrities themselves?*

I didn't know the answer to those questions. Growing up in the suburbs of Cincinnati with a middle-class family, I'd never been faced with celebrity or fame.

Quinn's gaze moved toward mine, and once our eyes locked, he smiled.

As I forced my feet to move toward him, he signed one last autograph, took one last selfie, and politely excused himself from the small crowd, saying goodbye to his fans.

It took a minute for his path to clear and people to leave him on his own, but once it did, he met me halfway.

"You waited for me?" I blurted out, and immediately, I wanted to slap a hand over my mouth.

But he didn't falter at my question, his full lips turning up at the corners and his blue eyes brightening by two shades. "I did," he answered and slid his hands into the pockets of his jeans. Rocking back and forth on his feet, he asked, "Want to get lunch?"

"I can't," I blurted out…*again.* But this time, it was with a lie.

Ever so slightly, the corners of his lips dropped.

Instantly, I felt like an asshole. "I have to get home," I added lamely in an attempt to soften the blow I'd just delivered.

Good Lord, I sucked at this.

I had no idea why I'd lied, or why I'd avoided him on the plane like a toddler, but both just felt necessary in the moment. Like, self-preservation had taken over or something. I wasn't too fond of the hopefulness I'd been feeling about the possibility of some sort of relationship with Quinn. It all felt a little too fast for comfort.

And, if I was being honest, I was still a little overwhelmed by the fact that he was some uberfamous football player.

It was a complete one-eighty from the type of life I'd imagined he led when I'd first spotted him on that initial flight. I'd just thought he was a normal, everyday kind of guy. Well, a really amazing-looking, normal, everyday kind of guy. But that was neither here nor there.

He is just a guy, Cat. One who appears pretty damn determined to spend more time with you.

Quinn assessed my face for a quiet moment, his eyes inquisitively taking in my features until he quirked a brow. "Boyfriend?"

"No." I shook my head, an amused smile playing at my lips. The fact that he was inquiring about my relationship status made me want to laugh like a lunatic. I dismissed the reaction with force.

"Husband?"

"Definitely not." A quiet laugh escaped my lips. Not a whole giggle; just a little squeak of crazy. "My work schedule is too insane for that. The closest thing I've got to a husband or boyfriend is my ficus. But he does need regular maintenance."

"I'm also unattached," he offered with a soft, knowing smile. "I can relate to the crazy work schedule sentiment."

Unattached? I found it hard to believe he didn't have someone in his life. Or many someones, for that matter.

"Yeah, but you're probably seeing someone on like Fridays, Saturdays…"

"I'm a single guy, Cat," he responded with charm oozing from his voice. "Obviously, I find the time to enjoy female companionship, but I can tell you once preseason training starts, I generally only find time for football."

"When does preseason start?"

"It started in May."

It was July…

My eyes went wide with surprise. For a man who only found time for football during the season, he sure appeared to have a lot of free time to track me down today.

"Walk out with me?" he asked with a little nod toward the exit.

"Okay."

He grabbed my carry-on out of my hands and led us away from our gate and toward the terminal exit.

For a few quiet moments, we walked side by side, sneaking glances at one another, and occasionally, when our eyes would meet, sharing smiles.

God, I loved that smile of his.

"Since you're refusing to have lunch with me," he said once we reached baggage claim, "and you were noticeably absent during the flight…" I blushed at the way he said that like he knew it wasn't a coincidence. "I'm demanding you share a cab ride home with me."

Considering that RoyalAir provided all of its NYC metro area flight attendants a free shuttle service home, I never took cab rides from the airport.

But I didn't want to tell Quinn that. I'd already reached my lie quota for the day.

Hell, I was starting to regret declining his lunch offer so quickly.

"So, you're *demanding* that I share a cab with you?" I asked in a teasing tone.

"I just want to spend some time with you." He shrugged and ran a hand through his shaggy brown hair. "Pretty please?"

He held out his hand, and I took it. The warmth of his palm and the way his big hand engulfed mine only solidified my decision. Being in his presence just made me feel so fucking good.

Next thing I knew, we stood in front of the taxi line, still hand in hand, and I was letting our driver know the address to my house. Quinn hadn't offered an address of his own, but he hadn't seemed inconvenienced either. *Maybe he lives in Hoboken too?*

I started to ask, but the feel of Quinn's hand on my hip, pulling me gently to the side robbed me of any and all speech capability.

He offered a wink as he swung open the door and helped me inside the cab while our driver filled the trunk with our luggage.

Not even a minute later, we were off, heading in the direction of my place. A million questions fought for supremacy in my mind, but in the end, only one came out victorious.

"So," I started and flicked my gaze toward him, "you're the quarterback for the Mavericks?"

"Yeah." He grinned. "I guess I've been caught, huh?"

Incredulous, a small burst of giggles fell from my lips. "Uh… You didn't think that was something you should've maybe mentioned?"

He shrugged. "You said you weren't interested in sports."

I looked out the taxi window as fondness threatened to make me do something foolish.

Wasn't interested in sports?

The times…they were about to be changing.

Chapter Eleven

Quinn

Cat's knuckles wrinkled as she squeezed the worn leather of the taxi seat. She was nervous, I could see that—I'd have to be an idiot not to be able to see it—but it wasn't quite so obvious why.

Was she upset with the way she'd found out who I was?

It didn't feel that way. When she'd broached the question, she'd seemed amused and entertained by my response.

Or was she thinking she'd made a mistake, getting in a cab with a virtual stranger and actually fearing for her safety?

God, I hope not.

I scooted a little farther away, just in case, and cleared my throat, trying to come up with some small talk that might put her mind at ease.

"So," I muttered, "have you always had a green thumb?"

Her gaze swung from the window to me, and her eyebrows were drawn together. A little jagged line ran from her hairline to the top of her nose—a tiny, almost imperceptible hint of an old scar.

"A green thumb?"

I smiled at her confusion. "You know…the ficus. You said he requires regular maintenance. I can't keep bamboo alive, and all you have to do is stick it in water."

Surprise over the change in topic of conversation made her answer sound robotic. "I, uh, keep a watering schedule."

"Like in iCalendar?"

"Google."

"Oh, groovy," I said easily. "Does that mean you're an Android user?"

She shook her head, still trying to follow the direction of our conversation, but her fingernails had stopped digging into the leather.

That's it, kitten. Just relax.

"No, I have an iPhone. Google calendar still syncs."

"I'm terrible at keeping a schedule," I admitted after a nod. "My assistant, Jilly—Jillian—she keeps all that shit organized. Otherwise, I'd be missing games and practices and all kinds of shit, and she wouldn't get a paycheck."

"Your assistant…Jillian," she murmured, and I had to laugh. I could see the direction she was going, and yeah…the idea of romance with Jillian was hilarious.

"I see what you're thinking, but Jilly would rather, uh…*cut off* that appendage than play with it."

The cab driver cleared his throat, obviously listening in on our conversation, and Cat blushed.

"I drive her crazy. She's in charge of things like making sure I don't run out of shampoo, have clean clothes for practice, de-smelling my gym bag…" I made a face that said how terrible a job that really was. "Hard to believe, but apparently, all that sucked all the romance out of good ol' Quinn Bailey for her, Cat."

Just a hint of a smile curved the corner of her mouth, and white-hot victory surged in my chest.

"Hard to believe, indeed," she murmured.

"So, I guess you don't have any manservants…pool boys…that kind of thing?"

She barked a surprised giggle. "Manservants? No, that'd be a negative."

I held my expression serious and thoughtfully pursed my lips.

"That's good. I mean, I'm not the excessively jealous type, but thinking about you getting, like, fanned and bathed by some other guy—"

Her eyes widened. "Bathed by someone?"

"Well, you know. Whatever it is manservants do. I'm no expert because I've never had one, but I imagine if I were yours, I'd try to be accommodating."

"Accommodating…" she muttered.

Starting to sound a little creepy, Quinn, I warned. *Dial it back.*

I cleared my throat and shifted uneasily in my seat. Somehow, I'd become the one who was uncomfortable.

"I, uh…" I rambled. "Sure, sure. Did you say you had a roommate or—"

"We're here," the cab driver announced, pulling to the curb in front of a brick-faced apartment building.

Wow. This maybe wasn't the note I'd wanted to end on.

I looked over at Cat to see her digging in her purse for some money to pay for the cab, so I reached over quickly to stop her with one hand and dug into my pocket with the other.

"No way, Cat. I got it."

She smiled and shook her head, so I just nodded mine. "Go on, get out. And don't even think about grabbing your own bag."

"Or what?" she asked through a laugh, her face *finally* fully relaxed, smiling, and goddamn beautiful.

"Or…" I thought quickly, trying to come up with something, but I had nothing. I sighed. "Geez, kitten, you're just supposed to take the threat at face value."

"So sorry," she murmured cheekily, sliding out the door gracefully.

I looked forward to the driver, my intention to ask him to wait so that I could say goodbye before we headed to my place, but he was already turned all the way around in his seat, watching us and grinning.

"Quinn Bailey, huh?" he asked.

I tried not to grimace. "Please, wait here while I say goodbye and save any commentary until she goes inside, and I'll give you as many pictures and autographs as you want. I'll even get you a fucking game ball," I pleaded.

"Fuck *yes*. Consider your game uninterrupted, dude," he agreed, turning back to the front and putting both his hands on the wheel obediently.

I rolled my eyes even as I celebrated internally and climbed out of the car.

The trunk popped as if on my command, and I pulled Cat's bag out and left my own.

As I set it by her feet, I asked, "Can I carry it upstairs for you?"

She smiled but shook her head. "I'm on the first floor."

"Yeah, well," I said with a laugh. "I guess that means you're all set, huh?"

She tucked her hair behind her ear and then reached out a hand, her eyes frantically looking anywhere but directly into my own. I went with it, moving my head around in chase until I caught them.

Her face melted into a cute crinkle, astonished wonder making her deep brown eyes shine.

I took her extended hand in mine and gave it a squeeze. "Thanks for sharing a cab with me, Cat."

"Thanks for paying for it, Quinn."

I wanted to touch her. Pull her body to mine, smell her hair—breathe her in. But a woman who extends a hand, gets a hand back. The last thing in the world I'd ever want to do was barrel through one of her boundaries without permission.

I gave her one last smile and waited to get one in return before turning back to the cab and climbing inside. When I settled into the seat, the door to her apartment building was closing behind her.

"Where'm I headed, boss?" the cab driver asked. I stared at the closed door, wondering if even a small part of her had wanted to linger, to stay and talk some more—to get to know me.

"Mr. Bailey?" the cab driver questioned again when my thoughts kept me silent.

I turned back to him then and settled into the seat, letting the overanalyzing die. I could question myself until my brain bled, but Cat still wouldn't be around to give me any of the answers.

"Far Hills."

He whistled. "A little out of your way, huh?"

A wealthy New Jersey town in relatively close proximity to the Mavericks stadium, Far Hills was south and west of Cat's Hoboken neighborhood by just under an hour and home to several of my teammates. New York was short on space, and since stadiums tended to take up a lot of it, the Mavericks stadium was actually located in New Jersey. It always confused people that a New York athlete actually spent all of his time in New Jersey, but it was the way of our world.

Still, my daily life wasn't just around the block from Cat's.

I thought about Cat and her shy smile and the way her hand had felt in mine.

"Just a little," I answered while my mind silently added, *But most definitely worth it.*

Chapter Twelve

Cat

The faint sounds of a garbage truck beeping its arrival and my upstairs neighbor Becky Mayes's raised voice slid their way into my living room. Too curious for my own good sometimes, I shuffled my bare feet across the hardwood floor of my apartment and stopped in front of my living room window. With two fingers, I flipped two slats of the blinds out of the way and gave my best impersonation of a voyeur.

Becky *without the good hair* stood in the middle of the small, fenced yard of our apartment building, her pink fleece robe and UGG boots showing signs of overuse and discoloration. A true sight to behold, it took a certain kind of strong, confident woman to give zero fucks about standing outside in her bathrobe, *or* the fact that she was wearing fleece in July.

I admired her gall and self-assurance.

"Oh my God, Bob," she huffed. "Just go already. I have to get back inside."

Her face grew tired with frustration as her miniature schnauzer Bob refused to do anything but sniff the grass.

Becky tapped her foot in quick succession. "Bob, you know I'm on a deadline. I don't have time for you to dillydally. Piss or get off the pot, dude."

Bob was unfazed by her demands. His pepper gray beard shook at the ends as he continued to sniff his way around the entire yard.

Becky and Bob. The dynamic duo of grumpy and obstinate.

I never exchanged more than a few sentences with my neighbor, but from what I'd witnessed and overheard—*via watching through my blinds*—and what she'd shared with me, I knew she was a writer. A contemporary romance author who published several books a year and had a fairly big female following.

I'd never read any of her books, though, but that wasn't out of disinterest. I just didn't know her pen name.

While the Becky and Bob show continued to entertain, my phone pinged with a text message notification from my coffee table. I shuffled back to the couch and plopped my ass down.

Dad: We need a business meeting soon, Caterpillar.

To my dad, I'd always be *Caterpillar*.

I smiled, nostalgia and memories glittering my thoughts, and savored the blanketed warmth of comfort inside of that constant.

Me: I know. I feel like things are finally settling down. How about August when I take the training trip to Cincinnati?

My dad and I ran a small—*more of a hobby*—business together. It wasn't anything big, just a cute, personalized greeting card shop that mostly sold its goods through Etsy.

Caterpillar & Co—a company established back in my grade school days. It'd all started out as *Dear Santa* letter responses to unanswered letters in my dad's mail room. Not his *own* mail room, mind you, but the mail room of one of the postal offices in Cincinnati that he managed and oversaw.

Somehow, someway, what had started out as a fun little Christmastime tradition had developed over time into something more as my interest in calligraphy and art grew.

If anything was a passion of mine, it was art, any and all versions—paintings, sculptures, sketches, doodles. Any form of creative release and I was one hundred percent in.

Honestly, it was exactly why doing the doodles and sketches for our greeting card line had become one of my favorite things to do. I looked forward to our quarterly plans, when I could finally put my pencil to paper and *create* something.

And my dad—*thank God for him*—had been holding down the fort and doing most of the work for Caterpillar & Co while I'd experienced several life events—flight attendant school, starting my career, moving to New York. *Almost. Hoboken might be in New Jersey, but it's only across the river from the Big Apple and about a thousand dollars a month cheaper. It counts.*

Dad: Sounds good to me. I've got something in the works that I think you'll be really excited about.

Me: I can't wait to see what it is :)

Dad: Everything else going okay?

Me: Yep. All is good in NYC. I'm currently enjoying a much-needed day off.

Dad: Glad to hear it. Love you, Caterpillar.

Notorious for keeping text conversations short and sweet and to the point, I knew this last text was his version of goodbye.

Me: Love you too, Dad. Tell Mom I said Hi! And that I love you!

Dad: Will do. :)

I clicked my phone to lock it and tossed it down onto the couch beside me. Normally, I loved that my dad always kept conversation concise, but today, I wouldn't have minded the distraction.

I'd been home for four hours. My apartment was clean. My carry-on was unpacked. My laundry was done. And the clothes that required dry-cleaning—*my RoyalAir uniform*—had been dropped off at Park Cleaners, a little family-owned, neighborhood business that I'd pretty much fallen in love with the second I stepped into their shop.

If you ever want to meet the nicest woman in Hoboken, go there. You won't be disappointed. Maria will greet you like you're already best friends, and treat you like you're family. Seriously, Hoboken natives, if you're taking your dry cleaning somewhere else, you're missing out.

Oh, *and* I'd watered my ficus.

Considering I'd started the day on an early flight from Birmingham, and it was only a little after six, it had been a productive day.

But now, I had no idea what to do with myself.

My brain, on the other hand, seemed far too content with thinking about *him.*

Quinn Bailey.

Mr. Quarterback.

Possible flight stalker.

I still didn't really know if he'd purposefully been on my flight, but the fact that he'd waited for me after said my gut instinct was right.

A man that seemed to have attention following him everywhere had wanted my attention via a lunch date, and when I'd abruptly declined, he'd demanded a cab ride together instead.

I didn't want to be self-deprecating about his apparent interest in me, but still, it was a bit of a mindfuck.

His life was worlds apart from mine, and I wasn't sure how I felt about that.

How was a simple flight attendant from Cincinnati supposed to compete with the hordes of enthusiastic fans following him around?

I imagined even a simple trip to the grocery store turned into a photo and autograph session for his fans.

My mother would chastise me for sounding insecure. I could literally hear her voice in my head. She'd probably say something along the lines of, "*Catharine*, get it together, girl. I don't want to hear that garbage coming from your mouth. You are a strong, beautiful, and confident woman. Any man, no matter how famous he is, would be lucky to have you on his arm."

My mother, Alexa Wild, was a special kind of person. A confident, African-American woman who lived her life with strength, beauty, and grace.

It was times like these that I missed living under my parents' roof. Missed the ability to just walk downstairs and sit at the kitchen table and savor the comfort that only home could provide.

Sure, I didn't have regrets about my current life choices. I loved living near the city, and the traveling capabilities my job provided were unreal. Last month, I'd managed to fit in a four-day trip to Paris just because *I'd felt like it.*

Not many twenty-four-year-olds had that kind of freedom.

But every once in a while, even though things were pretty fucking good, it was normal to get a little bit homesick, especially when your family was hundreds of miles away.

With a rerun of *The Kardashians* playing on the television, I grabbed my laptop off the coffee table and set it on my lap as I nestled my back and shoulders against the cream pillows of my sectional. A few taps to the track pad and my eyes started browsing the home page of *Vogue.*

Meghan Markle and Prince Harry's engagement photos.

An article about Rhianna's Fenty makeup: ***Why is Rhianna's Red Lipstick Line so Groundbreaking?***

The 13 Best Celebrity Hair Transformations.

Eventually, when I spotted ***The 15 Best Fashion Instagrams of***

the Week headline, I clicked the track pad with my index finger and scrolled through the celebrity pictures. Salma Hayek, Bella Thorne, Alton Mason, and then, to my surprise, when I reached photo number fifteen, Quinn motherfucking Bailey.

Jesus Christ in a peach tree, I felt like he was following me around. I had been mindfully avoiding anything sports-related, and yet, somehow, some fucking way, his face pops up on my laptop, in a *Vogue* article, mind you.

Dressed head to toe in a sleek suit designed by Calvin Klein, a throwback Thursday photo of Mr. Quarterback himself filled my screen. He stood outside of a gas station, pumping gas, while a beautiful, older woman with sleek hair shaped into a bob smiled from the driver's seat of the SUV.

The caption on the Instagram photo: ***Mom (my date) got me pumpin' gas before the show. #ESPYAWARDS***

I had no idea what an ESPY Award was, but that didn't matter. He'd brought his mom to an awards show.

Thick, sculpted muscles covered by smooth, gray, and expensive-looking material, he was wearing that suit. My eyes had never experienced an easier sight to digest.

Mamma Mia. No wonder the editors of *Vogue* knew who Quinn Bailey was.

I was starting to feel a little stupid I hadn't known who he was until *after* I'd taken a four-hour, midnight train ride to Birmingham with him.

My eyes stared off into a distant corner of my living room, focused on nothing in particular, while my brain tried to comprehend what the odds of meeting a man like Quinn Bailey in the middle of the night on a train actually were. I'd probably have more luck getting my own Instagram pictures to be spotlighted by *Vogue*.

Kim Kardashian laughing on the television caught my attention, and I watched as she chatted with her sisters about how hard their life was before they had their own chef.

Sheesh. Not everyone is fed via a silver spoon, Kimmy.

I glanced back at my computer screen to find sleek-suited and handsome as hell Quinn still front and center, and then the questions started flowing in like cold water from an open faucet. Did Quinn have his own personal chef? Did he know the freaking Kardashians? Holy hell, what does his place look like? Is it crazy elaborate with gold furniture and a Lamborghini in the garage?

How much did an athlete like Quinn Bailey make?

I wasn't proud of it, but I found myself pulling up a new tab and typing *Quinn Bailey net worth* into the search bar. But when the results filled my screen, I didn't have the strength to actually click on anything to find the answer.

I didn't want to know his net worth.

But I did want to know a little—*okay, a lot*—more about him.

So, I tapped the track pad, following the hyperlink from the *Vogue* article to his actual Instagram profile, and browsed like a little secret stalker. The small verified blue check beside his name stood out instantly, and then, his follower count.

3.1 million.

Holy guacamole. That was a lot of fucking people.

I cruised through his pictures—various shots of him in game situations, a ton of candid videos, and other various things that showed Quinn Bailey truly did reach out to his fans.

Should I follow him?

I hesitated, my index finger hovering over the track pad.

Would he know if I followed him? Would that be weird?

The man has 3.1 million followers. Surely, he won't notice one little fish in his sea of millions.

That was true. I mean, the odds of Quinn even noticing that I, a random girl with all of fourteen followers, was following his Instagram profile were minuscule. Pretty sure I'd just blend in with the other three fucking million.

I shut my eyes and clicked follow. When I opened them again, the world still looked the same. My living room hadn't changed, and my laptop hadn't blown up.

See, that wasn't so bad.

I smiled to myself at how ridiculous I was being about this whole thing, but before I could relax back into the sofa and browse more of Quinn's Instagram, my laptop chimed with a sound I'd honestly never heard before.

A notification popped up on my screen: *Quinn Bailey is Live Now.*

"Oh my God," I muttered and shoved my laptop halfway down my thighs.

With my heart pounding erratically inside my chest, I assessed the screen and quickly realized it was just live video notification, as in, a live video for all three million of his followers.

Relax, crazy pants. He's not going to pop out of your laptop and yell "Gotcha!"

Holy hell, that had scared the crap out of me.

Like a kid being caught with her hand in the cookie jar, I had to place a hand to my chest and wait for my heart rate to slow back down to a normal, less erratic rhythm before I could even think of doing—*stalking*—anything else.

Fuck, it's stressful social media stalking someone.

Despite my better judgment, and without any concern for my heart's well-being, I clicked on the Live Now notification and found myself face-to-face with Quinn Bailey.

Behind him, televisions hung from the walls, and as he turned the camera toward the right and left of him, he appeared to be hanging out with a few of his buddies—possibly fellow football players.

I honestly didn't know who they were, but none of that should come as a surprise at this stage in the game. I mean, I didn't even know Quinn Bailey was a fucking NFL quarterback. Hell, I don't think I really realized the Mavericks were a professional football team until I'd Google searched his name.

"I just wanted to say a quick Instagram hello," he greeted into the camera, that handsome smile of his causing my heart to flitter inside of my chest. "And let you guys know that Cam Mitchell and

Sean Phillips just finished up the hot wing challenge." He waggled his brows, and then his full lips creased down at the edges into a disappointed frown.

The background noise filled with cursing and shut-ups, but Quinn just laughed a toothy grin and continued talking into the camera.

"It was pathetic, guys. Mitchell didn't even make it through six, and Sean required five glasses of water just to reach ten. Let's just hope they're saving their A game for the Mavericks preseason."

Several pretty girls behind him started jumping up and down, their boobs bouncing dramatically underneath their skintight attire, and chanting *Mavericks! Mavericks! Mavericks!* behind him.

The comments section of the live feed starting blowing up with various versions of *Go Mavericks!* but my eyes couldn't stop themselves from finding their way back to the gorgeous—and extremely busty—women standing near his table.

Of course there're just a bunch of girls hanging around him...

Hell, this was probably a daily occurrence for a man like Quinn.

"All right, friends," he announced into the camera. "It's been real. But I gotta get off of here to check in on my kitten." He grinned, wide and proud, before waving goodbye with his left hand and ending the video.

And the comments section of the video switched gears, leaving their Mavericks victory calls behind and going straight for everything kittens.

@therealdiva Quinn Bailey has a kitten?
@unicornMaverick OMG I want to see Bailey's kitten!!!
@hollylovesmavericks Post pictures, Quinn!!!
@MrsQuinnBailey Awwwww he has a kitten! That's so cute!!!

Eventually, once I spotted the Instagram handle of @ ***MrsQuinnBailey***, I clicked out of the video and shut my laptop screen.

It was all a little too much for me to take in.

How could I compete with all of that?

Instead of fixating on things that were beyond my control, I decided a distraction in the form of a drink and a snack was much-needed.

As I headed into the kitchen to grab a can of Mountain Dew, my phone pinged and vibrated across the counter. I picked it up and almost choked on my own saliva when I saw the text message.

Quinn: Hey, kitten, how's the ficus?

Chapter Thirteen

Quinn

After the cab ride home, a good thirty minutes of pictures and promises for my cab driver, and a quick shower, I'd jumped in my car to head over to the bar, Doolan's, where at any given moment—when we weren't at work—you could find at least one of the Mavericks hanging out.

Noise buzzed around me as the bar got busier by the minute.

This always happened after I posted on social media, essentially confirming to droves of local followers that I was somewhere they could come see me.

It never stopped me, though, from posting when I felt like it, telling it like it was, or even giving away my location.

I lived a public life, and I knew full well that I'd signed on for it. I didn't resent it like some people did, and I certainly didn't think I was above the consequences. Instead, I embraced it. I lived at the center of my bubble and did my best to look out for both my interests and those of the people around me.

Unfortunately, sometimes, my cavalier attitude about social media etiquette and personal privacy led to fights with my publicist and agent and even Jilly from time to time. Apparently, she was tired of opening packages with women's panties inside at my home address.

Thankfully, Sean and Cam Mitchell were doing a good job at distracting the droves while I focused on my phone as it buzzed with a response from the woman I wished would stalk me the most.

Catharine: He's watered and sleeping like a good boy.

Me: Is sleeping the only thing good boys do?

Five minutes passed without a response, and the fans started to infiltrate the invisible barrier around me. I was good at staring at my phone, keeping my focus, and doing my thing until I was good and ready to interact with the public, even when people were staring at me, but having nothing to actually do on said phone while waiting for a response from someone that might never come made it a hell of a lot harder.

Finally, by sheer force of will, I suspected, as my eyes were moments away from turning into lasers and my hand was starting to cramp up from randomly scrolling through my apps, a text message popped up on the screen.

Catharine: I...have no idea. I was just talking about my plant. I'm confused and completely blank as to how I should answer you. I tried to think of something cute, but...I've got nothing.

I smiled, completely tickled by her unease—especially the fact that she'd shared it with me.

Me: Well, I can tell you. According to Cosmopolitan magazine, good boys do the following: they put the toilet seat down, bring home flowers for no reason, listen when you're talking to them, and plan surprise vacations.

Her response was immediate and made me laugh embarrassingly loud.

Catharine: :(My ficus doesn't do any of that.

Sean was looking at me funny and a couple of fans were creeping in, but I did something I hardly ever did and turned my back to all of them. I just wanted this moment, a couple more exchanges with Cat, and then I'd get back to them.

Me: Looks like I'm going to have to give him some lessons.

Catharine: You mean to tell me YOU do those things?

Me: I can do almost anything when truly motivated, kitten.

Catharine: Wow. I think I'm impressed. Maybe a little scared.

I looked up as someone bumped into my elbow, creeping so far into my personal space that they'd be able to read my screen despite my special privacy cover soon.

I tilted my phone away and leaned, hoping the moment would hold long enough to tell her goodnight.

Me: Sounds like the perfect combination to me. I've gotta get these guys off their barstools and into cabs, but we'll talk in the morning, okay?

Catharine: Um, okay. Have fun.

I felt unbelievably unsatisfied, like I had conversational blue balls, but I knew what had to be done. If I waited any longer, there'd be hell to pay and teammates to bail out of jail.

"You done?" Sean asked, shouldering in between me and the nosy fan without shame. He wasn't rude, but he wasn't overtly accommodating like I was either.

I nodded, noting the lipstick smears on his neck and the spot where the missing button at the top of his shirt used to be.

He'd disappeared earlier, for the better part of an hour. And given the opportunity now, I asked about it, even though I was fairly certain his disheveled appearance said the answer. "Where'd you go before?"

His cheeks dimpled as he smirked before draining the dregs of his bottle of beer.

"Nowhere."

Nowhere was code for *somewhere* with *someone* doing a few *sexual somethings*. He was highly sexually active in a way even I didn't really understand.

And trust me, I loved to fuck.

I shook my head and smiled, a loud slap to his shoulder my kickstarter to the end of the evening. It was time to get this show on the road.

"All right!" I shouted as I spun around on my stool. Everyone in the bar's attention came to me.

"If you belong to me," I started, "down your drinks, pay your tabs, tip Amber," I nodded to the bartender, and she bowed at me, "and get your ass outside."

Murmurs started up immediately, and a couple of the guys rolled their eyes, but everyone moved. They were used to this and used to me, making sure they kept their act together, got home safely, and didn't ruin a good thing for the whole fucking team by being an irresponsible drunk asshole.

I grabbed a few sheets of paper that hit me in the chest on the way out and gave them a quick sign, and then herded the guys together on the sidewalk. When I did a count, we were a couple over.

I took another look, and when I really paid attention, it was pretty easy to tell who didn't belong—their breasts were a dead giveaway.

"Okay, ladies. Time to hit it," I instructed, giving a wink and a smile as I indicated they should exit the group.

This always seemed to happen when I did the roundup, a couple of women trying to blend into our flow. Sometimes they had help from the guys, and sometimes they did it all on their own. Either way, it wasn't a good idea.

Oran Wells, the Mavericks middle linebacker, frowned at me and pulled his companion closer. I looked into his eyes to see they were glassy and dilated.

"Sorry, Oran. Practice starts at five sharp. That's zero five hundred in military speak. You think she's gonna *help* you get out of bed?"

"Negative," Sean muttered, and the rest of the guys laughed.

I stepped up and pulled Oran away, wrapping my arm around his shoulder as I led him to a cab.

"Look, I'll give you a free shot tomorrow," I offered, my tone conciliatory. "Seriously, I'll make sure Sam lets you come right through. But tonight, I've gotta block you."

"Cockblock!" he accused, and I laughed.

"A descendant of the devil, I know. But if it's any consolation, every time I do it to another man, I get one in return added to my curse. It's like a séance of male sex bonding or something."

"You're twisted, QB," he mumbled as I dropped him down into the seat of the cab and gave the driver directions.

"I will be when you take your free shot," I returned easily and slammed the door.

After a double tap to the metal top of the cab, they were off like a shot.

I looked back at the group on the sidewalk and sighed.

One down, five to go.

Chapter Fourteen

Cat

The remnants of my dream faded away, and the tinglings of reality started to seep in through my senses. The warmth of my down comforter reminded me that I was far too cozy to get out of my bed. Streaks of morning sunlight penetrated the window and, if I'd allow my eyes to open, would probably blind me.

It felt early.

Slowly and reluctantly, I uncovered my face. I blinked, closed my eyes, and blinked again. And the sun did exactly what I'd guessed it would, damn near blinding me back into a closed-lid state until I could turn my head and partially cover my face with my cupped hand.

What in the hell time is it?

Groggily, I snagged my phone off my nightstand and checked the time: 7:05 a.m.

"Seriously?" I questioned into the silence of my bedroom.

I groaned. Most days, unless I had an early flight, I didn't wake up until a little after nine. Seven a.m. was a time only tolerated for work purposes. Not days where I didn't have to be to the airport until two.

My phone vibrated and shot off an alarm in my hand. I startled and dropped it on top of my mattress and just kind of stared down at it in a sleepy, "What the hell is happening?" kind of state.

I had no idea what that alarm meant, but as my mind started to filter memories into my brain, I quickly realized it had been that very alarm—that godawful sound—that was the culprit behind my early morning wake-up call.

I really needed to learn to use the Do Not Disturb option.

With my phone in hand, I finally found the strength to sit up in bed, drag my feet off the mattress, and rub the knuckles of my free hand onto my eyes. I stretched my arms above my head and yawned until I found myself just watching my legs dangle above the hardwood floors of my apartment.

If the director of *The Walking Dead* was in my room looking for extras, no doubt, I'd be cast in a starring zombie role.

Despite my tired as fuck, ready to complain about every-fucking-thing state, the unknown alarm on my phone didn't seem to give a rat's ass. Its sound reverberated off the cream walls of my bedroom and vibrated in my hand like it was actually meant to alert me to something.

For fuck's sake! What do you want?

Finally, with *sort of* focused eyes, I stared down at the notification. It had the little Instagram icon and the words: ***Direct Message from Quinn Bailey.***

Huh? My eyes squinted in confusion as I reread the notification, only to find that I'd read it correctly the first time.

I tapped the screen, and it took me directly to the social media platform.

Apparently, Instagram had an inbox section where you could send and receive messages. It was news to me. Not to mention, my inbox was filled with no less than ten messages, all from Quinn Bailey.

How did he even know I was on Instagram?

Holy hell. My eyes popped wide open of their own accord. Was it because I had social media stalked him last night?

Had he found out?

Oh. My. God. He probably knows I followed him.

One light tap to the heart icon, and all of my notifications popped up on the screen.

Quinn Bailey liked your photo.
1 new follower Quinn Bailey.
New Direct Message from Quinn Bailey.
Quinn Bailey liked your photo.
New Direct Message from Quinn Bailey.

That was just half of them.

And here I thought I was the social media stalker out of the two of us.

Apparently, that little bastard of an alarm that had woken me up at the butt crack of dawn was actually the Instagram notification chime. Go figure. It also showed just how much I generally paid attention to social media—*a big fat zero for anyone keeping count.*

As I pushed myself to my feet and stumbled toward the kitchen for coffee, I opened up the first message sent at 5:30 a.m.

It was a video, and I clicked play and watched in rapt attention as the screen of my phone came to life with Quinn Bailey.

Surrounded by mirrored walls, larger-than-life men moving about behind him, and every variation of weight-lifting equipment, it was pretty easy to ascertain, even for an anti-gym rat like myself, that he was in the weight room.

Providing me a bird's eye view of his workout, he proceeded to demonstrate the proper way to do bicep curls. It was like my own personal infomercial. Only, at the end, I wouldn't be asked to send in three payments of $19.99. Although, with the way his sculpted muscles flexed and rippled with each curling lift of his forearms, I imagined I'd be tempted to lick my screen and attach a debit card to arrange for monthly installments.

"Now, Kitty Cat," he instructed, "it is important that you never take more weight than you can handle. That's how injuries happen." He held the phone toward his face and grinned into the camera as he finished his current set with the opposite arm.

Entranced by all of the muscle, I kept my eyes glued to every flex and curl that was bestowed upon me. Good Lord, this was better than porn.

Once he set the weight down, I frowned but continued watching, secretly hoping there would be more muscle show-and-tell.

Show me the muscle! my pervy mind shouted like Jerry Maguire.

The video continued, and Quinn walked around the room, pointing the camera toward the large, muscular men that dominated the otherwise large space.

Yeah. Definitely better than porn.

"Everyone say hello to Cat!" he shouted and immediately received several loud Heys and Yos and What ups.

After he took me on a short tour of the weight room, showing me the equipment, the location of the water station, and introducing me to more men that I assumed were actual New York Mavericks football players, he turned the screen back to his face and said, "I'm going to finish up in here, Kitty Cat. But don't worry, I'll be sending you more messages this morning. See ya in a little bit." He flashed one blue-eyed wink, and a second later, the video ended.

My nose scrunched up, but the disappointment was brief until I clicked back to my inbox and remembered that it was still chock-full of more Quinn-style greetings.

With one tap to the screen, I opened the next—a picture of Quinn in the locker room, the words New York Mavericks prestigiously filling up the wall behind him.

The following message was yet another photo. This time, Quinn took a selfie on the field. The sun shone brightly behind him, highlighting the little blond hairs within his shaggy locks, and the green of the pristine turf framing his face only added to his presence, making him look like football royalty.

Another one had a video of him inside the therapist's room, getting his legs stretched out by a smiling man that Quinn introduced as "Denny, the best fucking physical therapist in the NFL."

And that wasn't the end of it. There were more. At least five more messages, to be exact.

What in the hell was happening?

I scrolled to the top of my inbox and opened up his most recent message—a selfie of Quinn drinking out of a Gatorade bottle. Delicious droplets of sweat on his chest shimmered under the sun's early morning rays.

I sucked my bottom lip into my mouth.

Dayum, Gina. He looked good with a capital G.

It was pictures like this that made me understand why women professed marriage and took his name via their Instagram handles.

Besides the sexy muscles and the urge to virtually lick the sweat off of his chest, I really only had one thing on my mind. And that's exactly what I sent him before setting my phone down and filling my coffeepot with fresh water.

@WildCommaCat: What is happening?

By the time I had Mr. Coffee filled with fresh grounds and hit his brew button, my phone shot off what I now knew was the Instagram chime.

@QuinnBailey: Good Morning, Kitty Cat. I was wondering when you were going to wake up. And I figured since I've seen you at work, I wanted you to see me at work. ;)

I chuckled at the ridiculousness of it.

@WildCommaCat: I'm pretty sure I could see that on ESPN.

@QuinnBailey: Pop Sports Quiz: What does ESPN stand for?

A snort left my nose. He knew I didn't have a fucking clue what ESPN stood for. Hell, I hadn't even known he was the freaking quarterback for the Mavericks until I typed his name into Google.

@WildCommaCat: Not a damn clue.

@QuinnBailey: Entertainment and Sports Programming Network.

I poured freshly brewed coffee into my favorite yellow mug and added my ideal amount of cream and sugar. As I stirred it together with a spoon, the coffee and cream mixing together to create a perfect color of creamy beige, I typed out another response with my free hand and hit send.

@WildCommaCat: Thank you. That is a valuable piece of information that I will hold on to forever.

@QuinnBailey: See? We're so good together. I can teach you everything about sports, and you can show me the ins and outs of airplanes. I've always wanted to be a pilot.

@WildCommaCat: LOL I don't actually fly the planes…

@QuinnBailey: Baby steps, Kitty Cat. We'll both learn together.

@WildCommaCat: Oh, yeah, of course. By this time next year, I'm sure we'll be working on our smooth landings. ;)

@QuinnBailey: When can I see you again?

My heart kicked up speed and pounded excitedly as I read the words. He wanted to see me. *Again.* Holy moly.

My heart screamed *Today! Right now!* But my brain stayed rational and reminded me with, *Girl, you've got a busy fucking week of flights.*

Stupid brain.

@WildCommaCat: Well…my next few days are pretty booked with work. I'll actually be doing another NYC to Birmingham and back again today.

@QuinnBailey: When do you fly out today?

@WildCommaCat: 2 p.m. I have to be to the airport by noon.

@QuinnBailey: And you'll be flying straight back to NYC after that?

@WildCommaCat: Yep. No overnights during this round.

@QuinnBailey: Can you make me a promise?

@WildCommaCat: I guess that depends on what the promise is…

@QuinnBailey: Oh, come on, Kitty Cat. You know I'm a total gentleman. I'd never make you promise to do something that would make you uncomfortable.

He had a point. Quinn had never been anything but extremely polite to me.

Well, and sexy and charming as hell, but that was beside the point.

@WildCommaCat: All right. You got me there. What do you need me to promise?

@QuinnBailey: As soon as you know your schedule is letting up and you can carve out a little time for me, let me know, okay?

Sugary-sweet and thoughtful as hell. I swooned.

@WildCommaCat: That I can do.

@QuinnBailey: Attagirl. All right, I've got to head out onto the field. But don't worry, we'll chat later.

@WildCommaCat: Promise me something?

@QuinnBailey: Anything.

Damn. So quick to respond. It was like he was trying to make me fall head over heels for him or something…

@WildCommaCat: Have a safe practice.

@QuinnBailey: You got it, Kitty Cat.

Kitty Cat. Apparently, that was my official Quinn Bailey-appointed nickname.

Well, that, and *kitten.*

And I'd be a liar if I said I didn't like both.

Chapter Fifteen

Quinn

I slammed my locker shut and swung my bag up on my shoulder, hair still wet and dripping onto my T-shirt-covered shoulders.

A wedding DJ would be extraordinarily proud of my version of the hustle as I rushed around trying to get my shit together and head out of the stadium in order to make it to my destination in time.

"Yo, Bailey, grab a bite with me," Jorge "Teeny" Martinez, my left tackle and the guy who often steamrolled the "me" from the other team, invited, but I was shaking my head before he even finished.

"Sorry, buddy. I've got some errands to run. Rain check, though, okay?"

As one of the leaders of the team, I made it a point to make time for all of my teammates. Practice time, life time—even time to share a meal or do stupid shit. In my experience, it kept them out of trouble, and it made them even more determined to protect me on game day. Both of those were very high up on my priorities list.

Just not today.

He jerked up his chin, and I motored again, weaving through the men strolling around in towels and various states of dress, all fresh from the showers after a vigorous morning practice.

Thankfully, we'd done most of the outdoor activity during the early morning hours, when the sun wasn't quite yet at its full strength, but it'd still been hot as balls.

"Q!" Sean yelled from behind me, my stride casually eating up the hall on my way out of the stadium as fast as I could go. "Wait up, dude."

I slowed to a normal pace, even though I didn't really have the luxury of extra time, and gave him a chance to catch me.

"What's up?" I asked as he finally made it to my side.

"Where you headed in such a hurry? You were moving around the locker room like your throttle got stuck, and I know you don't have any kids to take to the doctor and shit."

I shook my head and chuckled. "I have things to do today. They're time-consuming. I'm in a hurry. What's the big deal?"

He didn't look convinced, but he didn't push it. "Fine, fine. If you say so."

"I say so," I said, and without waiting, started walking again. He fell into step beside me, the bastard.

I shook my head again as we walked and asked, "What are you doing?"

"I'm coming with you."

"Sean—"

"You may have a busy day, my man, but I'm as free as that whale Willy."

"Great," I acquiesced. It was useless fighting him. Sean's undying persistence was what made him one of the best receivers in the league.

I smiled then, though, as I thought about how funny it was going to be when Sean figured out what the fuck he'd just gotten himself into.

Down the hall, through the lobby, and out the doors, Sean and I walked in silence all the way to the parking lot, stopping beside my car.

"What about your Jeep?" I asked.

He shrugged as he pulled the handle to the passenger door of my

F-150 and climbed in. I followed suit after tossing my bag in the back seat.

"I'll leave it here for now. You can either drop me by later today when we're done running around, or I'll get it tomorrow," he clarified when the ringing from both of our doors slamming shut silenced.

I smiled. *Yeah, it's probably going to be tomorrow, buddy.*

"Okay."

Something occurred to me, so I asked, point-blank.

"You have your driver's license on you?"

His cheeks climbed closer to his eyes, but he didn't question it—at least, not directly. "Yeah."

I nodded, and with one flick of my wrist, the engine fired to life, and we were off.

Next stop, JFK.

Sean didn't really start to get inquisitive until we crossed over the Verrazano Bridge onto the Belt Parkway. Traffic was thick, and the route was long as we weaved our way along the inlet shoreline, around Brooklyn, and past Coney Island. Summer was in the air, and the beach was thick with tan bodies and gelled hair. Rides spun and danced, and lights flickered and flared in bright, colorful patterns as people got in a little adventure at Brooklyn's favorite amusement park.

Everyone was partaking in all the recreational time they could before fall came and wrecked it all with colder temperatures and school schedules.

"What do you have to do all the way out here?" Sean asked, surveying all the people with languid eyes and propping a sock-covered foot up on my dashboard as I rolled down the windows.

I hummed, pursing my lips with a grin. I wasn't sure I could really say anything at this point without lying, and I wasn't keen to have him beg me to turn the truck around either.

I settled on the truth—a vague version of it anyway—knowing I'd just struggle to fill in the gaps in any other tale I tried to weave. "Just have to swing by JFK."

"Is your brother flying in?" he asked, his eyebrows drawn down into a funny little point. I glanced between him and the road, watching as traffic once again slowed to a crawl.

"Nah. His schedule's too busy with preseason training for Alabama."

He nodded in response to my non-answer, and thankfully, got stuck on a subject I was an expert at talking about in minute detail—football.

"How's he doing? He's starting this year, right?"

"Yep. Groover finally graduated, and they're trying out Den as the starting quarterback."

"How's he feeling about it?"

I shrugged. "He'd probably be better if he didn't hate football."

"What the fuck?" Sean asked, surprised. Apparently, we'd never discussed the real details of my brother and all his complications with the game Sean and I both loved. "What do you mean, he hates football? Why's he playing, then?"

"My dad," I said simply. "My brother both hates my father and hangs on his every approval at the same time. Den and I are complete opposites in a lot of aspects, and my parents would have him believe that I'm everything he should be. Which is complete bullshit. When it comes down to it, my brother's just trying to walk a line with being his own guy and getting a little parental warmth for himself."

"Wow."

I nodded, my fingers flexing on the leather of my steering wheel. "I know. The sad thing is, if my dad weren't so invested in football, Den would probably love playing it."

Sean sank his head into his hands and pretended to rub at his temples with a little chuckle. "I thought you said he's playing *because* of your dad. Why would he love it if your dad weren't invested?"

"Because then it'd have nothing to do with my dad."

"This is some twisted shit."

I nodded and hummed, trying to put the whole thing into words. "Den is doomed to unhappiness until he can let it all go. My dad is the factor that will forever taint everything. Den doesn't allow himself to love football because my dad loves football. But he's fucking good." I raised one shoulder cockily. "I *am* his big brother, after all."

"Wow, QB. I had no idea your family was so messed up."

"Lies and blood, Phillips. The best camouflage there is."

I pulled off the exit and followed the signs for short-term parking, and finally, Sean remembered why he'd been asking about my brother in the first place.

"Okay, so, it's not your brother. Who else is flying in?"

I smiled as I pulled up to the machine to take a parking ticket, and pulled through the gate as it lifted to let us by. "Nobody."

"All right, dude. You've been the most taciturn during this car ride that you've ever been in your life, and the ambiguity is starting to freak me out. If no one's flying in, what the *fuck* are we doing at the airport?"

He'd been patient—way more patient than I'd have ever been in bumper-to-bumper traffic—and as I pulled the truck into a space and cut the engine, I figured he was stuck there with me whether he liked it or not. It was time to tell him the truth.

"We're flying out."

He laughed. Just one quick burst that turned into a scoff when I didn't immediately start laughing with him.

"We have practice tomorrow morning!" he semi-yelled, reminding me of something I already knew.

I rolled my eyes and opened my center console to dig out my wallet. I couldn't tell you how many times Jillian had yelled at me for leaving it in there, preached about how someone was going to rob me stupid one day, but I couldn't be bothered. It was just so much easier to leave it in there for when I needed it. "I know. We're flying to Birmingham on the 2:15 and then right back on the 6:45. We'll be home by midnight at the latest."

"We're flying there and back again, back-to-back?"

I nodded.

"Why in the *fuck* would we do that?"

I smiled. "Sean, buddy," I murmured and then paused to squeeze his shoulder. "I'd like you to meet someone. Someone who I think might just be someone special."

Sean grumbled as we walked down the jetway, giving my Beats, wrapped conveniently around my neck, a flick. "I can't believe I'm doing over six hours' worth of flying, and I don't even have my headphones."

"I'll remind you," I said, the thud of our big feet on the extendable tube making the entirety of it shake, "You volunteered to come along. Chased me down at the stadium, as it were. I was supposed to be doing this alone."

"I didn't know I was signing up to fly to fucking Alabama and back!" he snapped. "I thought I was riding along to the goddamn post office. Maybe the grocery store."

"Oh, Seany, growing up with that sister of yours, I *know* you had to have learned what a bad idea it is to assume."

"Leave Cassie out of this."

"She is *insane*. An impromptu trip to Alabama should be like a walk in the park for you."

My most recent personal experience with her had been at the cabin in the Catskills last Christmas, but she was always coming to the games, cheering Sean on, and raising all holy hell. What I said was no exaggeration: Cassie Phillips, now Kelly, was off her fucking rocker.

He laughed and tried to touch the back of his head with his eyeballs. "It's been several years since we lived together. I guess I'm out of practice."

"Well, good then, ol' buddy. Your Captain Quinn is good for

practice any day of the week."

We were both laughing, wide smiles lightening our sometimes mean faces as we stepped up to the plane and a pretty flight attendant's eyes went wide at the sight of us.

"Quinn Bailey and Sean Phillips," she muttered, her breath soft and her voice even softer. Her eyes, though, they danced with light.

My smile turned polite as I stuck out my hand, offering it to the woman I'd never seen before—a woman who was obviously a fan.

Shit. I sure hope Cat didn't switch fucking flights with someone. I laughed a little to myself. *Goddamn, that'd be one hell of a joke on me.*

"Nice to meet you, ma'am." Sean nodded in kind.

"Carly," she said, blushing. "My name's Carly."

She turned her body and reached out a hand toward the aisle of the plane, but her wide green eyes never left me.

"Uh, um," she mumbled, trying to snap her fingers at someone down the aisle and failing. Finally, she got it together. "Cat!" she nearly yelled, turning to look down the aisle but stopping before actually making it far enough to look and jerking her gaze back to us.

I smiled and relaxed, knowing now with absolute certainty that my girl was on the plane. I could allow myself to enjoy the excited fan's bumbling.

"What?" Cat asked, looking down at her hands as she stuffed some garbage in a little bag, her step hurried. "Why are you snapping at me?"

Carly just pointed. Sean and I smiled, still outside the plane, having been barred by a dumbfounded Carly. In fact, a line of waiting passengers had started to form behind me just like last time.

Cat's gaze followed Carly's hand, and when it landed on me, her whole body jerked.

"Quinn?" she said on a surprised whisper.

I winked. "Hey there, kitten."

Sean, the asshole, nudged me from behind.

I shook my head slightly but smiled. "This is Sean."

Chapter Sixteen

Cat

"Tell me something," Nikki whispered into my ear as we stood near the entry doors, watching passengers from Birmingham file on to our plane. Luckily, she was on the flight back to New York with me this time, and Carly, a flight attendant for RoyalAir I worked with a hell of a lot less, was on her way somewhere else.

For three and a half hours, the enamored woman had chatted my ear off about Quinn and Sean and everything she knew about them—enough information to start a Facebook profile for each of them—and I'd had to smile and listen.

Because if I wasn't telling my close friends all of the details yet, I certainly wasn't telling her. Still, every swallowed comment tasted like vinegar.

Am I actually jealous of Carly's little fan trip?

Christ. I was.

Get it together, Cat. The man is into you. *He's flight stalking you, for Pete's sake.*

"What?"

"Those two guys," she responded quietly. "The ones that I saw get off the plane before I got on and are now *reboarding* the plane. They're here because of you, aren't they?"

"What guys?" I questioned dumbly, even though I knew full well who she was referring to.

How'd I know? Well, because Quinn, followed by Sean, was literally *re*-boarding the plane for their flight back to NYC. It was hard to miss two men that stood over six feet tall and had biceps the size of tree trunks.

"Lovely to see you again, Catharine." Quinn winked as he walked by, and Sean smirked knowingly. Good God, what had Quinn been saying about me while I worked during the last flight?

"Uh…*yeah*." Nikki rolled her eyes. "I think it's safe to say you know exactly who I'm talking about."

Shit. I'd managed to avoid the topic of Quinn Bailey and everything I felt for him for a couple of days, but that was done. Nikki wasn't having it anymore.

"Technically, they're not both here for me," I answered honestly, and an incredulous laugh slipped past her lips.

"I think now is the time to explain to me why two of the Mavericks are on our plane, and one in particular—who just so happens to be the fucking quarterback—appears to be on a pretty fucking friendly basis with you."

I turned toward her. "How do you know they play for the Mavericks?"

"Oh, come on." She huffed out an exasperated breath. "Everyone in America knows Quinn Bailey and Sean Phillips. The men, because they're considered to be the best team in the NFL, and the women, because, well, look at them."

"Well, I'll be honest, Quinn Bailey was on our last Birmingham to JFK flight, and you didn't seem to even notice who he was then."

"He was?"

I nodded.

"Jesus Christ," she muttered. "How in the hell did I miss that?" I watched as she mentally calculated the days in her head. "Oh, yeah, it was period week. I was probably just trying to not strangle passengers and hemorrhage through my uniform."

"Ew." I scrunched my nose. "Gross."

She rolled her pretty hazel eyes. "Like you don't know exactly what I'm talking about."

"Yeah." I grinned knowingly. "You got me there."

Every woman in the world had experienced her own personal version of period nightmares and the occasional murderous rage that menstrual cycles provided.

My gaze flicked toward first class, and I watched as Quinn and Sean filed into their seats, their wide, strong shoulders making the spacious seats in first class look more like a tiny house version of an airplane.

Speaking of which, if that tiny fucking house trend ever started to filter into the airline industry, I'd put my resignation in on the spot. Planes were small enough as it was, and anyone who didn't believe that needed to attempt to make coffee in the coach galley while passengers waiting in line for the lavatory surrounded them.

Nearly fucking impossible, I tell ya.

Nikki grabbed my elbow and led me toward the back galley of the plane, politely pushing us past the passengers who were still working on getting their carry-ons into the overhead bins.

The instant she had us behind the curtain, she released her death grip on my elbow, and I grimaced from the abrupt change in nerve pressure.

"Okay. Explain yourself. Why are two of the Mavericks stalking you?"

My eyes went wide. "They're not stalking me."

Well, technically, one wasn't stalking me. The other, well, I wasn't so sure. He appeared to be flying on a lot of my flights lately…

"Oh, come on," she muttered on a groan and proceeded to put her hands together in a praying position. "Tell me everything, Cat. *Everything*."

"There's nothing to tell…"

She pulled her cell phone out of her back pocket. "Do not make me get Casey on the phone right now. I knew you two were hiding something from me the other day! I'd thought it was my period paranoia, but now, I know I wasn't hallucinating that shit. This is why you switched cabins with me."

Ah, man. She was playing dirty.

I stared at Nikki, and she stared back at me.

Once she raised her eyebrow and started waving her phone around in the air, I folded like a house of cards.

"Fine."

Nikki's mouth morphed into a grin, her lips cresting and lighting up her eyes to shades of outright giddy. She propped one hip against the counter and settled in, far too excited for what I was about to tell her.

"So…I met Quinn Bailey on one of my flights a little less than a week ago," I explained. "Actually, it was the flight Casey and I were on that got detoured to Atlanta because of Tropical Storm Rita."

"Oh, yeah." She nodded in remembrance. "The flight with the sexy as hell guy in 2A."

"He told you about the guy in 2A?"

"Yep," she responded, popping the p. "He couldn't shut up about him."

Good Lord, he was such a little gossiper.

"So, I'm guessing he told you about the train ride too, then?"

"Uh-huh." She grinned. "*And* the Journey serenade."

"Does that diva keep any secrets?"

Nikki laughed. "When it comes to gossiping to me and you, no, probably not. But anyone *not* in his inner circle, he definitely knows when to keep his chatty lips shut."

"Well…" I paused, not really sure how to explain the situation. The strange coincidence of it all sounded a bit crazy inside my head. "Well…"

"Well, *what?*" The tip of her toe tapped against the carpet in quick succession.

"Uh…Well… Quinn is actually 2A."

"*What?*" she asked on a shout, and I held my index finger up to my lips to shush her.

"I'd prefer to keep this conversation between us, not the entire plane."

"Quinn is 2A? You mean Quinn Bailey? The flipping quarterback for the Mavericks?"

I nodded once in confirmation.

"Shut the fuck up!" she shouted again and proceeded to go Elaine Benes on me, shoving my chest with both hands until my ass bounced into one of the galley cabinets.

So much for keeping this conversation between us...

"Ow," I muttered and rubbed at the cheek of my ass. "No need to resort to violence."

But she didn't give a shit. She was too amped up over the news I'd just delivered.

"So, what is going on with you guys, then?" she asked, her eyes wide and inquisitive. "*Wait*...are you, like, dating?" Her eyes grew even wider at her own words. "Oh my God, if you tell me you're dating Quinn Bailey, I might have a stroke."

"Take a breath, girl. We're not dating," I responded honestly. "We just met."

I didn't really know what the fuck we were doing, but I knew we weren't dating. At least, we'd yet to go on an actual date. I was pretty sure him stalking my flights didn't really count...

Nikki stayed quiet for a long moment until her face brightened up like a light bulb. "Oh my God, I've got the best idea ever."

"What?"

"You need to date him."

"That's your brilliant idea?" I asked on a laugh. "Pretty sure I can't just decide something like that on my own. It takes two willing participants to equal a date."

"Believe me, Cat. He wants to date you."

"How in the heck would you know that?" I asked. "You literally just found out that I knew him. Not to mention, you're not the most observant. You didn't even recognize him the last time he was on our flight."

"Again, I was having a period rage moment. I was just trying not to strangle passengers during that flight. But I know what I'm talking about here." Nikki held open the curtain until both of our eyes could see directly down the center aisle of the plane. "And I know it because of *that.*"

"Because of what?"

"The fact that I can literally see the back of Quinn Bailey's head on our plane," she responded and shut the curtain again. "A man doesn't fly to Birmingham and back to NYC in the same fucking day because he just felt like flying. There is only one reason a man would purposely take a woman's flight without any need to go to the intended destination."

"And what reason is that?"

"Because he totally wants you," Nikki answered and clapped her hands together. "Holy hell, Quinn Bailey wants you. This is like one of those Lifetime Cinderella movies. Oh my God! I can't fucking wait to go to your wedding. Mr. Miller is going to lose his fucking shit when he finds out we're going to Quinn Bailey's wedding!"

"Whoa, whoa, whoa," I muttered and placed a hand over her mouth before the entire plane started listening to our conversation. "First of all, stop being so fucking loud. And secondly, slow your roll, Nik."

She pulled my hand off her mouth and just grinned.

"*Seriously,*" I stated firmly. "I barely know the guy. I'm definitely *not* Cinderella, and no one is getting married."

"No one is getting married...*yet,*" she answered with a wink and then headed back toward the front of the plane without another word *or* giving me the chance to refute her ridiculous prediction.

My friend had lost her freaking mind. Quinn Bailey wanted me?

That sounded a bit crazy...*right?*

It sounds crazy, but the proof is right in front of your eyes, sitting on your flight again, Cat...

Instead of driving myself crazy analyzing Quinn Bailey's

motives, I busied myself with getting both galleys ready while Nikki did final checks before takeoff.

Maybe by the time we landed in NYC, I'd find the confidence to just straight up ask him what the deal was…

Oh, hey, Quinn. How are you? This might sound weird, but it kind of feels like you're stalking me, and I'd really like to understand why…

Jesus. Yeah. I'd definitely need to work on my approach.

Besides the fact that everyone on the plane realized Quinn Bailey and Sean Phillips were on our flight, and an impromptu autograph and selfie session had taken place in the middle of first class, the ride back to JFK had been otherwise uneventful.

Kidding. It had been a bit of a whirlwind assisting Quinn and Sean with keeping passengers—*and apparent superfans*—from trying to take over the plane with their Mavericks mania.

But Nikki and I had been a good team, and the guys had been nothing but generous and patient toward their fans.

It was still pretty weird, though. Seeing Quinn signing autographs and being adored by his fans…*again.*

Even when you weren't the actual person, but the outsider watching situations like that unfold, I wasn't sure it was something someone could ever get used to.

I mean, how did he deal with it on a daily basis? How did his non-famous friends and family deal with it? How did someone like Quinn Bailey ever have a relationship when his life was surrounded by the constant potential for chaotic situations like the one I'd just witnessed on the plane, and before that, when he'd gotten off the train in Birmingham?

I honestly didn't know the answers to those questions.

All I knew was that we were nearly to the point in the flight where I'd have to tell everyone to strap in, do final checks, and clean the lingering trash from refreshments as we started our descent into New York.

I knew I was working and he was being watched by just about everyone on the plane, but it felt painfully anticlimactic that he'd gone to all the trouble of flying to Alabama and back and we hadn't even had a chance to talk.

I was pushing the coffee maker back into its cabinet and locking the door into place, my face a pout full of sad thoughts, when big hands grabbed on to my hips from behind and squeezed.

"Holy shit!" I whisper-yelled, my hair flying out in an arc as I spun around. Quinn's smile was downright roguish as he leaned forward and put his lips to my cheek.

His breath fanned warmth across my skin as he spoke. "So good to see you, kitten." My eyes widened, wondering if someone might be watching us, but Nikki pulled the curtain shut to the galley and gave me a thumbs up over Quinn's shoulder.

Minty notes flirted with my nose as Quinn shifted the gum in his mouth to the other side. "Five hours of seeing you I've gotten," he murmured softly. "Still, it's even better to be able to touch you."

Yeah, I agreed. My cheek still pulsed where his lips had touched.

"You took these flights just to see me," I said. It was fact, pure and simple, but still, I expected an answer to my non-question.

He had no problem taking the hint.

"Yep."

The captain sounded the bell to signal the beginning of our descent, and without prompting, my lips turned down into a small frown.

Quinn smiled and lifted a hand, smoothing the unhappy line in my cheek with his thumb. "That sound means I have to leave you alone, huh?"

I bit my lip and nodded, and he tucked my loose hair behind my ear, gave my hip a gentle squeeze, and disappeared back behind the curtain..

Good God, I'm fucked.

By the time Sean and Quinn had been safely escorted off the plane by airport security, and the last passenger had exited the main doors, Nikki and I had quickly finished up our final tasks before calling it a day.

"Ready to go?" she asked.

"Girl, I'm *more* than ready."

Grabbing both of our carry-ons from the flight attendant closet, I handed hers off and wrapped my fingers tightly around the handle of mine.

"It's a shame the guys got noticed on our flight and needed the assistance of airport security to leave the plane."

"What do you mean?" I looked at her curiously as we walked the long hallway toward the gate doors.

She shrugged one bony shoulder. "I was just kind of hoping you two would get to chat for a little bit longer than the half a freaking minute on the plane. Maybe grab a bite to eat after the flight. Get naked at his place."

I laughed and rolled my eyes at the same time. "You're such a romantic."

"I know, right?" Nikki grinned. "It should come as no mystery that Mr. Miller and I know how to keep things spicy in our marriage."

"And how exactly do you two manage that?"

She pushed open the gate doors. "A lot of Chinese takeout and Netflix and chill."

Soft giggles left my lips. "That sounds surprisingly amazing."

To be honest, it did. One day, I hoped to find that perfect someone to just spend nights in wearing sweats and eating Chinese without a care in the world.

"Well..." She paused, her words and her feet. "Maybe you should see if *he's* interested in something like that?"

I stopped and looked back at her. "Huh?"

Nikki nodded in the opposite direction, and I followed her eyes across the main aisle of the terminal until they landed smack-dab on Quinn.

There he stood, waiting for me outside my gate. *Again.*

I was starting to see a pattern here…

"I'll call you tomorrow." She patted my shoulder and leaned in to whisper into my ear. "And you better tell me every-fucking-thing."

"Deal. Although, I'm not sure my reality can live up to your fantasies of marriage and Lifetime Cinderellas." I grinned, and she just rolled her eyes as she started to walk away. "Oh, and have a nice night with Mr. Miller!" I called toward her departing back.

"I'm sure you'll be able to find us watching season two of *Stranger Things*!" She waved over her shoulder. "Night, Cat!"

I watched her walk away for a brief moment, before bringing my eyes back to Quinn. He still stood in the same spot, but this time, the smile on his face was what I noticed the most. It was infectious and seemed to make its way from his lips, across the tiled terminal floor, all the way to my lips.

Damn, he was good.

"You waited for me," I said once I made my way over to his tall frame. "Again."

"I did."

"And you stalked me today."

He smirked. "I did that too."

"Is there a reason for the stalking?"

Quinn's eyes sparkled, and instead of actually answering my question, he asked, "So, how about that date, Kitty Cat?"

I was lost for words as I wandered in the blue pools of his eyes, and he waited in silence as I stared at him mutely.

Quinn leaned forward, done waiting for the silence to break on my end, pressed a soft kiss to my cheek—*the second of the fucking day!*—and whispered into my ear, "Say yes."

Goose bumps rolled up my spine in delicious waves.

I couldn't hold back my answer any longer.

"Yes." One word. But a definitive one at that. I smiled as it left my lips, and his answering expression mirrored mine.

He wrapped his arm around my shoulder, grabbed my carry-on, and led us in the direction of the exit.

"Tonight work for you?" he asked, and a soft, amused laugh rasped out of my throat.

"Uh… It's like midnight, Quinn," I stated the obvious truth. "I've been on a plane all day. You've been on a plane for half the day. I'd prefer to go on our date not smelling like stale airplane air and peanuts…"

"Okay. You've got a point." He smirked. "How about tomorrow night?"

Thank everything, I'm off tomorrow.

"That sounds perfect."

"Any special requests?"

"Nope," I answered honestly. *Just you.*

The only thing I needed and wanted out of our date was more time with him.

"Don't worry, Kitty Cat. We're going to have fun tomorrow."

When it came to Quinn Bailey, I was pretty certain he could have taken us to an electric chair and it would have been fun, but I chose to keep that little remark to myself.

There was nothing wrong with making a man work for it, right?

Chapter Seventeen

Quinn

"Take a water break!" Coach Bennett yelled just after the sound of the whistle.

Sweat ran like a river over ninety percent of my body, so I didn't fucking argue.

Practice in the summertime heat reminded me why we played the regular season in the fall, and it made me a little less resentful at playing in the occasional snowstorm.

At a jog, I moved toward the side of the field, the rest of my team a flock behind me. Sean ran up close, slapping me on the back of the helmet before I could get it pulled off, and cut in front of me to grab one of the water bottles support staff had ready on the sidelines to pass out.

Cam Mitchell followed his lead and went to cut ahead of me, but Sean elbowed him back. "Hey, whoa," he said to Cam. "I earned this. Sacrifices were made for the greater QB good. You go behind him."

I rolled my eyes, but unfortunately, Sean's little speech got some of the guys inquisitive. "Oh yeah, Li'l Sean?" Jimmy Thompson, the kicker, asked. "What you'd do to earn the privilege?"

All of it was talk, a bunch of ballbusters flapping their gums about a pecking order that didn't exist. But once again, Sean played right into the game, outing me to everyone. "Bailey is a fucking legend, and I paid witness, that's what."

I bit my lip and tried to blend into the crowd, but several of the guys started shoving me from behind, trapping me in a churning semicircle as Sean continued with his grand tale.

"Two flights, down and back, we flew to Alabama yesterday, all so QB here could mack on the stewardess."

"Ohh," Teeny yelled dramatically, stirring the pot.

I shook my head, muttering under my breath, "They're called flight attendants now."

"Uh-huh," Sean hummed. "Little hot chocolate cutie with soulful brown eyes."

"Sean," I warned.

He just smirked. "*Kitten*, as he calls her."

The whole team crooned, catcalled, and hollered, and I worked hard not to blush.

"Wait," Cam said, pausing just long enough to smirk. "Is this the fucking kitten everyone on Instagram has been asking all of us about?" He raised his voice to mimic a female fan. *"Oh my God, Quinn got a kitten? What's its name, Cam? Have you met it? Have you had to cat sit?"*

"Holy shit!" Teeny yelled. "QB's been getting a little something something and keeping it to himself!"

"Cut it out!" I ordered, but I allowed my lips to curve into a smile to take some of the harshness out of it. "You're supposed to be hydrating, not gossiping. Unless you think gabbing about my love life is going to keep you from collapsing on the field?"

Sam Sheffield's smirk was ornery. "I don't know, QB. I'm pretty sure a little dirt on you could keep me going for a while."

I laughed and gave my mouthy center a shove in the shoulder. "How about two hours?" I asked. "That's how long you have left out here. And I know you've been losing water," I noted. "Every time you bend over in front of me to snap the ball, I see the line of sweat between the cheeks of your ass."

"Ohh," Teeny yelled. "QB got jokes today, fellas!"

In truth, what I had today was desperation. Time ticked like molasses as I tried not to think about my date with Catharine tonight. Of course, it wasn't that I didn't actually want to think about it so much as, if I let myself, it would be the *only* thing on my mind.

I wasn't really looking for that kind of physical pain. Because, trust me, any time spent on the field with the guys mocking me endlessly best be done with a whole fucking boatload of concentration. One misstep, one flicker of mental uncertainty, and I'd be flat on my back, trying to extricate my lungs from the back of my ribcage.

Plus, crutches wouldn't really match the outfit I had planned.

So I had to change the subject, and I had to do it fast, before I lost myself to thoughts about her and ended up showing up on her doorstep via stretcher.

Just in time, Coach Bennett blew three sharp bleeps on the whistle, and I didn't have to try to get my team's asses in gear anymore.

They moved all on their own, turning their bottles of water upside down and hosing their mouths like animals.

Empties littered the ground as players dropped them and took off toward the center of the field again at a jog. Just like during a game, when the whistle blew, time waited for no man.

That's why the team had people they paid to collect all the bottles, haul them in for cleaning, and come back promptly with an entirely new set.

Precision playing took over soon enough as we set up again, running hard and slamming bodies all in the name of getting a ball from one end of a field to another.

Sean was on fire today, picking balls out of the air like he was predestined by God himself to do so.

I hoped like fuck he'd keep playing like that as we headed into the season. After last year, a season where we'd found ourselves in the play-offs with the potential to go all the way—but come up painfully short—I was hungry for it *all* this year.

An undefeated season, flawless play-offs, and a win in the ultimate championship—the Super Bowl—at the end of it all.

With all that in mind, I pushed myself harder than I had in weeks, using speed I didn't know I had and putting everything and then some into the strength of my arm.

Coach Bennett pulled me aside as the rest of the team filed into the tunnel, heading to the locker room to shower up, when we finally finished a couple of hours later.

"Fucking outstanding performance today, Bailey." He looked me up and down, from the top of my sweat-drenched head to the shake in my tired thighs. "I see you're spent, so make sure you get good rest tonight, okay?"

I swallowed hard before reciting my lie. "Sure, Coach." I hoped to God I wouldn't be spending my date with Cat *resting*.

He gave me a hard smack on my shoulder pad. "Shower up."

I nodded and turned up the dark beckoning of the tunnel at a jog. Jell-O legs or not, I had a date to get ready for.

I was trying on my third shirt of the evening when Jilly slammed my front door so hard the house rattled.

An interesting way to enter a house, for sure, and an entire hallway and flight of stairs away from me, but I still knew it was her.

One, she was the only one with a key; two, she had a lot of rage toward me currently; and three, she'd made this exact entrance several times before.

Temporarily satisfied with the shirt on my back since it covered all my flesh, I hustled out of my room, through the hall, and down the stairs.

Jilly was waiting at the bottom, as expected, her toe tapping furiously on the travertine tile.

"Hey, Jilly-willy," I greeted playfully, watching as the tops of her ears turned a burning hot red.

"Cut the crap, Quinn," she replied. Her tone was remarkably less friendly. "Nathan's been chasing me around like a rabid dog since he can't get ahold of you."

I shrugged.

Her head looked like it might explode as she shook it violently back and forth, her blond ringlet curls bouncing as she did. Her hazel eyes looked amber and a whole lot pissed. I semi-feared she was going to transform into a werewolf, they were glowing so hard.

"I know you didn't just shrug," she said, eerie calm making me take a step back before responding.

"You need to make yourself less available like I do. It solves a lot of problems when it comes to Nathan."

Publicists, man. Hopped up on gossip columns, and like scavengers, they hunted everywhere for issues, opportunities, things to slide under the rug. They were an entirely different breed, and with as much as mine called me, I often wondered when Nathan found the time to sleep or take a shit.

"You pay me to be available!" she shouted.

I smirked shamelessly. "Oh, yeah, that's right. So what is it you're complaining about again?"

"One day, I'm going to murder you," she threatened and I laughed.

"Probably not a good long-term employment plan, but hey, you do what you gotta do."

For the first time since arriving, she noticed my appearance. From the button-down shirt to my nicest pair of jeans to the product in my hair, it was obvious I was making an effort. At least, it would be to her. She saw me on a daily basis in my regular gear, and trust me, this wasn't it.

"Where are you going?" she asked suspiciously, drawing a figure eight over my body with a point. "I don't like this."

I shook my head and headed for the kitchen, avoiding her eyes as she trailed me. "What's not to like? I'm wearing clothes. No big deal."

"Uh, no," she spewed behind me. "Those aren't just clothes. Those are going-somewhere clothes, and I'm still dealing with the somewhere you went yesterday."

I rolled my eyes, but in the interest of full disclosure, she was behind me. She couldn't actually *see* the action. I didn't have a death wish.

"What were you thinking, getting on a fucking plane to Alabama yesterday? Did you think no one would notice? That there wouldn't be videos of you all over social media? Because there were, trust me. I know because I've been fielding calls from your publicist all day about it!"

"Jilly, relax," I coached, pulling two bottles of water out of the fridge and sliding one across the island to her. She unscrewed the cap and took a big gulp, all while shooting laser beams out of her eyes at me. "I'll call Nathan."

"Tonight," she ordered, but I shook my head.

The lasers became death rays.

"I have a date tonight," I admitted. "So, no, not tonight. Tomorrow."

"I knew those were going-somewhere clothes!"

I laughed. "Come on, Jilly. Don't you want your best friend Quinn to meet a nice lady? Someone you can inspect carefully, fall in love with, claim as your new best friend, and then occasionally loan out to me?"

She shrugged and popped her eyebrows, grumbling, "Well, that doesn't sound *bad*."

I smiled, biting into my bottom lip as I did. "You're going to love her."

She rolled her eyes, disbelieving, so I pulled my phone out of my pocket and quickly clicked through to Cat's Instagram profile.

"Here." I shoved my phone across the island, and she caught it on the other side before it hit the ground—thankfully. "Look at her profile."

"Oh, great," she groused as she lifted the phone. "Probably some fucking YouTube star with forty million—" Her eyebrows drew together so sharply the gap between them disappeared. "Does that say she has fifteen followers?"

I grinned hugely, thinking about Cat's profile picture. Hair pulled back off her face, she grinned into the camera with paint streaks all over it and her shirt. She was a mess, but the light in her eyes was fucking brilliant.

"Yep," I confirmed, rounding the counter and snagging my phone from Jilly's hands.

"Hey!" she snapped. "I was still looking at that."

"Time's up. I have to finish getting ready and pick her up in Hoboken."

She sighed, but most of the fight had left her. Her scrutiny remained, however, and I shifted under her stare. "What?" I asked.

"What exactly do you have to do? You look ready to me."

I looked down at myself self-consciously. "I thought I might wear a different shirt."

She shook her head immediately. "Wear that one. The lavender goes with your eyes."

I scoffed playfully. "Are you saying you've noticed the color of my eyes?"

"Shut up."

I laughed and stepped forward, ruffling her hair and pissing her off enough to last the next two months. "Don't wait up, Jilly. I'll make sure you meet your new mommy soon enough."

She flipped me off behind my back as I strode from the kitchen. I could feel it burning heat through the fabric of my shirt, but nothing could break my stride. I tucked my phone into my pocket, grabbed my keys from the entryway table, and headed out the front door to my truck.

I started the engine and then had a thought before I left. I was a couple minutes early thanks to Jilly's arrival and interrogation—and her dismissal of my plan to try on forty other shirts.

I shifted in my seat, digging for my phone and squeezing it out of my pocket by a sheer miracle. A few quick taps and I was back on Cat's Instagram, where I clicked to open a direct message.

Phone up in front of my face, I pointed the camera at myself and tapped the button to record.

"Hey, Kitty Cat," I greeted. "I hope you're ready because I'm going to see you real soon."

Cat

The intercom buzzed, and unless someone had sent a Chinese delivery to the wrong apartment, those sounds signified Quinn's arrival…for our freaking *date.*

Holy moly.

"It's Quinn," he said through the speaker, and I tapped the intercom to let him inside.

I hurried my ass back into my bedroom, my heels click-clacking across the hardwood floor, and took one last look in the floor-length mirror beside the door.

Hair shiny and sleek? *Check.*

Makeup intact? *Check.*

Little black dress and heels? *Triple check.*

It'd taken two hours of fashion analysis to come up with the easiest, most clichéd choice: my one and only black cocktail dress paired with my favorite pair of nude pumps.

Honestly, I still wasn't certain it was the right choice, but I knew time had obviously run out when two knocks reverberated from my door. I couldn't dillydally any fucking longer; my date was here.

"Just a minute," I called out as I practically skidded across the hardwood floor of the hallway and toward the living room.

As I gripped the door handle, I gave myself another two seconds to take a big, calming breath and silently pray, *Please let tonight go well.*

The instant I turned the knob and opened the door, the nerves in my belly fluttered and flopped around at such an intense pace I felt like squealing. Son of a nutcracker, I was nervous. I hadn't planned on this much anxiety when I'd initially said yes.

It's because you like him so much...

Another calming, yet very discreet breath, and I schooled my face into a soft smile. "Uh...hi," I said lamely and instantly felt like face-palming.

Uh...hi? I was the queen of un-smooth and awkward.

And good God, why did he always have to look so fucking good?

Perfectly kempt yet shaggy light brown hair, those intense blue eyes, and a body that looked good underneath pretty much anything—*especially* his current choice of casual yet sexy attire of a lilac collared shirt and jeans—Quinn looked good.

And not just good, but *good* with an *extra-long* O.

"Hi." He greeted with a sexy little smirk. "Wow, Kitty Cat. You look amazing," he said, each word coming out of his mouth at a smooth and steady pace, mimicking his eyes' perusal.

I didn't know what to do underneath the intense, warm gaze of those blue eyes of his. So, I did the only thing I could think of. I motioned for him to step inside, the exaggerated movement of my arm more awkward than anything else. A bystander from the hallway probably thought I was inviting him inside for some line-dancing and a good old fashion hoedown.

"Please come in," I added. "I just need to grab my purse and keys."

He stepped inside my home, and I wasn't sure what he could possibly be thinking in that moment.

"So...this is where I live..." I said, and even I could hear the uncertainty and nervousness in my voice. Surely, my quaint little first-floor apartment inside a Hoboken brownstone-style building was nothing in comparison to his place.

I didn't have to know his net worth to understand a professional NFL quarterback could afford a whole lot more than my humble abode.

Stop being so self-deprecating, Cat.

My subconscious was right. Quinn knew I wasn't rich and my life wasn't surrounded by fame. I was a twenty-four-year-old flight attendant. The fact that I'd already achieved as much as I had, all without the help of my parents, and in my early twenties at that, was a huge accomplishment in my opinion.

He looked around my home, taking in the white walls and eclectic yet colorful furniture and accents. A soft smile kissed his lips when he noticed my favorite spot in the entire apartment—the picture wall I'd created. Various, candid photos, all of my closest family and friends, they took up the entire wall space surrounding my mantel.

"I love your place." Realness and authenticity coated his words like caramel. His eyes met mine, and I shrugged.

"It's a bit random for some people's tastes..."

"Really, Cat. It's fantastic, and I've only seen the living room."

"Thanks," I said in a small voice, his enthusiasm throwing me off guard a bit.

He smiled, and I strove to regain my equilibrium.

"I'd offer to give you the tour, but I don't kiss-and-tell *or* show my bedroom on the first date," I teased, and Quinn chuckled.

Wait...what? I don't show my bedroom on the first date?

Where in the hell had that come from? If this date went well, I'd be an idiot *not* to show Quinn my bedroom.

"I guess I'll start crossing my fingers for a second date now."

Giggles left my lips in a wave of melody and amusement. "How about you make yourself comfortable for a minute while I grab a few things?" I suggested and motioned—*casually, this time*—toward the small white sectional in the living room. "Can I get you anything to drink while you wait?"

Stop being weird, I mentally chastised myself for all of a sudden turning stuffy and formal and silently prayed he hadn't sensed my weirdness. Although, I knew that was probably an impossible feat, but who knew, maybe the Big Guy upstairs was feeling generous tonight.

"I'm good," Quinn answered and winked at me over his shoulder. "I'll just stalk your wall of photos until you're ready to go."

I smiled and headed back into the hallway. "You know, you're surprisingly good at the stalking," I called toward him once I reached my now-mess of a bedroom.

Clothes scattered across the floor and my bed like rag dolls, it looked like a bomb of H&M had gone off.

Quinn's chuckle echoed down the hall. "You say stalking, but I say tenacious!"

I grinned, but once my eyes took in the disaster of my bedroom again, it quickly faded. What in the hell had happened in here? It was like I'd deconstructed my entire closet and relocated it to my bed and floor.

I did my best to straighten up—*because, yeah, I didn't know how the date would end*—while Quinn remained safely unaware in my living room.

Once I'd tossed everything back into my closet and managed to shut the door, I grabbed my purse, keys, and phone and headed out.

"Okay, I'm ready whenever you are," I announced as I walked back into the room. Quinn still stood by my picture wall, his eyes intently examining each photo.

"Are these your parents?" he asked and pointed toward a picture from a beach vacation in Gulf Shores. With the sun in our eyes and the beach at our backs, the three of us stood huddled together, smiling down at the camera in my father's hand. I'd been twenty at the time, still unaware of who or what I'd wanted to be.

"Yep." I nodded and stepped beside him, my bare arm brushing softly against the soft fabric of his lilac shirt. "That's Martin and Gail."

My mother was a beautiful, dark-skinned African-American woman, and my father was the complete opposite—a creamy, white-skinned Irishman. When you put the two together, you got me—a creamy, mocha latte mix of both.

"You're a perfect mix of them," he said and glanced between me and the photo. "You have your mother's lips and your father's eyes."

"And a little bit of both when it comes to skin color," I added with a cheeky grin.

"That too." Quinn smiled knowingly. "Where did you grow up?"

"A little suburban town known as Mariemont. It's just outside of Cincinnati."

"Do your parents still live there?"

"Yeah. They'll probably never leave Mariemont. I can't really blame them, though. My parents' house is adorable, and it's located in this little ten-mile area where everyone knows everyone. Honestly, sometimes, it was like growing up in Stars Hollow on the *Gilmore Girls*."

Confusion slid onto his face, and he quirked a brow. "*Gilmore Girls*?"

"It's a TV show… Lorelai… Rory… Wait…" I paused and took in his now more puzzled expression. "You don't know the *Gilmore Girls*?"

"Should I know them?"

"Are you kidding me?" I questioned in damn near outrage. "*Everyone* should know them." I was only speaking facts. *Gilmore Girls* was one of the best television series ever made. Hell, I still watched reruns and was waiting on bended knee for yet another season to come out. And spoiler alert: I needed to know what in the hell was going on with Rory's pregnancy.

Quinn took his cell phone out of his pocket and summoned Siri with two quick taps to the home button. "Siri, add a reminder for tomorrow at four p.m. Title it, *Gilmore Girls*."

A shocked laugh left my lips.

"A reminder for *Gilmore Girls* added to tomorrow at four p.m.," Siri confirmed, and Quinn waggled his brows toward me. "All right. Now that that's settled, are you ready for our date, Kitty Cat?"

"You're ridiculous." I grinned and shook my head at the same time. "And to answer your question, yes. I didn't get all dolled up to stand around in my living room and look at old pictures."

"On the contrary, I like looking at your old pictures, but in the spirit of keeping my gorgeous girl happy, let's go." He smiled and reached out his hand, ready to start our date adventure together.

My gorgeous girl? Oh my.

I faltered on my heels a bit, stepping to the side to regain my balance, but luckily managed to pull myself together.

"Okay." I slid my hand into his, and the instant I felt the warmth of his skin against mine, I couldn't stop myself from *feeling* just how good this—Quinn and me, *together*—felt.

He led us out of my apartment and out the main door and gently helped me into the passenger seat with his hand pressed at the small of my back.

And the entire time, I wasn't thinking about the fact that Quinn's version of a vehicle was a decked-out F-150 with black-tinted windows, or the fact that the man sitting in the driver's seat next to me was an actual celebrity to the rest of the known world.

No. It wasn't any of those things.

It was the fact that I was going on a date with the handsome stranger from 2A. The one who'd serenaded me on a midnight train to Birmingham, Alabama. The guy who'd inserted himself on to more than one of my flights because he wanted to see me.

Hot damn. Tonight, I was one lucky bitch, and it had nothing to do with Quinn Bailey's celebrity status. It was just him, and everything that made him the man I was finding out had a heart of gold.

Two hours later, we sat inside a little art studio in New York, side by side on wooden stools, drinking wine from the bottle of Merlot Quinn had brought, and following Stella's—*our teacher for the evening*—step-by-step painting instructions.

With purples, blues, oranges, yellows, and reds filling our canvases, tonight, our Paint 'N' Sip masterpiece was called Times Square.

I had already finished up the billboard portion, but Quinn was a little behind, still focusing intently on the little people filling the sidewalks.

"Psst," I whispered toward him, while Stella moved on to the taxis.

"What?" Quinn questioned quietly, but his eyes never left the strokes of his brush.

"You're like *way, way* behind."

"No, I'm not."

"Yes, you are." I giggled. "Look at mine."

Considering that Quinn was still concentrating on the pedestrian portion of our painting, the one that had occurred three steps ago, he was most certainly behind. His canvas looked nearly bare compared to mine and Stella's.

"Is everything okay?" our instructor asked and rubbed a hand across her already paint-covered smock. With her brush still in hand, Stella paused to glance back at the only two people in her studio. Her hair, shades of fire red with wild ringlets, shone beneath the studio lights as her gaze moved back and forth between Quinn and me.

Not only had he planned a date at a painting studio, he'd also rented out the entire place for our session, giving us complete privacy. With the number of Mavericks fans who resided inside the city limits, I had a feeling it was more out of necessity than anything else.

"Yep," he blurted out quickly. "We're all good back here."

I fought the urge to burst into laughter when I glanced at his canvas again.

So bare.

"Okay," Stella responded. "Just let me know if you need me to slow down."

Slow down? Quinn probably needed her to start over.

"What made you choose Paint 'N' Sip for our date?" I asked on a whisper after taking a quick sip of my wine. Hints of chocolate and cinnamon pressed against my taste buds, and I swallowed.

"I got the idea from your Instagram."

"Seriously?" I questioned, surprised by his thoughtfulness.

Apparently, Mr. Quarterback had not only been paying attention to my flight schedule but my social media too. Most of the things I shared on my Instagram revolved around my own personal sketches, paintings, and pictures of the greeting card line my father and I sold through Etsy. Selfies and personal photographs were pretty rare.

"Yeah," he answered honestly. "Which, by the way, what is the whole 'Caterpillar & Co' thing I keep seeing pictures of on your profile?"

"It's a greeting card line," I said with a shrug. "Just kind of a fun, hobby thing my father and I do together."

"How long have you been doing that?"

"For a really long time, actually. I was twelve when we started it," I explained and dragged my brush across the canvas in the small, quick strokes Stella had instructed us to do from the front of the studio. "It didn't start out as a greeting card line, though. It just sort of evolved into it."

"Consider me intrigued. How did Caterpillar & Co start?"

"Well…my father runs the post office where I grew up, and I used to help with all of the Dear Santa letters that came through. When I was twelve, I'd pretty much made it my mission to answer every Dear Santa letter the post office received. I don't know, I guess a year or two after that, once I'd started taking art classes at the community center up the street from the house, it had all just kind of turned into greeting cards. And the rest is history."

"And Caterpillar? Is that a nickname?"

I nodded. "My dad called me that a lot when I was a kid. Hell, he still calls me that now, and I'm twenty-four."

"I guess there's just something about you," he said with an indulgent smile, and his eyes brightened with warmth. "You're just so damn cute and adorable. It's impossible to not want to give you a nickname."

"Yeah…*Kitty Cat*…*kitten*… Surely, there won't be any more, right?" I teased.

His smile grew wider. "Only time will tell, I guess."

"I should come up with a nickname for you."

"Do your worst," he said through a chuckle, and his eyes locked with mine. "I'll eat anything you dish out with a spoon and a smile."

I had no response to that, only a soft laugh and a shake of my head.

"Okay..." Stella's voice grabbed my attention, and I looked toward the front. "Before we move on to the skyscrapers, make sure you refill your blues and reds if you're running low."

Several minutes of focus passed, and I'd lost myself in the strokes of my brush as I added softened hues of red to create a dramatic shadow.

Once I'd managed to lay the foundation for my skyscrapers lining the street, I paused my painting and just watched Quinn for a few moments. He was still crazy behind but appeared unfazed by that fact.

So, while he painted, I watched, taking in the focus etched on his face. Lips firm in determination, he furrowed his brow, and a slight wrinkle formed above his nose.

Even superfocused, he was handsome.

Not to mention, he'd taken off his long-sleeved collared shirt and was now just painting in a white, cotton T-shirt that revealed enough of his biceps for me to be reminded that his body was ah-fucking-mazing.

All those hours on the field and in the gym had obviously paid off.

The muscles of his arm rippled and flexed as he moved his brush across the canvas. I licked my lips and silently wished I could take a taste. Hell, if we weren't in the middle of a Paint 'N' Sip, I might've actually attempted it.

"Stop watching me," he whispered mid-stroke, and I just grinned—half dazed and drunk off of my prolonged ogle time.

"I can't help myself. You're so..." *Hot...sexy...lick-able...* "Focused."

Yeah. Focused. That's exactly what you were just musing about…

"Because I'm painting a masterpiece here, Kitty Cat," he said, and his brow furrowed deeper.

I wondered if his sports fans were familiar with that determined face.

"Is this what your 'O game face' looks like?"

Instantly, he stopped painting and turned to face me. "My what face?"

"You know, your *O game face*," I repeated. "The face that your sports fans probably know all too well."

"I'd be surprised if my fans know what my O face looks like, but my *game face?* Yeah, they probably know that one."

"That's what I said."

"No," he said through a chuckle. "You said *O game face.*"

I snorted in shock. "No, I didn't."

Holy hell, I'd just said O game face? Was that some kind of Freudian slip?

It's probably because all of the sex and licking thoughts you've been having since this date started…

Quinn gazed at me with a smirk kissing his lips.

"Shut up," I muttered, but he only smiled wider. "Oh my God. Stop smiling at me like that."

"Is everything okay?" Stella questioned. "Are you guys good to move on to the next step?"

"Yep," Quinn answered for both of us, even though I hadn't even added my taxi cabs yet, and he was still stuck on the pedestrians.

While Stella started instructing us on how to properly paint the evening lavender sky, my painting partner just kept smiling at me, his eyes glimmering like diamonds beneath the studio lights.

"What?" I asked once I started to feel awkward underneath his intense gaze. For lack of anything better to do, I lifted my wineglass from the table and distracted myself with a sip of wine.

He brushed his finger down my cheek. "Thanks for coming on this date with me, Kitty Cat."

My heart pitter-pattered inside of my chest.

"Thank you for inviting me on this date."

"Can I ask you something?"

I set my brush down on my easel. "Of course."

"Tonight, after I've finished this masterpiece that you can hang on your mantel…and I'm walking you to your door…" He paused, and I waited with bated breath for him to finish.

"Yeah…?"

"Can I kiss you, Kitty Cat?" he asked on a whisper, and a sharp gasp escaped my lungs. He leaned forward, and with his gaze holding mine, he quietly added, "I need to feel how soft those perfect lips of yours are. They've been driving me crazy all night."

My skin flushed from the heat permeating his words. I blinked, but it wasn't a quick blink, it was a long, slow, trying to digest his words kind of blink.

Holy hell. And yes, please.

"Okay."

One corner of his mouth reached up toward his cheeks. "Okay?"

"Yes." Apparently, one-word answers were all my brain could handle in that moment.

"You'll save a kiss for me, then?"

"Uh-huh."

He just smiled in response and ran one lone finger slowly up the skin of my bare thigh. In rapt attention, I watched its ascent *up-up-up* my thigh, until it reached the hem of my dress. But instead of going farther, he pulled it away, picked up his paintbrush and resumed his painting.

Holy water in a petri dish. I fought the urge to moan out loud.

Thank God Stella was only one more step away from finishing up Times Square.

Just as Quinn pulled in front of my building, the clock on the dashboard clicked over, the neon green numbers glowing midnight. I'd been focused on the fucking time ever since he'd brought up the whole kissing thing.

And believe me, it'd felt like a snail, inching by at a sluggish pace.

It'd taken Stella a whole thirty minutes to finish up the final step for our Times Square painting, and then another thirty minutes for Quinn to catch up on all the steps he'd missed.

Although, I had to give it to him, his final product was pretty fucking adorable.

The people in his painting were us. And the billboards were all variations of Cat, Kitty Cat, and actual pictures of cats and kittens.

He'd joked about me hanging it up on my mantel, but I so totally was. The fact that it was the first thing I grabbed for when he put the car in park was proof of that.

With his hand on the small of my back, Quinn gently helped me out of his truck and up to my front porch. He nodded toward the painting—*his painting*—that I carefully set down by my door.

"Are you really keeping that?"

"Of course I am," I answered instantly, nearly offended that he even had to ask that, and he grinned.

I probably should have said something witty and cute and adorable in that moment, but my mind was far too busy going through my mental "Are you ready to have sex with Quinn?" checklist.

Sexy underwear? Check.

Legs shaved? Check.

Horny? Triple-Triple-Check.

Surely, the odds were really, really fucking likely that tonight, we'd end up inside my house, on top of my bed, and completely naked.

Normally, I would be a little hesitant over that fact, moving so quickly on the first date, but when it came to Quinn, I was ready to throw caution to the wind. And most importantly, I was ready to experience that kiss he'd asked me for.

"I had an amazing night with you, Kitty Cat." He reached out and slid his fingers into my hair, tucking a few loose locks behind my ear.

"I did too."

We should totally kiss over how amazing it was...

"No regrets?" he asked with a smirk, and I shook my head.

"No regrets."

"You should always live your life to avoid regrets, Kitty Cat," he mused. "You know, when I was twelve, my dad gave me the best advice I've ever been given. And it's prevented me from a lot of regrets."

"And what advice was that?"

"It only takes one minute of bravery. One minute of insane, embarrassingly crazy courage to change your life. Sometimes, it only takes that one minute for something great to happen."

I scrunched my nose in confusion at his sudden, serious change of pace, but he continued on.

"I've used that advice three times in my life. The first time, when I was in high school, and it was that advice that helped me play the game of my life in front of a college scout for the University of Alabama. The second time, I was in college, and it ended in a National Championship," he stated and then paused.

Wait...that's only two...

"And the third?"

"I was on a midnight train to Birmingham, and I ended up serenading the most beautiful woman I've ever seen."

He stole breath from my lungs, and I had to avert my eyes from his intense gaze for a brief moment because those words made me feel too vulnerable.

But carefully, tenderly, he slipped his index finger under my chin and lifted my eyes to his. Hesitantly, I looked up at him from underneath my lashes and the swirls of emotion I saw there urged a soft gasp from my lips.

Lust, desire, *need.* No doubt they mirrored mine.

"And do you know what right now is?" he asked, his voice quiet but his words vibrating with intensity.

"What?"

"The fourth time."

He didn't give me time to ponder it further. Between one breath and the next, Quinn wrapped his arms around my body and pulled me toward him.

Warm, oh so soft lips pressed against mine.

I was completely unprepared. You would've thought that after spending an entire evening with Quinn—watching him talk and laugh and smile—that I would've known all there was to know about his lips. But I hadn't imagined how perfect they would feel pressed up against my own.

My eyes widened, and it only took me about one second to fully realize that Quinn was kissing me, and another 0.8 of a second to understand that I was most definitely kissing him back.

Fluttering my eyes shut, I savored the feel of him. His mouth was so warm and the caress of his lips softer than I could have imagined. I opened my mouth with a low moan, and instantly, our kiss turned hungry.

Liquid warmth spread through my body as his fingers moved into my hair, gently holding me closer to him while his mouth danced with mine.

I slid my hands up his stomach, his chest, until my fingertips caressed the smooth ripples of muscle covering his shoulders.

The kiss was long and his mouth was hot and my heart was pounding. It obliterated every thought. For the first time in forever, my mind was locked into the present. The usual worries of the day evaporated like a summer shower on a hot car.

I had no other wish but for the kiss to never end.

A kiss like this should never have an ending, only a beginning, and a promise of much more to come.

I was drunk on endorphins, my only desire to touch him, to move his hands under my dress and feel him touch me. I moaned when his hands moved down my shoulders, my back, until they caressed the curves of my ass.

Instantly, my breath quickened, and my thighs grew damp with arousal.

Yes. Please. Touch me.

I wanted his fingers under my dress, beneath my panties, *inside of me*. I was ready to drag him inside my house, give him the official—*and naked*—tour of my bedroom, and spend hours upon hours worshiping his insanely muscular and fit body.

But he surprised me, knocking my equilibrium straight out of whack.

Instead of urging us further, Quinn softly ended the kiss. He pulled away, resting his forehead against mine. Our breaths mingled and danced as we both fought to slow our heartbeats and erratic pants.

"That was…perfect," he whispered.

Yes! Let's keep doing that…

"It was."

"Tonight was perfect."

"It was."

It really was. But God, I didn't want it to be over yet. I wanted more.

He pressed his lips to mine again, but before I could start getting excited over the prospect of more, he pulled away.

What is happening?

"Sweet dreams, kitten," he said, and before I could process the fact that we weren't going inside, Quinn pressed a soft kiss to my forehead and added, "I'll call you tomorrow after practice, okay?"

"Okay," I muttered and had the insane urge to shout, "*Wait! Come back and have sex with me!*" from my front porch. But I reeled in the crazy—and the horny—long enough to force myself back inside the house once I saw he'd made it safely to his truck.

That kiss. What in the fuck was that? And more than that, how in the hell had Quinn Bailey gone home after a kiss like that?

With my back resting against the door, I stared into the empty, dimly lit hallway of my apartment, confused, and if I was being honest with myself, really fucking disappointed.

I had been all kinds of ready to do a whole lot more than *just kissing* with Quinn Bailey.

Chapter Nineteen

Quinn

"Okay," I murmured to myself, my voice ringing out in the silent cab of my truck like a gunshot. "Okay," I said again, trying to slow my breathing and sort out the absolute cluster in my head.

"What the fuck is wrong with you?" I shouted suddenly, my voice box taken over by my dick. He was hard and hurting and a whole lot angry that I'd ended the night where I had. And when he had this much control of my blood, I had a really hard time forming thoughts to explain the situation to him.

I punched my steering wheel, a loud thud echoing throughout the empty space, and immediately regretted it, shaking my hand to ease the sting.

"Relax," I coached myself as I drove, trying really hard to focus on the road in addition to my one-man show. "You did the right thing. Fast fucking is short term. Groundwork is long term."

I shook my head in the dim glow of the streetlights and laughed maniacally. "I'm talking to myself out loud. I'm going crazy. It's official, I've fucking lost it."

Two hands gripped the wheel and tightened, making the leather wrap creak under the stress as I tried to sort myself out, and I looked over my shoulder to double-check the lane I was moving into.

"No, no, it's okay. You're not crazy, you're just crazy *about* someone. This is normal. Right?"

I laughed to myself.

"Well, I don't know, *Quinn*," I carried on, turning my rants into an actual conversation. "Seeing as we've never been in a serious relationship before, I don't really have a lot of experience with the feeling."

Good God. How far away do I live again?

I had the sense I wouldn't be able to stop the madness until I got home and could talk down my cock in another, more *physical* way.

"Just drive," I told myself. "Just focus on the road and the assholes on it and the radio—"

I slammed a hand against the console. "Yes, the radio! I just need music to drown out all the thoughts!"

I reached forward immediately and pushed the volume nob to turn it on. AC/DC filled the air, and some of the tightness in my chest released.

"Thunder!" I yelled, singing—*more like shouting*—along to the song and bopping my head so hard I almost got dizzy. "Thunder!"

Okay, wow. Not a good idea to headbang.

I scaled back the personal violence, but I sang even louder.

It helped a little—for about five songs—until "Sweet Caroline" started to play. Immediately, my mind changed the name to Catharine.

I coached myself to consider personal safety. "No, you idiot. Do not text and drive. Catharine will wait fifteen minutes to hear from you."

Convinced, I focused back on singing almost aggressively. "Sweeeeeeet Cath-a-rine, bum, bum, bum!"

God help me if someone snuck a surveillance camera into my truck.

The minutes ticked by, one by one, just as slow as the miles, but finally, I made it home.

The hot exhaust snapped lightly as I pulled into my circular drive and shut off the engine, all of the energy in my body draining like I'd opened up a faucet.

I hadn't realized how exhausted I was, how much I'd really taken out of myself until then. Practice, worrying about the date, having the time of my life with Cat, and then the fucking crazy drive home—I was officially spent.

The temptation to sink farther into the leather and sleep right there in my truck was real, but I knew I'd regret it in the morning.

Heaving the door open with a kick of my foot, I hauled myself out of the truck and trudged up the steps to my front door. I normally parked in the garage, but I'd just had the cement floor in there painted. All of 21 Savage's rapping about his garage had influenced me to do a little sprucing of my own.

The key slid easily into the lock, and the alarm beeped my arrival until I pulled up the app on my phone and shut it off. Jilly had obviously set it behind me when she'd left.

I reset it for the Stay setting and then backed out of the app, and the little red bubble on my messages caught my attention.

Eyebrows drawn together, I clicked my inbox to open them and went to the top of the list to see what was new.

Two new messages from Catharine sat waiting. Instantly, my energy renewed, exploding like a tossed water balloon in my chest.

Catharine: Um. What?

Catharine: Did you fall and hit your head?

What the fuck? What is she talking about?

Quickly, I scrolled up, hoping to understand. Unfortunately, it all made sense immediately. I'd sent her multiple texts, all in a row, and the content…well. Yeah.

Me: Sweat catheter Buns buns buns

Sweet Jesus. My fucking truck must have voice texted her! I didn't even know the thing had that fucking capability!

Me: Reaching ouch touching me touching you. so good so good so good

Me: Sweet Catharine!

I scrolled back to the bottom hastily and started typing.

Me: Sorry about that. Neil Diamond, you know? Apparently, my truck took over and texted you while I was doing some of my best vocal work.

Her response was immediate and made my cock jerk.

Catharine: Oh. I thought maybe you were thinking about touching me.

Okay. All right. *Sweet Jesus.* It was safe to say I was thinking about touching her now.

And to be fair, I'd most definitely been thinking about touching her then too.

Me: I AM. Good God, Cat, believe me, I am. Are you thinking about me touching you?

Catharine: It's all I can think about.

Fuckkkk. Taking them two at a time, I bounded up my stairs, ran down the hall, flicked on the light switch in my bedroom and dove headfirst into my bed. With a roll and a flop, I made it to my back, but my breath was still as thick as if I were facedown.

Me: Where am I touching you, kitten?

I looked down to my jeans to see if they were going to withstand the challenge my full-mast cock now presented. I thought better of it and undid the button, pushing them off my hips and tossing them on the side of the bed.

Pretty soon, I was going to need them to be gone anyway.

I palmed my dick over my boxer briefs and squeezed.

My phone lay still in my palm, so I moved my fingers over the keyboard again.

Me: Don't be bashful, baby. Swear to God, you're safe with me. Tell me what you're picturing.

Catharine: I want to...but...I don't know how to do this.

I'd been trying to give her the lead, just to make sure I didn't make her uncomfortable, but she'd handed me the reins. I could do that and handle her with care.

Me: Okay, Kitty Cat. Are you on your bed? What are you wearing?

Catharine: Yes... And pajamas.

I smiled and shook my head before working my fingers over the keyboard furiously as I bit into my bottom lip.

Me: Good. Take them off. In fact, take everything off. I need to see your perfect pussy.

Catharine: Oh God.

Nearly a minute passed by, and I started to wonder if she'd lost the nerve, but then, another text rang through.

Catharine: Okay, I'm naked.

Sweet fucking hell. I groaned and pinched the head of my cock through the fabric. He was a little too willing and a little too ready, but if this was going to be good for her, he needed to slow the fuck down.

Me: Are you wet for me? Aching?

Catharine: Yes.

Me: Touch yourself. Take those perfect, pink-tipped fingers and rub a sweet circle around your clit, baby. Can you feel yourself on your fingers? Slick and hot for my cock?

Catharine: God, Quinn.

Me: Yeah, kitten. I'm right here. Stick a finger inside, let your perfect pussy suck it in deep. Tell me how it feels.

Catharine: Soft. Warm.

My eyes tried to roll back in my head as I pictured it perfectly.

Me: I bet it is. I bet it tastes like the sweetest fucking honey too. Tell me. Take your finger out and suck it. Tell me if you taste good.

Catharine: Oh my God.

Me: Tell me, Cat. Tell me how good you taste. I'm dying. I want to eat you so bad it's painful.

I waited—not at all fucking patiently—as I imagined her finishing herself off. The seconds turned into a minute, and I thought I would die from the anticipation.

Catharine: I…well, finished. I can't believe how good that felt. You know, without you even here.

I totally fucking understood the sentiment.

Now, I had to catch up. I shoved my underwear off and grabbed myself, hot skin against the palm of my hand.

Hard and sweet, I stroked my cock as I pictured her hand taking the place of my own. On her knees between mine, which I held cocked high, hunched back on her heels while her breasts swayed in my line of sight.

Fuck, she's perfect.

Harder I stroked as my imaginary Cat licked her lips and moaned, thinking about swallowing my whole cock deep in her throat.

The silence in my bedroom came in broken sections, the sound of my groaning pants filling the gaps as I worked my hand over myself, paying special attention to the top.

I wondered if sweet Cat would be shy as she took me in her grip, or if she'd find a confidence she kept special for the bedroom. Would she be wild like her name or would she purr softly?

God, I had to know.

My balls ached and swelled, pulsing in my other hand as I gripped them hard and squeezed, rolling them between my fingers and giving them a hard tug.

Fuck yeah, I told imaginary Catharine, reaching forward in my mind to tweak one of her perfect brown nipples. *Put me inside that perfect pussy.*

Wet, bare, and glistening, she'd climbed up higher, straddling my thighs with her own so her juice would run all over my balls while she stroked my cock.

Goddamn, I could punch myself in the nutsac for leaving her apartment tonight.

Faster and faster, up and down I stoked, pulling at the head like the mouth of her pussy would until I couldn't take it anymore.

"Fuckkkk, Cat!" I shouted into the empty space, shooting a hot stream of come all over my hand and onto the ridges and planes of my straining abdomen.

I couldn't even bring myself to clean up before reaching for my phone with the only part of me not slick with come.

Still breathing heavily, I typed.

Me: I know. I need to see you again. Tell me when I can see you again, and make it soon.

Her reply came quickly, and I hoped that was a sign she was just as desperate as I was now that she'd had the teeniest of tastes.

Catharine: Yes. Soon, please…

Another text came a moment later.

Catharine: Call me tomorrow and I'll tell you my flight schedule? My brain is all 2 + 2 = Potato right now thanks to that delicious orgasm.

A soft chuckle left my lips. *God, she is something.*

Me: You got it. Sweet dreams, kitten.

Soon, I promised in my head. *I'll see you soon, and we'll both be naked in person.*

Chapter Twenty

Cat

As I fluttered my eyelids open and caught sight of the morning rays filtering in through the sheer white curtains of my bedroom, I felt the instant sensation that only zero sleep could provide. I had a feeling mothers with newborn babies feeding every two hours had slept better than I did. After tossing and turning for most of the night, my body was still reeling from my date with Quinn. Not only had he only kissed me at my door, but he'd left me with the kind of kiss people spent their entire lives trying to experience just once.

Literally, the unicorn of kisses.

And after that kiss, when I'd been heated with arousal and left unsatisfied, he'd engaged in a text conversation that had left me gasping, sated, and flushed with satisfaction.

His professional status wasn't just reserved for the field. Quinn knew and executed the art of dirty talk like it was his day job.

Imagine what those words sound like in person, when he's sliding inside of you...

My skin heated and ached at the thought.

But I refused to let my mind go there. It was the sole reason I'd slept like shit last night in the first place. As I'd lain awake, staring up at my ceiling, my mind had raced with the play-by-play of our conversation and the way his words had made me feel. By the time the clock had struck three a.m., I had wound myself up again to the point of frustration.

Thinking of time, I glanced at the clock on my nightstand and saw it was only half past eight.

Jesus. It was my day off. I should *not* have been awake.

With a sigh and half-assed attempt at throwing my hair up into a messy bun, I dragged myself out of bed and shuffled into the kitchen to make some coffee.

Right now, my coffeemaker was the only man that could offer any inkling of satisfaction. Mr. Coffee had been a good friend, oftentimes the only man in my life, for the past five or so years.

Once I'd filled him with enough grounds to brew six cups, I tapped his lid closed and pushed his start button, and then pushed again when he failed to respond.

The first initial trickles of hot water brewing filled my ears, and I smiled. He might've been slow and sluggish at times, and his buttons had seen better days, but I still loved him all the same.

While my coffee brewed, I plopped down onto my sofa and started scrolling through social media on my phone. Mentally, I told myself it was just because there was nothing better to do. And I also reminded myself that I should definitely *not* look at the text conversation we'd had last night.

But, apparently, my brain wasn't very good at remembering anything at eight o'clock in the morning because I somehow found myself exactly where I shouldn't be.

Our text conversation was front and center on my screen, and I couldn't stop myself from rereading his messages.

Quinn: Touch yourself. Take those perfect, pink-tipped fingers and rub a sweet circle around your clit, baby. Can you feel yourself on your fingers? Slick and hot for my cock?

Oh, sweet baby kittens in a pink basket.

His version of dirty talk was better than my own personal porno.

When the apex of my thighs started to ache and protest lack of stimulation, I closed out of my inbox and decided that if I wanted a virtual dose of Quinn, I needed to find it in less arousing ways.

One click tap to the Instagram icon, and I quickly navigated my way to Quinn's page.

I opened his most recent post—uploaded a little over an hour ago. It was a picture of him standing in the Mavericks' weight room with a big old smile on his face, dumbbells in his hands, and droplets of sweat dripping down his bare chest.

Heaven Almighty, no one should look that good sweaty.

Memories of the videos he'd sent from that very same weight room filled my head like visions of sugarplum fairies dreamily dancing for children on Christmas Eve night.

Eventually, my eyes found the strength to move away from his abs and read the caption.

@QuinnBailey: I be up in the gym, workin' on my fitness. #practiceday #weightroom #Mavericks #GoodMorningKittyCat

I blinked once, twice, and reread the last hashtag.

#GoodMorningKittyCat

I couldn't have stopped the smile that crept onto my lips and consumed my whole face if I'd tried. *Good Morning, Kitty Cat.* I probably shouldn't have been so damn smitten over it, but it was the sweet, thoughtful little things like that that put Quinn in a league all his own.

There was a Times Square painting highlighting various kittens and cats sitting on top of my mantel that proved that very truth.

I had the urge to send him a message, but quickly remembered he'd be at practice for the next few hours. He probably wouldn't even be able to respond.

I glanced toward the kitchen to see that Mr. Coffee had finally finished up, and I shuffled in there to get a much-needed dose of caffeine. And possibly, a little distraction from my brain's horny as fuck thoughts.

But while I fixed up my coffee, my brain couldn't stop thinking about Quinn.

God, I wanted to see him again. As soon as possible, to be exact.

Like a corn kernel turning into popcorn, a thought popped into my head.

What if I turn the tables on him and stop in for a quick hello visit while he's at practice?

He'd definitely shown up at my place of employment. Hell, he'd purposely flown on more than one of my flights to see me.

But was it a good idea?

Oh, geez. Stop worrying about the logistics, Cat. Be spontaneous.

Before I knew it, I'd convinced myself that stopping by the Mavericks' stadium to say hello was a good idea. And about fifteen minutes later, I was dressed, inside my car, and following the instructions of my GPS, en route to the stadium's location, and surprisingly, the *New York* Mavericks were located in New Jersey.

Once I pulled into the parking lot, I shut off the engine and hopped out of my car. It only took a few glances around the perimeter for my eyes to spot what looked like an entry gate. The giant security guards manning that entrance weren't too difficult to spot either.

Instantly, realization started to set in.

I'd just made a forty-minute trip to an NFL football stadium to say hello to Quinn, you know, like he was just some average Joe working at Target. Not a freaking professional athlete who probably required his own team of security when he went to highly publicized events, not to mention his team had their *own* team of security. Which, apparently, they utilized on a daily basis.

Basically, everyone but me had fucking security, and it was most likely impossible for me to get anywhere close to Quinn without him knowing in advance.

"Oh my God, you're an idiot." I loudly chastised myself—to myself—for going with the whole *don't worry about the logistics* mindset before I'd left my apartment to start this venture of crazy. "I mean, seriously? Who does this, Cat? Who just shows up to a football stadium on a whim?"

I kicked at a few loose pebbles of the gravel parking lot and groaned.

I wasn't sure which was worse: the frustration of wasting nearly two hours out of my day to drive back and forth to a stadium for no goddamn reason, or the mortification over the fact that I'd actually just gone through with this absurd, and let's face it, extremely impulsive plan.

"Can I help you?" a voice called over to me, and I looked up to find a man walking toward me.

Oh, great. That was just what I needed, someone to actually spot me in the fucking parking lot. I honestly didn't know what to say to his question, and I found myself blurting out something just as equally ridiculous as showing up to the stadium unannounced.

"Uh…I wanted to see Quinn Bailey…"

Way to let the impulsive and completely awkward cat out of the bag…

Why couldn't I have just said something simple like, *I got lost, so I just pulled in here until I could get my GPS straightened out?*

The man, who I quickly realized was pretty fucking good-looking once he'd closed the distance between us, tilted his head to the side in confusion. *"Quinn Bailey?"*

"Yeah…You know the guy that…uh…throws the ball…" I answered, and I even added a throwing motion with my right arm to really hit a home run of embarrassment.

An amused smirk crested the man's lips. "Do you know Quinn?"

"Uh…Yeah." I nodded and decided to just throw caution to the wind and see if maybe this man, whoever he was, could get me inside the stadium. "Quinn and I are friends…good friends… And he left this…uh…" I paused and quickly glanced into my purse for some kind of excuse for my random drop-by.

It was a fucking mess by the way.

Pens.

Lifesavers.

Random wrappers and receipts.

By the time I came across the most viable item—a half-empty bottle of Bath & Body Works hand sanitizer, I yanked it out of my bag and waved it in the air like I'd found Willy Wonka's Golden fucking Ticket. "This! He left this," I said way, way too loudly for the short distance between us. I took a breath and lowered my voice before adding, "He left this in my…uh…purse…and I wanted to give it to him."

"Hand sanitizer?" The man looked at it, reading the label, and grinned. "Citrus explosion? Hmmm, I always thought Quinn was more of a vanilla-scented kind of guy."

"Well…he really likes it. The citrus explosion, I mean…" I paused and internally grimaced at my own words.

God, I sound ridiculous…

But what the hell, right? I was already this far deep into the hand sanitizer/citrus explosion story. Why stop now?

"I think it's a good luck thing or something," I lied. "And he just…uh…lost it last night…and I have it…and I just thought I'd stop by real quick to drop it off for him."

He quirked a brow. "And what's your name?"

"Catharine Wild," I responded and held out my hand.

"It's nice to meet you, Catharine," he said and shook my hand. "I'm Wes Lancaster."

"It's nice to meet you, Wes."

I honestly had not a clue what Wes and the Mavericks' relationship was, but I was hoping he had some kind of job that gave us a security free pass.

"Give me just a sec to make a quick call?" he requested and I nodded.

Wes pulled out his phone and turned his body slightly away from mine as he tapped the screen and lifted it to his ear.

Oh God. I hope that security free pass I was just hoping for isn't actually a security pass to kick my crazy ass out of here…

"Hey, Bennett," he greeted into the receiver. "Is Bailey close by?"

I stood there awkwardly, uncertain of what I should do with myself as he continued his phone conversation.

"Let me talk to Phillips, then," he said curtly, and a moment later, he asked, "Does Bailey know a Catharine Wild?"

Wes stayed silent for a moment before adding, "No shit?"

I had no idea what had just been said, but whatever it was, it had him turning back toward me with an intrigued smirk on his lips. He ended the call shortly after that and slid it back into his pocket.

"Well…" He grinned and motioned toward the gate entry doors I'd spotted earlier. "If you follow my lead, I think I can help you find Quinn Bailey."

"Really?" My eyes widened in surprise. "Do you have friends in high places or something?" I asked, teasing, and he just smirked.

"I guess you could say it's something like that."

It didn't take us long to make our way past the giant security guards manning the front entrance, and honestly, they didn't even bat a fucking eye or ask for any kind of identification when Wes walked toward them.

All it'd taken was a simple, "She's with me" for them to not be disturbed by my presence.

We walked in the direction of the center of the stadium, and besides the occasional staff member that passed us by, the place was an empty shell. The boring concrete walls absorbed any contact sent their way and made our footsteps sound louder than normal.

People waved and greeted Wes as he walked past them, and he returned the sentiment with a simple nod or quiet hello.

Apparently, he was a pretty popular guy inside this stadium.

Maybe he's like one of the concessions managers or something?

Once he directed us down the cement tunnel that led to the field, my initial view of the pristine green turf urged a rush of butterflies into my stomach. They flitted and flipped, and if I went by feeling alone, they reproduced like fucking rabbits until they moved up into my chest and tightened my breaths.

Any minute, Quinn would realize I'd driven all the way down to the stadium to say hello.

All of a sudden, the realization of what I'd just managed to get myself into was too overwhelming. Personifying a cat with dew claws still intact, anxiety clawed at my throat.

Would this come across as too weird?

Would he be concerned I was secretly some crazy, obsessed fan or something?

Oh. My. God.

Abort! Abort! This is not a good idea!

I shuffled my feet in place, at any second, ready to turn and high-tail it out of there.

But my hourglass of time had run out once we reached the end of the giant tunnel.

"Just wait right here," Wes said. "I'll be right back."

Time to face the impulsive music, Cat.

Chapter Twenty-One

Quinn

"Hut, hut!" I called around my mouthguard, one sharp spike of my toe into the turf beneath me. Sammy hiked the ball, a perfect spinning spiral to settle right in between my waiting hands.

One step, two, I dropped back and shuffled my feet as my eyes scanned the field in front of me. Pads clashed and grunts sounded, and with a quick shove off of his coverage, Sean broke free into the open field twenty yards out.

I snapped my arm back and let it fly, and I got in a millisecond of watching the ball sail through the air before my back met the ground and a harsh burst of air left my lungs.

Fortunately, this was one of my guys doing the tackling, so he shifted off of me quickly and reached down with a helping hand to get me back to my feet.

Game situations were a little different. Tackles ten times harder, insults and shit-talking filling the air like a thick fog, and I hadn't even gotten started on the behind the scenes—away from the refs' eyes—pinches, kicks, grabs, and little maneuvers meant to cause pain. Things most people wouldn't understand until they were stuck under a pile of bodies, holding the football tight to their chest, while everyone within their reach tried their damnedest to make them drop the fucking ball.

"Sorry, Quinn," Martinez apologized. "Couldn't stop my momentum."

I smiled around my mouthpiece and gave him a sound slap to the helmet. "Don't worry, Teeny. I need a little warm-up for all the bell-ringing Pittsburgh is gonna do."

His smile turned menacing. "Not if we have anything to say about it, QB."

The whistle sounded, two sharp bleats in a row, and I turned to look for the culprit. Coach Bennett had a hand in the air and Mr. Lancaster, the owner of the Mavericks, was standing next to him—both of their eyes were on me.

I glanced back to Teeny, but Mr. Lancaster called my attention back with a shouted, "Yo, Bailey!"

Spitting out my guard and pulling my helmet from my head as I moved, I picked up the pace to a jog and headed for the side of the field. Mr. Lancaster turned and headed for the tunnel, and Coach Bennett jerked his head to indicate I should follow.

I turned my jog into a run.

Getting called over by the owner of the team during practice wasn't exactly a regular occurrence. He was a good-natured guy, and he joked around with the best of us, but he was also my boss, and I'd skimped a little on sleep last night even though I'd *physically* needed it. I hoped he couldn't tell.

I sure as hell couldn't. In fact, I felt like I was on top of the world today, and my arm had been even better than usual. Apparently, late-night text-sex with Catharine Wild was good for my game.

I wonder what the real thing will do for it.

Shaking off those thoughts and preparing to face my boss, I made it to the mouth of the tunnel in no time. Half of what I found was expected.

The other, pacing, muttering, fucking adorable half I couldn't have guessed for all the money in the world.

Mr. Lancaster's eyebrows rose as he jerked his head toward the interior of the tunnel. The air was electric with energy as my gaze locked with Catharine pacing back and forth across the concrete. A few locks of her dark hair shook across her shoulders as, unless she had magically started hearing voices, she berated herself.

My heart beat wildly in my chest, almost out of control, really. Just last night, I'd come all over myself to thoughts of being inside her, and she'd brought herself to the brink with a few hot words from me.

But now her skin was real, and the light that poured out of her didn't have to transcend cellular waves to seep into me.

God, she's something, I thought as she fell a little deeper into her personal torment. Ironically, I imagined she looked now much how I'd looked as I'd gone on a one-person trip to Crazy Town within the confines of my truck last night.

I was hesitant to stop the show, but the hard lines of my boss's face said, quite strongly, *Get the fuck on with it.*

"Cat?" I called softly, hoping to ease the roughness with which I startled her.

Her body jerked violently and whirled, before settling into a pose of casual indifference—a very forced, false, comical version of casual indifference.

"Hey, Quinn." She gave a little, arched wave.

I smiled, and Mr. Lancaster looked down to his feet.

"What are you doing here?" I asked gently. She looked like a frightened animal, all tense limbs and quivering fur, and I didn't want her to think I didn't like the fact that she was here.

I was surprised, but by all accounts, I was fucking *thrilled* to see her.

"Uh…You're… This hand sanitizer," she stuttered. "You…left it. And I wanted to make sure you had it so you could be…uh…clean."

Mr. Lancaster's eyes climbed back to mine, and they were positively dancing.

I focused my attention on him, wading through any embarrassment by knowing it would all be worth it when I finally got to put my hands on Cat. "Could you maybe give us a minute?"

He smiled without shame. "Not really. I want to know why someone showed up here in the middle of practice asking for my quarterback."

Cat's question was no more than a mutter, but in the silence of the tunnel, neither I nor Wes Lancaster had any trouble hearing it. "*His* quarterback?"

I pulled my bottom lip into my mouth, raked my teeth over it, and popped it back out before scrubbing a hand on the back of my neck and explaining. "Uh, yeah, kitten. This is Wes Lancaster. Owner of the New York Mavericks."

"Oh, son of a bitch."

Mr. Lancaster looked down to his feet once more, but I knew by the ear-to-ear smile I caught on his face before it disappeared, he thought she was just as amusing as I did.

"I'll just..." Cat paused, fighting to gain enough composure to keep going. Her embarrassment was potent—at a nearly lethal level—enough that the walls seemed to be moving in and the air felt thicker. But she didn't run as fast as her cute sparkly sandals would take her, and she didn't avoid my eyes. She was magnificent. "I'll just go. I'm so sorry I interrupted like this—"

"Cat, wait," I said, just as Mr. L chimed in at the same time. "No, no. I'm going."

Cat and I both shut our mouths as Mr. L looked between us and made up his mind. "Practice is practically over anyway. I'll let Coach Bennett know you'll be back tomorrow."

Gratitude nearly blinded me with its ferocity. "Thanks," I said sincerely, hoping he knew how much I appreciated his understanding.

He nodded and let his lips curve up into a barely there smirk. "Looked good today, Bailey. Keep it up."

"Yes, sir," I agreed. I'd maintain anything I could that pleased the owner of the team, and I'd do it double if the thing I suspected was the cause was getting sexual with Catharine Wild.

She was silent as he stalked back out of the tunnel and toward the field until he reached the end. "Um, thank you!" she yelled suddenly, like the feeling took a while to take hold but had finally overcome her.

Mr. Lancaster turned back and flicked out a wave. The sun at his back made it hard to see his face, but I had the strong sense he was smiling. Thank God his wife, the team physician, Dr. Winnie Lancaster, had a spirit similar to Cat. She was playful and fun, and showing up at a professional football stadium unannounced was exactly the kind of thing one of her nutty friends—especially Sean's crazy sister, Cassie Kelly—would have done.

Thanks to that, he had experience in letting things go.

I walked the few steps that separated us, my helmet dangling from my fingers on one hand. The other set buzzed with my adrenaline, and when the ache inside them became too much, I had to pinch them together to relieve some of the pressure.

"Cat," I whispered, heat and sex and *feeling* inside that one guttural word.

"Quinn, I'm so sorry. I can't believe—"

I started shaking my head as she spoke, but her words only got faster.

"I showed up and asked your boss to get me into the stadium to see you. I assure you I don't normally do things that are this crazy—"

Her gasp was sharp but short as I closed the rest of the distance between us with a mere step and sealed my lips over hers.

The hand sanitizer fell from her hand and hit the floor with an audible snap, and her arms wove their way around my neck. I dropped my helmet, put my hands to her hips, and pushed her back until her body hit the wall.

Arousal flooded my entire body, hardening my cock beneath the layers of football gear and sending my tongue delving deeper. She tasted perfect, just as I'd remembered, like freshness and sugar-coated candy. I breathed her in, clenched my fingertips into her hips, and groaned.

Fuck. We needed to find somewhere private, and we needed to

do it fast. If we didn't move before the rest of the team came into the tunnel, there'd be hell to pay and mockery to endure.

No doubt a good razzing by a few of my teammates would ruin the moment.

"Come on," I whispered against her lips, just barely coaxing my tongue to come out of her mouth. I skimmed the skin of her arm before interlocking our hands, and I grabbed my helmet with the other. "Come with me."

Her nod was slight, but her body made up for it in willingness as she moved her legs at a jog to keep up with me. I scoured the hallway, looking for the door I knew I'd seen hundreds of times on my way to the locker room but had never opened.

Ah, there!

Pure joy made a bid to make me jump when I saw the words *Supply Closet* in big, block letters. But for once, the blood in my dick problem inhibited a brain signal and the result was *good.*

My breath stuck in my throat as I put my hand to the handle and twisted. The knob moved with ease, clicking the lock out of place and going with the door as I opened it into the room.

I made a mental note that Santa sometimes granted really important wishes for good little boys year-round. If I ever had any free time, I'd have to pen a strongly worded thank-you letter.

I pulled Cat inside with a soft tug and shut the door behind us. Silence rang out so loudly, I truly thought it had a noise.

Seconds passed as we stood there staring. I found the means to come unstuck first. Just like before, I pushed her back with a gentle grip of her hips until her body met the support of the wall. Her eyes burned, everything she was anticipating bold and bright and right out in the open for me to witness.

My skin hummed, waiting for her touch as if her hands on it were its only destiny.

I leaned in close and nipped at her ear before skimming my nose along the smooth skin just below. She shivered, and a hint of lemon settled into my sinuses.

"Hey, Kitty Cat," I whispered, watching as her nipples pebbled beneath her thin tank top.

That was all it took to make her steal control. Her arms wound around my neck, and the rest was history.

Lips, teeth, and tongues, I gave her everything I had as I marked her as my own. Nibbles to her throat, soft tugs on her lower lip, and a *thorough* exploration of her tongue with my own, and I was just getting started.

Unfortunately, the sound of cleats and shouting in the hallway as the team filed in widened her eyes and took her focus away from where I wanted it—namely, on me.

I sighed and dropped my forehead to hers, my dick rearing like a wild stallion in my uniform pants.

Our breaths eased slowly, dialing down the volume of our panting, and I smiled. "Does you showing up here mean you're ready for another date?"

She smiled. She tried to limit it to a grin, but her happiness refused to allow it.

"Maybe."

"Tonight?" I asked, and she nodded before I finished the word.

My chest felt light enough to make me float.

I kissed her again and let our lips linger there well after the real action was done.

"I have to go," she whispered softly. I nodded.

I didn't want her to, not even a little, but my fucking teammates would be out of the showers and littering the halls in no time.

I pulled her to me again, sealed our lips, and gave her a closed-mouth kiss.

My body didn't want to extricate itself from hers, but I forced it, making a swift, clean break and opening the door slowly to check for people.

With the coast clear, I grabbed her hand and pulled her out, back down the tunnel toward the field and the hallway that led to the parking lot.

She smiled and waved as I sent her on her way.

"I'll text you about tonight," I promised with a wink. Her dimples sank in the center of her cheeks. And then she was gone.

I watched the space where she'd been, willing my body to calm down enough to go hit the showers with the rest of my team. It took some work, but I finally got myself under control after a couple of minutes.

With a smile and a small shake of my head, I turned to head back to the locker room and spotted it. Right there, against the wall of the tunnel, where I'd had her body under mine and my lips against hers, lay the bottle of hand sanitizer she'd used as an excuse to see me.

With a few steps of effort, I had in my hand. I swiped my thumb over the name.

CITRUS EXPLOSION.

Chapter Twenty-Two

Cat

My phone pinged with a text notification, and I snagged it off of my bed to find a message from Quinn.

Quinn: ETA 5 minutes.

It was the fifth text I'd received from him in the past hour, all of them similar in nature, each one noting an official countdown to his arrival.

Me: Sheesh. Are you in a hurry tonight or something?

If speed to start our date was his motivation, I couldn't fault him.

After the make-out session we'd engaged in at the stadium, when I'd made it to my home and realized I still a few hours until our date, I'd felt like time had stopped—the hours ticking by slower than molasses sliding out of a mason jar.

Quinn: Just excited to start our second date, kitten.

Ditto, buddy. But seriously, he needed to do less texting and more driving.

I preferred him to arrive safe and in one piece, thank you very much.

Me: Stop texting me while you're driving!

Quinn: I'm at a stoplight. ETA 3 minutes.

I smiled and hurried my ass into the bathroom for one last glance in the mirror. I'd chosen a more casual approach for tonight, keeping my makeup natural and my outfit—a knee-length, breezy white skirt, lavender tank, and nude flats—cute but comfortable.

Although, with the hopes of sex in mind, I did go all out for the bra and panties that lay beneath my clothes. Thanks to a trip to the mall—which not only was necessary, but served as a nice distraction from time's snaillike pace—and a hundred-dollar receipt from Macy's lingerie department, I'd found the sexiest little pink and *very* sheer silk panties and bra.

Fingers and toes crossed Quinn actually got to see my underwear tonight.

Fuck, he better see my underwear tonight. On me, off me, on my fucking floor.

With a quick flip of my hair to add some extra volume to my natural waves, I added one final coat of hair spray and headed out of the bathroom with my purse and phone in hand.

As Quinn pulled up in front of my building, I beat him to the punch and walked outside. I had my front door locked and was heading down the stairs when he managed to meet me halfway.

"You didn't even give me time to knock?" he asked, and I grinned.

"I felt like your ETA text messages were code for 'Hurry your ass, Cat.'"

Quinn chuckled and shook his head. "That's not *exactly* the point I was trying to get across."

I put a hand to my hip in response to his words. "And what point exactly were you trying to get across?"

"Well…" he said and stepped toward me, closing the distance between us. "I just wanted to make sure we didn't spend too much time inside your house or else…" He paused, and his lips brushed mine.

"Or else, what?"

Quinn's lip brush turned into a full-on kiss, soft and slow, and my mind danced with memories of the kissing we'd engaged in inside the supply closet at the stadium.

I wanted to experience *that* brand of kissing again.

Also, a whole lot *more* that was far, far dirtier.

Wrapping my arms around his neck, I attempted to take it further, pressing my hips against his, but he pulled away, a small, knowing smirk cresting his pink and slightly swollen lips.

"Or else," he started to finish his original thought, "I was afraid we wouldn't actually make it out of your house, and we'd have to change our date plans from Plan A to Plan B."

A little giggle of amusement left my lips. "Oh, so what you're saying is this ETA business was all for a noble cause?"

He winked. "Exactly, kitten."

"Well…" I paused and feigned a little frown. "I kind of disagree…"

The skin between his eyebrows creased. "You don't think I was trying to be noble?"

"No, I think you were being *too* noble," I said, and his face lit up like the morning sun—a smile wreathed in happiness, with rays of excitement shining out for good measure. "I would've enjoyed the scenario where we never left my house." The admission felt vulnerable and risqué, but I worked hard not to focus on either. Instead, I pressed a hard, smacking kiss to his lips and let his gaze hold mine. "But let's stick with Plan A and enjoy our second date together."

With Quinn's jaw slack and his eyes wide, I pointedly sashayed my ass toward his truck and hopped into the passenger seat.

That's right, buddy. It's on tonight. Tonight, I was Cat Wild, tigress. I would be bold, I would be confident, I would be irresistible. *Hear me roar!*

He opened my door, I hopped in, and he jogged around the hood to get to his side.

Furrowed brow, firm lips, and that little crinkle above his nose, his face morphed into the focused and determined expression I'd seen at the Paint 'N' Sip on our very first date as he settled behind the wheel of his truck. He had his sights set on something. I wasn't sure what, though.

I silently prayed it was sex. With me.

Me and my vagina, Lord, hear our prayer.

A loud squeal came from the tires as he pulled away from my building and took a right onto the main road, and a couple of pedestrians' heads popped up to find the source.

Boy, someone's in a bit of a rush…

"So…uh…where are we headed?" I asked, thrilled by his rushing and trying not to feel like Wonder Woman at being the cause of it.

"To Plan C," he responded and flashed a grin in my direction. He weaved the truck in and out of traffic, driving a good ten miles over the speed limit but still managing to do it safely and with ease and finesse.

"Plan C? I didn't even know we had a Plan C."

How many fucking plans were there? And which ones included the sex?

"Trust me, there's a Plan C."

"Mind clueing me in here, Quinn? What exactly is Plan C?"

Is it just me or could we play a drinking game of how many times we've said "Plan C"?

"Consider it a combination of Plan A and Plan B." That was his version of an answer.

Incredulity made me giggle like a deranged chimpanzee. For some reason, tonight, Quinn was allergic to providing any kind of useful information. "Can you at least tell me where Plan C is located?"

"It's a surprise, kitten." He shook his head as he took a left turn at a stoplight. *"But,"* he added and handed me his phone. "Feel free to play DJ while I drive us there."

"Is there a reason why we're in such a rush to get to the illustrious Plan C location?"

He winked.

He was acting so weird it was cute.

Choosing patience over nagging, I shrugged and made myself comfortable in the passenger seat while I scrolled through his phone. I smiled when I saw his various playlists related to football: Game Day, Practice, PreSeason, Play-offs, etc. It was a pretty long fucking list, but when I spotted "Bodak Yellow" by Cardi B, I clapped my hands together and tapped play.

With a flick of my wrist, I turned the volume way up.

The speakers vibrated with the bass, and I quickly realized his truck had one kick-ass sound system, Cardi's voice ringing out crisp and clear.

I sang along, and Quinn's blue eyes flashed toward me for a brief second as he grinned at me out of his periphery. Me and Cardi B weren't exactly sisters in sound and appearance, but by God, I was definitely a soul sister. *Make that lettuce, Cardi.* I loved money and I could make moves.

For the next three minutes of the song, we cruised through the streets of Hoboken, rap music bumping behind the blacked-out windows of Quinn's truck, headed in the direction of God only knew where.

It didn't come as a surprise that he sang along to the entire song too, tossing out lyrics like he'd written them himself.

And when that song ended, I chose another; this time, Selena Gomez, "Good For You."

But the singer or the song didn't matter to him. Full of emotion, and even hand gestures on display, Quinn sang the opening lines while I giggled my ass off. And, eventually, sang right along with him.

We'd only managed to get through three more songs before he pulled into a McDonald's parking lot and got in line for the drive-thru.

"What sounds good, kitten?" he asked, and I sat up a little in my seat, glancing around the parking lot.

"Huh?"

"What sounds good to eat?" he repeated, and I scrunched my brows together, still surveying the parking lot beneath the famous golden arches.

"This is Plan C?"

"It's not *all* of Plan C," he comforted, and a laugh flew from my lips.

"We're eating dinner here?"

"Yep," he answered but then closely assessed my face. "Is that okay with you?"

Was it okay with me?

They had McFlurries here. Of course, it was fucking okay with me.

"I'll take a cheeseburger, chicken nuggets, small fry, and an M&M's McFlurry," I said, giving him my order in a clear, concise tone.

Quinn's full lips stretched up into a grin, even reaching the corners of his blue eyes. "Anything to drink with that?"

"What the hell, give me a small Coke too."

If I was going to eat fast food, I was going to fucking enjoy it.

He nodded in confirmation, and once a lady's voice crackled through the speaker, he proceeded to give her my order, along with his—two double cheeseburgers, ten chicken nuggets, a large fry, and a large water.

I smiled as he finished rattling off his meal request. I guessed I wasn't the only who was hungry or ready and willing to enjoy some greasy fast food.

He pulled up to the first window, paid the teller with cash, and moved on to the second. A teenager with a name tag that read Doug handed off our bags, and I didn't miss the fact that Quinn was pointedly ducking his head away from the window as the exchange of food occurred.

With bags of food making sweaty steam in my lap and the drinks nestled in the cup holders, Quinn exited the drive-thru. "Hold on tight to the food, Kitty Cat. I've got one more stop before we're ready to eat it."

In enough time for me to sneak three French fries from the bag, he pulled the truck into a Mike's Car Wash and stopped beside the automated pay machine.

A car wash? Was he serious right now? With amusement kissing my lips, I glanced around the empty lot to try to understand what in the hell was happening.

Is this Plan C?

I looked into the side mirror, inspecting the exterior paint. If Mr. Clean stood outside the truck, it would only take one quick swipe of his beefy index finger to deduce that Quinn's truck was already clean.

Like, pristine clean.

I wonder if car washes are part of his assistant Jillian's weekly tasks?

One swift slide of his credit card and a quick shift into neutral, and the truck eased forward for a good old-fashioned cleaning.

Just as the overhead jets squirted pastel-colored soap onto the windshield, Quinn turned in his seat, rubbed his hands together excitedly, and grinned. "Let's eat."

A shocked laugh escaped my lungs.

"What?" he asked and rummaged through one of the bags for his food.

"McDonald's and a car wash?" I questioned, and my giggles turned infectious, one right after the other, I had to hold in my diaphragm to calm them down. "If you tell me this is Plan C, I might lose it."

He nodded. "Pretty genius, huh?"

His smile was so bright and warm. *I wonder if I can swim in it forever?*

Eventually, my laughter eased, and I tilted my head to the side, trying to make sense of the situation. "Mind explaining your reasoning…?"

He offered a simple shrug. "Less date time outside of your house equals more date time inside of your house, particularly while you're giving me a naked tour of your bedroom."

Oh boy.

Without a second thought, I rummaged through the second bag and handed him his chicken nuggets. His fries followed soon after.

A questioning smirk crested his lips, and I waggled my brows in response.

Be bold, Cat, I coached.

"Eat up, buddy. You're going to need your strength."

Chapter Twenty-Three

Quinn

Her front door slammed open, splintering into the wall. I moaned and took a quick breath, pushing her into the damaged Sheetrock as I apologized.

"I'll fix it."

She jumped up, wrapped her arms around my shoulders and her legs around my hips, and crashed the door back into the frame. "I don't care."

To say I had Cat worked up would be an understatement. After drive-thru chicken nuggets and the car wash, we'd headed straight back to her apartment as fast as the speed limit would allow.

Traffic was our ward, and the truck was our prison, the two of us slowly combusting from the inside out.

From the moment I'd come to a stop in the spot directly in front of her building—acquiring such had been a God-ordained miracle—we'd been at each other like animals.

I had no idea if someone saw me while we'd groped our way into the apartment, but I didn't really care.

Her pussy would be mine tonight—more than once if I could swing it.

"Oh Jesus, *fuck*," I groaned as she rubbed herself against my dick. Her motions were hurried and eager, and my chest felt like a balloon thanks to all the air I was taking in without letting it back out. "My kitten's in heat, huh?"

She smiled against my lips and grabbed my shirt by the material near the collar. Her small hands felt like anchors, sinking into the fabric with the intent to keep me in place. "Take me to the bedroom, Quinn."

Fuck yeah.

"Yes, ma'am," I agreed, careful to employ my best Southern manners. If she was going to be polite enough to invite me to fuck, the least I could do was accept the offer like a gentleman.

Her giggles rang out in rolling waves as I took off at a run to her room, hands at her ass for a little extra support—and for fun. She bounced and wiggled in my arms, but it'd take a nuclear bomb to actually pull her away. My iron grip made sure of that.

The door was pulled shut when I got to it, so I shoved it with a knee. That one snapped around and hit the wall just as hard as the first. "Dammit!" I shouted through a laugh. "I'll fix that too."

"Hurry," she advised, teasing laughter softening the rims of her eyes, "Get me on the bed before we turn my whole apartment to rubble."

As a professional athlete who followed a playbook and partook in a game with rules, I was already really good at following orders. When a woman told me to put her on the bed, I got even better.

Quick as a cat—thanks to the motivation of *my fine as hell feline*—I jogged the three steps from the door to the mattress and dropped her down with a plop. She laughed, her face alight with adoration and arousal, and her breasts—well, they did magnificent things.

Up and down and then around in a swirl, they moved until the momentum of her body slowed. Her thin purple tank top did little to inhibit the visual.

I had ideas she might have a thin bra underneath, but I swore to my dick I wouldn't make any assumptions until we had the evidence to prove it to ourselves.

She shifted to lie on top of me, and I wriggled my fingers under the hem of her tank top and skimmed all the way up her side. She took the opportunity to shove her chest farther into my own. She wanted to be touched.

God, *yes.* I had every intention of indulging her desires.

I did some of my best exploration from on top, though, so I rolled, taking her to her back and driving my fingers into her hair. Her mouth was pliant, inviting, downright heavenly as I worked it with my tongue from one corner to the other. She moaned, then writhed, and I couldn't take it anymore.

I had to have some part of me inside some part of her or I wouldn't be able to keep breathing. The physics were sketchy, but I was absolutely certain. My existence now hinged on joining our bodies, one way or another.

I moved from between her legs, falling to my hip in the bed and shifting her over so I could get a hand underneath the hem of her skirt. I wholly approved of her attention to easy access when choosing her date attire.

Cold and wet, my hip immediately felt weird, and her once-agitated but fully aroused movements paused beneath me.

"Quinn," she whispered hesitantly, a tremor of concerned laughter making the double n's shake. "Is that…did you…"

I threw my head back with a roar of hilarity before falling forward to bury my mouth in her neck. I was tremendously thankful I had a real reason to assuage her fears.

"Don't worry, kitten. The gun is still fully loaded. That mess that you feel is nothing more than a citrus explosion."

"A citrus explosion?" she questioned.

I smiled and shifted enough to pull the decimated bottle from my pocket, holding it up for her inspection.

"The hand sanitizer?" she squeaked with a laugh.

I shrugged. "I planned on carrying it around with me for a while." I turned the mangled plastic to the right and the left and then tossed it away over the bed. "I guess that's done."

Her whisper was sweet and sentimental. "I'll get you another one."

I kissed my thank you, fusing our mouths and licking at the seam. She opened to let me back in, breathing so hard, her air became mine. I knew we weren't built to run on carbon dioxide, but I couldn't give a fuck. I'd take oxygen in through my nose.

Heavy and sensitive, her breasts taunted me as I grabbed at the hem of her tank with both hands and ripped it upward to get it off. She complied cooperatively, moving her arms up and away from my shoulders to ease its removal.

Pink lace, thin and intricate and fucking sexy as all hell, covered her breasts like a foggy film. I could still see the hard points of her nipples, the brown of the skin around it beckoning to my mouth.

I didn't wait to give verbal confirmation to my dick about the bra—trust me, he already knew—I just closed my mouth around one perfect nipple and sucked. Her skin felt hot through the fabric, and I felt like I was on fucking fire everywhere else.

I'd never been this turned on in my life.

"God, Cat," I moaned, moving my mouth from one nipple to the next. "You have the most perfect tits I've ever seen."

She smiled, coy confidence making her features beckon me closer. "You haven't even see them bare yet."

I pulled her nipple between my teeth and held it gently as I looked up at her. She gasped as I let it go. "Let's change that now."

Smooth like her skin, I slid a hand around to her back and popped the clasp of her bra open on the first try.

The shoulder straps slip off easily as I pulled it forward and off and tossed it over my shoulder.

"I think," she breathed. "Maybe you've done that before."

I shook my head. My admission didn't even catch in my throat before making its way out. "It's never been like this."

Her eyes widened noticeably before I lost them, the draw of her naked breasts too strong. I had to see them, touch them, taste them. And I had to do it now.

All lips and tongue, I buried myself in them, moving my face around until I'd licked and nibbled on every square inch. Red-rashed with my attention, they looked perfect as I took them in both of my hands and squeezed.

A full fucking handful, in my giant hands—it was all I could do not to take my cock out and trap it between them.

Filled with thoughts of the fantasy, I told her. "I'm gonna fuck these tits one day, kitten. Come all over them."

She gasped.

"But not right now," I murmured. "Right now, there's only one place my dick wants to be."

She nodded, her eyes lighting as her body begged. "Please."

Shifting my focus from her top to her bottom, I slid down her body and undid the zipper of her skirt at the side of her hip. She lifted for me as I slid it off, and I didn't bother with leaving the panties. They were the same cock-hardening lace, but my cock was already hard and ready for bare pussy.

"Fuck, kitten," I whispered, running a finger through her wetness and giving myself over to sensation. Her pussy was as smooth as silk. "I have died and gone to heaven."

I shoved back off the bed, leaving her momentarily to undo the button on my jeans, grab the condom from my pocket, and push the denim and my boxer briefs off my hips.

My cock sprang free, saluting all the way up to my belly button, and she gasped.

"Oh my God." Her swollen lips formed into a perfect little O. "You're *huge,*" she muttered, more to herself than to me.

I bit my lip with a smile, trailing my eyes down her naked body like a caress. "Damn, baby. It's not even my birthday."

Her brows drew together, and I laughed. "Every man loves to hear his dick is huge, Cat. Most of them only hear it on their birthday." I winked.

Condom on and free from my pants, I pulled my shirt over my head with a hand between my shoulder blades and crawled back on top of her. She opened her legs to ease my way, and I yanked her legs up high with clenching hands in the flesh of her thighs.

"Knees high," I ordered. She nodded.

I reached between us to guide my cock to her pussy and then slowly pushed inside. Not hard and quick, but definitely not slow.

Just one smooth stroke.

She cried out on a deep and raspy moan, her nails raking over the skin of my back like sand.

I stilled there, fully inside her body, our bodies as close as they could possibly get.

A more perfect moment had never existed.

"Quinn," she whispered, so directly in my ear, I could feel the moisture of her mouth.

I framed her face with my hands and looked directly into her stunning chocolate eyes. "Yeah, baby?"

"Can you please…move?"

I smiled and pulled my hips back, slamming forward again in one, quick thrust.

She gasped, her lips parting as her eyes glazed.

"Like that?" I asked.

Her nod was minute, but her grip on my shoulders was bone-breaking.

I did it again, swift and strong, once again settling all the way to the root, my balls against the skin of her ass.

Her moan was delicate—so fucking soft—as I leaned forward and pressed my mouth to hers. I worked at it, just barely moving my lips over hers until she was chasing my tongue. I gave it to her, spearing it into her mouth and shifting my hips in and out to match.

Her moan tasted like sex, and my hips, unable to stop themselves, fell into a steady rhythm.

The bed shook, squeaking with every thrust and making a song with the sounds of our flesh slapping. It was loud and wholly erotic, hearing nothing but the melody of our connection like that.

I sat back on my haunches, eager to put my hands to use on her tits and her clit and her ass and anything else I could get within reach, but she followed, hanging on to my neck like a monkey.

I smiled, unwrapping her arms from around my neck and laying her back down. Her face pinched in worry, but I smoothed it out with my thumb, explaining, "I just wanna play with you, baby. Lie back, okay?"

She nodded as I picked up my rhythm, and a bead of sweat ran down my spine so distinctly, I could feel it.

Suddenly, I'd never been more thankful for all that fucking football conditioning.

With her knees still high, I widened her legs and watched as my cock disappeared inside her body and came back out coated in her.

"We're beautiful," I told her. "Fucking beautiful."

Her tits bounced with my momentum, so I reached up to get a feel of them. Her nipples were hard, and I gave them both a pinch and a tug.

"Quinn," she moaned, already close. Her face was flushed and her eyes were cloudy, the space with which they were open thinning by the minute.

"Oh, come on," I teased. "Not yet, kitten."

Truthfully, my release was barreling out of my balls as we spoke, but I wasn't fucking done. I wanted to play with her tits more, suck them inside my mouth while I reached around to put a finger in her ass.

I wanted to turn her on her knees and give both perfect cheeks a slap while I watched my cock disappear inside her from behind.

Oh, *fuck*.

Her pussy squeezed, gripping me like a vise as she screamed, the volume of it nearly ringing in my ears.

My release listened.

Hard and fast, it raced down my spine and out of my balls, straight through my cock and directly into her.

I pounded, my movements harsh, as we both finished, the veins in my neck standing out. I could feel them threatening to pop as I growled my release.

Dear God, I was in trouble.

I could spend the rest of my life losing myself between her legs.

Cat's finger moved slowly, sketching an imaginary picture on my chest.

I wasn't sure how I could tell it was more than a random pattern, the lines erasing as soon as she'd drawn them, but I could. Somewhere on my skin, a masterpiece lay undiscovered.

"What are you thinking about?" I asked.

Four times we'd made love throughout the night, and I easily could have done more. My dick didn't know if he had the energy, but if I hadn't been afraid of hurting her from overuse, I would have talked him into trying.

"Nothing," she lied.

I chuckled. "I don't believe you."

She sighed then, both exhausted from the sex and whatever was weighing on her mind.

"Just say it, Cat. You can tell me anything."

Her body pulled at my arm as she shifted up, leaned into my chest with her own, and looked me in the eye. "All right. I'm worried about how this is going to work. We both have insane schedules, and you've got a horde of followers." She frowned, and I reached up to smooth the line between her eyebrows.

"How'd you get this scar?"

"What?" she asked, perplexed by the change in subject.

"The one right here." I traced it with my finger. "It's superfaint, but it's there."

"Oh," she mumbled, reaching up to touch it self-consciously. "I fell off my bike when I was six. Face first."

I smiled. She frowned. "What are you smiling about? You like the idea of me falling off my bike?"

I shook my head and pressed my lips to her scar. "I just like picturing you as a kid."

She sighed again, long and deep this time, before settling her head on my chest. I played with her hair and rubbed at her back until she was almost asleep, her breathing deep and even, and then I laid it out for her.

"We're going to be fine, Kitty Cat. Hectic schedules, hordes of women, men who no doubt pursue you—none of it matters."

Her sleepy voice was a soft puff of air against my skin. "Why?"

"Because I won't let it."

"You think just because you decide something, that makes it so?" she asked.

"I know you don't follow my career, baby, but there's something you should know about me."

"What?"

"I don't follow my destiny. I choose it."

Chapter Twenty-Four

Cat

It was midday, which meant it was the worst time to arrive at any airport inside any city in the entire world. Nikki, Casey, and I exited our plane and headed toward the next gate of departure. Fluorescent lights from the ceiling guided our path with a breadcrumb trail of yellow and white hues.

I pulled my phone out of my pocket and checked the time.

1:04 p.m.

We had an hour until we'd need to board our plane and get ready for our next departure out of Birmingham.

This time, though, we weren't going to New York. Well, at least not on this leg.

All three of us were at the beginning of a five-day stretch, with four overnights scheduled at various airports throughout the South and Midwest. Atlanta, Louisville, Chicago, and Detroit. Those cities would be our home away from home for the next week.

"I'm famished," Casey said and abruptly swerved right, his black loafers tip-tapping in the direction of the food court. "I need to eat something substantial or else you girls are going to have to carry me on to the plane."

Nikki and I followed his lead, not even questioning his motives. When Casey was hungry, it was always in your best interest to go with the flow and give him the time he needed to choose his next meal.

Otherwise, he'd go Diva Smash and start demanding candy bars while simultaneously whining about anything and everything.

Trust me, it was a situation that needed avoidance.

Our terminal had the usual hustle and bustle of midafternoon on a Monday.

Airports, no matter what city or country they were located in, encompassed the same vibe—plasma screens with arrival and departure times covering the walls, people—excited, bored, and half-asleep—waiting at their gate with their suitcases and baggage resting beside them, and a cacophony of sights and sounds that provided the background music, all revolving around one thing: *going somewhere.*

A sea of faces that moved in an unseen current, flowing like water to their destinations and creating a wide river down the aisles. Small groups sometimes stopped and caused an eddy, but the others kept the current moving, flowing around the outside and continuing on their way.

Once Casey spotted the Great American Bagel shop, he became a man on a mission, swerving through the crowd and heading straight to the counter.

No doubt, his sights were set on a chicken salad bagel. He went nuts for anything chicken salad, especially if it was placed on a lightly toasted sesame bagel.

"Want anything?" he questioned over his shoulder before giving his order to the lady at the counter.

"I'm good. I packed my lunch today," Nikki answered, and Casey redirected his gaze to me.

"No thanks," I said and pointed toward the Hudson News Shop. "I'm going to run over there real quick and grab an *US Weekly* or something equally gossipy to read."

"Grab me a *Cosmo*?" he asked.

"Sure thing." I nodded. "I'll meet you guys at the gate."

Once I stepped into an empty Hudson News, my eyes quickly

located the book and magazine section—an entire wall full of every popular magazine in circulation. For a little airport store, they had a nice selection, even organizing their books and magazines into genres with staff recommendation cards.

As I reached out my hand to grab the newest issue of *Cosmopolitan* for Casey, I paused mid-movement when a set of familiar blue eyes stared back at me from the cover of a magazine. *Sports Illustrated*, to be exact.

Instantly, I redirected my hand and pulled the sports magazine down from the rack.

With both hands clutching the magazine, I stared down at the cover graced with a closeup view of Quinn's handsome face—black paint smeared below his eyes—shielded behind a football helmet.

The Quinn Bailey Connection: A Champion on and off the Field.
Get to know the best quarterback in the league,
and find out why his Mavericks are our Super Bowl pick this year.

It was surreal seeing his name and face on one of the most popular sports magazines in the country. Hell, for all I knew, it was a worldwide publication.

I flipped through the pages until I found the six-page spread with Quinn's interview, more pictures of him on and off the field, and the sports magazine's Super Bowl predictions for this year. Which, out of ten analysts, eight of them voted in favor of the New York Mavericks bringing home the championship. And every single one of them attributed that possibility to Quinn's quarterbacking abilities.

When my eyes caught sight of a photo with Quinn's back to the camera, his body clad in football pads, helmet, and Mavericks uniform, my brain fixated on the thick, veiny muscles of his forearms until it moved down to his strong hands.

I knew those hands. They'd touched every inch of my body.

Images of hot kisses and greedy touches and soft caresses filled my head, and I pretty much lost myself after that, floating inside the memories of spending an entire night wrapped up in Quinn.

Our first night *together* had been engraved inside my brain, painted on my skin, every little moment memorized to the point of obsession.

My skin hummed and vibrated with cravings for more.

More Quinn. More nights like that. Just *more.*

We'd both been busy, too busy since that night a week ago, and I'd only gotten to see him one night in the entire seven days. And trust me, after you'd had Quinn Bailey inside you, once a week wasn't enough.

"No doubt, Bailey is going to get a Super Bowl ring this year." A voice pulled me from my daydreams, and I looked up to see a young, twentysomething guy standing behind the counter of the store. He nodded toward the magazine in my hands. "Are you a Quinn Bailey fan?" he asked, and I internally smiled at his question.

Does having his dick inside me make me a fan? I thought sarcastically, but luckily, I cut off the signal from my brain to my mouth before offering up that information to a complete stranger.

Instead, I just shrugged. Sarcasm was better in secret anyway. "He's all right, I guess."

"Just all right?" the guy, whose name tag read Devon, questioned in outrage. "Homeboy broke league records last year with his laser-sharp arm. And that was *before* the postseason."

I smiled at his words, and my heart twitched inside my chest as it grew bigger with the intensity of my pride. I was honored to know Quinn. In that moment, with a magazine spotlighting his career in my hands, everything he'd accomplished settled inside me with undeniable clarity. After getting to know the man behind the football persona, I knew, without a doubt, he deserved all of the recognition he received.

"I take it you like Quinn Bailey," I responded, and Devon grinned from ear to ear, pointing toward himself proudly.

"You're looking at one of his biggest fans right here."

"Is that right?" I asked and refocused my attention on getting the things I actually needed.

"Yep," he answered. The honesty in his voice rang clear. "In my eyes, Bailey is a legend. The best quarterback that's ever lived."

I grabbed Casey's *Cosmo* off the rack and an *US Weekly* for myself, headed toward the counter, and set my magazines—*including the* Sports Illustrated—onto the glossy white surface. Just before Devon started ringing up my goods, I spotted Twizzlers on the candy rack down below and snagged a pack for Casey and added them to my items. "So, do you ever go to the Mavericks' games?" I asked as he started to scan my goodies.

"Ah, man, I wish." He sighed a disappointed breath. "Game tickets are expensive. Flights are expensive. Hotels are expensive. Hell, pretty much everything is expensive," he said with a chuckle. "Plus, I don't think my car would make it all the way to New York." He placed my magazines and candy into a plastic bag. "What about you? You ever see QB play live?"

I shook my head. "I've never been to a game. Hopefully, this year I'll go."

"You live close by?"

"I just moved to New York, actually. So, no hotel or flight necessary," I added with a grin.

"You work for an airline," he mused. "It shouldn't matter where you live, you can probably get your flights for free."

I laughed. "Yeah, I guess you got me there, huh?"

Once I swiped my credit card, I slid the bag over my arm and leaned my hip against the counter. "If you could say anything to Quinn Bailey right now, what would you tell him?"

Devon thought it over for a minute. "I guess I'd just wish him luck this year. And let him know that that seventy-three-yard throw to Phillips in the last twenty seconds against Baltimore was the single best play I've ever seen."

"Seventy-three yards?"

I was no expert in distance, but that sounded pretty damn far.

"Seventy-three yards and Phillips had triple coverage. Bailey is a fucking monster out of the pocket."

I had no idea what out of the pocket meant, but I chose to keep my mouth shut and not reveal my idiocy on football-related topics.

While Devon filled my ears with another play-by-play of *another* "seventy-yarder by Quinn" my phone pinged in my uniform pocket. Discreetly, and without disturbing Devon's man-crush gush session, I pulled it out and checked my inbox.

Quinn: I just left a shop called Bath & Body Works with a bag full of Citrus Explosion. That place is nuts, by the way. Everything smells like fruit, and the ladies working there never stop smiling. I think they might all be high from the fumes. What are you doing right now, kitten?

Citrus Explosion. I nearly burst into laughter at the memories those words brought to the surface. Not to mention, the hilarity an image of him standing inside of Bath & Body Works and shopping for hand sanitizer provided.

Me: LOL. I love that you just went to Bath & Body Works and actually purchased something. And, you'll never guess what I'm doing right now...

Quinn: Are you doing the same thing I'm doing right now?

Me: I don't know. What are you doing right now?

Quinn: Thinking about the two best nights of my life (so far) and how much I miss you.

He misses me? I swooned.

Me: Besides those two things. ;) I miss you too, by the way. <3

Quinn: Glad I'm not the only one. :) And I give up. What are you doing?

Me: I'm currently in the Birmingham airport talking to your biggest fan.

Quinn: My biggest fan?

Me: His name is Devon, and he works at the Hudson News shop in Terminal C.

A minute later, my phone started ringing, and I almost dropped it out of my hands.

"Oh my God, I'm so sorry," I apologized to Devon, who had now stopped talking about Quinn's last season stats and stared at me in confusion. I looked down at the screen to see ***Incoming FaceTime: Quinn*** flashing on my screen.

He's ridiculous. I smiled. I tapped the screen, accepting the call, and crazy curious where the conversation would lead.

"Well, hello there," I greeted.

"Hey, kitten." Quinn grinned. "You still with Devon?" he asked and I nodded. "Mind if I talk to him for a minute?"

"Uh..." I couldn't not smile at his request. "Okay," I agreed and turned the phone to Devon, who was now standing behind the counter with a still very puzzled look on his face. "This call is actually for you."

"Me?" he questioned. "You have a phone call for me?"

"Yep." I nodded toward my phone, which now displayed Quinn's gorgeous face. "Trust me," I said, "I know this is all very random, but you want to take this call."

Hesitantly, he took the phone from my hands, and his eyes flicked down to the screen. Once realization set in, his mouth dropped open, and his bottom lip practically hit the display of Skittles on his counter. *"Quinn Bailey?"* he practically shouted.

"Hey, man," Quinn responded with a hint of amusement in his voice. "How's it going?"

"It's…uh…great…how are y-you?" Devon asked while his eyes kept moving between the screen of my phone and me.

"I'm good. Just finished up practice. Cat here tells me you're a Mavericks fan."

"I'm a…" Devon paused and swallowed hard. "I'm a huge fan. Probably your biggest fan. You're my favorite quarterback of all time, dude. Seriously. You're a legend." The rambling way he delivered his words was downright adorable, and when he lifted up his Hudson News polo to reveal a Mavericks T-shirt underneath, I couldn't believe the odds of the situation. I'd literally found the world's biggest Quinn Bailey fan while in an airport shop in Birmingham, Alabama.

"See what I mean?" Devon said and pointed toward his T-shirt. "Big-time fan. I always find a way to support my team."

"That's awesome." Quinn chuckled. "And thanks, man. We appreciate the support."

"I mean, that pass you threw to Phillips in Baltimore last year, holy fucking shit. It was the best play I've ever seen," Devon said, astonishment in his voice.

"The seventy-three yarder?"

"Hell yes! Phillips had *triple* coverage. My mind was blown when I saw you guys pull off a win like that in the last twenty seconds of the game."

"Good thing Phillips's hands are sticky like glue," Quinn mused. "That bastard can catch anything."

"You guys are going to win it this year. I just know it."

"Can you do me a favor, Devon?"

"Anything," the adorable superfan responded, and I believed him. He looked so amped up that he'd probably run through the airport naked if Quinn asked him.

"Grab a pen and paper."

"Okay," Devon muttered as he hurried to find something to write with. He damn near knocked over the candy display when he snagged a pen out of a mug near the register. "Okay, I'm ready," he said once he'd set a blank piece of paper down on the counter and looked at the screen again.

"Write down this email address," Quinn instructed. "J-i-l-l-i-a-n at Quinn Bailey dot com."

Devon scribbled. "Got it."

"Now, check the Mavericks upcoming schedule and figure out the date and location that works best for you. Then send an email to that address with your full name, phone number, and game date choice. Oh, and make sure to put the words *Unicorn Tickets* in the subject line so my assistant won't miss it."

"Wait...what?" Devon questioned in surprise. "I don't understand."

"I'm making sure one of my biggest fans comes to a Mavericks game this year. Flight, hotel, and food—it's all on me, dude. All you need to do is get off work, put on your luckiest Mavericks gear, and have an awesome time."

"Holy. Fucking. Shit. I can't believe this is happening right now."

"It's happening, man. Well, as long as you follow through and send that email."

"Dude. It'll be the next thing I do today," Devon said, his voice equal parts certain and still amazed that this call was happening. "Wow. Just. Thank you. Thank you so much."

"No, *thank you*," Quinn responded. "Consider this thanks for your Mavericks support. All right, man, it was really nice meeting you. Mind handing me back to my girl now? I'd like to chat with her before she has to get on her next flight."

"You got it, man. And seriously, thanks again. This conversation made my whole freaking life."

As Devon handed me the phone, he smiled, huge and wide and thankful. "I have no idea how you just managed that. But thank you," he whispered. "Thank you so much."

"Drink a beer at the Mavericks game for me, okay?" I said and shot a wink in his direction, and he nodded enthusiastically.

I smiled at his excitement, offered a polite wave of goodbye, and as I turned toward the exit, I brought the screen back to my face. The sight of Quinn's blue eyes urged my smile to grow. "You're pretty amazing, you know that?" I asked, and he just shrugged.

"I wouldn't be anything if it weren't for fans like Devon."

"You're a good man, Quinn. Don't ever forget that," I said, sincerity in my voice. "And now I'm curious, what's with the subject line *Unicorn Tickets*?"

A soft chuckle slid past his lips. "It's a little inside joke with Jillian. The first time I did something like that, she got all pissed and said, 'What do you think happens when you offer shit like that? A fucking unicorn just magically makes it happen?'"

"So now, of course, you can't stop yourself from calling them unicorn tickets."

"Exactly."

"You're such a smartass," I said through a laugh. "It's a wonder she can deal with you on a daily basis."

He just grinned. "So when do I get to see your beautiful face again?"

"Right now." I fluttered my eyelashes and winked.

"I mean, in person and preferably *naked*," he said, and his voice grew deep with anticipation. "I need more, Kitty Cat."

More. It was my sentiments exactly.

"Well…this is the first of five days on the road so…"

"Fuck."

I nodded in confirmation. "Yeah. I know. It's a real bitch."

He paused for a moment before requesting, "Promise me something?"

"Anything."

He grinned at that. "Send me your flight info for day five and let me pick you up from the airport."

I scrunched up my nose. "But I usually just take the employee shuttle…"

"Kitten, promise me."

How could I say no to that?

"Okay. Promise."

"All right," he said, satisfaction in his voice. "I'm going to let you get back to work. Call me when you make it to your hotel in Atlanta tonight?"

"You got it, bossy pants."

He winked one blue eye at me. "You can bet that delectable little ass of yours that I'll show you just how bossy I can be in five days."

Oh, yes, please.

A soft moan escaped my lips before I could stop it. "Promise?"

Quinn groaned. "You're driving me crazy here, kitten. How's a man supposed to focus on football?"

"I'm sure you'll find a way," I teased. "Bye, Quinn."

"Bye, Kitty Cat."

The instant I disconnected the call, I realized I still hadn't thought of a clever nickname for him. I mean, how in the hell could I find a nickname for a professional quarterback whose initials were literally *QB*?

It was difficult, to say the least.

With a brain full of Quinn, I click-clacked my navy pumps toward my gate. I took a quick glance at my watch and saw I still had twenty minutes before we'd have to board our plane and get ready for the flight.

I found Casey and Nikki sitting in the polyester upholstered seats closest to the currently empty gate agent's desk.

"Girl, where were you?" Casey asked as I set my bags in an empty chair and plopped down beside him. "And what's got you smiling so big?"

"What? I'm not smiling." I definitely was. My cheeks were starting to hurt from it.

I blamed Quinn. A man shouldn't be allowed to be so damn charming.

"You're totally smiling," he retorted, and Nikki agreed.

"Like the fucking sun."

"Whatever," I retorted for lack of anything better to say. "And I was at the Hudson News store."

"Did you read an entire book while you were there?"

I rolled my eyes. "I also took a phone call."

"And who was on the other end of that phone call?" Casey asked, grinning. "Was it someone who just so happens to be a professional quarterback?"

"It might have been someone like that…"

"I knew it!" Casey cheered, and Nikki smiled.

"If you tell me he's your freaking boyfriend, I might stroke out from shock and happiness."

"He's not my boyfriend…" At least, I didn't think he was.

Wait…is he my boyfriend?

"If he's not your boyfriend, then what is he?"

"Uh…" I paused, unsure how to answer. "A guy that I'm dating, I guess?"

"That's the definition of boyfriend, honey!" Casey cackled. "Tell me this, have you guys had sex yet?"

My silence revealed everything.

"Oh my God!" Nikki exclaimed. "You totally had sex with him!" she added on whisper-yell. "Cinderella Lifetime movie marriage, here we come!"

"Girl, that man is six foot six," Casey stated with wide, shocked eyes. "You had that *monster dick* inside of you?" he asked on a whisper and proceeded to look around my body like he was inspecting it for something. "Where in the hell did it fit?"

"Oh my God. Stop it, you nutjob." I slapped his hands away when he started lifting up my arms and investigating my armpits.

Casey just laughed.

"You're crazy. And being superweird right now." And I was blushing. *Big time.*

"I'm just curious," he said through a soft laugh. "And now, I'm even more curious… How are you going to blow him?"

"What?" I asked on a shout. "What in the hell do you mean by that?"

"I mean, how are you going to *blow* him? Girl, he's gotta be huge. No way deep-throating is an option," he said, but then quickly added, "Although, I bet plenty of women have managed it when they landed Quinn motherfucking Bailey."

Nikki giggled and nodded her head. "There are a lot of women who would do much more than just deep-throating for Quinn Bailey."

Blow jobs? Deep-throating? My friends were fucking perverts.

While the two of them went off on a tangent about *Cosmo's* latest article related to something called the Grapefruit Technique, I completely zoned out because my brain wouldn't stop thinking about what it would be like to give Quinn a blow job.

Even though he'd never actually seen Quinn naked, Casey's words held merit.

Obviously, I was no expert by any means, but I'd seen Quinn naked, and, well…he was pretty fucking blessed in the nether regions. I'd gained quite the plethora of intimate knowledge of Quinn's dick during our two amazing sex-filled nights.

I'd felt it deep inside of me. I'd cradled it in my hands and stroked. I'd even run my tongue up its length. But I hadn't fully wrapped my lips around it.

Holy moly, how was I going to wrap my lips around that monster while still managing the whole sucking—and apparently, deep-throating—thing that went along with blow jobs?

It wasn't that I had never given a blow job. I had. But this felt like approaching the Mount Everest of dicks. I wasn't sure if my mouth was up to the climb.

And deep-throating? Was that an actual thing?

Did girls deep-throat every time they gave a blow job?

Did they really have the ability?

The last time I'd attempted the illustrious deep-throat, I was a freshman in college, and I'd gagged. Like, *a lot* of gagging.

And you know what happened when you gagged? Your tear ducts turned into geysers.

I'd basically looked like I'd started crying mid-BJ, and my then-boyfriend, Jimmy Wallace, hadn't stayed turned on much longer after that.

I guessed dick-themed tears weren't the most arousing thing.

Most girls could have dug into their bag of sex tricks and found the self-confidence to attempt the blow job on Quinn, but I had no bag. I had no tricks. And the more I thought about it, the more I started to freak out.

I mean, we were dating. We'd had sex. Ah-fucking-mazing sex, at that.

But, eventually, we'd exchange a *just* oral session or two. It was inevitable.

"Come on, Cat." Casey's voice pulled me from my thoughts. "It's time to board."

Without a word, I nodded and stood up from my seat. And with my bags in my hands, I followed my friends past the gate agent, down the boarding hallway, and on to the plane.

All the while, my mind was still freaking the fuck out.

Holy shit. How am I supposed to give Quinn Bailey *a blow job?*

How could I even compare to all of his previous blow jobs?

Chapter Twenty-Five

Quinn

"Come on, QB," Teeny called. "Getcha ass in gear. We're gonna be late to the field, and you know Coach don't care if your balls are sore from all that rubbin' they been gettin'."

I threw my hand towel at Teeny and chucked my bag into the bottom of my locker while the rest of the guys laughed. Good-natured teasing was part of the locker room experience, and it wasn't personal. It wasn't about disrespecting anyone or making light of personal relationships. It was about elevating the mood and keeping your mind active. Teeny had been teasing me about having my balls rubbed before Cat existed, and I knew, if I played my cards right and somehow managed to keep playing at a professional level for a while, he'd be talking about it for years to come.

"Don't be jealous," I teased back. "I'm sure you'll find a woman with small enough hands to rub your balls soon, Teen."

He flipped me off with a smile and climbed to his feet before merging into the crowd of retreating players as they made their way out of the locker room.

I scooped my phone up off of the bench, and it buzzed in my hand.

Seeing that the message was from Cat, and knowing she was still gone on a five-day stretch of flights with limited contact, I checked the area discreetly for nosy eyes and then clicked to open it.

Cat: Do you like blow jobs? Or are they kind of blah to you?

Um…what?

I smiled to myself, amused and confused all at once.

Me: Never really met a mouth around my dick I didn't like, kitten.

I waited for her response, even though I knew I didn't have time. I was just too curious to spend all practice wondering about it.

Cat: Right.

Me: I'll like anything you do, Cat. Or don't do, for that matter.

Sean peeked his head in the door of the locker room, making me realize I was the only one still there.

Shit. I was going to be Coach Bennett's fucking dog food.

Me: I gotta get to practice. I'll call you after, okay?

Cat: Yeah, yeah, Of course. No worries here. Two thumbs up.

I smiled at her awkward rambling, even via text, and threw my phone onto the top shelf of my locker before slamming it shut. Scooping my helmet off the bench, I broke into a jog and caught up to Sean just as we were about to exit the tunnel.

"I told Coach you were on your period, and you were worried about starting a fire in the locker room if you didn't get your heating pad shut down."

"Oh, good. Thanks."

"No problem. That's what friends are for, true?"

"Bailey!" Coach Bennett bellowed as soon as I cleared the darkness of the tunnel. "Over here! Now!"

Oh, *shit.*

Practice ran longer than usual, thanks to my late arrival. Apparently, Coach Bennett had a little bit of my father in him.

Sprints, suicides, push-ups, drills. You name it, we did it, and we did it until our bodies were so ready to give up, they'd have gladly merged with the ground.

I got a few glares from the guys, but nothing too callous. They'd all been late once in their life. The whole point of this exercise in pain was to teach us not to be again.

And I had learned.

Sweet merciful Jesus, had I learned.

I was moving at a snail's pace out of the tunnel and down the hall toward the locker room when Jilly found me. Her lips turned up at the ends when she realized I was in great physical pain.

I shook my head at her lack of sympathy.

"I'll warn you, Jilly. Now's not the time to push my buttons," I told her as she fell into step beside me.

"I disagree. Now looks like the perfect time to do a little poking." I raised my eyebrows, and she laughed. "I might actually be able to outrun you."

I grinned and then nodded. "Yeah…true." I had to give her that.

"Anyway," she murmured, "As much fun as it is, I'm not here to mess with you. I'm here in an official capacity because Georgia Brooks called today to say that she had to move up the recording session for player intros."

Georgia Brooks was the marketing director for the Mavericks. She got us into all sorts of stuff, some unorthodox on occasion, but player intros were a standard thing we did every year. They were the little videos on TV toward the beginning of the game that the commentators would play when introducing the starting lineup. Mine had been scheduled to film the following week.

"To when?" I asked, praying it wasn't today.

Jilly could read the opportunity to crush my dreams in my eyes. She smiled sweetly. "Today. Now, actually."

"I have to shower."

Jilly nodded. "Yeah, I can tell. You smell like a cesspool."

Such compliments. I grinned acerbically. "I don't have my team jersey here either."

"Georgia has an extra."

I shrugged then. Resigned. My player intro was obviously happening today, whether I liked it or not. Might as well roll with the punches. "Fine. Where?"

She scrolled on her phone, using a stylus to mark things off on her to-do list. "Upstairs in the main lobby."

"I'll be there in twenty minutes." Jilly accepted that, moving away without a word when I thought better of it. I'd wanted to call Catharine after my shower. If I didn't, she'd probably end up on a flight, and I wouldn't be able to talk to her.

And not talking to his kitten didn't make Quinn Bailey very happy. She'd been gone for four fucking days, and I missed her.

"Yo! Jill!" I called. She stopped walking and turned her head with an exasperated sigh. "Make it forty-five minutes."

She nodded. "No problem. I'll just tell Georgia you had to get your bikini wax in first. Gotta look good for the camera."

Teeny just happened to be walking up behind me at the time. Of course, though I was caught unaware, Jillian had known full well what she was doing.

"Whoa, QB. You waxing your balls before you let 'em get rubbed now?" He whistled. "That's really considerate of you."

I narrowed my eyes at Jilly, fully contemplating firing her again. That only lasted fifteen seconds, though—the time it took to remember all the shit she dealt with for me that I didn't want to, and how well she did it without even having to be asked.

She gave a falsely friendly finger wave before disappearing from sight. With a twist on the ball of my foot, I turned tail and headed for the locker room. I didn't have any illusions that she hadn't set a timer on her phone for forty-five minutes exactly, and if I had anything to say about it, most of those minutes would be spent on the phone with Catharine Wild.

After breaking land-speed records for a shower and shave—an important part of the process now that I knew I was going to be on camera—I grabbed my shit and headed for the field. The stadium was big, but people were plentiful. Support staff lingered everywhere, and someone was always listening.

But the stands were huge and the seating was abundant, and if I couldn't find a spot within the hundred thousand fold-down chairs where I could get a little privacy for my phone call, I wouldn't be able to find it anywhere.

Sunlight speared and spiked through the darkness at the end of the tunnel, and I pulled out my sunglasses to prepare for the glare. It was past midday now, and the sun was high enough in the sky to come up over the top of the stands. I knew from experience that if I didn't shield my eyes, one wrong look could put spots in my vision for the rest of the day.

The grounds crew was working when I walked back out and onto the turf, but the stands were blessedly empty.

I wandered for a while until I found a spot about halfway up, right on the fifty-yard line. I very rarely got the opportunity for the view. I loved football, always had, and wished I got to watch it, live and in action, more.

But that was the twist of playing—you very rarely got the opportunity. If someone else had a game for me to attend, I usually had my own to play. One day, when I retired, I'd be right back here, every game, every season, being the most obnoxious fan I could imagine.

With a quick scroll into my contacts, I put my thumb to Catharine's name and moved the ringing phone to my ear. She answered on the second ring.

"Hello?"

"Hey, kitten."

Her voice was soft and sweet and melted right into me. "Hi, Quinn."

"How's my favorite Cat doing?"

She giggled a little. "I'm good. Ready to be done with these flights—"

I cut her off with a tsk. "Uh-uh, baby. I'm not talking to you."

Her confusion made her voice sound even raspier than normal as she asked, "You're not?"

I smiled to myself and glanced around to make sure no one was within earshot. "Your pussy," I clarified. "I want to make sure you're taking care of her while you're away."

Some indistinct shuffling muffled the phone. Her voice was breathy when she came back on the line. "Quinn, I'm already on the plane. Stop turning me on."

I smiled, picturing her trying to find enough privacy to have this conversation while on something with distinct limitations in distance from other people.

"Sorry," I apologized easily before dissuading the validity of it entirely. "But I'm fucking aching to put my tongue on you. Suck your clit. Cover my face—"

"Quinn!" she snapped, and her voice echoed.

I smiled. I wasn't sorry at all.

"Where are you right now, kitten?"

"The bathroom," she admitted unhappily. I couldn't help it—I laughed.

"This isn't funny. You think you can just call and get me all worked up before I have to go out there and serve people drinks! I—"

"Cat," I interrupted quickly, saying her name again when she struggled to hear me over her own talking. "Cat!"

"What?" she snapped.

"I miss you. Have a safe flight. FaceTime me tonight from your room, and I'll make all the teasing up to you. I promise."

Her voice was so soft it was practically a whisper. "Okay," she agreed.

"Bye, baby."

"Quinn!" she called, panicked that I'd hung up. I smiled into the phone and shook my head. There was no fucking way I'd have removed that phone from my ear until I knew for a fact that she was gone.

"Yeah?" I asked, waiting as she paused before saying it.

"I miss you too."

A warm glow joined the longing ache in my chest, and then the line clicked dead.

I pulled my phone away from my ear, and a text message came in from Jilly right then.

Two words shone like a taunt.

Time's up.

Chapter Twenty-Six

Cat

Tonight had been the light at the end of a grueling work schedule tunnel.

Quinn had picked me up from the airport, and after I'd kissed the daylights out of him in his truck, he'd driven me home. He'd dropped me off at my apartment, and while I'd showered the stench of airplane off my skin, he'd run out and grabbed us takeout.

Just a simple, quiet night in with Quinn—it was fucking heaven.

Although, the cheesecake he'd picked up from Carlo's Bakery tasted a lot like heaven too.

I took the very last bite of the decadent dessert and moaned.

"God, it's so good," I announced and felt melancholy over the fact that I didn't have any bites left. Hopeful, I glanced toward Quinn's plate, but to my dessert-addict dismay, we'd both finished off our cheesecake slices at the same time.

He chuckled beside me. "Were you just eyeing my plate to see if I had any cheesecake left, you little vulture?"

"I have no idea what you're talking about," I retorted, but the giggles that snuck past my lips revealed my truth.

Quinn grinned and took my plate out of my hands, setting it down on the coffee table beside his. Next thing I knew, he was in motion, lifting me up, and I squealed in response. But he ignored my dramatics and pulled me into his lap, adjusting my body so my legs straddled his thighs and our faces were left mere inches apart.

He gazed at me, and I felt like I could swim inside the pools of blue that made up his mesmerizing eyes. "I missed you," he said and rubbed his nose against mine. "Five days was too long."

"I missed you too," I whispered against his mouth and placed a long, soft kiss to his lips. "You want to know something crazy?"

"Of course."

"I found out this week that work is a lot more fun when you're stalking my flights."

Quinn smiled, and his eyes lit up my living room. "I found out this week that life is a lot more exciting when I'm stalking your flights."

It was my turn to smile.

We stayed like that for a long, quiet moment, me in Quinn's lap, his arms wrapped tightly around my waist, and our gazes locked. The silence was comfortable, a peaceful space of sweet and tender. And I savored the warmth of his companionship. There was something special about being able to enjoy someone's presence without the need for conversation. It was a rare kind of thing, one that was generally reserved for only your nearest and dearest.

As the silence stretched thinner and thinner, like a balloon blown big, the temptation to rupture it grew too great to resist.

"What are you thinking about right now?" I asked.

"How insanely pretty you are."

I had to give the man credit where credit was due—he was smoother than silk.

And to sweeten the answer, he flashed that smile that had me tied up tighter than a banker's money. But unlike a vault, it wasn't claustrophobic at all. His smile, his presence, only provided a sense of comfort and safety.

The more time I spent with him, the more time I wanted to spend with him.

I wanted to ask him a thousand questions. I wanted to witness all of his smiles and hear all of his laughs. And more than that, I wanted to be the person on the receiving end of those reactions.

"Can I ask you a question?"

He tapped my nose with his index finger. "You know you can ask me anything, kitten."

"Why do you like me?" I asked, and he furrowed his brow. "Wait…before you answer…I want you to know I'm just asking that question out of curiosity, not insecurity," I added, and honestly, I wasn't sure if that was one hundred percent the truth. My uncertainty over my own truth stirred an awkwardness in my belly, and I found myself tracing the freckles of his arms, connecting them with invisible lines, in order to distract myself from my own thoughts.

"How could I *not* like you?" he retorted and lifted his arms off of my waist to cup my face, lifting my eyes to meet his again. "You're beautiful. Intelligent. Funny. And so fucking cute that it takes my breath away. If anything, I should be the one asking you that question. Why is a gorgeous girl like you giving a guy like me the time of day?"

I snorted. "A guy like you?"

"Yeah." He nodded. "A sometimes stubborn, sometimes stalker—" he grinned "—not the world's greatest singer, goofy guy like me."

"I'd love to know how you consider yourself stubborn."

"I got you to go on that first date with me, didn't I?"

"I figured that fell into the stalkerish category," I teased.

"Okay, okay." He chuckled. "You got me there. I guess it's a little bit of both. But it was my stubbornness that led to the semi-stalking."

"I liked the stalking," I said through a giggle. "That probably makes me sound crazy."

"Well, I liked doing the stalking, so I think that makes my crazy crazier than your crazy."

I laughed. "You're crazy."

"Apparently, when it comes to you, I am." He pressed a soft kiss to my lips. "Completely crazy for you," he whispered against my cheek as he peppered my skin with kisses, moving his lips across my jaw, down my neck, until his fingers slid my T-shirt out of the way so he could place kisses across my collarbone.

A soft moan fell from my lips when he reached my chest, hovering between my breasts. The warmth of his breath against my skin urged goose bumps to burst up my arms. My nipples pebbled and hardened beneath my clothes when his fingers slipped under the hem of my shirt and lifted it over my head, revealing the sheer white material of my bra.

"God, you're beautiful," he whispered.

Deftly, he unhooked my bra, sliding it down my arms and off my body. He leaned forward and sucked my right nipple into his mouth, swirling his tongue around and around until my skin flushed with arousal.

"I need you, kitten," he said against my skin. "Let me taste you. *All* of you."

"Yes," I moaned.

We were in motion after that, Quinn standing up, and with my legs still wrapped around his waist, he carried me into the hallway. His long and quick strides ate up the hardwood floor until he reached the threshold of my bedroom.

Between one pounding heartbeat and the next, Quinn had me on my back, my body sinking into the mattress of my bed.

He kneeled above me, his fingers unzipping my jean shorts and his hands sliding both denim and silk panties down my legs. He haphazardly tossed them onto the floor and gripped my thighs with strong hands, spreading me wide and baring me to his heated gaze.

In one fluid motion, he took off his shirt and added it to the clothes pile on my floor. My gaze moved down his body, taking in his broad shoulders, his toned chest, the way his abdominal muscles rippled and flexed with each subtle movement, until they locked on to his visible arousal, heavy and hard beneath his jeans.

While Quinn moved up my body, pressing openmouthed kisses against my thighs, my mind started wandering, thinking, *obsessing*, over the idea of giving him a blow job.

Was this about to be an oral exchange?

And if so, could I even give him a blow job that would be worthy of a climax?

Do I have to do that whole deep-throat thing?

My brain was fucking me over, making me focus on the absolute wrong things at the worst time. I should've been enjoying the fact that his lips were now moving up my inner thighs. I should've been losing my mind when he slipped his tongue out of his mouth to take a long, soft lick over my clit.

When he sucked me into his mouth and spurred tingles up my spine, I should have gotten lost in the pleasure he was providing. I felt his moan against my skin, and I gripped my breasts with both hands and arched my back.

It all felt so good. His lips, his tongue, his hands running up and down my aching skin felt *so fucking good*. Instead of focusing on that, my manic mind jumped to a subject that catapulted my anxiety.

Can I make him feel this good?

My incessant and stupidly insecure thoughts might as well have been a bucket of ice water, drowning my pleasure and forcing me out of the moment.

It was official. My brain and my vagina were at fucking war.

One wanted to overanalyze blow jobs, while the other just wanted a fucking orgasm.

Frustrated with myself, *my stupid brain*, I abruptly sat up and maneuvered my body away from Quinn's oh so perfect mouth.

He looked up at me in shock, his mouth parted and his brow furrowed.

Oh God, now I've really screwed this up. Hurry up. Do something.

Quick as a rocket, I switched positions, forcing Quinn to lie back on the bed while I kneeled between his thighs, unbuttoning his jeans.

"W-what are you doing?" he asked, words stuttered, eyes still shocked.

"I need to taste you," I whispered and didn't give him any time to decide, sliding my hand inside of his boxer briefs and pushing them down his thighs. His cock was bared, still hard, still ready, standing tall and proud and directly in front of my face.

I licked my lips. He looked delicious.

Can I do this? Can I make him come with my mouth?

Still, my mind was at war with itself, my damn blow-job insecurities wreaking havoc on my confidence.

You can do this, Cat. Just suck him like your own personal lollipop.

Yes. I *could* do this. And I did. I wrapped my lips around the thick and rounded head, swirling my tongue around to taste velvety silk.

"Uh…Okay…" Quinn moaned. "I g-guess we can do this now…"

Okay. Good sign. Keep going.

I moved my lips down his shaft, sucking and softly flicking the tip of my tongue as I went. Again, I was rewarded with more Quinn-toned moans.

And I loved it. His moans. His cock. The way he filled my mouth.

Okay, we can do this, my brain and vagina agreed. I could suck him deep *and* enjoy it at the same time. I was already halfway there.

Wait…halfway? I don't have his entire dick in my mouth yet?

With a quick inventory of my current mouth-to-penis location, I realized I was, in fact, only *half*way. But good God, my mouth was full, and the tip was already saying hello to my throat. If this were a hot dog eating contest, I would've stopped taking in wieners about an inch and a half ago.

But, fuck, I didn't want to disappoint. I wanted more of his moans. I wanted to blow his mind. Literally.

Deep breaths, Cat. In through your nose, out through your…well… nose because your mouth currently has a dick in it. But you got this. Just close your eyes and take it all the way, baby.

Throwing caution to the wind, and with Quinn's pleasure my top priority, I attempted to take all of him, moving my mouth all the way down,

Down,

Down.

Good Lord, it was a long way, but I was doing it. I was owning this blow job. Completely rocking out with Quinn's cock out.

But before I could start doing a victory dance with my tongue, my throat abruptly decided things weren't working out.

Oh, no…

My gag reflex kicked in, and then, worse than just gagging, my throat outright spasmed against the foreign object—*aka Quinn's dick*—blocking its entrance.

Asthma flared. My chest tightened, and my eyes felt like someone had just poured a gallon of water directly into them. With tears streaming down my cheeks, I tried to stay strong, keep sucking, and reeducate my lungs on how to breathe. But they had gone on strike, tightening and wheezing in response.

Oh, fuck. This isn't good…

This was like freshman year and Jimmy Wallace all over again.

But worse. Way, way worse.

Chapter Twenty-Seven

Quinn

Deep and wide, her mouth opened farther to take more of my cock inside. I was lost to the sensation, so fucking into it that I had to close my eyes and drop my head back onto the top of her headboard.

She was warm and wet, and with every passing second, her nails dug harder and harder into the flesh of my thighs.

Sweet merciful Jesus.

And then, her grip got painful.

One second it was hot and lusty, and the next I was considering if I'd need a blood transfusion once she got done draining me.

"Cat," I choked, trying to ease into telling her to let up on the grip a little, but the feel of a tiny drip of moisture hitting my balls pulled at my awareness. *Am I actually bleeding?*

Blinking rapidly and fighting for some visual focus, I reached forward to pull the curtain of hair away from her face so I could look into her eyes.

Every muscle in my body pulled tight as it hit me that she was crying.

"Jesus, Cat," I called, pulling her off me and trying to lift her to my chest.

She fought me, though, choking violently as my dick popped

free and air filled her lungs.

I chased after her as she crawled on all fours to the other side of the bed.

This is horrifying.

What the fuck had I done?

She's crying!

She pushed me away but held up a finger as she scrambled to the nightstand, yanked open the drawer, and came back with an inhaler in hand. With practiced ease, she put it to her mouth and pumped to inhale while I watched. Life bleeding back into her face, she pushed to inhale again and took another hit of the fast-acting medicine. I didn't know what I could do to make it better.

Finally, her breathing came more evenly and her coloring returned, so I took a chance by pulling her into my naked lap.

She didn't fight me this time, cuddling into me as I rubbed at her back.

The skin was smooth, but the more I rubbed, the more pebbled it became. Goose bumps ran rampant, and the longer we sat in silence, the longer I feared she was too cold.

I grabbed the comforter from the side of the bed, where we'd thoroughly balled it up through activity, and wrapped it around us like a cocoon.

"Are you okay?" I asked, rubbing at her through the blanket and using the other hand at her jaw to lift her face to my own.

Embarrassment overwhelmed her, changing the shape of her face from its normal happy heart to a sad little triangle.

"Why do you look like you just killed my puppy, kitten?"

She shrugged, but I wasn't having it.

I pushed. "Cat, come on."

The twist of her head was violent, mortification turning to anger at my persistence. "Are you kidding? How can you not know what's wrong? How can you not know how fucking horrified I am that I just…that I couldn't even… Oh my God! I tried to give a simple blow job, and I fucking choked, Quinn! How am I ever going to get over this? How are you? It can't make you feel good things that I can't seem to fit you in my mouth."

I laughed, even though I knew it was dangerous.

If I hadn't had the blanket so tight around us, I think she might have slapped me.

"Baby, my dick is so big you literally choked on it. I'm trying really hard to see the horrible, upsetting part of this, but it's just not happening."

"Quinn!"

"My dick is literally too big for your mouth, kitten. I feel like I can die now. Like I'll be remembered for millennia. Like my purpose has been forever fulfilled."

She slapped at me, pushing me in the chest so hard that I fell to my back with a laugh.

"This isn't funny! This is… I can't even—"

I cut her off. "Interestingly enough, I know something that *is* big enough for my dick."

"I can't believe you're joking right now," she grumbled. I eased the line between her eyebrows with a kiss to her lips.

"Best time to joke is when you feel like crying, Kitty Cat. That's a fact. I can't stand to see that sad fucking look on your face, and I'll do exactly what I have to do to change it."

Finally, her affliction turned to affection. "Quinn."

"How about that pussy?" I asked, and she roared, my blunt delivery taking her all the way to amused. "Can I get some? Is it open for business? It's been a few days."

She shook her head with a smile. "You're terrible."

"I'm fucking aching," I corrected.

Her smile turned coy.

I was seconds away from getting some, I could feel it, when my phone started ringing on the nightstand.

I was gladly prepared to ignore it, but Cat was too curious not to look. I guess it went with the name.

"It says Denver," she remarked, picking it up, and in the process, her finger accidentally tapping the green icon button. "Oh, shit," she muttered and quickly handed it to me with a cringe sweeping across her face. "I didn't mean to do that," she whispered, and I just smiled in response as I put the phone to my ear.

Happiness suffused me. I knew without a doubt he was the only caller in the universe that didn't make me feel murderous thanks to his poor timing.

"Hey, brother. To what do I owe this honor?"

Cat's eyes widened at the mention of my brother, her fingers raking frantically through her hair, so I clicked the button to put it on speaker. Her cheeks were pinker than normal, and I had a feeling I knew why. Leave it to a woman to get nervous about being presentable for a meeting with a family member *over the phone.*

"Oh, not much. Just that Skeletor and her burly friend decided to pay a visit this weekend for our Crimson versus White game, and you'll never guess who they brought with them," he announced, voice rising with each word. But before I could even attempt to guess who our parents—*yeah, Skeletor and her burly friend was their given nickname of the moment*—Denver answered for me on a shout. "Gerdie freakin' Hawthorne!"

The Crimson versus White game was an Alabama preseason tradition where we played ourselves, usually a mix of second and first string on both sides, and the fans came to watch for fun. Families often came up, intermingling in the stands with students and other diehards.

"Jesus," I whispered. "I'm sorry, Den. Why would they do that?"

"Why wouldn't they do that?" he yelled hysterically. "This is the exact kind of thing they do!"

Cat bit her lip and gestured to the phone, obviously uncomfortable that I was allowing her to listen without his knowledge.

"He won't care," I told her immediately, just to ease her mind.

"Who won't care about what?" Denver asked. "Who are you talking to?"

I laughed. "Den, meet Cat. Cat, meet Denver."

"Cat?" he asked. "Are you in bed right now?"

I looked around at the covers and down at our naked bodies. *Busted.*

Cat blushed as I answered, "Maybe."

"Oh my God! Tell me you interrupted the bang-bang to answer my call?"

"The bang-bang?" I coughed through a laugh.

Denver's yell made me laugh. "You know what I mean! I was trying to be polite to the mixed company on the phone by not saying fucking."

"But it's polite to ask us if we're in the middle of it?"

Cat rolled her eyes as we went back and forth, learning pretty quickly that if she wanted to get a word in, she'd have to force it. "Hi, Denver. Nice to meet you telephonically."

"Oh, shit, Quinndolyn!" he hooted. "Telephonically. You found yourself a smart one."

I shook my head and changed the subject. "Her friend Casey is the one I wanted to set you up with."

"The random gay man Quinn bonded with so easily belongs to you?" Denver asked Cat immediately.

"Guilty." She smiled. "But, I should add here, when it comes to Casey, Quinn isn't an exception. He pretty much bonds with everyone. He's a charismatic kind of guy."

Denver sighed and then sat silent, likely considering it. "Fine. Set it up."

I pulled Cat to me and smashed our lips together, catching her by surprise. She had no idea how many times I'd tried to set my brother up with someone and been shot down. She'd officially turned the tide.

"Sweet Jesus, a miracle has just occurred," I teased.

Denver's grumble was comical. "Yeah, yeah. Live it up. I gotta go anyway. You can continue celebrating when I get off the phone. I just called to complain."

My face softened at his words. "You know you can call anytime, Den. I'll always listen."

"I know. Go fuck your girlfriend, you big softy."

Cat's laugh was the last thing he must have heard before the line went dead.

Her eyes were alight with warmth. "I love your brother," she said as I set my phone back on the nightstand, turned out the lamp, and scooted us down in the bed.

"I know," he replied. "If he weren't gay, I have no doubt he'd be stealing all my women."

"All your women?" she asked carefully with a raise of her brow.

I kissed it smooth. "Well, just the one now."

And I meant that. Ever since I'd met her, I had zero interest in other women.

Silent and reflective, we both lay in the dark for long moments before a random thought made me laugh.

"What?" she asked, her invisible picture on my chest almost complete.

"Nothing." I smiled into the darkness and gently moved my body over top of hers. She was warm and soft, and my cock started to ache once it glided across the apex of her thighs. "That blow job text message just makes a whole lot more sense now."

I'd never seen a woman glare and moan at the same time as I slid inside her. It was mesmerizing.

Just like Cat, she did everything better than anyone else.

And the instant I filled her to the hilt, I knew, without a doubt, she felt better than anyone else too.

Chapter Twenty-Eight

Cat

"Good morning, kitten," a warm voice whispered into my ear, and I fluttered my eyes open to find Quinn sitting on the edge of my bed, wearing only black boxer briefs and a smile.

"Mornin'," I squeaked out past the sleepy cobwebs in my throat. I rubbed at my eyes and sat up, resting my back against the headboard. "What time is it?"

"Breakfast time."

"Huh?" I quirked a brow. "Like, actual food?" Unless he managed to bring the breakfast in, the odds of finding anything remotely resembling breakfast foods were slim to none in my kitchen. It wasn't for lack of eating, though. I blamed it on the five-day work stretch I'd just gotten done with the day before.

"I snuck out for a little bit and grabbed us some rations from that mom-and-pop shop up the street," he updated. "Which, by the way, you're running low on food, Kitty Cat."

"Trust me, I know. The grocery store is on my to-do list for today," I said and internally groaned at the thought.

Why was the mere idea of going to the grocery worse than getting a tooth pulled?

Consider it an affliction, but I'd hated grocery stores and grocery shopping all of my life. Unless it was Target. Then, I could make an exception. Although, my bank account always felt the aftereffects.

"Good plan." He grinned and rubbed his hand up the bared skin of my thigh that peeked out beneath the sheets. "Now, are you ready to eat something?"

"Yep." I nodded. "I just need to throw on some—"

Before I could finish, Quinn slid his arms under my body and lifted my naked ass straight out of bed. "No need for clothes," he said with a wink as he carried me out of the bedroom and toward the kitchen.

"Quinn!"

He completely ignored my squeals of protest, moving us into the hallway, past the living room, and into the kitchen. He sat my bare ass on the counter covering the small island in the center, and I squealed.

"Oh my God! That's cold!"

"Here," he said and slid a kitchen towel toward me. "Lift that cute ass up, you little complainer."

"Oh, hell no," I retorted and hopped off the counter. "I refuse to cover my kitchen towels with my ass. Pretty sure that's unsanitary."

Quinn just laughed, and with his arm wrapped around my waist, he pulled me back toward him like a fish on a line. "Fine. Fine," he said through a chuckle. "I've got an even better solution. Close your eyes."

"I'm not sure I trust you…"

"Close your eyes, kitten," he demanded, and this time, I listened. "Stay right here, okay?"

"Okay."

"I mean it," he added. "Don't move an inch. Or try to peek."

"I said *okay*," I answered, and my lips creased at the corners in a half-annoyed, mostly amused smile. "My eyes will stay closed until you say so."

The sounds of his bare feet trodding across the hardwood floor filled my ears until they disappeared completely. And moments later, he was back, his footsteps moving toward me. "Hold up your arms, kitten," he instructed once his voice got closer, and I assumed he'd closed the distance between us.

With eyes still closed, I listened and held both arms up in the air. Carefully, Quinn placed something soft and cottony over my arms and head, until the material slipped down the rest of my body and landed just below the cheeks of my ass.

"Oh, yeah," he stated. "That's perfect."

"Can I open my eyes now?" I asked and put my arms down.

"Yep."

Fluttering my eyes open, I found Quinn standing there, smirking at me like the devil. He waggled his eyebrows. "My kitten is so fucking sexy. Especially in my number."

I glanced down at my new shirt to find the word *Mavericks* scrolled across my chest.

"And if you could see the back, you'd find out that you're wearing my number on your back."

"And what number is that?"

"What the fuck, kitten? You don't know my number?"

"Uh…" I paused and bit my lip with a little shrug to my shoulder. "I'm not big on sports, remember?"

"I can't believe my girlfriend doesn't know my number," he said with a frown, but I didn't miss the teasing tone highlighting his voice. "I'm number nine, by the way."

"Wait…" I said once his words sank in. "Did you just say girlfriend?"

"I did," he responded, tone precise, eyes certain.

"So…I'm your girlfriend?"

"Well, I hope you're my girlfriend, kitten. Otherwise, I just lied to about three million people on Instagram this morning."

"You…*what?*" I questioned. "What do you mean you lied to three million people on Instagram this morning?"

He moved toward me and wrapped his arms around my waist, lifting me off my feet. "I posted about you this morning. My adorable, sexy, beautiful girlfriend."

"You posted about me?"

"Uh-huh."

I prayed to God he didn't post something that included my current state of bed head.

"Tell me it wasn't like an up-close shot of me asleep and drooling..."

"Nah." He grinned and wrapped my legs around his waist. "It wasn't anything like that," he said and squeezed my ass beneath his T-shirt.

"Then what was it?" I asked and tapped his nose with mine.

"You know what I think is even more important than whatever I posted on Instagram?"

"What?"

"That whole thing about you being my girlfriend," he whispered into my ear. "Are you my girlfriend, kitten?" He leaned back and looked into my eyes. "I'm really hoping you say yes to that question."

"I guess that depends."

"On what?"

"Are you my boyfriend?"

"*Hell yes.*" He leaned forward to press soft as silk kisses to my lips, my cheeks, and my nose. My skin tingled where his lips touched, and my heart beat erratically in my chest, so hard that I thought it might fly straight out of my body.

Without hesitation or doubts, when Quinn's eyes met mine again, I whispered, "Then, *hell yes,* I'm your girlfriend."

His grin grew wide and all-consuming, raising his cheeks and lighting up his eyes. He spun us around the kitchen a few times until he stopped, set my ass on the island again and kissed the hell out of me.

Boy, oh boy, I liked him.

It's way, way more than like...

"So we're giving this, *us*, a shot?" I asked, and he nodded.

"I'm all in, baby," he said, no hesitation or doubt revealed in his words or expression.

"I'm all in too."

"I just want you. *Only* you."

His words hit me straight in the heart, and I couldn't stop myself from saying exactly what was on my mind in that moment. *Approximately.*

"I-I think I l-ick you."

Holy God. I'd almost just told him I loved him. Panic made my heart race and my cheeks turn red. *Christ, Cat. Nice save…I think I lick you. Fuck.*

Eyebrows drawn, Quinn pulled his lips up into the most adorable smile. It was too bad I was too busy dying of embarrassment to get a chance to fully enjoy it.

Quinn pressed another kiss to my lips and then whispered against them, "I think I lick you too, kitten. I think I lick you a lot, and I think I need to do it more."

If it was possible for my cheeks to get even redder in a matter of a second and a half, they'd done it.

I had a boyfriend and his name was Quinn Bailey, and I was no doubt head over heels for him. He probably knew, by the bumbling fuckup of a line I'd put in its place at the last minute, but at least he'd had the decency to go with it.

Sigh.

"But first, beautiful girlfriend of mine," he said, and his smile was infectious. "How about some breakfast?"

"Sounds perfect."

"Go get cozy in the living room, and I'll bring everything in."

"Oh boy," I said with a grin and hopped off the counter. "This whole boyfriend thing is already off to the best start ever."

He playfully spanked my ass as I walked past him, and I giggled all the way to the living room. Once I plopped my ass down onto the couch and grabbed my phone off the coffee table, I realized I had several missed calls and social media notifications.

The first one was from Instagram.

I clicked open the app to find a notification that Quinn Bailey had posted a new photo. It was a photo, *of my freaking bare feet peeking out from the covers of my bed*, with a caption that read: ***My girlfriend has the cutest little feet I've ever seen. #mykitten #tinypaws***

What an adorable...*weirdo*. I had no idea when that picture had been taken, but I imagined it'd occurred while I was sleeping. Honestly, I wasn't sure if I wanted to smack him or kiss his face off for showing the world my pink painted toes.

Before I could playfully give him hell, my phone started vibrating with an incoming call.

Incoming Call: Mom

Immediately, I tapped the green phone icon. "Hi, Mom."

"Hi, sweetheart." Her warm and smooth-as-honey voice made me smile. "Your father's on too."

"Hey, Dad."

"Hey there, Caterpillar."

"So," my mom chimed in, skipping any other pleasantries and getting straight to the point. "Is there anything you want to tell us?"

I scrunched my nose up in confusion. "Tell you?"

"Yeah," my dad answered. "Anything new going on in your life...?"

"Uh...?" I honestly had no idea what they were talking about.

"Just tell her, Martin," my mom said eventually.

"Caterpillar, do you mind explaining why your mother and I just saw your pretty face on the cover of a magazine in the checkout line at the grocery store this morning?"

"I'm sorry...*what?*" I damn near choked on my own saliva.

What in the hell were my parents talking about?

"I'm feeling a little left out of the loop here. I mean, when were you going to tell us you're dating that football star, Quinn Bailey?" my mom asked, and my jaw dropped open like I was going to start catching flies with my mouth. "Well...at least, that's what the tabloid magazine says..." She trailed off, and my dad didn't hesitate to pick up the conversation where she left off.

"Caterpillar, is it true?" he questioned. "You can be honest with us. We won't be mad."

My mom's sigh filled my ears, and my chest tightened from the discomfort. My parents had been through all of my stupidest moments with me. I didn't want them to think this was another one. "We just want to know what's going on with you, sweetheart."

"What tabloid magazine was it?" I asked.

"Uh..." my dad muttered, and the sounds of rustling filled the receiver. "It's called *U-S Weekly*."

My stomach dropped. My parents had found out I was dating Quinn through a freaking magazine in the grocery store.

I'd always loved that my relationship with my parents was close. I didn't hide things from them. And this, well, it made it seem like I had been.

I didn't like it one bit. And my brain hadn't had the chance to actually process the fact that I was in a gossip magazine. That felt too surreal to comprehend at the moment.

"Oh, wow..." I said more out of shock than anything else. "Well...the, uh...the tabloid is right. And I swear to God, I wasn't trying to hide anything from you. I wanted to tell you about Quinn in person when I came to Cincinnati for my quarterly training."

"So, it's true?" my mother questioned, surprise filling her voice. "That is...quite a turn of events, Catharine..."

Tell me about it, Mom. I was getting used to my life as a spinster too.

"I know, I know. I'm sorry you guys found out about it this way, but I promise my lack of telling you wasn't out of secrecy or choice, though. It's a new relationship."

The line grew quiet until, finally, my dad broke the silence.

"Is he treating you right, Caterpillar?"

Quinn walked into the room and set our breakfast and fresh coffee onto the table in front of my sectional. He sat down beside me, handed me my mug, gently patted my thigh, and otherwise, left me to my call while he started eating his breakfast.

"Yes, Dad," I answered with complete honesty. "Quinn treats me very well. And I promise when I come to Cincinnati for my quarterly training we'll have dinner and I'll tell you all about him."

"I like this plan," my mom said, and my dad agreed.

"I miss you guys so much." Most days, I didn't realize it because I was too wrapped up in my work schedule, and lately, Quinn, but I did miss them. I loved living near the Big Apple, but it wasn't without sacrifice. The distance from my family was hard. "Is everything going okay back home?"

"We miss you too, sweetheart," my mom said, only love in her voice.

And Dad quickly added, "Everything is great, Caterpillar. Your mom and I are doing just fine."

"Good. I'm glad," I said. "Well…I have to get off of here, but I'll see you soon, okay? I love you tons and tons and tons."

They both offered their love and ended the call shortly after that.

Once I set my phone down on the coffee table, Quinn looked over at me and smiled softly.

"You have to go to Cincinnati?"

I nodded. "Yeah. Four or five days from now, I can't remember which." He looked unhappy, and the reality of my life hit me like a brick wall. "I guess it's safe to say I'm always going somewhere…"

My own words made me feel sad, and I watched the corners of his mouth turn down even farther.

Eventually, his eyes met mine, and a teensy tiny smile kissed his lips. "Well, you're not going somewhere right now, are you?"

I leaned over and replaced his smile with a kiss. "Nope. I'm not going anywhere right now."

"Perfect. Eat your breakfast, and then go get dressed," he said with a little wink. "I'm taking you somewhere fun today."

Somewhere fun sounded like exactly what I needed. It'd be a nice distraction from the whole gossip magazine situation that was apparently happening around me.

"Wherever we go, can we make a quick stop on our way?"

"Of course," he said and took a sip of his coffee. "Errands to run?"

"Sort of…" I paused, hesitant over the next words that I wanted to say. "Well… Apparently, my parents found out about us through a gossip magazine at the grocery store. So, I just kind of wanted to see what exactly was written in the article…"

Or at least, I thought I wanted to see. Hell, the more I thought about it, the more uncomfortable I became. I wasn't sure if I'd like seeing my face splashed across the cover of a magazine.

What if it was an awful photo? What if they said mean things?

"Oh, shit," he muttered with wide, surprised eyes. "I had no idea, kitten. No wonder Nathan called me six times this morning. I would've answered if I would have known it was about something like that."

I shrugged. "I guess I shouldn't be surprised, by it. I mean my boyfriend is Quinn Bailey."

"True." A half-happy, half-sad smile kissed his lips. "But I can't stop myself from feeling responsible for the fact that you got blind-sided by that news, through your parents, at that." He reached out and held my hand in his. "I'm so sorry, kitten. I'll call Nathan after we eat and get it all straightened out."

"It's okay." I leaned forward and pressed a soft kiss to his lips.

The discomfort in his blue eyes hit me straight in the chest.

Obviously, I wasn't a fan of the idea of being in a gossip magazine, but that took a back seat to seeing Quinn sad.

I nudged his arm with my shoulder. "You better eat up and get your strength, buddy."

He tilted his head to the side, puzzled. "And why's that?"

"Because I'm expecting you to bring your A game when it comes to the surprise of fun you just promised me."

"Surprise of fun?" he questioned, a smile teasing his lips. "I don't remember using those words…"

Ha. The liar. He knew he'd promised me that exact fucking thing.

"The pressure is on, Bailey."

He barked out a laugh. "Challenge accepted, kitten," he said. "Consider my *O game face* already on."

Chapter Twenty-Nine

Quinn

Today was about tradition. Team bonding. Pride of membership.

Today was about bringing in a group of fifty-three men and turning them into a unit.

Today was the day we took our annual trip to Walmart.

I know. I sounded like a lunatic. But there was truth in each and every one of my words, no matter how mismatched they seemed together.

Three years ago, when Sean had been drafted to the Mavericks and become a staple in my life, we'd invented this ritual. Every year, as the structure of the National Football League rarely changed with any real significance, the order of our schedule became more and more predictable. We had an idea of when we'd have practices, when we'd be expected to do endorsement deals, when we'd have team photos and film to shoot, and when we'd be traveling and confined to team rules. But every year, in the week before the first preseason game of the year, there was always one day that managed to prevail, one day that saved itself for tomfoolery and hijinks—one day that had birthed an institution.

The Twenty-Five Dollar Challenge.

Fifty-three men. One Walmart. Twenty-five dollars. And ten

minutes to make the best fucking outfit you could manage. The crazier, the better, everyone ran around like a bunch of kids, trying to find the unicorn among the mundane. I'd managed a Minion onesie last year with a pair of sparkling pink flip-flops, but I'd still tasted defeat.

Sean, the fucker, had won the game the last two years running, so I'd spent the off-season contemplating a new judging system. AKA, creating one, since before, one didn't exist. Usually, the team just fell into pandemonium until someone declared themselves the winner and the team accepted it or not.

Of course, I'd come up with nothing but shit, because there was no one to choose who could be an impartial authority, but when I'd woken up with Catharine this morning, the answer had come sweeping in.

Get ready, boys. There's a new judge in town.

Luckily, after we'd caused a near-riot last year, the Edison Walmart had finally learned to plan for our arrival, coordinating it with my assistant and shutting down the store. No one got in while we were in the heat of battle, and the security was tight as Catharine and I slipped seamlessly in the back door.

It made the process much more enjoyable, not worrying about who was watching or what might get posted to some tabloid site, but after all was said and done, we did a three-hour meet-and-greet with the fans. Unlike on game day, everybody won.

"Are you sure it's okay that I'm here?" Cat asked apprehensively. I'd explained the game in the car on the way over, and once she knew it was an actual "official" team activity, she'd started to question having a role in the whole thing.

"I told you, baby. I have a job for you. No one will mind that you're there, I promise."

She nodded as I pulled her along the back hallway toward the aisles in the rear of the store where I knew the guys would be gathered. Starting in the automotive section, we'd decided last year, made sure no one had an unfair timing advantage.

It was a weird sight, finding so many giant humans among car oil, air filters, and batteries, but it definitely wasn't a bad one. I loved when we were all together—especially doing stupid shit like this. It gave me an excuse to act a little bit like an overgrown kid.

"Hey, guys," I greeted with a smile as we came to a stop just outside of their grouping. Catharine's body melded to the back of mine, trying to stay out of sight.

Honestly, it worked pretty well for her, she was so much smaller than I was, until a peek of her feminine hand crept around the side of my body to clench the material of my shirt.

Cam Mitchell, one of the most observant of the group, noticed first, his eyebrows popping to his hairline. "You got a stowaway you want to tell us about, QB?"

Catharine's squeak was chipmunk-worthy as I pulled her out from behind me with one swift hand.

"Guys, this is Cat. Cat, these are the guys." With wide eyes and a circular wave, Catharine almost peed her pants when fifty-three guys said hello all at once.

"Holy shit," she whispered quietly, but those of us closest to her heard her almost perfectly. We smiled.

"Wow," she murmured then, and I nudged her gently with my body.

"Don't swoon, baby," I said with a laugh. "You're already taken."

She looked at me then, mischief in her eyes. "Yeah, but they're pretty."

I bit my lip, my eyebrows pulling down to my nose, and challenged, "So am I."

If struggling dancers couldn't find jobs doing backup for the newest music act, I was certain they'd be able to find work in her eyes.

"Yeah," she agreed finally. "You are."

Cam's throat rattled loudly as he cleared it to get our attention. "Easy on the romance, QB. Unless you brought us companions and you're hiding them in the back."

Sean's ears perked up like a fucking puppy. "You have women?"

"No," I denied, dashing his dreams instantly. His face fell, and

Catharine let out a giggle beside me. "Sorry, buddy," I apologized. "But I brought an impartial judge."

Sean's and Cam's eyes jumped to Cat and narrowed. Cam was the first to burst out laughing. "Impartial, my ass."

"Don't worry," I assured. "Cat's got an evil spot really deep inside her. She'll probably blackball me from the win just for the hell of it."

Cat nodded beside me gleefully.

God, I'd never seen her smile that big, her eyes that uninhibited. My heart dropped in my chest, falling a little farther into a pit with walls it wouldn't be able to scale.

"Plus, if she does, by some miracle, pick me as the winner, the team will have to vote to confirm, majority rule."

Sean's smile was indulgent. "I see you've thought this through, bro."

"Your streak is coming to an end," I taunted. Sean, embodying one of Missy Elliott's best hits, took his jazz hands, flipped them, and reversed them, wiggling his fingers in a response of *Come and get me*.

Half an hour later, after going over the rules and regulations with all the new guys on the team, we took off into the store at the sound of the whistle.

Cat had abandoned me, claiming she'd be providing me with an unfair advantage if she tried to help at all, and headed off in another direction.

Tunnel vision in place, I'd scoured the children's costume section, looking for a tiara, before heading to the long underwear.

If I had a prayer of getting Cat to choose me, I'd have to make sure my dick was visible through my pants.

At seven dollars a pop, I chose a pair in a dusty rose color, about twenty sizes too small, and did my best to hoist them up to my waist. A quick glance down told me everything I needed to know. The twig and berries were definitely on display.

Sean yelled as he ran by, a quick, "Suck it," to keep the spirit of our rivalry alive, and then he was off to parts unknown.

"One minute!" Cat called over the bullhorn, making me realize I'd yet to grab a shirt.

Knowing I didn't really have the time to scout one, I headed back for her without. I'd automatically be disqualified for failing to buy an entire ensemble, but if I were really sweet, maybe Cat would console me by sneaking away to have sex in the bathroom when all the judging was done.

"I can't believe Sean won again!" I complained, dragging Cat in a very strategic direction as I did.

She came along without protest. "He had the best outfit! I'm sorry, but he looked just like fucking Katniss."

"I'm going to have to invest in training for these guys if any of us ever has any chance of beating him."

She shrugged. "Either that or get him kicked off the team."

I barked a laugh, loud and riotous at her callousness. "Wow, kitten. That's cold."

She smiled unabashedly, and I pushed her against a shelf, well away from the guys, to put my lips to hers.

Her sigh, expelled directly into my mouth, tasted like contentment.

"Good day?" I asked her, nipping at her bottom lip while she smiled.

"Definitely."

"You sure you want don't want to come out to the meet-and-greet with me? I hate the idea of leaving you alone to do nothing."

She shook her head. "I think seeing my face inside an *US Weekly* was enough attention for the day."

My heart spasmed inside my chest. I still felt bad for how that went down. I should've answered my phone when Nathan had called this morning, but God, Nathan always called. Every fucking morning. His persistence wasn't out of the ordinary.

I was just thankful Cat's first dose of media attention—because let's face it, there would be more now, she *was* my girlfriend—had been, if anything, a positive one.

Quinn Bailey's New Lady Love, the headline had read, and inside were a few candid photos of Cat and me from when I'd last picked her up at the airport.

If nothing else, the pictures were fucking cute.

And, Cat? Well, she'd looked beautiful. But that was no surprise; she always looked beautiful.

But I didn't underestimate how that probably felt for her, seeing herself in a gossip magazine. I knew it was a lot for anyone to process, and all I could do was give her the time she needed to do it. And most importantly, reassure her that she had nothing to worry about.

I wrapped my arms around her and hugged her tightly to my chest. "The meet-and-greet shouldn't take too long."

"I'll be fine, Quinn," she said and leaned back to look into my eyes. "I'll sketch. That's why you brought me paper and pencils, isn't it?" she asked. My chest tightened, overcome by how good the affection in her voice over that seriously simple task sounded.

I nodded. "Okay."

She touched my lips with her thumbs, smoothing them from the center out to the sides. "You're really something, Quinn Bailey."

An irrational urge to keep her in my pocket all the time made me blurt out my next request. "Our first preseason game is this weekend in Pittsburgh. I know it's sports..." I stuck out my tongue, and she laughed. "And I know they're not your thing. But maybe, just maybe, you'd make an exception if it meant getting to watch me play?"

Her frown took over her entire face, even turning her eyes down at the corners, and disappointment bled out of me through an imaginary wound.

"I want to," she assured me quickly. It was pretty clear I'd known what she was going to say. "It's just, I have work. I'm still too new to take any official time off, and I don't know anyone but Nikki and Casey to switch with. And they're already working the flight with me."

If I was disappointed, she seemed devastated. Perversely, that was enough to make me feel better. Wanting to be flesh-to-flesh, I joined our lips and ran my tongue along the seam with a barely there touch. *An apology and acceptance all at once.*

"It's okay, kitten." I brought her hand up between us, splaying it on my heart so she could feel the way she made it race. "You and me? We're gonna last."

I smirked, kissed the corner of her mouth, and fell a little deeper. "You'll have plenty of chances to come watch something you have absolutely no interest in. I promise you that."

Chapter Thirty

Cat

Another day and another round of NYC to Birmingham flights.

Normally, I wouldn't have minded it at all. But today, I was annoyed. Internally irritated that my flight schedule had gotten in the way of seeing Quinn in all of his quarterback glory.

Sure, I didn't really like football. But I *did* like Quinn. If I was being completely honest with myself, I'd probably use a different, more encompassing word to describe how I truly felt about him.

Love.

But I wasn't ready to verbally say that word to him. Not without the cushion of "I think" in front of it, at least. Hell, I was having a hard enough time keeping my girlish impulses of planning out my dream wedding and naming future kids under control.

I'd gone all *Cinderella Lifetime movie marriage* in my thoughts, and I wasn't sure that was the best-case scenario for me or my heart. We were still so new. If our relationship was a child, we'd said our first words, but we hadn't really taken our first steps together.

I hadn't even been to his house yet, which I tried to tell myself had nothing to do with him not wanting to let me all the way in, and was more of a timing and scheduling issue. But I didn't really know. How could I? I wasn't inside his mind or hearing his thoughts.

And I hadn't met his family either. But that statement was true in the reverse. The only thing my parents knew about Quinn occurred between the pages of tabloid magazines and ESPN.

When it came to the uberfamous quarterback, who just so happened to be my current boyfriend, I needed to keep my outlook realistic.

I needed to keep all of my future tense daydreams true-to-life—no weddings or babies or professions of love. I just needed to focus on the day-to-day and enjoying our relationship for what it currently was—in the early stages.

"Excuse me, Cat?" a female passenger in 6B caught my attention.

"Can I help you with something?" I asked as I moved down the aisle and stood beside the woman's seat. She smiled up at me, her brown eyes soft and gentle yet still encompassing confidence and self-assurance. Young and attractive, she couldn't have been a day over thirty.

"I have something for you," she responded and nodded toward the small package she held out toward me with her right hand.

"You have something for me?" I furrowed my brow. Unless it was complaints, drink requests, or disasters in the bathroom, it wasn't exactly the norm for passengers to come bearing gifts.

"Yep. Definitely for you." She nodded and shook the box in her hand a little—a universal gesture for *take it.*

Hesitantly, I took it. "I'm not trying to come across as rude right now, but should I know who you are?"

She grinned. "Probably. We have a mutual acquaintance. Although, I'm pretty sure you enjoy his company a lot more than I do."

I didn't really know how to respond to that. An acquaintance? Who could I possibly know that she knew?

"Quinn Bailey," she offered, and I tilted my head to the side. "I'm Jillian, his personal assistant."

"Oh," I said, and my mouth formed a perfect little O.

"And," she continued with a soft smile, "to be honest, this was a nice change of pace from my usual tasks of cleaning up after him and making sure he's where he needs to be at all times. Which, you'd think that'd be an easy assignment, but Quinn is sometimes impossibly stubborn."

"But doesn't he have a game today?" I asked and looked at the time on my watch. "Like, right now, to be exact?"

She shrugged. "He does, but he wanted me here. This was his number one priority for today."

"This was his number one priority? Delivering this package?" I glanced down at the small cardboard box in my hands. "*To me*?"

I was Quinn's priority number one for today. On a game day?

My brain honestly didn't know what to do with that information. It was stuck between two very strong reactions: tap-dancing down the aisle like a loon or swooning right out of my heels and falling face first onto the rough, most likely bacteria-infested carpet of the aisle.

"Yep," she responded with a smile.

A shocked laugh left my lips. "Wait…" I paused when the seat belt sign dinged off once we'd reached our intended altitude. "You do realize you're now stuck on a flight to Birmingham, right?"

"I have plenty of music and books on my iPad to keep me occupied. *Plus,* I didn't agree to this task without getting paid a little extra. Honestly, I should probably be thanking you." She winked, and a little grin crested her pretty pink lips. "I'll finally be able to buy that Michael Kors purse I've had my eye on for months now."

A quiet laugh fell off my tongue. "Girl, if it's the Cynthia, I will be so jealous. I saw that purse in Bloomingdale's and started drooling in the middle of the handbags."

I'd spotted the Cynthia after Casey had basically dragged me to Bloomingdale's on one of our rare off days. She was gorgeous, all soft pink leather and gold accents, but a little more expensive than what I normally spent on handbags.

"Oh, I *love* the Cynthia, but I need something smaller to use on date nights," she said. "My sights are set on the Ruby."

Michael Kors's newest quilted leather clutch, it was a kick-ass choice.

"Tell me you're going for the gold one instead of the black or silver…"

"Of course. Without question, gold is always the way to go." She winked and then nodded toward the unopened box. "Anyway, enough about my handbag obsession. I think it's time for you to open that box."

I glanced down at it, and slowly, amusement kissed my lips with a smile. "I guess I'll go do that now."

"Good plan." Jillian grinned. "You can find me here, reading this book one of my friends demanded for me to read." She held up her iPad, and I could see the sleek orange cover of *Bright Side* on her screen.

My eyes grew wide in surprise. I *loved* that book. Kim Holden's words were pure magic.

Bright Side was the kind of book that even after you'd finished reading it, its mark was still engraved on your heart. It just…changed you. In the very best way.

"Girl, get tissues and be prepared for an epic, amazing, love-filled, all-consuming ride."

"That good?"

"Trust me," I said. "Your friend was right. You need to read it."

"I knew there was a reason I liked you from the start," she said with a little secret smile, and then she swiped to the first page of *Bright Side* and started reading.

Liked me from the start? Was Quinn gossiping about me to his assistant?

Weirdly enough, I smiled at the thought.

With the box still clutched in my hands, I walked to the small, yet perfectly hidden confines of the first-class galley and rested my ass on a ledge near the window. Without anyone around to watch, I peeled the tape off the box and opened it.

Inside, rested a small, folded-up piece of paper, and below that, *a freaking inhaler.*

A laugh escaped my lips at the sight.

Cheeky bastard. I had a feeling the blow job turned asthma attack would be an inside joke he'd never let die.

I unfolded the paper and read the note silently.

My cute little kitten,

Please be nice to Jillian. Give her an extra cookie or something during the flight. She wasn't too thrilled when I asked her to fly back and forth to Birmingham just to deliver a package to my girlfriend. And, in order to get her to agree, I'm pretty sure I'm providing a shopping spree to Macy's or something…

My assistant is a ballbuster, I tell ya.

Anyway, eventually, after a solid negotiation, she was kind enough to deliver this to you for me. Not sure if she mentioned it, but this little box was priority number one for the day.

Now, I'm not sure if you remember, but I play football for the New York Mavericks. That's an NFL team, Kitten.

What a smartass, I thought to myself but kept reading, an immovable smile on my lips the entire time.

And NFL stands for National Football League, otherwise known as the professional league for American football. It's kind of a big deal.

Let's see what else can I tell you about football…

There are four quarters in a game. And the quarterback (that's me) throws the ball, and sometimes when I'm feeling frisky, even runs the ball.

While you're reading this, I'm in the middle of a game. I've already thrown for two touchdowns, and it isn't even halftime yet. Yes, I know while I'm writing this it is just a prediction, but trust me, I know those two touchdowns are now facts.

God, I loved his confidence. I imagined it was why Quinn Bailey was a household name in football.

Right this very second, Pittsburgh is wondering what to do with themselves. They'll try to adjust their defense, but it won't work.

By the way, a touchdown is how you score points in a football game. It's worth six points, and if our kicker is doing what he's supposed to, he converted the field goal for an extra point, which has brought us to seven points.

And since I said two touchdowns, we are beating Pittsburgh by 14 right now.

I know, it's a lot to wrap your cute little brain around, but we'll get there.

A soft giggle left my lips. I'd probably never understand football, but for Quinn, I'd try.

But, guess what? I didn't just write you this little note to talk about football.

I wanted to tell you I miss you. Yes, kitten, I miss you.

And, even though I'm in the middle of a game right now, I'm thinking about you.

But that shouldn't be a surprise. Lately, your sexy little ass is always on my mind.

I can't wait to see you again.

I can't wait to kiss you and hold your hand and just be all cute and shit with you.

Your adorable boyfriend, (Admit it, I'm fucking adorable.)

Quinn

P.S. The inhaler is a "just in case" kind of thing because I plan on ravaging your sexy ass the second you're

back in New York. And let's face it, we know what happens sometimes when you get all worked up. ;)

I held the note to my chest, and I sighed. And believe me, if that sigh could talk, she would ramble on and on about Quinn in a girly, dreamy, head-over-heels voice.

This man, he was the perfect amount of sweet and adorable yet knew all of the right moments to be sarcastic and cocky and sexy and alpha as fuck.

He wanted to ravage me once I got back to New York?

Um, yes, *please.*

Before Casey trotted his nosy ass into the galley, I hurriedly folded the note back up and slipped it into my jacket pocket, along with the inhaler, and tossed the small box into the trash.

For some reason, when it came to Quinn, I was territorial over all of our sweet and adorable moments and inside jokes. Hell, I guessed I was pretty fucking territorial over our hot and sexy moments too. Even the ones that ended in asthma attacks and tears.

I just didn't really want anyone else to be in on the secret, I guessed.

It was things like these, like the cute note he'd managed to have hand-delivered to me on my flight, that felt too damn special to share with anyone else.

It's because this is love.

Yeah. That's was probably exactly why.

God, I wanted to see him. But the opportunity wouldn't present itself for a few more days. I wished this flight was a one-off and straight back to NYC for a few days, but unfortunately for me, it wasn't.

Once I arrived in Birmingham, I'd fly back to NYC, then back to Birmingham again, where I'd have the pleasure of an overnight in a Marriott.

I wouldn't make my final leg back home to New York until the very next afternoon where I could finally enjoy some much-needed time off. Well, time off in the form of one day before I'd need to head to Cincinnati for training, but still, it was time off.

And one full day to be ravaged by Quinn…

Yes. *That.* I needed that.

The flights had felt long, and the passengers tired and cranky, and by the time I'd made it back to Birmingham—*for the second time today*—it was nearing midnight and my ass was practically dragging on the floor.

Bright and early, my day had started at nearly six in the morning, and now, I was more than ready to call it a fucking night.

"Thanks for flying with us," I said goodbye to passengers as they walked out the main doors. "Have a nice night."

Casey stood beside me, doing the same, until the last two passengers managed to get themselves off the plane safely.

"What do you think, Cat? You ready to get some drinks?" Casey questioned as he walked up and down the aisles, double-checking all of the seats and overhead bins.

"Hell no," I responded without a second thought. "I'm going straight to the hotel, checking in, getting my ass a hot shower, and calling it a night. I'm dead on my feet."

"Oh, come on, girl," he retorted with a smirk. "You're twenty-four, not sixty-four. All you need is a Red Bull or something, and you'll get a second wind."

"I don't want a second wind. I don't want any wind unless it's from my freaking hair dryer after my hot shower."

He huffed and frowned and flashed puppy dog eyes in my direction.

Normally, those things would make me cave, but not tonight.

Tonight, I didn't care. I wanted a shower and a bed.

"Not gonna work," I answered as I shut off all of the power in the front and back galleys. "I'm going to walk my ass off this plane and go straight to the hotel, where I will be getting twelve hours of uninterrupted sleep, and there isn't a damn thing you, *or anyone else, for that matter*, can do to change my mind."

I guessed the flights and missing Quinn were making me a bit grumpy.

"Well, okay, sassy pants." He grinned and handed my carry-on to me. "I guess I'll have to hang out with Captain Billy tonight."

"Good plan," I agreed, and Casey just laughed.

"All right, I think we're all set for you to leave this plane and give your best impression of an old lady. Sound good?"

"Sounds perfect. Let's hit it." I nodded, and side by side, we walked off the plane and down the long hallway until we reached the now empty area that was Gate C2.

The instant my heels reached the tiled floor of the terminal, I stopped, dead in my tracks, and my lips parted in outright surprise.

There he stood, my boyfriend, in all of his smiling glory.

Quinn.

My heart pounded rapidly in my chest, like it was trying to escape from my body and crawl into his.

A vision in sweat pants, a gray hoodie, and shaggy hair hidden beneath a ball cap, and I'd never seen anything better in my entire life.

He started to walk toward me, his smile getting bigger with each step, and I felt like my breath was stolen straight from my lungs.

"I have a feeling someone is a little liar who isn't going to be getting any sleep tonight," Casey teased, but I ignored him.

I couldn't do anything but smile. Right at Quinn.

Before I even drew in the air my body needed, I was dropping my carry-on and purse to the floor and running straight at him until I crashed right into his strong arms and melted into his muscular form. "Kitty Cat," he whispered, the nickname enveloping me in its warmth.

"I can't believe you're here," I whispered. Beneath his sweatshirt, I felt his firm torso and his strong and steady heartbeat within his chest. He folded his hands around my back, drawing me in closer, until he lifted me off the ground and swung us around in a circle.

I knew I'd missed him, but I hadn't realized how much.

Until *now.*

Being without him was hard.

And being with him was starting to feel a lot like home.

Chapter Thirty-One

Quinn

She hit me like a wave, all citrus bursts and sweet shampoo, and my arms closed around her tightly. Her body felt familiar and warm and like it was made to be pressed close to mine.

"Kitty Cat," I murmured softly into one giant swirling curl in her hair.

"I can't believe you're here," she whispered back, the vibration from her heartfelt words making my swallow even thicker than normal.

If I was being honest, I couldn't believe I was here either. The team plane had landed in Newark nearly four hours ago after a resounding win in Pittsburgh, and every minute since had been spent finding a way to get here. To be fair, Jilly did most of the actual plan-making, but a quick drive to Teterboro—a smaller airport in New Jersey—a chartered private plane later, and here I was. It wasn't planned, and it wasn't calculated; it was all feeling-driven action, and I was powerless against it.

"I missed you," I admitted into the top of her head, bending over to let her toes make contact with the ground again.

"I missed you too." She stared at me for a minute, searching my eyes so intently I had a hard time letting myself blink. She broke the contact to look down at her feet and rambled self-consciously. "I wanted to come to your game, really. But I couldn't figure out how to get someone else to cover my schedule and—"

"Cat," I interrupted, putting my hands to her jaw and applying gentle pressure.

Her chin came up so that her warm brown eyes could meet mine.

"What?" she whispered.

"Be quiet."

She nodded, her gaze flicking down to my lips for barely a moment—that was all I gave her before crushing them to her own.

Her mouth was pliant and inviting and tasted like every fantasy I'd ever had. My throat rattled with a groan, and my hands skimmed down her sides to meet her hips. She was all flesh and sweater, and my fingertips dug in, eager to brand themselves into her being and stay there.

She tasted like water, if I were a man dying of thirst.

Though, if I weren't particularly parched, she tasted like something a lot less bland.

Her lips worked under mine, stretching and molding to make my access to her tongue as easy as possible. Secretly, I didn't need the advantage. With the amount of longing that had been burning in my lungs for the last few days, I would have plundered.

Eyes were on us as I pulled away—I could feel them.

When you were in the public eye for as long as I'd been, you didn't need to see to believe. The stares were weighty, and all that energy focused on you made the back of your neck pulse.

My gaze stayed with Cat, despite the feeling, as I took both of her hands in mine and rubbed at her knuckles.

I'd done my best to stay incognito with the hat, but better disguises had failed. I had hope, though, that the attention had more to do with the public display than anyone really knowing who I was.

"Can I take you somewhere?" I asked, not knowing I was going to say it before the words were out of my mouth.

Just like the decision that had brought me here, the drive to take her home—to introduce her to my family—wasn't one of careful planning.

It just felt right.

She nodded her yes without even asking where I meant.

I smiled. "You don't even know where I want to go."

The soft curls of what I knew was carefully straightened and smoothed hair swayed with the motion of her head. "It doesn't matter." She giggled a little. "I'll go anywhere, as long as you're going with me."

Awareness of us ticked up, and people started to take out their phones behind Cat's back. I grabbed her hand and started to walk. "Come on, then. We've got a little ride."

As I pushed my parents' front door open with a gentle hand and put a finger to my lips, it was clear Cat was starting to regret her impulsive agreement to go anywhere with me.

But I was sneaking her into my parents' house in the middle of the night, without said parents knowing we were coming. I didn't really know a lot of people who wouldn't balk at that.

Her eyes glowed with annoyance while I pushed the door closed and took her hand to guide her to the stairs.

She mouthed something into the darkness. I could see her mouth moving—and I even had a pretty idea of what she was saying as she pointed to a picture of me on the wall—but I acted as though the dark of night was too much. "Sorry, kitten. I can't hear you."

She shook her head and squeezed my hand—pretty fucking hard for such a little thing—and I had to turn away to hide my smile.

When we finally made it to my room, shut the door, and turned on the light, her body was a snake, ready to strike.

"Tell me this isn't your parents' house," she whispered, and my silence was more than enough answer. She looked at more pictures of me on the wall and tossed a glare in my direction. "Oh. My. God.

I can't believe we came to your parents' house in the middle of the freaking night! Are they even awake? Do they know we're here?"

"Well…tomorrow, when they wake up, I'll definitely tell them we're here."

I didn't think it was possible, but her glare grew stronger.

"You said you'd go anywhere," I reminded her, knowing full well I was taking my life in my hands a little bit.

"Yeah, well," she whisper-yelled. "I thought we'd at least be going somewhere where the people knew we were coming!"

"Where's your sense of adventure, kitten?"

Her eyes were sharp, and her mind was better. "Back at the airport."

I burst out laughing, and she dove on me, her tiny hand doing its best to muzzle my mouth. "There's seriously something wrong with you."

I smiled under her hand and mumbled my response. "Youb glub pee."

"What?" she asked, her eyes wide and a little bit frightened as she pulled her hand slowly off of my mouth.

I didn't stumble, I didn't stutter, and I didn't hold back. "I said you love me." I grabbed her cheeks and brought her face to mine, touching our lips together in the sweetest kiss I'd ever been a part of. "And I love you too."

"Quinn," she whispered, unshed tears shimmering in her eyes.

"Quiet, baby," I ordered with a shake of my head. "I know how you can agree with me, without having to talk."

I left Cat sleeping in bed as I crept quietly out of my room and made my way down the stairs to the kitchen. It was just before six in the morning, but I knew my parents would be awake, just settling in at the table for breakfast.

The newspaper cracked as my dad shook it in front of himself, and my mom picked at a half of a grapefruit with a spoon.

I paused at the entry and cleared my throat, hoping to ease the intensity with which I startled them.

My mom turned with a gasp, and my dad pulled the paper down sharply, rising to his feet.

"Hey, Mom," I greeted. "Dad."

"Quinn!" my mom said, her voice as excited as I'd ever heard it. It went up at the end, almost like a question, and the sheer power of it brought her to her feet.

My dad's face, however, turned down into a scowl. "What are you doing here? Why aren't you in New Jersey, at practice?"

Always the strong, stubborn father who never wanted his sons to fail at *anything*, sometimes my dad had a hard time remembering I was a full-grown adult.

I kept my voice even, stretching it out straight like a pipe running across the room. "It's the day after game day, Dad. We don't have practice until tomorrow."

His eyebrows didn't look any less like a cartoon. "I'll repeat. What the hell are you doing here?"

"Beau," my mom chastised quickly. "It's good to see him."

I ignored my mom, knowing she wasn't the one I really needed to win over in this situation. She might be cold at times, but she was almost never harsh.

My father could be both, and he could be vicious in his method.

And the point of this visit wasn't to argue. I needed him calm and relaxed before I introduced him to Cat.

"I..." I paused, swallowing thickly before admitting, "brought someone to meet you."

"One of your teammates?" my dad asked hopefully. My mom, however, had a firmer grip on the situation.

"Beau, he's brought a woman home."

My dad looked behind me, dramatically meeting my eyes when he came up empty. "I don't see one."

I stepped farther into the room before speaking then, leaning into the island with a hand and meeting them both in the eyes. "She's upstairs sleeping."

The sound of a soft swallow from behind me brought my head around.

Cat, dressed demurely in her pajamas, thankfully, stood in the entry to the kitchen, my phone extended in her hand. She looked to me and then glanced nervously to my parents. "I'm so sorry to interrupt." She focused on me before whispering, "Your phone wouldn't stop ringing."

I took it from her hands and scrolled through the notifications.

Nathan and Jilly, a dance of calls between them, their siren song on repeat.

I put my phone facedown on the counter and ignored it. Both of them could wait. There was absolutely no way I was going to abandon Cat to fend for herself with my parents now. I'd been hoping to have more time to prep them—to implore that they be on their best behavior with the woman I was in love with.

But this would have to do.

"Mom, Dad…this is Catharine Wild. My girlfriend."

Chapter Thirty-Two

Cat

We'd arrived at the Bailey home late last night, his parents not even knowing we were there, and now, after being introduced to them this morning—all of forty minutes ago—I had never felt more uncomfortable.

When Quinn had brought me here after we'd left the airport, I'd had a moment of sheer panic. I mean, meeting the parents was a big deal, and of course, I wanted to give a good impression.

This was the man I love—*yes, love*—and I wanted his parents to like me.

Any sane human being would want that.

Once we'd gotten some sleep, and I'd freshened up in the bathroom, I'd felt excited to meet his mom and dad. Happy, even. It was a huge step in our relationship.

But then, I'd met them.

And that's where things had taken a nose dive.

If I'd calculated their welcoming attitude on a warmth scale, it would have been a frigid five degrees. Any second, I felt like I'd start seeing my breath leave my lips and icicles forming on their windows.

His mother and father appeared more interested in the television, the kitchen, hell, anything besides even looking in my direction.

The worst part of all, I had no idea where any of it was coming from.

Initially, when Quinn had first introduced me after I'd interrupted their conversation in the kitchen because his phone wouldn't stop ringing, I thought maybe we'd caught them on a bad or busy morning. And I hadn't judged or gotten discouraged, *at first*.

People had the right to have bad days sometimes. Lord knows, I'd had my share of shit days. And sometimes, even when you had the best intentions to make a good first impression, the stressors of a bad day could hinder your ability to be positive and happy.

Not to mention, it was first thing in the morning. They'd just woken up. We'd caught them off guard. Usually, it took me a full cup of coffee before I could fully engage in human interaction.

I'd understood all of those possibilities and mentally convinced myself that was probably what the initial uncomfortable meet-and-greet had been caused by.

I'd figured that once we spent a little time with them, chatted over coffee or lemonade or sweet tea or whatever it was Southerners liked to drink, everyone would loosen up, and the ice would be broken.

But the ice hadn't broken. It'd only grown thicker, colder, and more rigid with each small-talk exchange.

And now that I was fully dressed, we sat side by side at the formal dining table, with Mrs. Bailey directly across from us. Her posture rigid, her eyes looking everywhere but directly at us, and her husband, well, he was nowhere to be found.

Prior to our sitting down at the table, Mr. Bailey had muttered something about a carburetor and oil check and disappeared to the garage. That was fifteen minutes ago.

Quinn cleared his throat. I took a sip of sweet tea—apparently, a Southerner's drink of choice, even in the morning hours. And Mrs. Bailey tapped her fingers across the white lace tablecloth of her dining table while her eyes unceremoniously moved around the room, the house, basically, anywhere but the in direction where I sat.

A heavy silence settled over us, thicker than the tension that had already accumulated in the air, and I felt like a morgue held more conversation than this dining room. I swallowed hard against the unease that was working its way up from my belly.

"Mom," Quinn announced in the otherwise deadly silent room, "Do you remember how much you loved the old Allied airline flight attendant uniforms?"

"Yes." She nodded, one curt, very short nod, at that.

"Cat is a flight attendant at a newer airline, and you'll never believe this, their uniforms are uncannily similar to those old Allied ones."

Internally, I grimaced. I knew what he was trying to do here, but apparently, his parents wanted nothing to do with it, or me. I mean, his mother couldn't even look at me, and his father had hightailed it for the garage not long after I'd arrived.

"That's nice, dear," she responded, and her cheeks strained as she forced a brittle smile to her face.

"How long have you been with RoyalAir, kitten?" Quinn asked, and his blue eyes met mine.

"Uh…a little over seven months now."

"Mom, you'd love RoyalAir's uniforms," he stated, in another attempt to draw any sort of interest from his mom. "Personally, I'd never fully taken the time to appreciate flight attendant uniforms until I was sitting on a flight that ended up in Atlanta." Quinn flashed a smirk in my direction while his hand discreetly gripped my knee under the table.

But his mother, well, she didn't offer anything but a clear of her throat and a glance in the direction of the garage. "Beau!" she called toward the closed door. "Do you need any help in there?"

Holy hell, now she was trying to find a way to get the hell out of dodge—*aka far, far away from me*—too. This woman was not the kind of woman who helped in the garage. From the pearls around her neck to the perfect winter white color of her sweater, Mrs. Bailey was a *woman*.

"Hey, Dixie!" Mr. Bailey called back. "Mind coming in here for a second?"

"Sure thing, honey!" she responded and hopped out of her chair like her life depended on getting to the garage as quickly as humanly possible.

I bet if I'd timed her, she would've broken records for quickest woman in the house.

Air sawed at my lungs, the war between upset that she couldn't stand to be in the same room with me and relief that she'd finally gone tugging the blade back and forth. I tried to find the strength to ask Quinn what in the hell was going on in a nice, neutral way. I needed to understand what was happening, but I didn't want to insult him. Family was always a touchy subject, and questions could seem like an attack.

But I had things on my mind.

Was there anything I could do differently?

Did they feel ambushed by our showing up in the middle of the night and just appearing at their kitchen table during breakfast?

Did I smell like a garbage can, and I didn't even realize it?

Anything to help get some peace of mind.

Before I could verbalize my thoughts, his mother's voice filled my ears. "Hey, Quinn," she called. "Come into the garage for a minute! Your daddy needs some help!"

He furrowed his brow, and his gaze met mine. "Uh…I'll be right back," he said, and I nodded.

"Okay." I silently thanked God he hadn't tried to drag me in there with him. I feared the instant I stepped into that garage, his parents might try to hop in their car and peel out of the driveway.

I watched Quinn walk out of the dining room, through the kitchen, and into the garage, shutting the door behind him as he went.

I decided to use that time to take a bathroom break and try to find the strength to get through the rest of this visit.

As I walked through the kitchen and took a left past the garage,

I could hear the muffled sounds of Quinn's voice, and with each step toward the bathroom, his voice grew louder, clearer.

By the time I walked inside the first-floor bathroom and closed the door behind me, I could literally hear everything they were saying inside the garage.

"What's going on with you, Quinn?" his mother asked, concern etching her voice. "Are you feeling okay?"

He sighed. "Of course I'm feeling okay."

"Then why did you bring *her* to our house?" his father chimed in, and I watched my own face react to that question in the mirror, brow furrowed, lips slightly parted.

Her? What did he even mean by that?

"What are you talking about, Dad?" Quinn questioned, and irritation creased his voice. "What do you even mean with that question?"

"You know what your father means," his mother responded. "Obviously, this isn't the type of girl you'd settle down with, so why would you even bother bringing her to our home to meet us? That's not very nice to give her hope like that, Quinn."

My eyes grew wide, and my cheeks stretched down as my bottom lip dropped farther open. Any second now, I might have to catch my jaw with my hand before it hit the bathroom sink.

"Mom, she *is* the exact type of girl I'd settle down with. She's my girlfriend. That's the whole reason I brought her here. I was excited for you to meet her. I wanted you to meet her because she's really fucking important to me."

Tears pricked my eyes. This entire situation was beyond uncomfortable. What should have been a nice, simple meeting of the parents had turned into this ugly, cold clusterfuck of confusion.

I felt painfully out of place, like a pepperoni that had mistakenly made its way onto a vegetarian pizza.

"Language," his mother tittered under her breath.

"What is going on?" Quinn questioned. "Seriously, what is fucking going on with you guys? Why are you acting like this? Please, someone fucking explain to me what is happening right now."

"Quinn Bailey," his mother stated in disapproval. "I do not want to hear you talking to me or your father that way."

"Well, I didn't want you guys to act so cold and distant toward Cat, but I guess we can't always get what we want, huh?" he retorted and then paused. "Look, I'm not trying to be disrespectful here, but your behavior is ludicrous. It doesn't really add up. I feel like there is something you're not telling me here…"

Instead of standing there and listening further, I turned on the faucet at full blast to drown out their voices. Dabbing cold water on my face and quietly humming the theme song to *Star Wars*, I did everything but let my ears hear the conversation occurring in the garage.

By the time my hands had been washed and my face dried, I stepped out of the bathroom and found Quinn standing in the kitchen.

"Ready to go, kitten?" he asked, his voice sad and quiet, but his lips somehow managing to offer a soft smile in my direction.

"Um…sure…I just need to get changed real quick," I answered with a nod, even though, technically speaking, we were leaving a little earlier than we needed to. "Anyway, it's probably better we get to the airport sooner rather than later so I'm not late for work and we don't miss our flight." My stomach clenched as the words left my mouth. I knew his sudden need to leave had nothing to do with airport arrivals.

Nor did my desire to escape. The entire visit had taken its toll on me, the suffocating tension making it harder to breathe by the second.

"Yep. I think you're right," he agreed far too quickly. It was like he couldn't stand still in this house for a second longer. "How long will it take you to get ready?"

"Just a few minutes."

I only needed to change into my uniform. My hair and makeup had already been done in the name of making a good first impression.

Which, obviously, hadn't occurred.

I walked upstairs to his bedroom, and anxiety forced my brain to focus on simple tasks: get dressed, brush teeth, spray on perfume.

It'd only taken me a couple of minutes to switch out of my clothes and repack my small carry-on. By the time I made it back downstairs, Quinn met me near the entry with his keys in his hand.

"Hey, Mom, Dad!" he called toward the living room. "We're going to head out!"

Both Beau and Dixie Bailey managed to meet us at the front door. His mother hugged Quinn tightly. His father shook his hand. And both just offered brittle smiles and halfhearted waves in my direction.

"It was nice meeting you," I whispered, and even I couldn't hide the sadness in my voice. "You have a beautiful home."

I didn't receive more than a nod in response.

Instantly, nausea filled my stomach.

God, this is awful.

With his hand pressed gently to my back, Quinn led me out of the front door and toward the car.

Once we were buckled in and he reversed out of his parents' driveway, leading us down the long dirt road that led away from his childhood home, I snuck a glance at him out of my periphery.

His lips were firm. His brow furrowed. And his knuckles gripped the steering wheel tightly.

I understood his silence.

I'd accidentally overheard most of his conversation with his parents, and at one point, I'd had to stop listening out of fear, because of the choking anxiety that what they had been about to say would have been too painful for my own ears to digest.

I honestly didn't know what to say or do in that moment.

I had no words of encouragement, no reassuring thoughts to share.

All I could do was stare out of the window and watch the trees pass by as Quinn drove us out of Boone Hills and in the direction of

Birmingham's airport.

Ten minutes into our drive, he reached out and gripped my panty-hose-covered thigh with his hand, squeezing it gently, but other than that, all stayed silent between us.

Both of us were too lost in our own thoughts to share.

Chapter Thirty-Three

Quinn

Cat had been painfully quiet as we'd driven to the airport to catch our flight back to New York, and I had no trouble understanding why.

My parents were people I'd respected my whole life. I knew they had prejudices, and I knew they often closed their minds to anything outside of what they'd grown up thinking was normal—Den and everything they'd done to him was more than proof of that.

But, shamefully, I'd never fully understood the depth of their bias, the strength with which they held on to the evil of intolerance.

In all other scenarios, I'd always been the first person to stand up for the equal rights for people of all backgrounds, all proclivities, all lifestyles, all sexual orientations, and all races.

Cat's skin didn't register as different; it was just beautiful.

I was a man in love, and anything Cat had to give, any life Cat had lived, I wanted to be a part of it.

I'd naïvely assumed my parents would feel the same, such was the saturation of my emotion in my every move, thought, and choice. Surely, I'd thought, they would know that by bringing Cat home, I was making a statement. One that said this person was worthy, she was meaningful, and she was *mine*.

Beyond all other things, all preconceived notions and

long-standing misconceptions, they should accept Catharine as theirs—as a future member of the family.

But naïveté was a mighty and devious conduit to dissatisfaction. For, my parents—people I'd loved nearly indiscriminately for my whole life—weren't any of the magically accommodating things I'd wanted them to be and couldn't see the worth of a woman whom I considered to be worth everything.

I felt ashamed and wholly disappointed in myself that I'd been so ignorant to the situation for this long. I'd taken Cat into the lion's den of toxic bigotry, and I'd done it without warning.

Me, though…I'd had advanced notice. I'd just ignored it.

Denver had been going through this for *years*.

I suddenly felt like crying for all I hadn't given him, for how profoundly I hadn't understood.

Catharine's comfort was my first priority, but it seemed impossible to achieve when I'd created this.

How did I explain to the woman I loved that, deep down, I'd *known* my parents would not treat her with human decency and acceptance?

Inside, I felt tortured. The sharpest knives, the ones that cut the deepest and would never truly heal, were the ones they'd used.

"I, um…" Cat said into the silence of the rental car. The fog in my head cleared, and I snapped into awareness. Unwittingly, while lost to my own thoughts, I'd been leaving Catharine to wallow in her own. After an hour of near silence, there was no telling what she was thinking. "When we get to the airport, I'll have to check in like I would for work and then board the plane before you, obviously."

I glanced between her face and the road, squeezing the hand I'd placed at her thigh nearly an hour ago. "No problem, kitten. I know you're working. I just shanghaied you for your layover."

And how splendidly it had gone.

Fuck, why hadn't I just taken her to a hotel and spent all night making love?

"Right," she murmured. "Okay, then."

I didn't like the way her words weaved and danced with distrust in my head.

Just how much damage have I really done here?

"Wish I could be with you, though," I added. It was a statement of truth as much as any time since I'd met her, but now, it felt like she *needed* to know.

She nodded and then spoke, her sad words weighty. "Me too, Quinn. Me too."

Why did it feel like she wasn't just talking about the airport?

Mr. Lancaster peeked his head out of his office, and I lifted mine from the spot where I'd had it leaning against the wall. His voice cracked like a whip. "Get in here, Quinn."

I nodded and replied, "Yes, sir."

It was time to face the music after one of the longest nights of my life.

After arriving at the airport, Cat had gone her way, and I'd gone mine. She'd checked in through work, and I'd gotten my ticket like a normal passenger, and even when we'd gotten to the gate, she had things to do. As she'd disappeared down the jetway, I'd marveled at how you could be so close to someone, be in the same fucking building, and yet feel so far away.

My laugh had been mordant as I'd realized how *precisely* it mirrored where we were emotionally. We were together. We were in love. And yet, we were fucking miles apart, her lost to her thoughts while I floundered in mine.

But then a bad day had turned worse, our flight, in the end, delayed by eight fucking hours. We'd finally taken off in the wee hours of the morning, and by the time we were wheels down, I was already an hour outside of my window for making it to morning weight lifting on time.

Because of the rush, Cat had taken RoyalAir transportation

home from the airport, and I'd gone home in an Uber and then driven my truck—delivered to my house in Far Hills from Teterboro by my trusty, ever-complaining assistant, Jillian—straight to the stadium. Because of that, in all of the ten hours we'd spent in close proximity to each other, we'd barely spoken a word. My gut felt rotten, discarded, and left for dead; I'd gone against it during every time I'd caught Cat's eyes. It told me to reach out, to flag her down, to pull her somewhere private and set our world to rights. I'd convinced myself giving her time was the better option.

I was a stupid bastard.

If that scenario itself had been hell, someone was about to turn up the fucking heat.

I settled into the soft leather of the chair in front of my boss's desk and waited for him to speak first. I didn't think anything I had to say on my own would be appropriate.

"Coach Bennett tells me you missed most of morning weight lifting this morning."

I nodded. Unfortunately, it was fucking true. It wasn't like I could pull the wool on this one.

"He also tells me your concentration was all over the place today."

"Sorry, Mr. L. Maybe it took an impromptu trip to Alabama." Oh, but the truth was comical sometimes.

"You can't joke your way out of this, Quinn."

I bit into my lip and swallowed.

Mr. Lancaster's voice was gentle but unyielding as he went on. "You know I like you. My wife and daughter adore you. And you've been one of the best leaders this team could have asked for. But this kind of behavior is poisonous. Not only is it unacceptable on an individual level, but the other players on this team look to you as a role model. Your behavior affects theirs, and when you don't take the team, its time, and its schedule seriously, the rest of them don't either."

I nodded, struggling to find my voice enough to choke out a, "Yes, sir."

"I'm not taking any immediate action, but you should consider yourself on probation. Any other indication that you don't take your job and the time of others seriously, and I'm going to have to do something about it none of us will like."

"Yes, sir," I said, finding my voice somewhere close to my boots—right along with my pride. "You have my word. This is the end of it."

His eyes gentled, and I swear, it was a look I'd only seen him give two people before—his wife and his daughter.

"You've been around for so long, Quinn, I think of you as more than just my quarterback. I'd like to think I know you pretty well, and it doesn't take a genius to see where this is coming from."

I nodded. I knew he knew. She'd been in his stadium, in his tunnel, rambling along as I fell in love with her right before his eyes.

He was no idiot, and I'd be one if I tried to deny it.

"Is she worth all this?"

I looked to the door, my jaw hard as I worked through how best to express my thoughts. It was all a mess in there, my brain scrambled with the dogged determination that I could have *both* the girl and the dream job. Things were haywire today, but I just needed to find a way to manage it better. To put them both at the top and accept nothing less from myself.

He waited patiently until I found the words I was looking for and turned back to him.

"You know I love the Mavericks?" I asked. I'd dreamed of playing in the National Football League my entire life. And this team, this family, was more than I'd ever envisioned.

He jerked his chin up in ascent.

"You know I don't go home during the season?" I went on, questioning his knowledge of everything me.

This time, he nodded.

"Then you know there's only one reason I'd do anything to challenge either of those commitments."

Finally done with practice, I strode from the stadium and out to my truck, intent to call Cat and touch base. After arriving late, my day had gone from shit to even shittier, and I was desperately hoping hers was a little better.

I'd played terribly—which meant I ate a lot of fucking dirt and ached like a premenstrual woman from getting literally destroyed by the entire defensive line—had a meeting with my boss I'd happily never relive, went to five promotional shoots Georgia Brooks had set up for game day photos, team photos, the Mavericks merchandise line, and so on. It'd been the longest ten hours of my life.

The team had been quiet in the locker room, and everyone gave me a wide berth. They didn't tease, they didn't taunt, and they didn't question.

No doubt, part of it was the toxic cloud of energy I found myself cloaked in with every passing minute as I let the despair of this whole fucking thing weigh me down. And the other part, I suspected, was that they were disappointed in me. Being late wasn't the behavior of a team leader, certainly not this close to the season, and it wasn't what they'd come to expect out of me. And to top it off, I'd been like a fucking lump of shit on the field, tossing interceptions up like I was Oprah. *You get an interception, you get an interception!*

I unlocked my truck and tossed my bag in the back, climbing inside before pulling my phone out and lighting up the screen to check the time. It was just past four p.m., and Cat was leaving for Cincinnati today.

My chest clenched as I realized I also had a missed call from her while I'd been occupied. I scrolled to her name, ready to hit the button to dial when a sharp knock on my passenger window scared the living fuck out of me.

"Jesus Christ," I cried as Jillian climbed into the passenger seat and, horror of horrors, Nathan, my publicist, climbed into the back.

"No," Jillian denied. "I am awesome, but I am *not* Jesus." She jerked a thumb over her shoulder. "And he definitely isn't."

"Are you crazy? You can't just ambush me and climb into my

truck like this."

She rolled her eyes. "I can do anything I want. But, if you'd have been paying attention instead of looking down at your phone, you'd have seen me waving my arms like a fucking wind sock for the last thirty seconds as I approached."

"We have a problem," Nathan broke in from the back seat, his voice nasally and judgmental in one.

I waited for him to go on, as did Jilly, but he didn't. She got frustrated. "What do you want? An invitation? Tell the man what's going on, for shit's sake!"

"Photos of you on the flight home from Alabama surfaced last night, speculating on why you'd be so willing to miss practice. People are theorizing about injuries, even saying you're not taking the game seriously anymore. Partying, fucking your way around the globe, that kind of thing."

I scoffed a harsh laugh. "Well, that's fucking ridiculous. It's not true, any of it, so what does it matter?"

"Because your image matters, Quinn. Now that you're causing a stir, people are going to be coming out of the woodwork, trying to smear your reputation. You're going to have even more public scrutiny, and everything you do will be used against you."

My chest suddenly felt like it weighed as much as the stadium. "Fucking great."

"I just read on a site that you're falling down on your training and your game is slipping. There's speculation that you've lost your touch."

"I had a bad practice! One!" I shouted. "Today. How the fuck would they know this?"

Nathan shrugged. "There are a ton of people who work within these walls who are willing to share little snippets for money."

I shook my head as I tried to gather my thoughts, fought against all the demons circling my intestines and squeezing, and actually won. "It doesn't matter. Today was an anomaly. All of this shit will settle, and then I'll fucking destroy it when we play Minneapolis this weekend."

Nathan and Jilly shared a look, but I was done. I couldn't waste any more time talking about this garbage and letting it infect me any further. I had more important things to worry about.

"Do your jobs. Jilly, you know what I care about. Clean socks, food in the fridge, and a schedule I don't have to keep. And you…" I looked at Nathan. "I pay you to deal with this so I don't have to. Don't fucking call me unless the sky is falling." He looked shocked, but I was so beyond caring it wasn't even funny.

I grabbed my phone from the cupholder and turned in my seat to face the steering wheel. "Now, both of you get the *fuck* out of my truck." I sighed, let go of a little of the anger, and added some manners for good measure. "Please."

Thankfully, they both knew I was serious and followed orders immediately, leaving me to the silence of the cab of my truck once again. I relit the screen, pushed Catharine's name, and put the phone to my ear.

I'd never heard a more mocking ring.

In fact, it'd mocked me straight to her voice mail.

Chapter Thirty-Four

Cat

The midafternoon sun filtered in through the sheer curtains of my window and gently lit the room in softened hues of orange and gold. Normally, I'd savor such a soothing, beautiful sight, but today, all I could do was lie in my bed and mindlessly stare up at the ceiling.

After being delayed by eight hours yesterday, flying through the night, and arriving home from the airport just before morning rush-hour traffic would've started to hit the highways, I'd attempted to lie down and get some much-needed sleep before I'd have to leave for my afternoon flight to Cincinnati.

Just yesterday, I'd experienced the most uncomfortable meeting of the parents in my entire life, and I still couldn't really process what happened.

The car ride from his hometown to the airport had been silent, both of us reflective and lost in our own thoughts. The flight hadn't been any different and couldn't have gone any worse, considering we'd been delayed and only had time for a quick goodbye before Quinn had to rush off to the stadium.

It felt like the number of words we'd exchanged easily could have been counted with two hands.

And after overhearing the things his parents had said about me, I wasn't really sure what to do or say. Hell, I wasn't sure there was anything I *could* say or do in that situation to make it better or provide some semblance of reassurance.

They didn't like me. That was clear as water.

Their reasoning why, on the other hand, might as well have been covered in mud.

Was it the fact that I was a flight attendant?

My age? My *skin color*?

I guessed it could have been any of those things. Or it might not have been any of them. But the idea that it could have been an issue of race and the color of my skin was the most painful.

I was proud of my skin. I was proud that my mother was a strong African-American woman with beautiful, dark skin. And I was proud that my father was a playful Irishman with a golden smile and a white complexion that almost always burned underneath the sun's rays.

My roots were my roots. And I wouldn't change them for anything.

But even though I had my suspicions, I still didn't really know why Mr. and Mrs. Bailey were so visibly frigid toward me.

When I took into account how charismatic, warm, and openly friendly their son was to anyone and everyone he met, their cold demeanors were nothing like I'd expected.

But no matter what I'd expected or what had occurred, I had no idea what was going through Quinn's mind. His family was important to him. And it was very apparent they were not thrilled that his girlfriend was me.

I'd called him when I'd gotten home from the airport this morning and settled in, hoping we'd be able to put a swift end to the dark cloud that had enveloped us. I'd wanted to talk to him. I'd wanted to hear his voice and his thoughts and find the fucking sun.

But, just as I'd suspected he would be, he'd been too busy to answer.

All I could do now was wait for him to call me when he was done with all things New York Mavericks.

As I tossed from left to right and then back again, my legs got caught up in my sheets, and I struggled to untangle them. With an audible groan, I kicked myself out of my inadvertent restraint and sat up in bed.

I glanced at the clock. 2:00 p.m. I'd literally spent hours in this bed, and I was certain I hadn't slept a wink. My mind was too on edge, and anxiety had my heart pounding inside of my chest like a hummingbird's wings.

Giving in to the madness, and knowing it was time to get ready, I slid out of bed. The hardwood floor of my bedroom was cool against my feet as I walked into my closet and pulled out my suitcase. I had an early evening flight to catch to Cincinnati for RoyalAir's quarterly flight attendant training, and I still needed to shower and pack.

As I unzipped my empty suitcase and threw it onto my bed, my eyes caught sight of Times Square painted in colorful hues of red and blue and orange and purple.

It was the painting from our first date.

Quinn's colorful version was in the living room, hanging proudly on my mantel.

My heart ached at the mere memory of us, together, laughing and painting while Stella tried to teach us how to create a New York cityscape. The muscles in my chest tightened and constricted like a noose, and I forced a deep inhale of oxygen into my lungs to relieve the pressure.

God, this is awful.

I had no idea what was going to happen, where Quinn and I would go from here. I didn't know if we were still an us; I didn't know if we could still be an us. And the uncertainty of our future, of the state of our relationship, only stirred insecurities, allowing them to pick the lock on the deep recesses of my brain.

Why would he want to be with me? He's a fucking NFL quarterback... He's a celebrity... Millions of people adore him... His family doesn't even like me... We both travel so much...

It was a vicious fucking cycle.

God, I just wanted to be with Quinn.

But I also didn't want to feel so fucking insecure either.

Flying through the sky at five hundred miles per hour, I felt like my mind was racing faster than the plane I was buckled inside. With Cincinnati as our destination, Nikki, Casey, and I were heading toward RoyalAir's headquarters for our training.

I should've been enjoying the fact that I was inside of a plane but I didn't have to handle passenger issues or pass out drinks and snacks.

I should've been laughing and joking around with my best friends.

I should've been excited that I'd get to see my parents.

But I was none of those things.

The clusterfuck of emotions that came along with the current uncertainty over my relationship with Quinn had made it impossible to feel any emotion besides melancholy.

"Girl," Casey said on a sigh. "You have got to tell us what's going on."

I looked up from my magazine and saw both Casey and Nikki staring in my direction from the seats beside mine.

"Nothing's going on."

He rolled his eyes. "You've been quiet the entire flight. And you've flipped through that *Cosmo* at least four times, and I don't even think you've read a single word of it. Something is up, girlfriend. Spit it out already."

I sighed and rested my head against the seat.

Nikki offered a reassuring smile. "You can tell us anything, Cat. We just want to make sure you're okay."

I nodded. "I know that."

"Did something happen with Quinn?" she asked, and I nodded again.

Casey furrowed his brow in confusion. "But I thought things

were going good…?"

"They were," I answered, and I could already feel the liquid emotion forming behind my eyes. I hated that I was so fucking emotional over the whole thing, but I couldn't help it. Quinn was important to me. I wanted him in my life. But I had no idea where we stood. It hurt like a motherfucker, to say the least. "I met his family yesterday, and well, it just didn't really go all that great."

"What do you mean? How could it have gone badly? You're like a walking, talking ray of adorable sunshine. Everyone who meets you adores you."

"Well, if you really believe that, I can tell you that Quinn's parents are the exception to that rule."

Nikki's mouth turned down at the corners. "It went that bad?"

"It was pretty much the worst-case scenario," I said, and before a tear could slip past my eyes, I quickly swiped and rubbed at them.

Do not cry, Cat. We're about ten minutes away from landing; now is not the ideal time to have a mental breakdown.

"I don't really understand…" Casey said and then paused, looking at Nikki and then looking at me. "What exactly happened, pretty girl? What makes you think it went as terribly as it did?"

"Well…" I began, and pretty much word-vomited the entire summary of events to them. I told them everything, how cold his mother had been. How his father had done everything in his power not to stay in the same room with me. I even told them the worst part, the one that included me eavesdropping on their conversation in their garage.

And with each added detail, Casey's and Nikki's facial expressions changed. From reassuring to confused to shocked to completely disheartened, I watched each emotion cross their faces before getting replaced by another.

"So…" Casey muttered once I'd finished. "Well…" He paused again and stared at me with tender eyes. "What…What did Quinn say about all of it?"

"I think we were both too shocked by how it went. We didn't

really talk about it then," I answered honestly. "And we haven't had a chance to talk about it since. By the time we'd gotten home from our delayed flight, he had to head to the stadium, and then, after I tried to manage some sleep, I had to catch this flight."

"Wow," Casey mumbled.

"Yeah. Wow," I agreed. "It was pretty much a disaster, and now, I have no idea where we stand."

"I wish I had something valuable to say here," Nikki said in a quiet voice and reached out her hand to hold mine, resting it on her thigh. "But I just don't really know the right words..."

"It's okay," I whispered. "The fact that you guys were concerned and let me unload all of my drama on to you was enough. It's a relief not keeping all of that bottled up inside."

"We're here for you, pretty girl," Casey whispered, leaning over and adding his hand to the pile. "Anything you need. Hugs. Cuddles. Hookers. Booze. We're here."

I giggled at that. "I'm good on the hookers, but I might take you up on the hugs and cuddles once we get to the hotel," I said, and then added, "Hell, maybe the booze too."

He winked. "Don't worry. I got you, girl."

In that moment, even though my heart was aching and my brain was racing with insecurities, I was grateful—so fucking thankful for such amazing and supportive friends.

Twenty-four hours ago, I'd landed in Cincinnati and dived headfirst into all things RoyalAir. Our first day of training had been a whirlwind of meetings, presentations, and hands-on training with the newest pieces of airplane equipment that would soon be implemented on all RoyalAir aircrafts.

Work had been a much-needed distraction. I'd lost myself completely in my job, and for a short while, my brain had let the whole Quinn dilemma rest.

By the time I'd arrived in Cincinnati, jet-lagged and tired as hell, I'd seen the missed call from Quinn. I'd had all intentions of talking to him once I'd checked into my hotel and found some privacy, away from Casey and Nikki.

But my sleepless night had caught up with me, and I'd pretty much passed out the instant I'd stepped into my hotel room. And then, today, when I woke up, I had to be at training bright and early.

I had tried to call him back, though, before I'd started my day, but knew before I'd even tapped his contact on my phone he was most likely occupied in the Mavericks weight room.

We might as well have been passing ships in the night.

As I pulled up in front of my parents' two-story suburban home in my rental car, memories of Quinn and me doing this very same thing at his parents' house a few days ago filled my head.

At least, this time, I knew what to expect.

The only greetings I would receive would be those of love, acceptance, and open arms. And for that, I was thankful. It'd been nearly four months since I'd been home, and this was a much-needed visit to see my parents.

As I stepped out of the car and made my way down the stone-paved pathway toward the front door, my mother walked onto the porch, a huge smile kissing her beautiful face.

"Catharine!" she greeted, and I hurried my pace to meet her at the steps.

She engulfed me in a tight hug, and a relieved exhale escaped my lungs.

"I missed you so much," I whispered, and she leaned back to meet my eyes. Her hands cupped my face, and she examined me in a way only a mother could.

"You look so pretty," she mused. "A little tired, but still as gorgeous as ever." She tugged at the ends of my hair. "I love what you've done with your hair."

"Thanks," I said and glanced behind her, my eyes searching inside the house. "Where's Dad?"

"Oh, he's probably upstairs in the office," she said with a soft smile. "He's been hard at work updating the Caterpillar & Co website."

I laughed. "Of course he is."

Ever since I'd started my flight attendant career, my dad had been the sole reason Caterpillar & Co had continued selling greeting cards. Between my initial training, moving to New York, and getting used to my new flight schedule, I'd barely had time to keep up with anything else but work.

Luckily, my dad was sentimental as hell and kept our little greeting card business running.

Following my mom's lead, I walked inside my childhood home, and in true Caterpillar fashion, I shouted for my dad just like I used to when I was a kid. "Daaaaad! I'm hooooooome!"

"Caterpillar!" he answered on a shout, his voice echoing from one of the upstairs bedrooms. "Come up to the office! I've got something to show you!"

"See?" My mom grinned. "He's hard at work."

I jogged up the steps, and just as expected, found my dad sitting in his favorite leather chair, behind what looked to be a new Mac.

"New digs?" I asked, and he smirked.

"I'm trying to stay with the times," he said as he hopped up from his seat and greeted me with a big hug. "I've missed you, Caterpillar."

"I missed you too."

"Now, before we eat dinner and you update your mother and me on all of the new, amazing things going on in your life, I need to show you the new website." He moved back around the desk and sat down. With a click of the mouse, the screen came back to life, and a brand-spanking-new, sleek as hell webpage filled my view.

"Oh my God," I muttered as I stared at the new Caterpillar & Co logo and the gorgeous display of our top-selling greeting cards on the home page. "Did you do all of that?"

"Well…" he started with a knowing smirk. "I did some of it, but one of the new guys from the post office helped me. He has a background in graphic design and coding."

"This looks incredible. Like, we look like a legit business. Not just some freelancers selling stuff on Etsy."

"Awesome." He chuckled. "That's the exact look I was going for."

"So…just out of curiosity…what made you do it? I mean, I thought our setup on Etsy was working pretty good."

"I'm guessing you haven't had time to check our sales numbers…"

I quirked a brow. "What do you mean?"

He just grinned. "We've increased our sales by nearly sixfold. Apparently, Caterpillar & Co is catching on, and I'll be honest, the last line of holiday and birthday cards you designed were a huge hit."

"Really?"

He nodded. "People loved them."

"Wow. That's pretty awesome."

"So, either tonight or tomorrow, do you think you can etch out a few hours of your time to go over business plans?"

"Definitely."

"Dinner is almost ready!" my mother's voice echoed from the kitchen. "And Cat, I think your phone is ringing!"

Thinking it was Nikki or Casey calling to tell me something work-related, I jogged down the steps and to the front door, where my purse sat on the bench in the foyer. I grabbed my now-silent cell phone and checked the screen for missed calls.

The one and only notification on my lock screen glared back at me.

Missed Call: Quinn

Before I could even contemplate whether to call him back before or after dinner, my phone started ringing again in my hand.

Incoming Call: Quinn.

Hesitantly, I tapped the green phone icon and held the phone to my ear.

"Hey," I greeted, and I hated how uncertain and small my voice sounded.

"Hey, Cat," he said. "How are you?"

Cat? He never called me Cat. It was always kitten or Kitty Cat.

The absence of my nickname urged unease to fill my gut.

"I'm okay," I half lied. I wouldn't say I was one hundred percent okay, but at least, I was still riding out the happy vibes the conversation with Dad had just given me. "How are you?"

"I'm okay."

Wow. This conversation was off to an exciting start…

"So…" He cleared his throat. "You made it safely to Cincinnati?"

"Yeah," I answered and discreetly went back upstairs and into my childhood bedroom for some privacy, shutting the door behind me with a quiet click. "I'm actually at my parents' house right now for a visit."

"That sounds nice. I'm sure they're happy to see you."

Yeah, pretty much the complete opposite of how your parents feel about me…

"Uh-huh," I muttered. I had no idea what else to say. The fact that we still hadn't talked about how things had gone with his parents hung thick and heavy over our conversation, choking my words and depleting my brain's ability to maintain any form of small talk.

Silence filled the line, until eventually, Quinn cleared his throat and said, "I'm sorry how things went at my parents', Cat."

"Me too."

"I'm not sure what was going on with them, but I'm sorry that it was awkward."

I grimaced at his words. He knew what was going on with them. And I wasn't sure if he wasn't being honest to protect me, or if there was another reason for his lie of omission.

"It wasn't just awkward, Quinn," I said on a near whisper, the words too difficult to say at normal volume. "It was uncomfortable. And it felt like they didn't want me there at all."

"I know," he said, and I could hear the melancholy in his voice. "I'm so sorry, Cat."

Tears filled my eyes. I was still Cat. And he was still tiptoeing around what had happened.

Or was his "I'm so sorry, Cat" his way of saying that things weren't going to work out between us?

"What do you mean by that, Quinn?"

"What do I mean by what?"

"'I'm so sorry,'" I repeated. "What are you sorry about? The way things went at your parents' house, or the fact that you don't think our relationship can work out?"

He stayed quiet, too fucking quiet.

"Are you ending it?" I asked, my voice growing more strained from the emotion migrating up my throat.

"No," he whispered. "Don't get upset, Cat. That's not what I'm saying at all."

"Then what are you saying?"

"I'm not sure," he said. "I know that things are difficult and complicated between us right now. I'm in the middle of preseason, and you're always flying somewhere. Hell, I completely missed a weight-training session because of my impulsive behavior and lack of focus. I want us to work, Cat, I'm just trying to figure out the logistics."

"I want the same," I agreed. "But I also don't really know how either." What Quinn was saying wasn't false. We had mountains of obstacles ahead of us, and that was just our work schedules. When I factored in all of the other things, it felt like we were trying to climb out of the Grand Canyon.

Silence consumed the line again, and I decided this wasn't something we were going to solve on a phone call. This wasn't something we could figure out while I was miles away in Cincinnati.

"Quinn, I think I'm going to go, okay?" I whispered through my tears. "I just need to get off the phone right now."

"Kitten?" he questioned, and the sound of my nickname stabbed me right in the chest. "Are you okay?"

"No," I answered honestly. "But I think it's best if I just get off the phone and try to enjoy the night with parents. I'll try to call you tomorrow, okay?"

"Okay," he responded, and I couldn't miss the sadness in his voice if I wanted to.

"Bye, Quinn," I said, and before the tears started to stream down my cheeks and clog my throat, I hung up the call.

Face to my pillow, I cried. I only hoped the cotton of its case would be absorbent enough to get rid of the evidence before I went downstairs to face my parents.

By the time I'd pulled myself together and made my way into the kitchen, both my mom and dad were sitting down at the table, the chicken pot pie my mother had made front and center.

"So..." my mom started, "tell me all about Quinn Bailey." She glanced at me out of her periphery and smiled as she put a steaming hot helping of food onto her plate.

Just the mere mention of his name threatened another crying jag, but I swallowed hard against the discomfort.

I hated lying to my parents, hated hiding anything from them. But today, after that painful phone call with Quinn, my heart felt too damn broken to relive the discomfort I'd just endured over the past few days.

One day, no matter if Quinn and I were together or not, I'd tell the truth, tell them about Quinn's parents and the way they'd treated me, tell them about everything that had gone down. But today wasn't that day.

God, were Quinn and I going to make it?

My heart cried in the form of a breath-stealing ache while my mind whispered, *I'm not sure if that's possible.*

Before they caught on to my sadness and uncertainty, I forced a smile to my face and quickly told them a little bit about Quinn. I told them how we'd met. I even gave them a small insight into what the man behind the football god status was like.

But most of all, I kept it short and sweet.

And I skirted around any question about our future.

It was fucking painful.

But I guessed I'd heard enough people say it before... Love hurts.

Chapter Thirty-Five

Quinn

I wandered my house, waiting while my individual lasagna heated in the oven, a beer hanging from my fingertips.

The space was way too big for me, five bedrooms, five baths, and an entire finished basement, and I explored the square footage like I'd never seen it before.

In some ways, I guessed, I hadn't.

I'd never really paid attention to the four guestrooms down the opposite hall from my own bedroom, and I hadn't been responsible for the decorating. Jilly had hired the interior designer for me, requesting a clean, masculine look, and I'd approved it with a nod. None of the stuff around me was really meaningful. I'd hung no personal pictures on the walls, and as I settled onto the bed in my room, I realized sardonically that I hadn't even had time to bring Cat here.

My girlfriend—the woman I was in *love* with—had never even seen my house. Psychoanalysts would probably have a lot to say about that, but I wasn't sure there was some deep-rooted hesitance to bring her that close to me.

No, the truth, I feared, was that it didn't matter whether she'd been to this house or not because, to me, that's all it was. A house.

A big, nice house, with a large garage for my truck and a fancy kitchen that I barely cooked in.

But a simple house all the same.

Homes, on the other hand, tell a story about the person who lives there. They reminisce with pictures past and point to things that matter. What tastes make a person feel at peace and what gets their blood stirring. What artwork moves them in such a way that they have to see it *every* day.

All my house said was that I didn't really have time to be in it. It was big and empty, and right now, on the heels of such a horrible phone call with Catharine, all it did was make me feel alone.

Resigned to my thoughts, I stood up from my bed and headed for the door, eager to be in the kitchen where the smell of food could at least fool me into thinking this place had something to offer.

I was halfway down the stairs when my phone started to ring in my pocket.

Eager, fucking desperate, I clutched my beer bottle in one hand and dug into my pocket with the other, yanking the phone out and reading the screen as hope shocked me. I hadn't spoken to Cat since last night, and to say the ending of our conversation could have gone better was putting it mildly. I'd called and left a message when I got out of practice, but she was just as fucking busy as I was. Catching one another on the phone was starting to feel like trying to catch a shooting star from the sky.

But optimism's exit was swift as I read a name other than Catharine, and I settled firmly back into the depths of reality, where she wouldn't be calling me back tonight to tell me that she loved me—that'd we'd work things out, no matter the hurdles.

Remorse flooded me as my phone continued to ring, time ticking away and almost robbing me of the opportunity to answer the call that *was* coming in—from my brother.

Quickly, I swiped to answer and put the phone to my ear. "Hello?"

"What's good, Quinndolyn?" my brother said in greeting, and I smiled despite the unwelcome weight in my chest.

"Not much, Den. Not much."

"Wow. That was seriously depressing. All's not well on Romance Island?"

"Why does it necessarily have to do with Cat?" I deferred, wondering how he could so easily read me, but after so many years, I'd still been clueless enough to fail him.

I resolved to do better. To be better for him. He deserved a champion who didn't provide different support based on conditions. He deserved my conviction, not hesitancy, when it came to dealing with my parents, and I swore to myself right then I would change. Denver would never feel like he was fighting that fight alone.

"Well, for one, it's always about the girl. Watch a chick-flick, for God's sake. And for two, you never ever sound glum unless it's about something important. Ergo, new hottie in your life."

After a deep sigh, I sat down, leaned into the stairs behind me, and explained, "I took her to meet Mom and Dad this weekend."

"And you didn't call me?" he shrieked.

"It was a spur of the moment thing," I said with a wince. My eardrum would be ringing for days.

"Well, no wonder you're in a bad mood. A visit to the Wicked Witch of the Deep South and one of her royal monkeys will do that to you."

I smiled at his colorful description of our parents, despite the leaden memories of our visit running through my mind. "They weren't welcoming."

"What a shock," he deadpanned.

"They're not *always* terrible," I said automatically, my default setting to defend them. I slapped myself mentally for the offense.

"Yes, yes, they are. Not to you, maybe. Mr. All American, football, perfect, straight son. But to a boy who likes boys or a little mixed-race hottie—"

I was all ready to jump in and tell him I was sorry—tell him he was right about my parents—when what he said registered fully.

"Wait a second. Did I tell you she isn't white? Did Mom and Dad tell you?"

His voice was blunt. "No, honey. The tabloid I'm looking at right now while waiting in line to check out at Kroger did that."

"What?" There'd been one blip of a picture in a tabloid a little while back, but the impact had been relatively little—at least, for me. I winced as I recalled Catharine's parents finding out about our relationship that way.

"You've got some big problems, Quinndolyn. And they ain't got shit to do with dear old Mom and Dad. Your girl's just been served up to the *wolves*."

Fuck. What the hell was in this thing? Were they tearing her down?

I swear to God, I'd rip those fuckers apart…

"Holy hell, the two of you were in a *clinch*."

"What? Where?" I asked, feeling fucking helpless that I couldn't actually see the pictures he was talking about and trying desperately to remember when we might have been so public with our displays of affection.

"I'm not sure. Looks like a hallway maybe. The picture's a little grainy. *But* I'm having absolutely *no* trouble seeing that your hand is on her ass and squeezing more than a handful."

"Shit!" I yelled, and he laughed.

"Since when do you care if someone knows about your grabbing a woman's ass, one who's *clearly* asking for it."

"Since it could hurt the woman whose ass I'm grabbing." The last photo they'd published of us had been PG at best, and all of the commentary had been relatively harmless. I had a feeling from Denver's initial reaction that this was different.

"Aww," he murmured. "That's pretty swoony, bro."

"Can you just send me a picture of this shit? Please. And tell me why you were being so dramatic about wolves! What are they saying about her?"

"Sure," he acquiesced. "Just a sec."

He disappeared from our call while I suspected he was taking the picture and sending it. A text notification signaled in my ear as he came back on the line. "Okay, sent."

I clicked to put him on speaker and opened the text, pictures of Cat and me at the Birmingham airport the other night spilling out like all of Pandora's evil. "The fucking airport."

"Yes!" Denver shouted. "That's it! It's an airport!"

I rolled my eyes as I scrolled through the other photos, a bunch of horseshit, meant to do nothing other than tear at Cat's value and worth. "I was there, Den. I didn't have to solve the mysterious clues once I saw the picture."

"Right, right."

He waited silently while I flipped through the pictures he'd procured, reading headline after headline that went after Cat. They called her trashy and fixated on her race, and I felt a little like I was going to throw up.

I swallowed thickly, murmuring, "Oh God."

Denver didn't need to ask what was wrong. He already knew. "So what are you going to do?"

I shook my head and tried to focus. Tried to understand why people tried to tear others down for no reason other than entertainment value. I wanted to go back in time and fix all the wrongs—the visit to my parents, the way they'd treated her, the tasteless fucking article. But none of it could be wiped away, no matter how many calls to Nathan I made.

Maybe I should call him anyway.

"Just keep calling, I guess. Keep being there, ready to talk to her, until she's ready to talk to me."

"How uneventful," he grumbled, and I sighed. My hands were tied. She was in Cincinnati and I was here, and thanks to my probationary status with the Mavericks, there wasn't a goddamn thing I could do about it.

"Den," I called before he could hang up.

"Yeah?"

"I'm sorry for defending Mom and Dad. Just now, and for all the times before."

His voice was gentle to the point of tender. "You just want to see the good in everybody, Quinn. It's one of the things I love about you. Honestly, I hoped you'd never understand the real root of them because I knew it would mean you hurting."

My head dropped forward, the grains of the wood on my stairs swirling before my eyes.

"Just be you. Be the brother I've *always* adored, and Cat will come around. Trust me, I know. It's absolutely impossible not to love you—even when you're an idiot."

"Right back at you, Den."

Chapter Thirty-Six

Cat

"Girls," Casey announced and flopped down onto one of the beds in our adjoining hotel rooms. "I'm fucking exhausted. I don't think I can move an inch for the rest of the night."

We'd completed our last day of mandatory training, and to say we were tired as fuck of anything and everything related to RoyalAir was an understatement.

But two twelve-hour days of mostly boring meetings and presentations would do that to anyone, I guessed.

Nikki grinned. "Good thing we're officially done with training, huh?"

"God, you have no idea," he said on a groan. "I refuse to do anything but eat takeout and watch reruns of *Friends*."

"My vote is for *The Office*," I interjected, and he rolled his eyes.

"That's only because you have a girl hard-on for Jim."

"A girl hard-on?" I questioned on a laugh. "That sounds more gross than good."

He shrugged. "Look, no offense to you ladies, but I'm not the biggest fan of the illustrious pussy. Nothing related to a vagina ever sounds appealing to me."

"That's because you're into dicks instead of chicks," I teased, and he winked at me from the bed.

"What are we going to eat?" Nikki asked as she slipped off her heels and threw her hair up into a messy bun. "I hope it's something with fast delivery because if it takes more than thirty minutes to get here, I might start eating my arm."

"How about," I started with a teasing grin, "no one sacrifices any appendages in the name of food, and I'll run downstairs to the little store in the lobby to grab some rations while you guys call in a pizza delivery."

"As long as the rations include Doritos and Twizzlers, I'm down," Casey announced, and I gave him a thumbs-up.

"You got it."

"I swear to God you're the only person I know who still uses the thumbs-up."

I switched fingers and lifted my middle one instead. "What about this? Am I the only one who does this?"

He laughed. "Nope. I actually see that a lot more than you think. Especially when I'm working the late-night flight from Atlanta to JFK."

Nikki giggled and groaned at the same time. "Good Lord, I hate that flight."

"Preaching to the choir, sister." Casey raised both arms in the air. "I swear I get stuck with that flight more than anyone."

I just smiled and headed for the door, calling over my shoulder, "I'll be back, you little complainers!"

As the door closed behind me, I received several shouts and requests for other things besides Doritos and Twizzlers.

I rolled my eyes as I walked toward the elevator. I wasn't a delivery service. Those little bitches would be happy and thankful for anything I brought upstairs.

Lucky for me, the little hotel gift shop was still open and completely empty.

Like a vulture looking for its next meal, I scanned the aisles and pulled anything and everything that looked good into my arms. By the time I walked to the counter, both of my arms brimmed with junk of the sweet and salty variety.

"Hi," I greeted the woman behind the counter as I carefully attempted to drop my snacks near the register. "How are you doing tonight?"

"I'm good," she said as she shut the magazine she was discreetly reading behind the counter and stood up from her wooden stool. "How are—" She paused midsentence the instant her eyes met mine.

Her eyes went wide for a beat, and like a spectator at a tennis match, she glanced back and forth between me and something on the opposite end of the register.

I furrowed my brow at her odd reaction, even glancing down at my clothes to make sure I didn't have something on my blouse, or God forbid, my uniform skirt tucked into my underwear.

Nope. All good.

Confused, I followed the path of her eyes until I found the source—a gossip magazine. On the cover, a candid picture of Quinn and *me* at the airport. But it wasn't like the last cover; this was different. To an outsider, we were basically making out, and his hand was directly on my ass. And above the main cover photo was an up-close profile picture of me that had been taken when I'd gotten my employee badge from RoyalAir.

Oh God.

"Is…is that you?" she asked, and I didn't know how to respond to her question. I was still trying to process the fact that my face was on another gossip rag.

"Uh…"

She lifted the magazine and held it directly next to my face. "That's you!" she exclaimed. "You're Quinn Bailey's girlfriend!"

"Uh…"

"Can I get your autograph?" she blurted out.

"Uh…"

As the woman reached for a pen and paper, I did the only thing my brain would let me do in that moment, I fucking ran—out of the store, through the lobby, and into the women's restroom near the entrance.

It was an irrational reaction, but I blamed it on the culmination of everything that had occurred over the past few days. It felt like I'd just hit the rock bottom of the situation.

Could this get any worse?

Like a coward, I locked myself into one of the empty stalls and rested my back against the door.

My heart pounded wildly inside my chest, and I felt like someone had reached their hands inside my throat and closed a vise-like grip around my lungs.

I leaned forward, resting my elbows on my knees, and did my best to breathe through the panic. I wasn't sure why I was freaking the fuck out, but that wasn't a question I could reason through in that moment.

Anxiety had taken the wheel, and all I could do was grip the "oh shit" handle and endure the ride.

Once my breathing had slowed and my heart rate had calmed down to a more normal pace, I stood up straight and pulled my cell phone out of my jacket pocket. Even though I knew it was probably the very last thing I should've done, I clicked open my Safari icon and typed Quinn's name into the Google search bar.

Instantly, the most recent articles populated on the screen, and I clicked the one that had the word girlfriend connected to it.

My screen filled with that candid, invasive picture of the two of us kissing. We were in the Birmingham airport, and I knew it had occurred the day he'd surprised me and taken me to his parents' house.

I hadn't even known there were paparazzi in the airport, much less that they were snapping photos of us.

The headline of the article: ***Quinn Bailey's New Girlfriend: We've got the scoop, and it looks like our favorite quarterback isn't going for his usual taste in women…***

And the subheading: ***Could this be why his game is off?***

What in the fuck was that supposed to mean?

I flicked my finger down the screen, scrolling past the headline and photo of us, until I reached more photos, but this time, they were of Quinn's girlfriends of yore.

Models. Actresses. Pop singers. It was a plethora of the same three variations: blond, famous, and *white.*

Wow. Now, I understood what they meant by that whole *not his usual taste* comment.

Is this why his parents don't like me? Because I'm not white?

I cringed at those thoughts. I didn't want to think that was their reasoning, but my gut instinct told me otherwise. And now, after seeing this article, it appeared his parents had never seen him with anyone besides blond, white women.

I tried to read through it, but I had to stop when I was forced to come to the hard realization that the paparazzi knew a lot more about me than any sane human being who wasn't in the limelight would want. They knew my name, my age, where I grew up, my work schedule, even details about my family and Caterpillar & Co.

This spread was much different from that initial article. It was like they'd hired a private investigator to find out *everything* about my life. Not to mention, the overall tone wasn't exactly positive since they were questioning if I was the reason Quinn's game was off and comparing the skin color of his other girlfriends to mine.

It was all too much to process.

As I tapped the screen to close out of the page, an Instagram notification popped up on the screen, and my finger managed to hit that instead. The screen redirected, moving from the article to my Instagram account at a rapid pace.

And that was where things got ugly.

Hundreds, probably even thousands, of notifications appeared. It was too many to count, and included new followers, likes and comments on my photos, and requests for direct messages.

Morbid curiosity running the show, I tapped on one of the notifications, and instantly, one of my photos from last Christmas appeared. It was a photo of my mother and me, wearing our favorite Christmas sweaters and smiling toward the camera.

What originally had all of a handful of comments was so cluttered with new responses that I couldn't even view them all. It was pages upon pages of comments from random strangers that I'd never met in my entire life.

Some were nice.

Some were there to just tag their friends to come stalk my photos with them.

And a lot of them were really fucking mean.

All related to one thing: the recent news of my relationship with Quinn Bailey.

His superfans, his haters, and even people who just enjoyed following celebrity gossip had made their way on to my Instagram profile and sifted through my photos like my personal life was there for them to dissect and comment on.

It was awful. I'd never felt so violated in my life.

Too overwhelmed, I shut my phone off completely.

And by the time I made my way back to the hotel room, Casey and Nikki had apparently already heard the news.

It was no surprise. Casey followed BuzzFeed and *Cosmo* like his life depended on it.

"Are you okay?" Nikki asked as Casey stood up from the bed and pulled me into a tight hug.

"I'm not sure," I whispered. "Honestly, I'm not sure."

I'd had all intentions of calling Quinn tonight, once things had settled down and I'd managed to eat some dinner. I'd seen his missed calls over the past two days, and my avoidance wasn't because I didn't want to talk to him. I *did*. I just didn't know what to say. Honestly, deep down, I think it had more to do with the fear of hearing him say the one thing I didn't want to hear: *We can't make this work.*

But now, I wasn't so sure that was just a fear.

It felt more like a reality.

I stared out of the window, watching the wings of the plane slice through the sky.

After spending an entire night crying into Casey's and Nikki's arms, and not sleeping for shit, I was ready to get home and attempt a full night's rest in my bed.

The fact that I was on a tabloid wasn't the main thing that had upset me.

It had been the headline, the content of the article, and the fact that paparazzi had managed to sneak pictures of us at the airport and I hadn't even realized it. Not to mention, the thousands of horrible, mean comments on my Instagram photos from random strangers.

No matter how confident, how self-assured you thought you were, it wasn't easy seeing people say cruel things about your appearance, your life, your social-class status, your skin color, and pretty much anything else they could find.

Sure, some people had said nice things, but that wasn't what my brain focused on.

No. Only the negative things stuck in my mind.

Between the media shitstorm and the way things had been left between Quinn and me, I felt like I'd reached a new low of insecurity.

With a deep inhale, I stopped scrolling through the *Cosmopolitan* magazine in my lap and shut my eyes, resting my head against my seat.

"You okay?" Casey whispered into my ear, and I opened my eyes to find him looking at me with concern in his eyes.

I nodded. "I'm just tired."

I hated that both he and Nikki had to deal with my quiet, reflective, moody ass.

I knew I'd basically been mute the entire flight, but I just couldn't help it.

I couldn't seem to snap myself out of it.

C'mon, Cat. Stop fixating on the negative. Think of the good things. Focus on the positives...

I couldn't deny that, despite the whole tabloid debacle, my trip to

Cincinnati had been much-needed. I'd spent time with my two best friends, laughing and having fun in our hotel room when we weren't training, and even when we were training, we still found time to dick around and be goofy.

And my parents. God, I'd missed them.

I'd managed one dinner, several hours of catching up, and a fun, exciting work session with my dad, talking anything and everything Caterpillar & Co. And, I had to be honest, I was excited for all of the things happening for our tiny company.

What had started out as a little hobby my dad and I had shared when I was a kid had turned into something viable and had the potential to have huge success. I was thankful he had managed to keep the ship sailing while I'd been busy jet-setting and starting my flight attendant career.

Fingers and toes crossed that more good things came for Caterpillar & Co.

I sure as hell would start making it a priority and already had plans of setting time aside on a weekly basis to work on more sketches and cutesy tag lines.

The pilot announced our nearing departure, and by the time our bird safely fell from the sky and executed a smooth and steady landing at JFK, I'd packed up my snacks and phone and magazines, sliding them safely into my purse.

Nikki and Casey were the first two out into the aisle, and I followed their lead.

We walked out of our gate, through the terminal, and by the time we reached baggage claim, flashes of light filled my view until it became blinding.

"Catharine! Catharine! Over here!"

"What's it like dating Quinn Bailey?"

"Are you going to his game in Minneapolis?"

Questions and more flashes came from what felt like every angle.

I couldn't even blink past the assaulting lights from their cameras to put actual faces to the paparazzi who were asking the questions and snapping the pictures.

"Cat." Nikki's voice startled me out of my shock. "C'mon, girl. My husband is just outside. He'll drive us home." She grabbed my hand and led me through the obnoxious crowd and out of the airport.

Once she spotted Mr. Miller, we ran over to his car at a jog, and it was only then that I realized Casey had kindly retrieved our bags from baggage claim and was tossing them in the trunk.

The three of us slid into the car, and the instant my ears were hit with the silence and safety of the car, I looked toward Nikki in the front passenger seat and asked, "Nik, can I stay at your house tonight?"

"Of course."

"I just don't think I can go home right now."

I didn't want to go to my house for fear there'd be cameras waiting for me.

I wasn't even sure if I wanted to talk to Quinn in that moment.

I didn't know what I wanted.

Chapter Thirty-Seven

Quinn

The beep was like a taunt in my ear as, once again, my call to Cat rolled to voice mail.

I pulled at the fabric of my suit pants and smoothed it needlessly over my knee. The team plane was rowdy as everyone else spoke excitedly about the upcoming game, so I cupped my hand around my mouth and turned away from the noise as much as possible.

"Hey, Cat. I'm on my way to the game in Minneapolis. We're about to take off, and it takes about three hours to get there. I'll call you when I land, but I have Wi-Fi all flight, so send me an email if you want to get in touch before that. I…" I paused, trying to figure out what to say that would get through to her. "Just… Call me back, okay? I really want to talk to you."

I'd been trying to get her on the phone for the past three days, all to no avail. When my call went unanswered the fifth time, desperation had set in, and I'd driven all the way to her apartment to try to confront her in person—only, my truck had never stopped rolling.

A crowd of fifteen to twenty paparazzi stood outside her apartment like vultures, waiting for a sign of a wounded animal. To them, that's all Catharine was—someone to capitalize on, someone with a sordid story to sell. Knowing my showing up would only make things worse for her, I'd kept on rolling and driven right back home. I hoped she'd found somewhere else to go, somewhere to shelter since she obviously didn't want it from me.

Dr. Winnie Lancaster, the team physician and my boss's wife, took the seat across from me as I scrolled from calls to messages and clicked to draft one to Cat. Apparently, Winnie was the only one not put off by the waves of disgruntlement rolling off of me.

Swiftly, I typed out a note and hit send.

Me: I know you're busy with your own life and the problems I've caused for you, but I'm hoping that you'll please, please call me back. If you can't get me and don't want to email, I'll try calling again later. I love you.

I sighed and pushed my head back into the headrest as the plane taxied to the runway. I knew I sounded desperate, but I didn't mind. I *was*. Desperate to make this work by any means necessary. I wanted Cat to know that.

Winnie glanced my way, I could feel it, but she was courteous enough to stay silent as I ran through my thoughts and tried to compose myself.

The nagging, sinking feeling of knowing I might have lost Cat for good wouldn't ease its grip.

My parents had been awful, and I hadn't done a good enough job of apologizing for it. Their thoughts didn't reflect my own, and I should have skywritten it if I had to. Then, on top of that, the locusts had come out of the media woodwork. Both official, in the capacity of tabloids, and social, via Instagram and Twitter and every other goddamn thing, people had been on the attack. Her clothes, her skin color, her very involvement in my life—you name it, they picked at it.

I'd made a post discouraging the behavior strongly and asking for, just this once, some privacy in my personal life. Anytime I saw a negative comment directed at Cat on my social media, I deleted it and blocked the responsible user, but it was all just a drop in the bucket. I couldn't fucking protect her from all of it, no matter how hard I tried.

The engines roared and the cabin shook as the pilot hammered the throttle and sent us barreling down the runway toward the sky. Planes, understandably, had turned into something of nostalgia to me. I tried not to focus on all the memories as I stared out the window and watched the ground fade farther away.

"Okay," the good doctor finally remarked, turning in her seat to face me. The cabin leaned as our plane made a wide sweeping turn to head back in the direction we needed to go, and I inclined into it to avoid her eyes. "I've let you sit over there and stew, thinking it was none of my business," she went on. "But now I'm thinking you need someone to help you climb out of the tailspin."

I struggled against it, but as her voice grew softer and softer, it got harder to avoid meeting her eyes.

"Quinn," she implored, and finally, with a throaty sigh, I gave in. When I looked across the aisle, her eyes were patient and kind.

"What's going on?" she asked.

Thirty minutes of intensely one-sided conversation later and I'd laid it all out for her. Her eyes were shining with moisture, and her posture was sunken. I'd left nothing out—the good, the best, and the ugly—and apparently, Winnie was feeling personally attached.

I understood. I was fond of our story too.

"I'm honestly not sure how to fix it," I admitted, the words that lent themselves to my painful lack of control burning as they made their way out.

Her body was nearly pliant with kindness. "You obviously care about her."

I shook my head. "I *love* her."

Her shoulders squared as she reached a conclusion, thanks to my words. Her lips curved up, and all the unshed tears in her eyes cleared. “It’ll work out,” she declared. “Right now, she’s feeling overwhelmed and scared, and talking to you is like confronting the problem. As long as she avoids you, she can avoid this. She’ll get over that once she gets her bearings.”

“How do you know?” I asked, afraid to water the little seed of hope in my belly. Once it sprouted, it’d be a lot more painful to kill.

“Because when a man feels about a woman like you feel about her, we know it. I know because of my experience with Wes and my friends’ experiences with their men. Somewhere, under the layers of smoggy doubt and vulnerability, she’s got your love to see her through. Just keep loving her, and she’ll find her way out.”

“But I feel like I should do something, say something, *fix* something.”

“Can you fix the whole world? No. Can you change the opinions of your…” She frowned. “*Closed-minded* parents? No.” It was pretty apparent she’d wanted to use a ruder word but had deferred out of politeness. “But you can love her. I can see it with my own eyes, and she’ll see it with hers too. Be patient, Quinn,” she advised. “That’ll put you where you want to be in the end.”

Emotionally exhausted and ready to get some sleep, I settled into the bed in my hotel room in Minneapolis and picked up my phone one last time.

I had to try, to make the effort, just in case she decided to answer.

The rings bled together in my ear, and anticipation fizzled like a soda going flat.

She wasn’t going to answer.

I took a deep breath, in through my nose and out through my mouth, preparing to leave her another voice mail, when the phone clicked, and the sweetest voice I’d ever heard came on the line.

“Hi,” she whispered. Not a question, not a doubt. She knew I was the caller, and she knew the conversation.

I squeezed my eyes shut and tried to slow my heartbeat enough to sound relatively normal. "Hey, kitten."

"Quinn," she said, her voice brittle enough to break in the middle of even my short name.

"I know, Cat. I know everything is shitty, and I haven't done enough to make it not be, but I think if we can just get together, talk everything out, we can find a way to—"

"No," she interrupted my rush to get everything out, the desperation in every word climbing higher.

"No? No, what?"

"I don't think this is going to work."

"No," I refused, sitting up in bed. Everything in my body was pounding. "I refuse to accept that. I can fix this. I don't care what all the other people think. I love you, and they'll eventually see that you and I are meant for one another."

She sniffed. "This isn't just about your parents or the magazines or the people online, Quinn." It almost sounded like she was apologizing—for all the things I was fighting to render obsolete. "It's more than that. It's the day-to-day of how we make this work. There's always going to be someone thinking they're more important than our relationship, and in some cases, like with your job, or my job, they might be right. We're both trying to be what the other needs, and we don't even have the time to be what we, ourselves, need."

"That's not true," I argued. "When you make something a priority, anything is possible. It's fucking possible to have it all. I refuse to believe anything different."

"I wish I could see it, Quinn," she whispered. "The way you do. But I'm not sure I can. I'm sorry."

Pain, powerful and swift, violated my every cell as the line went dead.

Winnie had said to have patience while I waited, and it would all work out. But what if I was the only one waiting in the end?

Chapter Thirty-Eight

Cat

By the time I'd made my way back home from Nikki's house, it was dinnertime, and I'd felt nothing but out of sorts and confused. My mind refused to stop running, like a hamster spinning along on a wheel, and I couldn't turn it off for just a moment of peace and quiet.

And nothing could distract me from my own thoughts.

Not food. Not a shower. Trust me, I'd tried both. I'd barely touched the turkey sandwich I had made, and the hot shower hadn't provided any semblance of relief or comfort.

Nothing helped.

All I could think about was Quinn and us and the horrifying feeling that what we'd started—the intense, beautiful relationship that had developed between us—had been for nothing.

When I'd moved to New York and started my career as a flight attendant, I'd never set finding a relationship as a priority. I genuinely thought it would be a while before I'd find someone who intrigued me enough to throw caution to the wind and dive headfirst.

But I'd never considered meeting Quinn.

A man who knew all the ways to make me laugh and smile. He was the one person who, when I was with him, made me feel comfort, safety, *home.*

The last true relationship I'd been in had occurred in college. And when that ended, I'd made a promise to myself. I wouldn't settle for anything that wasn't one hundred percent the right relationship for me.

Everyone had different needs, desires, wants. No one relationship was the same. But I knew the kind of relationship I needed was one that allowed me to still maintain my independence and stand on my own two feet. A relationship where both people were both a "we" and two separate "I"s.

Kind of like sitting on a teeter-totter, when you first got on, it was a little scary, but you had to trust that the other person wouldn't let you crash to the ground—that they wouldn't jump off or do something crazy to throw you off-balance. But together, you were balanced and counted on and supported each other.

And sometimes, everything was just even—balanced.

But there were also times when one person's life was on a real high, and the other person would do everything in their power to hold them there and let them ride the wave, all the while appreciating them in all their glory—loving them unconditionally.

But mostly, together, you just enjoyed the journey.

I'd honestly thought a relationship like that—the kind of relationship I knew I'd need—was a near impossible feat.

Until Quinn.

There was something about him that had made me feel so young inside, but not in a childish way. He had awoken the pure side of me—the best side, all the facets of myself that only required love to be healthy and whole.

And us, together, was pure magic. It felt like our energy vibrated in such a unique way, each the perfect complement of the other.

I wasn't simply in love with him; I was all fucking in.

Quinn was what made my heart feel strong. His smile alone could make me feel things I'd never felt before him.

Before we'd met, I was one, but when we were together, I was a half—yet somehow so much more than I ever was before. And now, the mere idea of not being with him was more painful than I thought I could ever allow myself to fully feel.

Our phone call last night had been heartbreaking. I couldn't muster the strength or willpower to visualize the picture he was trying to paint.

"*When you make something a priority, anything is possible.*"

His words blared in my memories.

During that phone call, he had been trying to fight for us.

I paced my living room, my feet creaking across the hardwood floor with each step.

Where did I go from here?

What would be the easy route to most—just giving up and trying to move on with my life without Quinn—seemed like an impossible task.

I thought about him, and I thought about the night of our first date when he told me his dad's advice.

Those words rang loud inside my head. *"It only takes one minute of bravery. One minute of insane, embarrassingly crazy courage to change your life. Sometimes, it only takes that one minute for something great to happen."*

The man might not like me, but apparently, in some ways, he was wise. I needed that one minute of insane courage.

I needed to understand that no one—not the paparazzi or Quinn's parents or random internet strangers with an opinion—should be able to control my life.

I was in love with Quinn, and I owed it to myself, and to him, to give us a shot.

When you loved someone, you didn't fucking let them go. You fought for them.

I needed to fight for us.

For once, my mind stopped racing, and it stayed focused on one task, the important task: *Get to Quinn.*

He had a game in Minneapolis tomorrow afternoon, and that was exactly where I was going to be.

Without second-guessing or any doubts filling my head, I jogged the few steps to my bedroom, and I ran through the possible available flights at this late hour of the evening in my head. As I packed a suitcase, throwing underwear, bras, clothes, and shoes haphazardly in my carry-on luggage, I called RoyalAir's customer service line to see what seat availability they still had for the 9:05 p.m. flight to Minneapolis.

It took five minutes of being on hold before a customer service agent finally took my call. Meanwhile, I'd already finished throwing random shit into a suitcase and set it by my front door.

"Hi, my name is Catharine Wild," I started to explain on a rush once Donna from customer service took my call. "I'm a flight attendant for RoyalAir, and I'm trying to get a seat on the 9:05 p.m. flight to Minneapolis," I explained quickly.

"Okay. Just give me a moment, Catharine, while I look it up," the female agent responded. The sounds of her fingers typing across the keys filled the receiver, and I waited impatiently in my living room, tapping my foot against the hardwood floor in an erratic rhythm.

"It looks like there are still six spots available on that flight this evening. Would you like me to add you to one of the first-class seats?"

Hot damn, I love when this happens. Being a flight attendant had its perks sometimes.

"Yes, definitely. Thank you."

"Okay, Catharine. I've got you added to the 9:05 flight to Minneapolis this evening. Just check in with the ticketing agents to get your boarding passes when you get to JFK."

"Fantastic. Thank you," I said and quickly ended the call.

Mind racing, I glanced around my living room, trying to run through a list of things I'd need for the flight and impromptu trip to Minnesota. Sure, I'd packed a suitcase, but that didn't mean I'd successfully put everything into it. I was too amped, had too much adrenaline running through my veins to remember really little details like makeup or hair product needs for my last-minute trip.

I just needed to get to him.

My heart pounded and my body hummed with anxious energy at what I was about to do.

Would he be happy to see me?

Would he be angry?

Had he given up on us…on me?

Those were all valid questions. And they all had valid responses.

But I refused to let any uncertainty stop me from trying.

As I started to move in the direction of my bathroom, three knocks against my front door brought me to a skidding stop.

I looked toward the entry and furrowed my brow.

Who in the hell would be at my house right now?

Quietly, I tiptoed toward my living room, peeking out through the blinds to make sure it wasn't something crazy like paparazzi or a disgruntled Quinn Bailey fan.

But to my surprise, it wasn't. At least, I didn't think it was. All I could see was a well-dressed, early twentysomething guy. No cameras. No one shouting questions or rude comments toward my door.

And when I looked closer, I had a strong sense of acquaintance. The light brown hair, the blue eyes, the strong jaw, the broad shoulders…it looked very familiar.

He looks so much like Quinn.

I opened the door, and blue eyes smirked down at me.

"Hey there, Cat," he responded with a wide grin. "I know we haven't met in person yet, but we've chatted on the phone. I'm Denver."

"Quinn's brother, Denver?" I asked dumbly. It wouldn't have taken a rocket scientist to know these two were related, but I wasn't employed by NASA, I'd spent the last few days heartbroken, and I was tired. I decided to cut myself some slack on asking stupid questions.

He nodded, lips smiling. "That's me."

"Uh…" I muttered as my brain tried to catch up with the situation. *Quinn's brother is at my apartment? Why? How?* "How…How did you find me?" I found myself peeking over his shoulder and looking out toward the street for the answer. "I mean, not that I mind you being here, but how did you know where I live?"

"Trust me," he said, waving a nonchalant hand toward me. "Quinn's assistant Jillian knows everything."

A shocked laugh escaped my lips. "Yeah, but my address?"

He shrugged. "No one knows how she finds everything out, but she does. I'm pretty sure she's a witch with the power of sorcery. I tell Quinn all the time he needs to watch his back," he said, and a teasing little smirk lit up his eyes.

He had the same playfulness as Quinn, and the nostalgia made my skin tingle with the need to get moving. If I was going to make my flight—*and by God, I was going to make my flight*—I had to roll out. "I don't want to sound rude, but…is there a reason you're here?"

Of course, all I did by qualifying my question with a statement like *I don't want to sound rude* was sound even more like a bitch. And according to Casey, *bitches get stitches.*

But he didn't answer that question, didn't even acknowledge it. Instead, he tossed one of his own, nodding toward the suitcase by the door. "Are you going somewhere?"

"Well…yeah…" I admitted. "I was actually just getting ready to head out."

"Head out? To where? Going on a vacation?"

"Uh…" I glanced down at my suitcase and then back at him, shaking my head. "I'm…well…I'm going to Minneapolis tonight. My flight leaves at 9:05."

"Really?" His whole body vibrated with excitement.

I shrugged and offered a little smirk of my own. "I like the Mavericks, what I can say?"

His eyes flashed with prior knowledge, a knowing smile on his lips. "Good God, I was hoping you would say that and not something tragically sad like St. Croix."

"St. Croix is sad?"

"Not always. But it is when Quinndolyn is in Minneapolis with a broken heart."

I frowned at the thought of Quinn being anything but happy. He was born to be smiling.

"That *is* why you're going, right?" Denver asked suddenly. "Because you like my brother?"

"No," I corrected. "I *love* your brother."

One of the biggest smiles I'd ever seen crested Denver's lips. "Well, thank God for that."

I smiled, but he didn't give me time to bask in it, shooing me out of the door and grabbing the handle of my suitcase.

"Let's move," he ordered. "Get your cute ass in gear and get on the phone on the way. I'm going to need a ticket, and you've got pull."

"What?" I asked with a laugh, practically chasing him to a rental car he had parked in front of my building as he tossed my bag inside the trunk and slammed it shut.

"You think I'm letting you fly to Minnesota alone?" He shook his head and pursed his lips. "No. I'm coming with you. This…" He swirled his finger in the air, pointed to me, pointed to himself, pounded his heart, and mimicked an explosion with his hands. "I gotta see."

Chapter Thirty-Nine

Quinn

Almost four whole quarters of effort, and it was still all going to shit.

I'd been sacked more times than I liked, and the passes I'd completed had been cobbled together out of nothing more than bullshit and hope.

I was off. My game, my head, my so-called muscle memory—all of it was shit. Apparently, for Quinn Bailey, a broken heart wasn't a good thing for good football.

By some kind of miracle, and the help of people like Sean, Cam, Sammy, and Oran, we were still within a touchdown of winning the fucking game.

Mouthguard clenched tightly between my teeth, I scanned my eyes across the defense, glanced up to check the play clock, and signaled for Sean to cross back across the field.

The seconds ticked down to five, and I called for the snap, Sammy letting it fly and sending it straight into the palms of my hands. I dropped back, one step, then two, shuffling my feet while I scanned the chaos in front of me. Blocks were holding, but only just barely, and Sean was in double coverage upfield. A quick scan told me a big fucking guy was coming for me fast, so I pumped to check Sean's position and let fly despite the coverage, hoping he'd give me a miracle.

He got close to producing one, honestly, touching the ball with a finger as he outjumped the two guys on each side of him and made a grab for it.

Unfortunately, that was the end of the good news. Tipped by his almost-touch, the ball bobbled and flopped off the side on a wild jag and straight into the arms of a waiting defensive end. He ran awkwardly, unused to being the man with the ball, but it didn't matter. The damage was already done as Jeremy Watts, our fullback, tackled him on the forty-yard line.

Frustrated and coming loose at the seams, I jogged to the side of the field with the rest of the team. Sammy gave me a slap to the ass, intended to let me know the guys were behind me despite my mistake, and then went on his way to leave me to my thoughts.

Coach Bennett's mouth moved wildly, likely with words of an unpleasant nature, but all I could hear was silence.

I was internally reaming myself enough for the both of us.

Jillian weaved her way through the crowd of players, coaches, and technical assistants as I walked to the back bench of the sideline and pulled my helmet off of my head. I watched her make her way as a water bottle was slipped into my hand, paying attention to the sounds of the game as our defense took the field in the background.

The fact that she was on the sideline at all stuck out like a sore thumb, and I wondered who she'd had to sweet-talk in order to make it happen. I braced myself for whatever she'd come to tell me that was important enough that she couldn't wait until the game was over to say it. My day was obviously already not going as planned, and I imagined whatever she had to say wasn't going to make it any better.

"Look up at the forty-five-yard line, south side of the stadium, halfway down the fifteenth row. Don't ask me any questions because I don't have time to explain, but I promise you won't be sorry you did."

And then she was gone. Like some kind of fucking ghost.

Jesus Christ. Sometimes her abilities scared me.

With no form to watch disappear, I did as she asked, looking up into the stands and scanning the crowd. It was thick with people, and

I did my best to make out their shapes and separate them into individuals. Even though it was the preseason and no more than an exhibition game, the fans came out in droves. With cheaper tickets and extra events, if you weren't there for wins and losses, sometimes preseason games were the way to go.

Sure enough, halfway across the row, I found my brother's smiling face as he waved wildly at the field and me. I smiled and raised my hand to wave back when he started pointing beside him.

I looked into the next seat and felt my breath catch in my throat as Catharine stood up beside him, a blinding smile on her face and the cutest, most awkward little shrug I'd ever seen.

My heart spasmed at the sight of her, here, at my game, smiling at me like she'd done exactly what Winnie had said and taken control.

I was so used to being in control, handling the ball, that I hadn't realized it was possible to give the control to someone else. Just like the wildcat formation, ***@WildCommaCat*** had surprised me with a completely new and exhilarating configuration—with her at the helm.

She watched as my face melted all its hardness and worry and morphed into a smile full of love. With Denver joining in beside her, my kitten jumped up and down then, her excitement fully unleashed as they both chanted, "Bailey! Bailey! Bailey!" together. Her shoulders as her focus, she pointed her two pointer fingers at the Mavericks jersey she was wearing, and then turned around to give me the full view.

She'd gone all out, apparently determined to convince me she was in, *all in*, and emblazoned there for all to see was my name and number.

To the rest of the crowd, she may have looked like a just another fan.

To me, she looked like *mine*.

Chapter Forty

Cat

The roar of the crowd vibrated the stadium, and I stared toward the field as Quinn and his team filed back onto it. They'd taken a short break after the last round of—*uh…footballing?*—to huddle together off to the side, near the team bench, while the Mavericks' coach kneeled in the center, gesturing wildly about something.

I looked around the stadium, taking in all the faces of men, women, and children filling up the stands, most of them standing on their feet, their gazes fixated on the field.

Walking onto the pristine green turf, closer to one end of the field than the other, the Mavericks looked like gods among men, standing strong and confident in their uniforms.

But my man—*God, I hope he's still my man*—he looked the most confident of them all.

After this game was over, I was going to do everything in my power to let him know I was all fucking in.

Number 9. Bailey. It only took one game for me to know that jersey like the back of my hand. I could spot it anywhere on the field, even when he was on the sidelines. It probably helped I had intimate knowledge of the man inside the jersey. And that I was wearing a reproduction of said jersey too.

"This is it, Cat," Denver said as the Mavericks lined up in a row, Quinn standing behind them. "Fifteen seconds, sweet cheeks."

"Fifteen seconds left? Like, in the whole game?"

"Yep." He nodded. "Quinn needs to convert for a touchdown on this play."

Convert for a touchdown? I assumed that meant score more points. My football-ignorant brain tried to think back to the letter he'd written and had Jillian deliver to me.

A touchdown is how you score points in a football game. It's worth six points.

I looked at the scoreboard on the opposite end of the field, directly below the upper section of the stadium.

New York: 20 Minneapolis: 24

"Couldn't they, like, kick the ball toward that pole thingy?" I asked, and Denver shook his head, a smile on his lips. *That kick thing scores points, right?*

"A field goal isn't an option, sweet cheeks. The only way they'll pull out a win is with a touchdown," he explained, even though it was all still kind of as clear as fucking mud for me. "By the way, I love that you have zero clue about football."

"I'm trying!" I exclaimed and hopped to my feet, getting too nervous to remain sitting. I stared at the field, trying to figure out just how far away they were from the touchdown box thingy. "Aren't they kind of far away?"

Denver nodded. "They could definitely be closer," he answered. "Quinn is probably gonna have to pull off a thirty-yarder here to pull this one out. If he can only manage another first down, they might not have any time left on the clock to complete another play."

Thirty-yarder? That sounded far. But then I remembered Devon in the airport gift shop talking about a seventy-three-yard throw.

"But…he's done it before, right?"

Denver nodded. "He's done more *and* with less time."

I let that information sink in, and Denver smiled, nudging me with his shoulder.

"You probably don't really understand it, but your boyfriend is one of the best quarterbacks in the league. Probably one of the best to ever play in the league," he said, pride filling his voice. "If anyone could pull this win out, it's Quinn."

God, I hoped he was still my boyfriend.

I felt like I'd fucked things up with the way I'd avoided his calls, but that was why I was here. I wanted him to know that I would fight for us. That I wanted this, him. And, most importantly, that I loved him. I truly madly deeply *loved* him.

When Denver and I had arrived at the game, the anxiety of the situation had started to overwhelm me. I had no idea what Quinn's reaction to my being there would be. I wasn't sure if he would forgive me for the way I'd handled things. I knew I hadn't made it easy on him.

But then, after Jilly had intervened, he'd looked toward the sideline, directly near our seats, and our eyes had locked.

I'd never seen Quinn smile like that. It was...*beautiful.* And the tension in my heart had eased a little. I just hoped I could see that smile again after the game, when I would finally get the chance to talk to him.

But right now, I'd just focus on cheering for him and keeping everything crossed that the Mavericks could pull this out.

The crowd grew louder, and both teams were lined up, New York on one side and Minneapolis on the other. I might have known zilch about this game, but I knew this moment, right now, was important. Anxiety and nervousness pricked at my fingertips. I wanted Quinn to do well. I wanted to see the Mavericks walk away with a victory.

But they needed a touchdown. And they only had fifteen seconds left to accomplish it.

My chest tightened, and I fidgeted on my feet, moving from right to left over and over again.

"Come on, Quinn!" I blurted out, my voice fading in with the rest of the now-screaming and enthusiastic crowd. "You can do it!"

Now, I was starting to understand why sports fans yelled a lot. It was the only outlet for stress when things got intense.

Quinn squatted down behind the player in front of him, and it just kind of looked like he was staring at his teammate's ass.

I'm pretty sure that guy is the snapper…? Although, that just makes me think of fish…

But, truth be told, he did have a nice ass. Pretty much everyone on the Mavericks had a nice ass. Obviously, Quinn's was number one in my mind, but a girl was allowed to make observations.

The snapper guy tossed the ball from between his legs and into Quinn's hands, and I grabbed Denver's arm as I watched number nine take two steps back with the ball in his hands.

Come on, Quinn.

The crowd grew louder, their chants and cheers and shouts banging against my eardrums. And my grip on Denver's arm grew tighter as I watched Quinn look toward the other end of the field, ball still in his hands.

A big, huge monster of a guy broke through the Mavericks' line of other big, huge monster guys, and that bastard started running toward Quinn like he wanted to kill him.

Oh my God!

I gasped, and my free hand flew to my mouth. "Stop doing that! Go away, you bastard!" I shouted as I watched with wide, fearful eyes as Quinn looked right and moved left, throwing the hulk-sized player from Minneapolis off-balance just long enough for Quinn to chuck the ball into the air.

It flew like a rocket out of his hands, spiraling high and a long, long way down until it landed, perfectly, in the hands of who I already knew was Sean Phillips.

"*Touchdown Mavericks!*" the commentator exclaimed from the stadium speakers, but I couldn't focus on the fact that Quinn had just won the game.

I was too focused on the fact that he was on the ground.

"Oh my God, is he okay?" I asked Denver, and he nodded, wrapping an arm around my shoulders and tucking me into his side.

"Don't worry, KitCat," he said, making up his own version of my nickname. "Quinn Bailey can handle anything, even hard-ass motherfucking hits from burly defensive linemen."

A few seconds later, Quinn hopped to his feet. A little slow at first, but eventually, I knew he was perfectly fine when he ran toward Sean to celebrate.

They high-fived and hugged each other briefly, before the rest of the team huddled around them and joined in. A few moments later, the kicker guy kicked the ball between those pole thingys, and it was then that the Mavericks victory celebration could ensue.

I looked up at the scoreboard again.

New York: 27 Minneapolis: 24

"Way to go, Bailey!" Denver shouted toward the field.

They'd won.

I smiled, big and wide and so, so proud of Quinn.

I guess football isn't so bad, I thought to myself as I watched the Mavericks celebrate together.

I looked up at Denver. "I can't believe they won."

"I can." He winked. "So, how was your first Mavericks game?"

I grinned. "It was fantastic."

"Well, guess what?"

"What?"

"It's about to get even better." He nodded toward the field, and I followed his eyes.

Number nine jogged toward us, his eyes locked on me and only me.

By the time he reached the edge of the stadium, he took his helmet off and motioned me down toward him. "Come here, kitten!" he shouted, a giant, all-consuming smile on his face, and the fans that weren't trying to file out of the stadium started looking around at each other, not sure who he was talking to.

But I wasn't concerned with those people.

I just cared about Quinn.

"Go get him, pretty girl," Denver whispered into my ear, and I nodded, the smile on my face mirroring Quinn's. "This is the part we came for."

With the aisles full of people leaving the stadium, I worked my way down toward the field by climbing over the rows of seats. Awkward and clumsy and close to falling on my face, I didn't care. I just kept moving, right for Quinn.

"Yo, Quinny!" Denver yelled from behind me. "I'll meet you guys outside the locker room!"

My gaze was locked firmly on Quinn, so I knew he didn't nod or acknowledge his brother at all. But I had a very strong feeling Denver didn't mind.

A few seconds later, I stood at the bottom of the first level, my hands gripping the metal railing that separated the field from the stands. I looked down at Quinn, and he looked up toward me.

"You're here," he said and reached up to wrap his hand around my leg, squeezing it gently. "I'm so fucking glad you're here, kitten."

"Me too," I said, my voice low and emotion clogging my throat. Tears started to prick behind my eyes. "I missed you so much. I'm so sorry—"

"Hold on, baby," he interrupted. "I need you closer."

A surprised laugh escaped my lips. "I don't think I can get any closer right now, Quinn."

"Yeah, you can." He grinned and then, with fast hands, helped me climb over the railing and into his arms.

But he didn't put me down, *no,* he wrapped my legs around his waist and held me in his arms, our faces mere inches away. "There," he said. "That's much better."

God, I love him.

"I'm sorry," I whispered. "I'm sorry how I handled things. I was just scared and freaked out, and I didn't know how to deal with any of it."

"It's okay, kitten," he said. "I know it was a lot for you to take in all at once. Not to mention, some of it was really uncalled for and pretty fucking awful. I'm sorry you had to deal with that, especially that for most of it you were completely ambushed."

"It's okay."

"Where do we go from here?"

"I'm not sure," I said, and his face started to drop a little. "But I know with everything inside me, that wherever we go, we go together."

His blue eyes locked with mine. "All in?"

I nodded. "All. Fucking. In."

"God, I love you," he whispered.

"I love you too," I said, swallowing against the emotion in my throat. "So much."

He pressed his lips to mine, starting our kiss off soft and slow, until he took it a little deeper, gently touching his tongue to mine.

We stayed like that, kissing and holding each other tightly, for a long moment, until the sounds of the stadium and crowd and onlookers around us started to filter in. We weren't in the privacy of our homes; we were on display for all of the world to see.

"Shit," he muttered, a smile on his lips. "I almost forgot where I was for a second."

I grinned. "Me too."

Someone cleared their throat behind us. "Excuse me, Quinn?"

With me still in his arms, he turned to face them.

"I'm sorry to interrupt," a woman dressed in a nice black dress with a sleek jacket started, a knowing smirk on her lips.

She held a microphone in her hand, and a cameraman stood right beside her with his big camera resting on his shoulders. "But ESPN would really love to have a short interview with you since that thirty-yarder to Phillips will be on the Top Ten List tonight. Mind if we get an interview real quick?"

"Sure thing, Louisa." Quinn nodded and gently set me down on my feet.

As the cameraman pointed the camera directly toward Quinn, I started to move off toward the side, but he grabbed my hand, holding it tightly, and kept me in place, right beside him.

"Uh..." I muttered and looked up at him.

"I need you with me, kitten," he whispered into my ear. The sincerity in his voice made me melt, and instead of freaking out about being anywhere near the camera, I just nodded in understanding and squeezed his hand to let him know I'd stay.

Louisa got right into it, asking him questions about the game, what happened in the first half, and how he managed to pull off that thirty-two-yard throw in the last fifteen seconds. And of course, in true Quinn fashion, he answered with charm and grace.

And I stood there, right beside him, with our hands intertwined, and listened to the interview, smiling along and even laughing when he said something amusing.

I didn't worry about being near the camera and possibly making a television debut.

With Quinn by my side, I had no worries. I just wanted to support him.

If he needed me, I wanted to be there. Always.

Before Louisa finished up the interview, she looked toward me and then back at Quinn. "So...any important news for your fans?"

"Well...I know a lot of people were wondering about my kitten..." He paused, smiling down at me. "So, I guess now is a good time to introduce her. Say hi to ESPN, Cat."

I giggled nervously and glanced at the camera. "Uh...hi...?"

This whole media attention thing was obviously something I needed to get used to.

But, for Quinn, I'd do anything, even being awkward in front of way more people than I wanted to know.

Louisa grinned, looking far too giddy about getting me, *us, together* on camera.

"Is it safe to say this is your girlfriend, Catharine?"

"Yes, this is Catharine," Quinn said, nodding, and then paused. "And she's way more than just my girlfriend."

What? My eyes popped wide in surprise, and I darted my gaze to his face.

"Oh!" Louisa responded excitedly. "Has there been an engagement you haven't told us about?"

Engagement? What the heck?

His blue eyes shone brighter than the stadium lights, and he locked his gaze with mine. "No engagement…*not yet,* at least." And right there, with Louisa and ESPN watching, Quinn leaned down and kissed me.

And I kissed him right back.

A future engagement to Quinn Bailey? Count me all in.

Epilogue

Cat

The last cardboard box found its way on to the moving truck, and before locking the door to my little Hoboken apartment for the very last time, I paused just outside the entry to look around the now-empty space.

Today was moving day. And I wasn't moving in to a new apartment; I was moving in with Quinn. Another big milestone in our relationship and I had never been more ready to take the next big leap with him.

Over the past six months, we'd made our way together. We'd worked hard to always find time for each other, and somehow, someway, found a good, balanced approach in dealing with the media and spotlight.

With one final smiling look, I walked out of my apartment and shut the door with a quiet click.

As I hopped into my car and headed in the same direction as the moving truck that had left an hour before me, my phone started ringing for the one millionth time today.

Most of the calls had been from Quinn. He was at the house, and apparently, growing impatient. I swear to God if I received another ETA text from him, I might strangle his sexy ass when I got home.

Home. I smiled at the thought. Yes, that's exactly where I was headed.

Figuring it was my impatient boyfriend, I was surprised when I saw ***Incoming Call: Mom*** on the screen of my phone. I clicked accept from the smart screen on my dashboard, and her comforting voice came through the speakers of my car.

"Are you all moved in yet?"

"Not yet," I responded with a slightly annoyed smile on my lips. I mean, between Quinn and now her, it was like everyone thought the process of moving occurred via teleportation.

Sidenote: Moving was one of those things that, in theory, didn't seem like a big deal, and oftentimes, was really exciting. But when you actually got down to the meat and potatoes of packing up boxes, moving furniture, and cleaning your apartment for the next renter, it was a real pain in the ass. A trip to the dentist would be more enjoyable.

"Where are you?" she asked.

"I'm in the car. I just left my apartment for the very last time," I answered.

"Where's Quinn?"

"He's at the house waiting for the moving truck to arrive. And probably doing the last final clean of what used to be his bachelor pad."

She giggled at that. "Well, I'm so happy for you two, sweetheart. I'm also relieved that your father and I will no longer have to worry about you living in the big city all by yourself. We've had some sleepless nights fretting about something happening to you."

Goodness, you'd think my apartment had been in Harlem.

"*Mom,*" I said through a sigh. "I lived in Hoboken. You guys had nothing to be concerned about."

"I'm just thankful you'll have a big, strong man around to keep you safe."

"Really, Mom? A big, strong man?" I questioned on a laugh. This was the opposite of what Alexa Wild would normally tell me. "What has happened to you? Are you feeling okay?"

"What do you mean?"

"My entire life, you've told me that no woman *needs* a man. That we are fully capable of being strong and independent on our own."

"Yeah, but that was before I met Quinn."

I grinned and laughed at the same time. "I'm glad you like him."

"I *love* him," she said. "He treats my baby girl like a goddess. He's like a son to me now."

Once Quinn and I had established our relationship, despite what the media said and his parents' passive-aggressive disapproval, we had taken a short trip to Cincinnati so he could meet my mom and dad.

It had only taken about five minutes before he'd charmed my mom right out of her heels. And another ten for my dad to invite him down to his man cave in the basement.

That day had been a little bittersweet, though. On one hand, I'd loved that my parents had accepted him into our family with open arms. Hell, some days, Quinn probably chatted with my mom and dad more than I did.

But, on the other hand, the love and acceptance my parents had showed only magnified the way Quinn's parents had acted toward me.

I wished I could say it had changed with them, but it hadn't. Even after several months had passed, the Baileys were still fairly closed off from our lives.

Shortly after I'd impulsively flown to Minneapolis to show Quinn I'd wanted to fight for us, he'd paid his parents a visit in Boone Hills. He'd gone alone, and I wasn't one hundred percent sure what had gone down, but ever since that visit, his parents had changed their behavior whenever the four of us were in a room together.

Now, I wouldn't say they were ever really thrilled to see me, but they weren't as cold as the fucking Arctic like they had been that very first time. But whenever I saw them, they showed me the respect that I deserved.

I guessed progress was progress.

"Well, your dad is chomping at the bit to take a trip out to New

York to see you guys. But don't worry, I'll make sure he stays patient until you're all moved in."

"Good plan." I grinned and took a right off the exit toward my new neighborhood. "But I would definitely love for you guys to come stay a few days with us."

"Oh, sweetheart, we'll get a hotel when we come up there."

I snorted. "Trust me, Mom, we have the room. And Quinn's Southern manners wouldn't allow it. He'll demand you stay with us."

Quinn's house, *my new house*, was pretty damn big. Five bedrooms, five bathrooms, a finished basement, and that wasn't including the lush terrace, pool, and Jacuzzi nestled in the backyard.

Not only did we have room for my parents to stay a few days, we had room to host a goddamn party for the entire football team. Although, feeding all those manly mouths would be a difficult task to tackle.

"Okay, sweetheart, I know you're pretty busy right now, so I'll let you go. But promise to FaceTime me in the next few days and show me the house once you're all moved in?"

"Sounds like a plan, Mom. Love you."

"Love you too."

We ended the call, and before I could start my favorite Selena Gomez Spotify playlist, my phone started ringing again through the speakers of my car.

Incoming Call: Quinn

I laughed and rolled my eyes at the same time.

"What do you want?" I asked once I clicked accept on the call.

Soft and amused, his familiar chuckles filled my ears, and my heart skipped three beats. Good Lord, I was so in love with this man it was stupid.

"When are you going to be home?" he asked, voice tender and sweet as honey. "It's been too long since I've seen you."

"I'm about twenty minutes away, *and* you just saw me this morning."

We'd spent my last night in the Hoboken apartment together,

eating Chinese takeout and surrounded by moving boxes.

"Yeah, but that was six hours ago," he said, and his voice dropped a few octaves then, growing deeper with each word. "Come home, kitten. I want to play with you."

Oh boy.

"Stop trying to make me horny."

"Is it working?"

Of course it was working, but I didn't need the distraction while driving.

"That's beside the point."

"God," he groaned, and that sexy as fuck groan urged goose bumps up my spine and hardened my nipples. "I'm already hard just thinking about putting my mouth on your pussy."

"Quinn," I tried to exclaim, but it was more like a half whine, half moan. "I'm trying to drive here."

"All right, I'll stop...*for now*. But I can't make any promises for when you get home," he said, and I could hear the smile in his voice. I was certain I knew every one of Quinn's smiles, and this one was his "I love teasing Cat" sexy little smirk.

"Well, unless you want the movers to get a show, I think you should probably keep that promise for at least the next few hours."

"It's a big house, kitten. I'm sure it won't be too hard to find a bit of privacy."

"Oh my God," I said on a sigh. "We're not going to do..." I paused, and my cheeks flushed.

"We're not going to do...what?"

"You know what I mean."

"Say it, kitten. Tell me what we're not going to do," he said, and like honey from a beehive, his words dripped with sex.

"I'm not saying anything."

"Oh, come on, baby," he coerced.

"Quinn," I chastised, but even I didn't believe it. My face heated, and if I weren't busy driving, I would've given in to the urge to clench my thighs together to relieve the ache between my legs.

Holy heavens, is it hot in here?

I glanced at the inside temperature of the car on the dash and found it was a comfortable seventy-three degrees.

"You know it drives me fucking crazy when my sweet little kitten gets a little dirty…"

When it came to me, Quinn was so damn intuitive it wasn't even funny. Sometimes, it felt like he had a direct line into my brain. And right now, he wanted me to say all of the dirty things I was secretly thinking about.

Fine. I could play his game.

Game on, Quinn.

"We're not going to fuck," I stated, and immediately, my mind shouted, *Wait…we're not? That sounds a little ridiculous… We should definitely fuck Quinn. Lots and lots of fucking Quinn, to be precise.*

"And what else?" he asked, voice husky.

I swallowed and tried to keep going, but holy moly, I was only getting myself worked up in the process.

"You're not going to put your mouth on my pussy."

Why am I even saying this?

"You won't let me lick and suck on my kitten's pussy until it gets all wet and swollen with the need to come?"

I was truly playing with fire right now. Any minute, I'd ignite into flames.

"N-no," I responded, and the uncertainty in my voice was so thick I could've cut it with a knife.

"God, Cat," he whispered. "I'm so fucking hard right now I could slice through concrete like it's fucking butter."

"See?" I giggled at that. "This was why I told you to stop."

"Later," he said, his voice low and determined. "Once the movers are gone and we're alone, I'm going to play with you. Make you come on my fingers. My tongue. My *cock.* Does that sound like something you'd be interested in, kitten?"

I wanted to say, *Yes, please.* Or better yet, *Tell the movers to come back another day.* But in the spirit of not letting this conversation get out of hand again, I played it cool.

"Okay."

"Just okay?"

"Shut up," I said on a laugh. "I'm refusing to let this conversation go any further or else—"

"Or else what?"

"Or else I'm going to need a new pair of panties by the time I make it home."

"Fuck, kitten," he groaned. "I want to bury my face between your legs and not come up for air until you come on my—"

"Okay…yeah…" I cut him off before he could get started again. "I love you…but, yeah. Bye, pickle! See you in like ten minutes."

Pickle. I grinned at the nickname I'd come up with for Quinn as I hung up the phone. I wouldn't say he was the biggest fan of it, but every time I used it, I was rewarded with one of his secretly amused smiles. It was growing on him. I knew that much.

The nickname had been created after two visits to a little deli up the street from the stadium led me to realize that Quinn Bailey loved eating pickles, and, if you had a pickle anywhere in his vicinity, he would steal it without an inkling of remorse.

Now, he was pickle. I was kitten. And, I might have been biased, but we were fucking adorable.

Our nicknames for each other had managed to reach the media after Quinn and I had done an exclusive interview about our relationship with *Cosmopolitan*. He'd gotten a lot of shit for it from his teammates, but deep down, I knew he secretly loved it.

And I knew exactly why. Because he loved me just as much as I loved him.

I'd never known a love like this could exist.

Until Quinn.

Somehow, someway, we'd found our way together, and it wasn't without struggle. We'd tackled so many obstacles—his parents, the media, our insanely busy schedules.

At one point, I'd honestly thought it wouldn't work.

I thanked God every day I'd eventually realized that, no matter how hard things were, Quinn was worth every bit of the fight.

And, luckily, over the past few months, we hadn't had to work so hard against outside obstacles.

The media had settled down. Any articles about us were generally positive, and most revolved around the question of: *When are they getting married?*

Our schedules weren't so hectic. Thanks to Caterpillar & Co's ever-growing success, and Quinn's blatant promotion of his girlfriend's company, I'd decided to resign from my position at RoyalAir. Hell, we'd been doing so well, I'd even been able to hire both Nikki and Casey on full time.

They both handled the promotion aspects of our company, often traveling around the States to find prime placement in stores like Paper Source and Target.

They'd just nailed both of those contracts a few weeks ago.

Things were good. Though, I had a feeling the RoyalAir Comedy Show was suffering a little these days.

And now, as I pulled into the private drive that led to my new home, I knew that with Quinn by my side, this was only the beginning.

I drove around the moving truck and found an easy parking spot in front of the garages. Five, to be exact. I still had no idea why we needed so many places to park our cars.

I clicked off the engine, grabbed my purse from the passenger seat, and made my way into the house. Just as I entered through the garage, I could hear Quinn's voice reverberating through the house.

"Thanks, guys," he announced, and it sounded like he was in the foyer. "I really appreciate the speed at which you managed this move."

"No problem," a man responded, his voice having that all-too-familiar fanboy tone to it. "Anything for Quinn Bailey," he added. "I'm…well…we're all huge fans of yours."

I smiled and shook my head as I set my purse down on the big island in the center of the kitchen. Instead of eavesdropping on the fan session, I walked into the living room to see what boxes I needed to start unpacking.

But to my surprise, there was nothing.

Not a single box or container or…anything besides a perfectly clean space.

Maybe they'd moved all of my stuff upstairs?

I took one last glance around the living room and stopped once my gaze reached the mantel.

Hanging there, front and center, was one of my paintings.

My *personal* paintings.

An abstract portrait of myself, it showed the female form without really showing the female form. I'd painted it shortly after Quinn and I had really become an *us*. He'd been at my place when I'd created it, and once it was finished, he'd asked me what it was.

And I'd responded, "It's me. In love. With *you*."

I honestly hadn't really thought much more about that painting. Until now.

My eyes filled with tears as I stared at it, taking in the little nuances of pastel-color hues and smooth brush strokes and the magnified bits of red and gold interspersed throughout.

God, he had my heart.

I walked into the dining room and found two more of my paintings, and when I'd made my way into the entry where Quinn stood, I spotted another three of my canvases.

He smiled as I moved toward him. It was his "I missed you, kitten" smile.

The instant I reached him, he enveloped me in a tight hug and lifted my feet off the ground. I leaned back and pressed a kiss to his mouth, and his smile grew wider against my lips.

"What was that for?" he asked.

"Because I love you," I whispered. "So much."

"I love you too, kitten."

"You put my paintings throughout the house."

"I did." He nodded and set me on my feet. "And I also hired an extra ten movers to bring all of your stuff in as quick as humanly possible."

I giggled at that. "That's why I overhead you saying something about speed to someone. And how in the hell did you manage that?"

He shrugged. "I guess you could say I had it planned about two weeks ago. I didn't want to spend my kitten's official move-in day actually moving shit."

"And what exactly did you want to spend today doing?"

"I have a special surprise to show you." He smirked when I quirked a brow. "The only clue I'll give you is that it's not my cock. Not yet anyway. I have a good feeling you'll be falling all over it later."

I slugged him in the shoulder—don't worry, not his throwing arm—and laughed. "And where exactly is this special surprise?"

"Upstairs," he said. He took my hand in his and led the way, up the staircase, down the hall opposite our master bedroom, and to the very last room on the left. With a quick turn of the knob, he opened the door, and I nearly fell to my knees at the sight.

"Oh my God," I gasped and looked at Quinn. "Are you serious right now?"

"Yes." He nodded. "Welcome to your new space, baby."

I stepped inside and walked around the room.

The walls were a beautiful cream, not at all like the stuff I'd pour in my coffee, but with a decadent and calming hue of beach sand. The floor, a dark walnut. And the two large floor-to-ceiling windows overlooking the back terrace were covered with sheer curtains that allowed sunlight to pour through.

In the center sat a gorgeous desk with a brand-new Mac resting in the center.

In one corner lay a gold velvet ottoman nestled in the perfect, coziest spot for me to sit and draw for hours. And in the other sat an easel with a stool, ready and waiting for me to put it to good use.

The paintings—*my* paintings—on the wall, the framed Caterpillar & Co logo, and our bestselling greeting cards hung across an adorable clothespin line along the wall. All of the little accents were one hundred percent me.

This room—*my Quinn-appointed space in the house*—had been created and designed with love and care.

I stepped over to the desk, and tears pricked my eyes when I saw a framed photo of Quinn and me, standing right beside the computer. It was taken a few weeks ago by Denver. We'd driven down to Alabama to see him, and he'd managed to snap that pic when neither of us was paying attention. We'd been locked in an adorable embrace, Quinn looking down at me and my chin resting on his chest, gaze locked with his.

Both of us had soft smiles on our faces.

The instant Quinn had showed me that photo after Denver had texted it to him, I'd said, "We look so in love."

It was my favorite photo of us. And thirty years from now, I imagined it still would be.

He'd remembered that photo.

He'd remembered *everything.*

"Did you do all of this?" I asked and looked toward Quinn. He stood in the doorway, his shoulder resting on the frame.

"I did." He smiled. It was genuine, sweet, and made my heart skip three beats. "Without any help either."

"Fuck that!" I heard from the room next door, jumping at the unexpected voice. "I helped!" I recognized him then, his raucous laughter echoing through the wall as we listened to him jog down the stairs and out the front door before slamming it.

I winced at the force with which it resettled in the jamb.

Quinn laughed. "Sean is such a fucking diva." I bit my lip as he explained. "He only helped with the heavy lifting."

"I can tell," I said, and he quirked a brow, slightly confused by my meaning. "That you did all of the important and special parts yourself," I clarified. "The only way to create a room this amazing is out of pure love."

With three strides, he closed the distance between us and placed his hands on my hips, his blue eyes shining down toward me like my own personal stars. "I love you, Catharine," he whispered.

"I love you too."

"You know, kitten, you're so perfect for me, but…" He paused.

My throat constricted around the words. "But what?"

"If there's one tiny thing I could change about you…"

I narrowed my eyes, prepared to give him hell, but his smile stole my will to argue right along with my breath.

"It would be your last name." His heart was right there in his eyes, vivid and bright just like the blue. And with painful, tedious care—his movement so slow it felt like time stopped—he took my left hand in his and bent down on one knee before me.

The black velvet box came easily out of his pocket, and I gasped.

The small hinges opened with the barest hint of a crack, revealing the most beautiful diamond ring I'd ever seen in my life. The huge, cushion-cut center stone winked flawlessly in the light—a true showstopper—and the two sapphires at the sides did their best to sing backup. All of it shone with a brilliance only matched by the exuberance positively fucking beaming out of me.

"Catharine Alexa Wild, will you marry me?"

Quinn

With big doe eyes and shaking hands, Catharine stood before me like a baby deer on its first day.

Words were beyond my capability, and movement wasn't an option either. She hadn't seen the question coming, not today, and the fucking thrill of watching all the love she had for me scroll across her face threatened to bring me out of my skin.

"Kitten?" I prompted gently. I was eager for her answer, eager to touch her, eager to slide my ring onto her finger and get started on the rest of our lives.

Lives where everyone would know she was mine, I was hers, and together, we were unstoppable.

Tears kissed her cheeks, leaving behind the cutest of trails as they fell unchecked off of her chin. Her head shook, just slightly, the motion completely unconscious, and my chest tightened.

"Baby, the word you're looking for is *yes*," I told her. "Fucking say it!"

My order wasn't harsh, but it was impatient, and my little bit of fire was enough to set hers blazing.

"You know, normal people do this one step at a time, Quinn," she accused, her brows quirking in a way that showed her faint childhood biking scar. "They move in, spend some time living together, and *then* they get engaged."

She was challenging and teasing me at the same time, all the while, her brown eyes—shining brightly with fresh tears—showed her truth.

I bit my lip to keep my smile in check. If I didn't, it was bound to run away from me, completely out of control.

*She's so...*everything. *I have never met a more perfect woman.*

"They give people time to get used to the idea—"

"People? What people?"

"Me, people!" she shouted, but it was more of an amused declaration than anything else. "I need time to get my bearings. Time to settle. Time to—"

"No, you don't," I denied, shoving to my feet and stealing her breath as I pulled her into my arms. Her eyes were wide and her mouth was willing. I took full advantage.

With long, sweeping drags, I sealed her mouth to mine and owned it. Every inch, every breath, every fucking corner of her tongue, I made it mine.

I pulled away, just enough to see her face in its entirety. My voice was rough. "You don't need all that shit, and I don't either. You need me and I need you, and the rest of it can go fuck itself."

She laughed. Just a tiny burst that lit up her face and sank her dimples into her cheeks.

And then she nodded.

My whole life—*the whole fucking thing*—had been lived for this moment.

"Yes?"

"Yes, Quinn. Yes to you. Yes to us. Yes to taking your name. Yes to all of it."

She didn't have to tell me twice. I pushed the ring onto her finger, and then, around her back and down to her ass, I slid my hands until all I could feel was her. The front of her against me, the perfect flesh in my hands, the beat of her heart.

It still wasn't enough. I lifted, forcing her legs around my hips and drove a hand into her hair.

Her squeal was so sharp, I could feel it ringing in my eardrum. I took off for our bedroom at a jog.

"What are you doing?" she cried through laughter, her arms tightening around my neck more and more with every bounding step I took. She didn't need me to answer, though. My intent was clear as crystal, thanks to my hard, thick cock.

Thank God my bed was soft and forgiving, because I dropped her without finesse and tore at her clothes. The jeans, the sweatshirt, every fucking thing underneath—it all had to go.

"I hope you're ready," I taunted as I found purchase on her jeans and panties and pulled them off in a rush. She helped with her sweatshirt and then came back at me, pulling my clothes off with no less intensity.

"I'm ready," she challenged easily, shoving me down and climbing up to straddle my hips. "With you, I'm ready for anything."

With one swift stroke, my dick found its home inside of her.

And with three more simple words, I did the same. "Me too, Cat."

With Catharine Wild as my wife, I'll be ready for everything.

THE END.

Love Cat, Quinn, and the rest of the hunky Mavericks?
Don't worry, we're going make sure all of our favorite Mavericks Tackle Love. ;)
Get ready for MORE MAVERICKS from us!
Next up, Sean Phillips in Pick Six.

Pick Six: A term used when a quarterback throws an interception and a defensive player returns it for a touchdown, resulting in six points.

Pick(ing) Six: An event where a dual threat, man-wh*ring baller meets his match.

Sean Phillips is one of the biggest dual assets for the New York Mavericks. Often playing positions on both sides of the ball, on the field, he can handle almost anything.

But he's never been up against a woman like Six Malone.
Will it be a last-minute Pick Six that seals his fate?

#PickSix #MaxMonroeRomCom #MavericksTackleLove
After Sean, get ready for Cam and Leo!
Trick Play.
4th & Girl.

2018 has been the start of ALL THE FUN THINGS.
Find out why everyone is laughing their ass off every Monday morning with us.
Max Monroe's Monday Morning Distraction.
It's hilarity and entertainment in newsletter form.
Trust us, you don't want to miss it.
Stay up to date with our characters, us, and get your own copy of Monday Morning Distraction by signing up for our newsletter:
www.authormaxmonroe.com/#!contact/c1kcz
You may live to regret much, but we promise it won't be this.
If you're already signed up, consider sending us a message to tell us how much you love us. We really like that. ;)

You don't want to miss sexy, manwhoring baller Sean Phillips, do you?
#PickSix #Mavericks
Trust us, it's about to get a whole lot sexy real soon. ;)

Follow us online:

Website: www.authormaxmonroe.com

Facebook: www.facebook.com/authormaxmonroe

Reader Group: www.facebook.com/groups/1561640154166388

Twitter: www.twitter.com/authormaxmonroe

Instagram: www.instagram.com/authormaxmonroe

Goodreads: https://goo.gl/8VUIz2

Acknowledgments

First of all, THANK YOU for reading. That goes for anyone who's bought a copy, read an ARC, helped us beta, edited, or found time in their busy schedule to help us out in any way.

Thank you for supporting us, for talking about our books, and for just being so unbelievably loving and supportive of our characters. You've made this our MOST favorite adventure thus far.

Thank you to Basil and Banana for joining the team! We know it's a wild fucking ride at times, but we love how you just grab the "oh shit!" handle and fly through the crazy journey with us.

THANK YOU to our amazing readers. Without you guys, none of this would be possible.

THANK YOU to all of the awesome and supportive bloggers. You're like the sparkling unicorns of the literary world, and we'd love to take you for a ride… Wait…what?

THANK YOU to our editor Lisa with the good hair, and our formatter Stacey with the pretty smile. Our words wouldn't look good without you.

THANK YOU to our agent Amy, the smart-as-a-whip woman with all the words of wisdom.

THANK YOU to our Camp Members. You gals are the tits. #CLY Say whaaaat? ;)

And last but certainly not least, THANK YOU to our family. We love you guys. Thanks for putting up with us and our moments of creative crazy.

Monroe: Wait a minute…last but not least? What about me? Shouldn't you be thanking me?

Max: You know I could say the same fucking thing to you right now…

Monroe: Hahahaha, true. Okay, everyone, I'd like to add a huge THANK YOU to Max. Without her, my life would be a blank empty canvas. Okay, maybe it wouldn't be that depressing, but it'd be horrible, okay? Max is the wind beneath my writing wings.

Max: Ditto, dude. And I wouldn't want it any other way. Writing together is my most favorite adventure so far.

Monroe: Awww, did we just have a moment? Right here inside the acknowledgments?

Max: Yep. We totally did.

Monroe: Should we go ahead and end the acknowledgments now and get to work on Sean's book?

Max: Hmm… I was thinking maybe I'd work a little on that hot cop book we were just talking about first…

Monroe: Oh, *hell* yes. I'm in. #HotPD

Max: Let's do it! Bye, everyone! And again, THANK YOU!

Monroe: Yes, THANK YOU! YOU'RE THE FREAKING BEST!

As always, all our love,
XOXO,
Max Monroe

Made in the USA
Columbia, SC
29 June 2018